I0532586

Gatehouse:
The Door to Canellin

by
E.H. Jones

©2011 Eric H. Jones. All rights reserved.
ISBN: 978-0615478760

This book is dedicated to my son, Hal.

Special Thanks To:

My sisters, Geri and JoEllen, for being my first readers and keeping me on track throughout the writing of this novel.

My family, for supporting my dream and giving encouragement every step of the way.

My son, Hal, who was my inspiration for writing this novel, and one of my strongest supporters in getting it to publication.

The generous backers at Kickstarter. Without Kickstarter, this novel might never have made it to print.
www.kickstarter.com

Cover art by Barnaby Bagenda
Cover Layout and Design by Raquel Lopez
Title/Logo design by Raquel Lopez
Interior layout and design by Eric Jones

The interior of this book is laid out in 12pt Garamond font

The drop caps and chapter headings are set in **Immortal** 36-48pt by Apostrophic Fonts

These fonts are provided royalty free for personal or commercial use at the following websites:
www.fontspace.com
www.abstractfonts.com

Kickstarter Backers

The following is a list of the backers who helped fund this publication through Kickstarter.com, and the reward each received

David Cole – eBook

Erin Siegel – paperback

Derek Sanford – eBook

John Staples – paperback

Bryant Garibay – paperback+eBook

Brody Matthew Hermann – paperback

Brian Gmutza – eBook

David Baker – paperback+eBook

Erick Marquez – paperback

Amber Anderson – eBook

Warren Peterson – paperback

Adam Durbin – paperback+eBook

Cody Peterson – paperback

Kenya Orr – paperback+eBook

Michelle Blandford – paperback

Steven Groves – paperback

Elizabeth – eBook

Jeremy Reppy – paperback

Jerri Alexander – paperback+eBook

Kathy Huser – paperback

Rob Carnevale – paperback

Michael Whitely – eBook

Robert Grimes – paperback+eBook

Mark Ashworth – paperback

Michael Felty – paperback+eBook

Mitch Harden – eBook

Kickstarter Backers

The following Kickstarter backers funded the book at $50 or $100, earning limited edition hardcovers, original manuscripts, signed posters, and other one-of-a-kind rewards

Mike Weatherford
John Ellis
Shannon Goodwin
April Hendrixson
Donna Letson
Andrea Freeland
Bryan Riordan
Kimberly Key
Kate Templeton
JoEllen Bush
Charity Davis
Pawel Goj
Jeffery Post
Christopher D. Sandford
Tricia Mintner
Cheryl Roos
Janice Jones
Melissa McLendon
Tonya Martin
Andy Jones
Carole Bellamy

A special thanks to all my Kickstarter backers for your support and dedication toward the publication of this book!

Contents

Prologue

THE LITTLE MAN STEPPED OUT of the doorway and closed the door behind him. He was dressed in a long, sturdy tunic and thick trousers, with brightly polished leather riding boots on his inordinately large feet. He was short, barely five feet tall, and what there was of his hair flowed down his back in white wisps. He took off his broad-brimmed hat and batted it against his hand a few times to get the dust off before giving it up as a lost cause. His beard, also snow white, hung over his broad belly to his thick belt. As he looked down over that broad belly, he grinned, reflecting on how paunchy he was getting in his old age.

He began walking down the long, seemingly endless hallway, musing to himself as he went. He had been away from the House for far too long. There was always work to be done beyond the doorways, and at the moment, there was no one else to do it. Now that he had returned, he needed to stow some things from his last few trips. Then there were the thousand other nagging little chores that had been left for later while he was away. And he would certainly need to consult the Book. But the most important thing he needed to accomplish was a good long rest, to recoup his strength and rebuild his waning mystical energies.

He came at last to a stairway and started down. Entering a large sitting room, the strange little man pulled his pack off his back. He sorted through its contents, placing things here and there on shelves or tables. Each of the objects he removed brought a different expression to his weathered face; here a figurine that made him smile, there an ornamental dagger that brought a look of sadness. A locket that transformed his expression to one of wistful melancholy found a prominent place in the largest glass case. When he finally placed an antique sextant on the drawing table in the corner, his pack was empty.

1

The man flopped down in one of several overstuffed chairs in the large sitting room. Gods, he was tired. But he rested only moments before slowly rising to his feet. There was work yet to be done, important work, before rest could come. Ah, but rest... rest would be welcome, when the time was right.

The little man headed toward the door just past the stairway, unaware of the sinister gaze following his every step. He shuffled through the doorway and made a sharp right turn into an abbreviated hallway that ended in a massive, iron bound door. Fumbling with a large ring of keys at his belt, he selected the largest and inserted it into the lock. It turned with difficulty, producing a loud click, and the door swung open on silent hinges.

Through the door was a small room, roughly eight feet wide by ten long. Along the far wall was a sturdy bench overflowing with coils of tubing and vials and decanters, hand tools, wires, and other unidentifiable odds and ends. In the center of the room was a lectern, and on it was a large book bound in material that gave off a faint golden glow. The little man casually flipped the book open, displaying the first blank page.

"Show me the champion," he said quietly, making an arcane gesture over the page.

Words appeared line-by-line, just long enough for the man to read them before fading away again. What he read disturbed him, and a look of dismay began to grow on his face.

He read about a boy. A boy who seemed to him the least likely prospect for a champion imaginable. As he read on, the little man learned more about the poor decisions this young champion was making, the bad ideas that seemed to plague him. The champion was supposed to be a bastion of goodness, a pillar of solid values and hopeful optimism. Instead, the little man was reading about a boy who couldn't seem to make himself do the right things in life. A boy who was sarcastic, caustic, ill mannered, and more than a bit selfish. Oh, the child had his good points, certainly. He was compassionate, despite his overall selfishness, and he had a strong moral sense of right and wrong. But the story was rife with bad choices, wrong-headed attitudes, and a self-centered streak that seemed to have grown all out of proportion in one so young.

"Oh, no...that's not right. This is who you've chosen for a champion?" He shook his head, looking around at the walls of the small room. "How am I supposed to turn this child into a savior?" No answer came, and the little man looked back at the book with narrowed eyes. With a strained sigh, he closed the book and leaned on the lectern for support.

"Well," he sighed, "that's that. I suppose we'll just have to take the direct approach. You have a great many lessons to learn, young man, and I have a great many preparations to make." Feeling very put upon, he sighed again and left the workroom, locking the door firmly behind him and looking at the walls of the House accusingly. "So much for a nice, long vacation."

From the shadows, a baleful gaze followed the little man, but he attributed the prickling on his neck to worry over what he must now do.

Chapter 1

Bullies and Brawlers

MRS. JENSEN WAS WAITING AT THE DOOR when Wes arrived for Social Studies. "Glad you could make it, Mr. Bellamy. You just missed the bell. Please take your seat."

Mrs. Jensen's Social Studies class was a pain. History, names and dates... dry, boring, and pointless. And the homework and reading were completely mind- numbing, normally leaving Wes with nothing to look forward to but a drowsy hour of her droning voice.

Wes could tell right away that today was going to be different.

"All right, class, I want you all to step over here and look over the items I've set out for display," Mrs. Jensen said as she gestured toward the long table that had been set up against the far wall. "Everything is tagged and labeled so you can identify it. You may touch, but please, be very careful, since these things are on loan to me from the collection of a friend at the museum." She led the way to the display, and her voice took on a dramatic tone. "These are all examples of items that early explorers used in their travels when sailing uncharted oceans and exploring the unknown wilderness. They range from simple methods of record keeping," she said, pointing at a leather bound logbook, "to this complex device, sort of a precursor to the modern Global Positioning System." Here, she pointed at a strange looking contraption of metal dials, mirrors, lenses and telescoping arms. The bizarre device caught Wes' attention immediately. He took a few steps nearer to that end of the table, trying to catch a better look.

"Your assignment is to pick one of these items, examine it, and figure out what it is and what it does. Learn everything you can about it, especially how the early explorers might have used it to help them travel the world. There will be a four page typed research paper due next Thursday, and oral presentations on Friday." Most of the class groaned, but Wes was too engrossed in trying to get a better look at the device to even take notice. "Okay, everyone, start examining. You have until the end of class to look everything over, decide what you want to research, and get started."

Wes immediately headed toward the strange little device at the end of the table. No one else seemed even vaguely interested in it, which was just as well as far as he was concerned. He gently picked it up and read the tag. The device was called a 'sextant'. He examined it minutely, swinging the arms along the gauge, looking through the lenses, trying to figure out what it was supposed to be for. Something told him he should know this already. He spent the rest of the class period looking up everything he could about sextants in his textbook. The passages he found were frustratingly vague. 'A measuring instrument used by early explorers to calculate their position on a map using the measurement of angles of elevation between a celestial object and the horizon'. Despite the vagueness of the definition, Wes couldn't shake the feeling that he could almost grasp how it worked and what it was for, if only he could examine the contraption long enough.

When the bell finally rang, Wes reluctantly replaced the sextant on the display table and filed out of the room with the rest of the class, his mind still whirling as he contemplated the complex device. He wasn't paying the slightest attention to where he put his feet.

"Watch where you're going, maggot!"

Wes tumbled to the floor, his books skidding away from him, papers flying.

"I told you yesterday to stay out of my way, Bellamy," said Cameron as he stood over Wes' prone form, Darren and Jimmy flanking him. "You're not careful, you're gonna' get yourself in trouble." He laughed at his own pathetic wit, Darren and Jimmy chortling at his side.

"Whatever," said Wes irritably as he gathered up his fallen belongings. "Hard to miss such a big target."

Cameron was Wes' physical opposite in almost every way. Where Wes was a small boy, just a couple of inches over five feet, and slender, Cameron was tall and bulky. At six foot two, he weighed in at nearly two hundred and thirty pounds, and was the largest sophomore in the school. He was also a bully, pushing around anyone who crossed his path. Even some of the teachers tread lightly around Cameron.

"Smart mouth, there, Bellamy," he said with a sneer. "Careful. You know you don't want any of this."

Wes stood, still trying to arrange his books, and gave Cameron a spiteful glare.

"What did I ever do to you anyway? Why do you have to be such a jerk all the time?"

Just then the chimes began to ring, and Wes groaned. The sound meant he had sixty seconds to get to the band room, in the opposite wing of the school. He shouldered his way past Cameron, beginning to trot, and then to run as Cameron, Jimmy, and Darren's laughter followed him down the hall.

Wes sprinted down the hallway, skidding around the corner and through the double doors into the instrument storage room. He made it into the classroom and into his seat, still struggling to open his trumpet case, mere seconds before Mr. Drummond stepped to the podium. He let out a sigh of relief as the latch on his case finally gave way. Out of breath, he pulled out his trumpet and prepared himself.

"Okay, everybody, let's work on number twenty-seven, starting in measure sixteen. Flutes, concentrate on precision during the arpeggios, and trumpets, watch your dynamics. Forte does *not* mean blast me off the podium." Wes grinned as Mr. Drummond tapped his baton sharply, twice, and raised his hands. "Ready? Horns up!"

Despite having been nearly late yet again, Wes soon lost himself in the music, playing by instinct. Cameron was immediately forgotten as the music danced around him, almost visible in the air. The trumpet was something that just came naturally to Wes, and it was pure joy just to let it flow through him. He was glad now that he'd let his Dad talk him into joining, way back in middle school. This was the thing in the world that he was best at, by far. His skill had made him the first freshman to be a soloist in the school's history, and he'd kept that edge all the way through until now, as his sophomore year was approaching its end. Forget about homework and tests, this was what he was meant to do.

Fifteen minutes before the end of class, Mr. Drummond called a halt, as Wes had known he would. Every couple of weeks it happened, like clockwork.

"Okay, everybody, good work today." Mr. Drummond applauded them quietly, clapping his hands as he beamed at his students. "Now, it's Wednesday, that means challenge day. I've already received one request for challenge, but is there anyone else who wants to take a shot at moving up a chair?" He waited a few moments, but there were no takers. "Nobody?" Silence. "Okay, then," he said, sounding disappointed, "today we have Miss Stephanie Coscoe, our second chair trumpet, challenging Mr. Wesley Bellamy, our first chair." He gestured to Wes. "Mr. Bellamy, you're up first. We'll be playing today's selection, number 27. Follow me."

Wes rose with a sneer and followed Mr. Drummond. He wasn't worried in the slightest. He knew beyond doubt that he was better than Stephanie. She was good, sure, but he didn't see any need to be concerned. Stephanie, a senior, had been stuck at second chair for the entire semester, unable to dislodge Wes. She seemed to take it as an insult that a sophomore could beat her every time.

Wes entered the small office behind Mr. Drummond and seated himself in the challenge chair, arranging his music on the stand, supremely confident.

"Well, Mr. Bellamy, I hope you've prepared today. Miss Coscoe has been practicing hard for the past two weeks in after school sessions." He grinned at Wes. "You've got your work cut out for you."

"Don't worry, Mr. Drummond. I got this." Wes grinned.

"All right, then, at your leisure," said Mr. Drummond, flipping on the metronome. Wes counted slowly, horn to his lips, and began to play.

The trumpet was alive in his hands, the music flowing forth in a graceful dance as he worked his way easily through the selection. The notes came pitch perfect. He knew he was doing well, he could feel it, and when the final note died off, he lowered the trumpet with a satisfied smile. Mr. Drummond was making notes on his tablet.

"Good, Mr. Bellamy, very good. Please send in Miss Coscoe."

Wes strutted out of the office like a peacock, confident and sure of himself. He walked back to his seat and looked toward Stephanie. "You're up. Good luck!" He smiled at her as she walked to the office. "You'll need it."

The class was waiting for the challenge to be over, most people chatting quietly. Wes turned to Doug Boerner, a freshman trombone player who sat behind him. "I nailed it. There's no way she's getting my seat." Doug grinned and gave Wes a quick thumbs up.

A few minutes later, Stephanie returned from Mr. Drummond's office and took her seat next to Wes, smiling. She obviously thought she'd done well. Still, Wes wasn't worried.

Mr. Drummond returned to the podium a few moments later and theatrically shuffled the papers he carried with him. "This was a close one, ladies and gentlemen." He looked at Wes and Stephanie. "Very close. Fingernail close." He placed the papers on his podium. "Ladies and gentlemen, I'd like to present your first chair trumpet, Stephanie Coscoe." There was a momentary silence, and then light applause.

Wes froze. He had been preparing to stand up and give a grand bow in front of the class. But this… this was impossible. This couldn't be right. No one had beaten him since the beginning of the school year! He was first chair!

Except he wasn't.

As the rest of the class got up and began filing out of the room, Mr. Drummond put his hand on Wes' shoulder.

"May I see you in my office for a moment, Mr. Bellamy?"

Wes didn't reply, just let Mr. Drummond steer him gently to the office and into a seat.

"I wanted to talk to you privately. I think there's something you need to understand." He sat in his own chair and steepled his fingers in front of his face. "You played better than Stephanie today, Wes." At Wes' shocked look, Mr. Drummond held up his hand to forestall him. "Not a lot better, son, but better."

"Then why did she win?" Wes' voice was soft, despite a sudden surge of anger. He couldn't seem to wrap his brain around what Mr. Drummond was saying.

"Because while you played slightly better than she did, you didn't play any better at all than you did at the last challenge." He shook his head. "You haven't practiced, and it shows. You haven't gotten worse, but you're not improving, either. You play on instinct and natural talent, which I'll admit you've got. But there's more to it than that." He looked Wes directly in the eye. "Stephanie worked very, very hard for this. And she improved, not a little but a very big improvement. And believe it or not, that's a lot more important to me than talent."

The anger suddenly burst forth, and Wes shot to his feet. "That's not fair! If I did better, then I should have won!" Wes could hardly contain himself. He was straining not to explode and get himself in trouble, but he couldn't keep his voice from rising.

"You didn't do better, Wes, you played better, and even at that, only barely. In fact, I'd say if I had given it another two weeks until the next challenge day, and you still were at the level you are now, Miss Coscoe would have easily beaten you.

"It's not just about being able to do something, Wes, and this isn't just about band, or a first chair challenge. It's about everything. Your other teachers asked me to speak with you, hoping I'd be able to get through where they've failed." Mr. Drummond stood and looked out his office window. To Wes, the whole thing seemed staged, and very melodramatic. "It's not about being the best, and it's not about being first chair in the trumpet section. I'd be willing to bet that if you practice for the next two weeks, you'll win, and that's what it's about." He took a deep breath and turned to face Wes. "Not the winning, but the trying. The striving to be better. Or just the plain, ordinary doing what you're supposed to do." He paused to let that sink in. "Let me ask you something. When's the last time you turned in any homework?"

Wes was thrown by the sudden shift in direction. "I don't know, I just always forget it. So what?"

"So, it's just another example of your choice to not strive. And it's why you lost the challenge today. And you do realize that if your grades don't come up, you won't be marching next season, right?"

Wes looked at Mr. Drummond, filled with anger, and another familiar emotion. Shame. "It's not fair." He clenched his fist by his side as he trembled. "So I played better than Steph, but you gave it to her because I haven't been turning in homework. It's not fair!" His voice had risen to a shout, and his eyes were beginning to fill with unshed tears. "If I'm better, I should be first chair!"

Mr. Drummond sighed. "Before you keep this going and end up regretting it, I'm sorry to say, you've missed the point entirely, Mr. Bellamy. You're not better than Miss Coscoe, when it comes down to it, because she will always try while you choose to coast. But you've heard my decision, and my explanation, and it's final. You may challenge Miss Coscoe in two weeks, but for now, she's first chair. Now get to your next class, you don't want to be late."

&cc&cc

Wes sat slouched at the lunch table, barely playing with his food as he doodled in his notebook. He was still trying to shake his fury at Mr. Drummond, and this sketch he was working on was frustrating. Drawing the sextant from memory was harder than he'd thought it would be. He couldn't seem to get the mirrors on the upper arm quite right, and the irritation wasn't helping his mood.

"Gimme your pizza, putz."

Wes turned at the sound of Cameron's voice. The big ox was at the next table over, his two cronies Darren and Jimmy at his side as he snatched the pizza off Doug Boerner's tray and used his other hand to shove the freshman trombone player aside. Wes sighed.

"Hey, come on, Cameron," said Doug. "That's mine!"

"Not anymore," said Cameron. He gave Doug another rough shove and laughed. "Fries look good too." He reached out and snatched a handful of French fries from the tray. "You got my algebra homework done yet?"

"Yo, Cameron," said Wes, rising slowly. He'd had more than enough. He walked deliberately around the table and moved face to face with the bully. "Why don't you pick on someone your own size?"

"Find me someone, I will," replied Cameron, and Darren and Jimmy laughed uproariously.

"Seriously, can't you ever lay off? Leave Doug alone."

"Why don't you get lost?" Cameron grabbed Doug by the back of the neck. "So what if I decide to make Doogie here my slave? What's it to you?"

"Brass section's gotta' stick together. Besides, I don't really like you all that much, so whatever I can do to screw with your day, I'm up for it."

Cameron let go of Doug and poked his finger into Wes' chest.

"You think you bug me, Bellamy? You don't sweat me even a little."

"Knock it off, Cameron. You're gonna' get us in trouble." Wes' tone was sharp.

The bully grabbed Wes by the shirt and pulled him close. "You're the only one that's in trouble, Bellamy. I'm tired of your crap, and I'm doing something about it."

Wes jerked free from the larger boy, his contempt plain. "Yeah, sure, what are you gonna' do, ugly me to death?"

10

Cameron's face clouded, and he pulled Wes close again, his hot breath making Wes wince.

"No, you little turd. I'm kicking your butt. Show up or shut up. Right after school, behind the gym. You better be there." He shoved Wes aside, turning his attention back to Doug.

"Yeah, whatever. You coming alone, or you bringing your two girlfriends along?" Wes gestured toward Darren and Jimmy. He held his forefinger and thumb about half an inch apart, showing Cameron. "Your cojones are about this big, and it takes all three of you to make one tough guy." With every word, Wes could see Cameron getting more and more angry, but he couldn't stop himself. "Bad enough it takes three of you to think up a comeback, but now it takes three of you to beat up somebody half your size?" He waved Cameron away dismissively. "You aren't worth the time."

"Shut up, you little…," began Cameron as he lunged for Wes. His voice was raised just a bit too much, though.

"All right, you two, that's it!" Mrs. Schultz stormed over angrily. "Out in the hall, now!" She took both boys by the arm and walked them into the hallway.

"Now, what exactly is the problem here, gentlemen?"

"He was insulting me, Mrs. Schultz," said Cameron. "He turned around and started talking nasty about my mom." Cameron smirked as he pointed his finger at Wes.

"Whatever!" said Wes indignantly. "He was picking on Doug Boerner, and I told him to back off, that was it!"

"Doogie and I were just having a little chat!" protested Cameron with mock sincerity. "What gives you the right to stick your nose in?"

"What gives you the right to pick on a little kid?" shouted Wes, his finger in Cameron's face. "He shouldn't have to take that crap!"

"Mr. Bellamy, you're right, no one should have to take threats from anyone, but that doesn't give you the right to make trouble in my lunch room! If someone is bothering you, you're supposed to come to me."

"Oh, sure, that's gonna' work great." Wes' voice still held the disdain it had when insulting Cameron. He couldn't seem to help it. He liked Mrs. Schultz, but she was blaming it all on him!

"Cameron, I've had enough of your bullying. You have detention today and tomorrow for threats and intimidation." She rounded on Wes as he chuckled. "Wes, you can't behave like this, and you know it. We've had this conversation too many times. You get a detention this afternoon. I'll be having a word with your parents, both of you." Mrs. Schultz looked at them sternly, but the boys seemed cowed. "For now, I want you in the office. I've had enough of this for the day. Finish out the lunch period there and then go to your next class."

"But I didn't do anything wrong!" Wes couldn't believe that she was sending him to the office, and worse, was going to call his father. Again!

"Not another word, Mr. Bellamy! To the office, now! You too, Mr. Jacobs!"

With that she went back into the lunch room and closed the door.

"I can't believe this crap," muttered Wes as he started down the hall. "She's so stupid! And you're worse than she is, Cameron! I can't believe you got me a detention!"

Suddenly Wes felt a shove from behind and was slammed face first into the wall, bumping his forehead so hard that his head jerked back. A heavy arm settled on the back of his neck, forcing his face up against the rough bricks.

"Who's stupid now, you little freak?" a whispered voice said directly in his ear. "I'm gonna' beat you so bad you won't be able to walk for a week. I'm gonna' make you hurt." He shoved harder against Wes. "I'm gonna' make you wish you hadn't got out of bed today."

Something inside Wes snapped. The weight of everything that had happened today, losing the challenge, Mr. Drummond's lecture, Cameron's bullying, Mrs. Schultz's unfair treatment. It was all too much. He shoved against Cameron, hard, with strength he didn't know he possessed. He flung his head back and felt a satisfying crunch as it made contact with the brute's nose. Turning, he felt satisfaction as Cameron staggered.

Wes looked at Cameron, seeing the blood starting to run down from the boy's suddenly crooked nose, seeing his eyes start to water, and a cold fury came over him. It didn't matter in the slightest that Cameron was ten inches taller than Wes, and outweighed him by a hundred pounds. Wes' blood boiled as he looked at the bully, and he was gratified to see astonishment growing in the bigger boy's eyes. When Wes charged forward, his fists flying, Cameron staggered

12

backward in surprise. The sheer ferocity of the attack even surprised Wes. He landed a couple of solid blows, one to Cameron's jaw, another to his midsection, before Cameron reached out and took him into a bear hug, squeezing the breath out of him.

"What do you two think you're doing?" Mr. Jarvis, the gym teacher, ran toward them from the other end of the hall, but the two boys were oblivious. They both fell to the floor, struggling, each trying to gain advantage over the other. Mr. Jarvis grabbed Cameron by the shoulder as Mrs. Schultz emerged from the lunch room at a dead run. She got there just in time to grab Wes and hold him back from trying to get at Cameron, who was straining against Mr. Jarvis' grip.

"That's enough!" Mr. Jarvis bellowed at the two boys. "Both of you, come with me, now!" He grabbed both of the boys by the back of the neck and propelled them down the hall and toward the principal's office.

Chapter 2

Amazing Discoveries

RYAN SAT AT HIS DESK, his fingers drumming an unsteady staccato on his computer keyboard. He hated working under a short deadline like this, especially on something that should have been done two days ago, and by someone else at that. But Dan was the boss, and Ryan was the low man on the totem pole. He checked his notes, grumbling, and typed a few more lines when his phone startled him out of his concentration.

"Tech support, this is Ryan."

"Mr. Bellamy, this is Mrs. Novack at the high school. We've had a problem here today that we need to discuss."

Ryan buried his face in one hand and tried to keep his voice level. "What is it?"

"Well, Wes has gotten into a fight here at school. Don't worry, he's fine, but I'm afraid he broke the other boy's nose."

Ryan groaned inwardly. "What was the fight about?"

"That's not really clear, Mr. Bellamy. But we have a zero tolerance fighting policy, as you know, so I'm afraid you're going to have to come and pick Wes up. He'll be suspended for two school days."

"Crap. All right." He looked at his computer, and the report he was supposed to have finished in less than an hour. "All right, okay, I'm coming. I'll be there as soon as I can. I'm leaving now." He hung up the phone. Gathering up his papers into a decent stack and saving the file on his computer to the share directory, he left his office and walked to the door next to his, poking his head in.

"Hey, Adam, listen, can you do me a favor?" Ryan stepped inside and waved the stack of papers. "I just got a call from my son's school. He got in a fight and I have to go get him, but Dan wanted this report by lunch. I'm almost finished with it. Do you think you could…?"

"Yeah, yeah, go. You need to kick that boy in the pants, man. He's gonna' be the death of you."

"Thanks, Adam, I owe you." Ryan turned to leave.

"Hi, Ryan," came Dan's irritating, nasally voice, and Ryan winced. "I just came by to, you know, see if maybe you had that report ready for me?"

"Yeah, Dan, about that. I just got a call from my son's school, and I have to go over there and pick him up. It's kind of an emergency. I asked Adam to finish the report. You'll have it by lunch time, and I'll be back as soon as I can."

"Oh, okay," said Dan, his brow furrowed as he sauntered down the hall behind Ryan. "Well, if you're going to have to leave now, I'll need you to stay over tonight and make up the hours. That won't be a problem, will it?"

"Uh, no, I guess not," said Ryan in resignation. "I suppose Wes can have dinner at my mom's."

"Good, good," said Dan. "You know, Ryan, this is the third time in three months you've had to leave work because of your son. Do you really think that's fair?"

"What do you mean?" Ryan was trying hard to hide his annoyance.

"Just that Adam hasn't ever had to leave to deal with his kids. If he's supposed to be at work, that's where he stays."

"Adam doesn't have any kids," said Ryan, his calm façade slipping.

"Maybe not," said Dan, "but that doesn't change the fact that he's here when he's supposed to be." He shook his head. "What I'm trying to say is that this has been going on for quite a while now, and it's starting to be a disruption. I just think you should consider that."

Ryan took a deep, calming breath.

"Listen, Dan… believe me, I know it's been a pain, me having to deal with my kid all the time the past few months, but he's just going through a rough patch right now. I'm sure he'll get it together before too much…"

"Maybe I should be a little more clear, so you can understand what I'm getting at," interrupted Dan, bringing Ryan up short. He poked his finger into Ryan's chest. "Get it together, be here when you're supposed to, or I'll find someone who will." With that, Dan turned and walked back down the hall, whistling tunelessly.

Ryan stared after Dan, suddenly struck mute. This situation with Wes was starting to get serious. His shoulders slumped as he realized that Dan wasn't out of line. He was running out of options. He didn't think Wes even realized how far off the track he'd gotten. Well, he was going to get an inkling today, that was for sure. This was the last straw.

Ryan mulled over his options as he drove the twenty miles from his office to the high school. What was left to do with the boy? Military school? Boot camps? Grounding never worked, and Wes was way too old for spankings. He had finally decided on talking to Wes again, trying one last time to get through to him. Not that any of the half dozen talks about behavior they'd had over the past two months had done any good.

When he got out of his car and walked into the school, Wes was waiting on a bench outside the office.

"Hi, Dad. Sorry, I…" Ryan cut Wes off before he got any further.

"Not now. Enough. Just, don't talk right now."

"But…"

"Enough."

Ryan walked into the office.

"Hi, I'm Ryan Bellamy. I need to take Wes home, I guess."

The receptionist looked up at him. "Yes, Mr. Bellamy, I'm Mrs. Novack. Do you have a few minutes to talk?"

"Not really, Mrs. Novack. I'm already in trouble for having to leave work, and I have to get Wes to his grandparents' house and get back immediately. I'll be available this afternoon, though, if you'd like to call me."

"Perhaps Wes' mother could come in for a…"

"I don't think so. Wes' mother lives four hours away. I'm sure she'll have some words to say about all this, but for now, I'm all you've got. And I really do need to leave, Mrs. Novack, so if you don't mind?" Ryan turned to go.

"Really, Mr. Bellamy, I think we need to discuss…"

Ryan turned back to Mrs. Novack. "Did Wes start the fight?" Ryan was having trouble keeping his voice level.

"Mr. Bellamy, that's really not the issue…"

16

"I'm asking anyway." Ryan hated being rude, and he knew this woman was just doing her job, but for some reason this question felt very important.

"The other boy started the fight and Wes defended himself, Mr. Bellamy, at least at first. But when Wes got away from the other boy, he kept the fight going when he didn't need to. Either way, though, our policy here…"

"I know your policy, and I agree with it in spirit. I just expect my son to be able to defend himself if he's attacked. Or for that matter, to be safe when he's at school! If that means a suspension, so be it. But I'd be more than willing to discuss it further, later, after I've had a chance to talk to his mother. I really have to go now, so may I please sign my son out and get back to work before I lose my job?"

Moments later, Ryan came out of the office and motioned for Wes to follow him.

"Dad, listen, I'm sorry."

"I don't want to talk about this right now, son. I have to get you to your Grandma's house and get back to work. I've already been chewed out for leaving, and Dan made it pretty clear what would happen if this keeps going on. If you keep this crap up, I'm going to lose my job."

Wes was silent for a moment.

"I just wanted you to know I was sorry."

"I know, Wes. You always are." Ryan regretted the words as soon as he said them. But it was too late to take them back, and he couldn't think of any way to soften the sentiment. And at that moment, he wasn't sure it should be softened.

The drive to the home of Ryan's parents, Jane and Tim, was not long, but it was long enough to get the story from Wes. Ryan's anger cooled a bit as he listened, and he felt a little guilty. But regardless of the reasons, the fact remained that Wes had gotten suspended again. This was becoming a definite problem.

Ryan considered how to deal with the inevitable afternoon phone call he would receive from the school, particularly in light of his rudeness to Mrs. Novack. And the equally inevitable call to Wes' mom, Ruthie, wasn't going to be pleasant either. He really couldn't blame Mrs. Novack for this, though. It wasn't a bad rule. But after hearing Wes' side of the story, he couldn't help but feel a little indignant over the school system's treatment of his son. That, and even a little pride in Wes.

They pulled into the driveway and parked, and Ryan cleared his throat.

"Listen... son..."

"I know, I'm grounded," said Wes sullenly. "Just about as fair as getting suspended when someone jumps you in school. Whatever." He opened the door and got out, walking quickly into the house.

Ryan gritted his teeth, biting back a quick surge of anger. He'd meant to tell Wes that it was all right. He'd meant to tell him that stepping in to defend Doug had been the right thing to do, and that defending himself... well, he shouldn't have to, but if he did, that was all right too.

He'd meant to tell him that he loved him, and was on his side.

With a sigh, Ryan decided that conversation could wait until Wes cooled down a little. And finding out he wasn't grounded after all might even be a good end to a bad day. He got out of the car and headed inside.

"Hey, Mom, you here?" called Ryan.

"I'm in the den," she replied. "What are you doing here? Shouldn't you be at work?"

Ryan walked into the den, leading Wes.

"Yeah, Ma, I really should."

Jane turned around to see Wes and Ryan, and noticed Ryan's stern expression.

"Well, I take it someone got in a bit of trouble at school today. Or is there some other reason my grandson is standing in my den in the middle of a school day looking like a dead man walking?" She put her hands in her lap, looking at Wes and waiting patiently for an explanation.

"I got in a fight, Grandma." Wes stared at his shoes.

"Well, that apparently wasn't a very good idea, was it?"

Wes turned away, ashamed. "Guess not."

"Listen, Ma, it's a long story, but I'm going to be in trouble at work if I don't get back. Can you handle Wes for me this afternoon? I didn't want to leave him alone after this, and I'm going to have to work late as it is to catch up." Ryan glanced at his watch meaningfully.

"Sure, you head back to work, we can handle things here. I think I can find a few things to keep our favorite prize fighter occupied." Her grin was almost sinister.

Wes groaned.

18

Wes wiped the sweat from his forehead, looking down in disgust at the row of cabbages he'd been hoeing. Well, at least I'm finished, he thought.

It had definitely been a long afternoon. His grandpa had gotten home from his morning yard sale trip and joined in with his grandma in finding more chores for the boy to do. They seemed to be of the opinion that hard work in the hot sun was good for disobedient young men. So far he had washed both their cars, hoed the garden, weeded around the house, and washed two loads of laundry. While he had complied with their orders without question, Wes couldn't find it in himself to agree with their philosophy as he walked wearily toward the house.

"Grandma, I'm done," Wes called as he walked inside to the cool air conditioning. He entered the kitchen to find that his grandma had a glass of sweet iced tea waiting for him, a smile on her face.

"Here you go. Good work out there today."

"Thanks." He took the tea and couldn't help but smile back at her beaming expression.

"Your dad called, and he's talked to your teachers. He's going to have to work late again tonight, but he said he'd talk to you when he got here." She sat down at the head of the kitchen table. "I thought maybe you'd like to tell me what happened before he gets back."

"It really wasn't my fault, Grandma," began Wes, but she stopped him with a hand.

"I'm not interested right now in whose fault it was. I want to hear what happened and how. Give me the story with just the facts, without trying to make yourself look better."

Wes shot her a petulant scowl.

"Fine," he replied, and he told her the entire story, from bumping into Cameron in the hall to the end of the fight, sparing no detail.

She looked thoughtful for a moment as she considered him.

"And after you'd bloodied his nose, got him off you and away from Doug, why did you go after him again?"

"I... I don't know. I was mad, I guess."

"I'd say that's an understatement." She poured him some more tea. "Well, does anything jump out at you as to what went wrong?"

"Yeah, I guess. I probably shouldn't have gone after Cameron in the first place. I should have gone to Mrs. Schultz. But that still doesn't feel right. Why should I have to be a rat? What's wrong with sticking up for myself, or for Doug?"

"Nothing at all," she replied. "But you should follow the rules, at least, don't you think?"

"Yeah. Yeah, I guess I should." He took a long swallow of tea. He still felt abused, and in his gut believed that none of this was his fault, he just wasn't about to say so to her. At that moment, he just wanted to be out from under her understanding eyes.

"Good. I think we're done for the day, then, as far as your chores go." She smiled at him as she stood, and he found himself smiling back at her.

"Cool." Wes sighed. "Mind if I go for a walk in the woods?"

"I think that would be okay. Try to be back before dinner."

Wes grabbed his backpack and headed out the door, trotting down the hill and into the woods. He trudged through the little forest, following his favorite paths and slashing at the underbrush with a stick, his mind going over everything that had gone wrong in his life lately. He was confused, his emotions in turmoil, and he needed solitude. He made it to one of his favorite clearings and sat down in the crook of a tree root, his back against the trunk. After a few minutes of silent contemplation, he pulled out his notebook and spent a little time sketching, still trying to draw the sextant from memory, but he just couldn't get it right. Grunting in disgust, he gave up and stuffed the notebook back into his backpack.

He wanted to be angry at the world, angry that everything was conspiring to turn his life into this mess, and yet the more he reflected on things, the more he realized there was only one person to be angry with. It was his fault. Some of it was, at least.

Suddenly, the weight of what had happened, and of how far he'd fallen, came crashing down on him. He felt himself on the verge of tears.

There was no way to fix this.

Wes was suspended from school. His father had almost lost his job. All the things Mr. Drummond had said to him…

When the tears came, they surprised him, but he couldn't hold them back. It was too far gone! There was nothing left for him to do. He couldn't stop the sobs as his body continued to shudder. He'd

20

been depressed before, he'd felt sadness, but nothing like this. This was utter despair. He hadn't cried in… well, he wasn't sure how long. But now the tears came freely.

A sound off in the brush caught his attention and he jerked his head up.

"Who's there?"

There was no answer. He wiped the tears from his eyes and stood, following the sounds of brush being trampled by someone who apparently wasn't that familiar with hiking.

"Hey, is anybody there?" He followed the sounds further, and eventually saw a small form perhaps fifty yards ahead. "Hey!" he shouted. "Stop, who are you?" It was hard to see the moving shape clearly as it struggled through the underbrush, but it appeared to be a small man, considerably shorter than Wes, but definitely bigger around.

Wes picked up speed to follow, trying to catch up to the little man. He shouted after him a few more times, but when it was clear he wasn't going to get an answer, Wes simply followed. For some reason, the idea of someone violating these woods, violating his privacy, made him angry again. He fought that off and tried to remain calm, but he couldn't help feeling as if someone had been spying on him.

Wes followed the little man for a good distance, up and down wooded slopes, zigging and zagging between the trees. The little man was pulling away from him with surprising speed, widening the gap between them, and then he disappeared over a rise just ahead. Wes began to run, struggling to get up the steep rise, and he breathed heavily when he finally reached the top.

All thought of the little man was driven out of his head. Something was wrong here. In front of him was a hollow that memory told him shouldn't have been on the other side of the hill he'd just climbed. There should have been another gradual slope leading up to a large flat area with several clearings where he liked to sit. Instead, there was the hollow, and most surprisingly of all, a dilapidated shack sitting dead center in the bowl shaped depression. As he watched, the little man hurried up the steps of the shack and vanished inside.

Wes started forward again cautiously, looking at this little house where he knew there shouldn't be one. It was a small house, very run down, but all the windows seemed intact. There was a porch across the front that leaned precariously to the left side of the entrance, and a large, solid looking door. He walked around the house, staying back a good distance, trying to figure out how he could have missed this all these years, but it didn't make any sense.

He made his way back around to the front of the house, looking up the three steps to the porch. He grew more determined as he explored the outside of the house. He wasn't going to let the little man get away now! He wanted to know why that house was there, where it had come from, and who the little man was. He wanted to know how a house could appear overnight in a place where memory said it should never have been. He inched forward hesitantly toward the porch, paused, and then made up his mind and walked the rest of the distance. He stopped at the foot of the steps and pondered them, wondering if they were safe to hold his weight. He lifted his foot and gingerly placed it on the bottom stair, when…

BOOOOMMMM!!!!

The lightning struck barely twenty paces off to Wes' right, and the sound of it nearly knocked him down. He immediately staggered back from the porch, looking around in panic, and noticed the darkening sky threatening to drop rain on him at any moment.

Screwing up his courage, he placed his foot on the stair again.

BOOOOOOMMMM!!! Another lightning bolt struck, even closer, and Wes scrambled up the steps to the porch, his eyes wide. It took him a moment to regain his composure. He stepped back from the door and reached his hand up to knock.

Before he could make contact with the worn wood, the door swung open.

⚬ℚ℧ℚ⚬

Ryan sat at the kitchen table with his father as his mother puttered around the kitchen fixing dinner. He'd managed to get out of the office only two hours late, but he'd spent most of the afternoon mulling over Wes' issues.

"So what do you think I should do?" he asked.

"I think you should give that kid a swift kick in the pants, is what I think," said Ryan's father, Tim, in a gruff voice.

"I don't know if that's such a good idea, Dad, and I really don't think it'd do any good anyway. I'm serious here. I'm at my wits' end."

"Well, there's always private school, but I'm not sure you could afford that," said Jane, his mother.

22

"I'd already thought of that," said Ryan, "and I kind of tossed it out for that very reason." He chewed his fingernail. "I just don't know. It's just… honestly, today, I didn't know whether to scream at him or pat him on the back. After what he did… I know it wasn't necessarily the best thing to do, but I can't help feeling a little proud of him. He stood up for someone, and he got punished for it."

"Then maybe you should tell him that," said Jane.

"I tried," said Ryan. "In the car. But he wasn't in the mood to hear it."

"Just give him time," said Tim, gripping Ryan's shoulder affectionately. "He'll listen when he's ready to. I seem to remember another young man who had his share of teenage troubles."

Ryan nodded. "I know, I know. It's just… ah, well, I guess I'll know more after I meet with his teachers next week. I'm taking Monday off work so that we can have a conference. We're going to talk grades and attitude, and see if we can come up with a solution to all this."

"That sounds like the best plan. Now, why don't you go call Wes for dinner?" Jane gently patted Ryan on the hand, giving him a reassuring smile.

Ryan stepped out onto the back porch and cupped his hands around his mouth.

"Wes! Dinner!"

He went back inside to wait. After about fifteen minutes, Wes still hadn't arrived. Ryan went back out on the porch and called again.

"Wes! Time to come in!" There was no answering call, or any sign at all. Ryan opened the back door and poked his head in.

"Hey, Ma, how long has Wes been out there?"

"Oh, I don't know, hun, I think he went out at about five."

"Mom! That was three hours ago!"

"I know, but he wanders these woods all the time. He's not a little kid anymore! I wouldn't worry, he's probably just out of earshot."

Ryan peered out into the deepening darkness, a strange sense of foreboding filling him.

"I'm going to look for him," he called, trotting down the back steps.

The air was cooling quickly, and there were storm clouds rolling in. If he didn't hurry, he and Wes were going to be drenched before dinner. He followed the path down through the hills and valleys, calling after Wes as he trudged through the tree-covered landscape.

As he wandered further through the woods, he began to get worried. How was he supposed to find Wes? He hadn't been out in these woods in years. He wasn't really much of a hiker these days, all things considered. Years of sitting at a desk had softened him more than he'd like to admit, not that he'd ever been terribly athletic to begin with. He was what you would call a husky man, well under six feet tall and pudgy. He'd only trudged through the woods for fifteen minutes, and he was already short of breath. But he couldn't just wait inside for Wes. The boy was notoriously irresponsible, and wouldn't bat an eye at wandering until well after dark, rain or no rain, and probably get lost at that. All Ryan could do was wander through the trees calling for his son, following the hills and valleys, trying not to get lost himself. He picked up his pace as thunder boomed nearby.

Before he knew it, he crested a rise and looked down into a bowl shaped depression with a gentle slope on one side and steep, almost cliff-like rises on the others. The slope in front of Ryan dropped about fifteen feet at a precarious angle. There was a rundown shack in the center of the hollow, its walls leaning at odd angles as if it might collapse at any moment. Had there been a shack here when he was growing up? He couldn't remember. It didn't seem like it, but if not, where had this one come from? From his vantage point, he could see the dilapidated condition of the house, although his angle only showed him the front and left sides. The porch looked like it might be ready to fall off the structure with the next gentle breeze.

At that moment, he saw Wes. The boy was standing on the porch, his hand raised to knock.

"Wes!" His voice didn't seem to carry to the boy. "Wes! Answer me!" As he stared in disbelief, the door swung open from the inside without Wes ever touching it. Ryan stood by in horror as his son stepped inside.

Ryan looked down the steep slope in front of him and judged the angle and distance. He crouched and stepped forward, intending to climb down and get to that house. What was Wes thinking, going into a strange place like that? He stepped over the edge of the slope, and his heel caught on an exposed root. He found himself tumbling out of control, trying to catch his balance, but it was a lost cause. He fell the entire distance, slamming into the ground below, and felt his head strike something hard and unyielding. And then there was only blackness.

Chapter 3

Of Dragons and Doorways

WES ENTERED THE RUNDOWN SHACK with some trepidation. He took a few steps inside and stopped in awe, not even hearing the door creak shut behind him. What he saw inside was both impossible and wonderful, but what he felt inside was by far more astounding and profound, and even somewhat moving. It was the most bizarre sensation he could have ever imagined, but it was a sensation that he wanted to continue.

Wes felt... safe, warm, comforted. It was almost as if the house were welcoming him inside like a long lost son. No, that wasn't quite right either. The house was conveying the sensation of a loving parent wrapping arms around him in safety and comfort. It was giving him a hug. There was a gentle scent in the air that he couldn't really place at first. Mint, and a hint of chocolate, perhaps, but whatever it was, it was soothing and sweet.

A few more steps took him out of the entryway and into a large, cozy sitting room. The high ceiling was crossed with large oaken beams, and there was a strangely inviting fire burning in the fireplace, despite the warm weather. Everything about the room, in fact, was inviting, and completely at odds with the house's outside appearance. He had been sure, on seeing it from the outside, that the house was nothing more than a small shack with an upstairs off the back of the main room. But from the inside, it seemed much larger. The sitting room was larger than he'd thought the entire house should be, and there were obviously other rooms in the back. Not only that, but he could clearly see a staircase that led up not two, but at least three floors that he could make out.

Still, the overall feel of the house was one of safety, comfort, and welcome. From the overstuffed armchairs to the large, thick rug before the fire, the room seemed designed to evoke a feeling of hominess. Not any particular home, or indeed any place at all that Wes had ever been or imagined, but something about this room resonated with him in ways he would never be able to explain, most especially to himself.

The room was filled with items both strange and commonplace, none of which seemed to go together in any semblance of order. A large glass cabinet contained hundreds of tiny carved figures of dragons, knights, warriors, wizards, all sorts of fantastic creatures and people. In a prominent display case was a scale model of what appeared to be some kind of space ship, straight out of a sci-fi movie. On a side table, he spied what looked to be a stack of comic books, and was absorbed in looking those over for a few moments, but he recognized none of the characters, or even the language of the text. These and other items, all as different from each other as possible, filled the room from wall to wall. But what caught his interest and held it was what he found on the drawing table in the corner. A sextant! He quickly strode over to examine it closely, picking it up off the table.

Yes, it was definitely a sextant, although the design was slightly different, more elaborate, than the one he'd seen in Social Studies class. It seemed to be more ornate, designed to be pretty, unlike the simple utilitarian device Mrs. Jensen had brought for their project. He walked around the room in wonder, the rest of the bizarre contents forgotten for a few moments, examining the sextant in great detail. Just as he passed the bottom of the staircase, however, he heard a thump and the rustle of someone moving. He had forgotten all about the bizarre little man! Suddenly, the strangeness of the situation hit home. He was alone in an unfamiliar house with at least one other person he didn't know. He almost fled then and there, but he could still feel that strange sensation of welcome, and despite his misgivings, he screwed up his courage to speak.

"Hello?" His voice only quavered a tiny bit.

Wes jumped back as a head appeared around the corner of the landing above him.

"Ah, good, you've finally made it!" The head disappeared back around the corner, only to reappear a few moments later. "Well, what are you waiting for?" Then the entire figure stepped backward onto the landing, and Wes saw that the head was attached to the little man he'd followed to the house. The man was tiny, barely five feet tall, and somewhat round. He had a long, flowing beard and scruffy white hair stuffed up under a dusty old hat. He wore an outfit that seemed to be out of another era, with a long robe or tunic held shut by a broad belt, a cloak thrown over his shoulder, and brightly shined leather boots. His boots were the only part of the outfit that shined, though, as all his other clothing seemed to have been left out in a storeroom for the past hundred years. Maybe two hundred. The dust literally wafted from the man as he moved.

"Come, come, boy, time is wasting and days are passing and we must hurry!" The strange little man beckoned Wes up the stairs.

Wes hesitated a moment, but he felt no danger from the little man. In fact, he mostly felt amusement, and still that comforting hominess he had felt since entering this strange house. He glanced back to the front door, thought for a moment, and then made up his mind. He started up the stairs toward the funny little man, who was bouncing impatiently from foot to foot on the landing.

When Wes reached him, the little man grabbed his hand and hurried him around the corner and up to the top of the stairs. "So slow, so slow you go, don't you realize there are people waiting for you to save them?" When they reached the top, Wes looked down a long, seemingly endless hallway.

"Wait a minute," Wes said, stopping and jerking his hand free, his mind racing after hearing that last comment. People here, people waiting for him, people he didn't know, and him in such a strange place... he was feeling the beginnings of worry prickling the back of his neck. "Where are we? What is this place?" The little man sighed loudly at him, exasperated.

"Yes, well, boy, there's a lot to do and not a lot of time, but I know you need the details, lad, I won't forget!" He led Wes over to an arched doorway before the actual hall and led him inside to a small study, the walls covered with bookshelves. There were several comfortable looking chairs and a long couch, with a couple of old tables between them. "All right, lad, take a seat anywhere, I'll be back in just a few moments. There's something very important that I've got to show you!" And with that, the little man hurried out of the room.

Wes was flabbergasted. What should he do? Should he wait, or should he make tracks down the stairs while he had the chance, and get out of this crazy place? He looked down at his hands and was surprised to see that he still held the ornate sextant. Well, a few more minutes couldn't hurt anything, just to find out what was going on.

Wes could never resist his curiosity, and maybe this man could tell him more about the strange device. He shoved the sextant into the open mouth of his backpack and settled down to wait.

⊷⊶ ⊷⊶

The little man was downstairs fumbling with his keys, trying to open the great iron bound door to his workroom. He wasn't quite as prepared as he'd hoped! He had just sent out the call, it seemed, and he wasn't ready for a smart mouthed selfish boy, no matter that he had called him here himself and needed him. He must show him the book! He finally found the key and inserted it into the lock, when he heard a rustling sound behind him. He turned, expecting to see that the boy had followed him down the stairs instead of staying in the sitting room as requested.

"You," he breathed in disgust, but no real fear, when he saw the small creature emerge from the shadows. Its wings were held tightly against its back as it skittered forward on all fours. He readied a spell to fling at the little beast, drawing as much power as he could manage, knowing it would be tricky.

"Yes, Pomander. Me." The little creature's voice carried nothing but contempt, and before the little man could react, the creature sprang.

Pomander's spell hit the black shape hurtling toward him, flinging it backward to slam against the wall. It was back up immediately, though, and rushing toward him again, zigging and zagging down the little hall.

"You must be mad, confronting me here," Pomander said, throwing lightning and fire at the creature without much success. "You can't hope to prevail." He flung another bolt of mystical energy at the beast, missing again and leaving scorch marks on the tiled floor.

"I do as my master tells me, Pomander, as do you!" The creature sprang the last distance toward him. Pomander was ready, though. His blast of pure energy hit the creature full on, bathing it in iridescence. The small form stretched out fully, wings spreading, its small mouth opening wide in a soundless shriek. The light around the creature continued to build until even Pomander could no longer see the thing, and then it faded, leaving nothing in its wake.

"Maybe so, Crowley, but my master doesn't tell me to do stupid things." He shook his head sadly and turned back to the door as an unseen tendril of shadow fell on his shoulder. He felt a sudden chill, and began to tremble. Without warning, he fell to his knees, the trembling becoming an uncontrollable convulsion as he gasped for breath. He pulled his arms and legs in around his chest as the cold grew inside him.

ᘛ⁐̤ᕐᐷ

Wes waited in the sitting room upstairs, not knowing whether to stay or run. All was quiet up there, no sounds intruding from either the outdoors or downstairs where the little man had disappeared. He had finally risen from the chair, making up his mind to leave, when the strange man appeared in the doorway. The man looked at him blankly for a moment.

"Well," prompted Wes, curious, "what was it you were going to show me?"

That startled the little man. "Show you?" He looked back at Wes, suddenly nervous, unable to meet his eyes. "Show? Oh, yes, oh, nothing boy. It was nothing." He stepped into the room, glancing about as he did so. After a moment, he looked at Wes, and a sly grin crossed his face.

"Well, boy, it's time, now. Come along!" He grabbed Wes by the hand and pulled him from the room, suddenly very animated and full of energy. Wes jerked his hand back out of the little man's grasp.

"No way, I'm not going anywhere till you tell me what's going on here. What is this place?"

"Talk while we walk, boy, we've a ways yet to go!" With that, the little man grabbed Wes' hand and tugged him back into motion, not allowing him the luxury of delaying them.

"Where we are," he said in quick, accented words, slightly British or maybe even a little German, "is simply the House. Or the House of Doors. Or the Gatehouse. It's not really important, and I'm fairly sure it doesn't care what we call it." He quickened his pace, pulling Wes along behind him. "As for who I am, which you didn't ask, you may call me Pomander, and I shall call you Wes."

Wes dug in his heels, determined to stop the little man tugging on him. "How did you know my name? What do you mean, it doesn't care? How could it care?"

30

"I know a great many things," said Pomander irritably, "not least of which is your name, young man." He tugged again, hard, and Wes stumbled into motion lest he fall and be dragged behind the little man. Pomander was most definitely stronger than he looked.

"Fine," he said quickly, stumbling along behind the little man. "But what am I doing here? What was that you said about people waiting up here for me to save them?"

"Ah, lad, that's the meat of the story!" For a change, Pomander was the one to slow their pace. "And I suppose you do need to hear the basics, at that, don't you, boy? Listen closely!" And Pomander began to tell his tale.

"The Gatehouse is a very special place. No one knows exactly who created it, or why. What is known is that these doorways we keep passing," he gestured to one of the many doors along the hall, "aren't what you'd consider normal doors in your average family home. No, no, not at all! You see, the universe is in no way, shape, or form the place you have been taught that it is in school all these years." He looked back at Wes, still pulling him down the hall, though more slowly now. "There are many worlds, you see, even worlds between those worlds. And each of these doorways here holds a gateway to hundreds, thousands of worlds, the like of which you've never imagined!"

Pomander stopped walking and approached one of the doors. He tapped the frame.

"Some of these, you see, open onto worlds in this particular plane. For instance, I might open this door here and find that on the other side was the surface of Jupiter, or maybe a planet orbiting Alpha Centauri." Hearing those words come out of a tiny man dressed in clothing that would have seemed ancient a hundred years ago struck Wes as very strange indeed. "Other doors open to worlds on other planes, other universes, if you will."

Wes thought he finally understood what was going on here, and adjusted his thinking. The guy was a nutjob! But it seemed to be a harmless kind of crazy, not the homicidal maniac kind, and he was really very entertaining. Wes decided to play along.

"It sounds like something out of a story," he said with a wide grin.

"It is something out of a story, boy, very astute of you! It's the basis of stories, as a matter of fact. Some of the greatest works of 'fiction' your world has produced were written by people who, well, I suppose you would say 'picked up' on emanations from the House. As far as I can tell, this is something unique to your world." He glanced away for a moment, and said, seemingly to himself, "Your world is unique in a number of ways, it seems."

"What ways?"

"Let's not worry about that just yet, Wes," he said, grasping Wes' hand again and resuming his quick pace down the hall. "What you need to understand is that these doors are gateways to imagination. The rules you might find behind one of these doors are different from the rules you've grown up with all your life. Maybe there's real magic behind that door there. Or perhaps great starships fly through the vast reaches of space faster than light behind that other door. Maybe people run around in skin-tight, brightly colored costumes, battling evil with their amazing powers and abilities far beyond those of… well, you get the idea, child! What I'm getting at is, think of anything a boy like yourself might have ever read or seen in your television or movies or in your imagination itself. Any of those things could possibly, even probably, be on the other side of a doorway!"

Wes couldn't stop himself from laughing. "So behind that door, there might be people flying or shooting lasers out their eyes!"

"Or you might find a powerful wizard, now you've got it! Now hurry, we're almost there!" And he quickened his steps yet again.

All this stopping and starting, hurrying and pausing, essentially being dragged who knew where, grated on Wes' nerves for a moment. A part of his mind kept tickling him, telling him that this situation should have been scaring him silly, and yet he couldn't seem to feel any fear here. Between the sense of warmth and safety he could still feel emanating from somewhere, and the little man's odd mannerisms, he couldn't help but feel amused by this whole adventure.

"Now, you must understand, lad, it's not all wine and roses on the worlds behind the doors, any more than it is here. They're all actually very much like this world, in that they're all filled with people. And people, of course, come in all types. Every world has its heroes, but every world also has its villains." He paused in his monologue here, as if for dramatic effect, and again stopped their forward progress. He looked nervously down the length of the hall from whence they'd come, and then down the seemingly endless passage ahead of them, and he spoke in a melodramatic stage whisper. "And then, there's Crowley!" He looked up at Wes, as if expecting the name to mean something to him.

"Ummm…" said Wes. "Crowley. Okay." Wes looked at Pomander blankly. "Who's Crowley?"

The little man's face showed his sudden annoyance, and he began walking again, dragging Wes along behind him with a great harrumph.

"Yes, boy, Crowley! Even here, that name should strike terror into your very marrow! A powerful demon, servant of the Unnamed, Crowley fills men's hearts with fear wherever he's found!" His voice took on a sonorous, almost reverent tone. "Ten feet tall, he is, with great black wings and row upon row of razor-sharp teeth! His terrible countenance drives mortals mad with a single glance! The arcane powers at his disposal are unmatched in all the worlds, and woe unto me, he is my nemesis!"

"So… he's the big bad guy in the story, then," Wes said chuckling, imagining this whole thing as a comic book or video game. At Pomander's crestfallen look, he quickly said, "He sounds pretty tough!"

"The Unnamed is the 'big bad guy', as you so eloquently put it, boy, but Crowley is his right hand, and quite enough to be getting on with. In most cases, though, Crowley works from the shadows toward the goals of the Unnamed."

"But you still haven't told me what it is you want from me, and who I'm supposed to save." Wes was enjoying the little man's story so much that the strangeness of the entire situation was becoming lost on him. "What is it I'm supposed to do, defeat this Crowley guy?"

"Ah, Wes," Pomander said, guffawing. It expanded into a laugh so hard that tears streamed down his face. "Heavens no, lad, you could never hope to face Crowley directly! If you ever see Crowley, you run the opposite way as fast as you can!" He got his laughter under control and wiped the tears from his beard, still rushing Wes down the long hallway and chuckling occasionally. "No, you see, Crowley works behind the scenes, sowing seeds of dissension and evil throughout the worlds to try and claim them for his master. My job, and your reason for being here, is to unplant those seeds and unravel the plans he hatches. Ah! We're here!"

Wes was startled by their sudden halt. He looked up the corridor, and then back the way they'd come, and couldn't see the end of the hall in either direction. "What do you mean?"

Pomander pointed proudly at the door to their right. "This is it, the one we need! On the other side, you'll find the kingdom of Canellin. Everything else you need to know, you will learn there. There is a man there who can help you. So, simply defeat the evil dragon and its minions and return home, job well done!" He looked Wes in the eye and opened the door to… nothingness.

A roiling, swirling nothingness, if you can imagine that. Wes couldn't tear his eyes from the sight.

"Do you, Wes, accept this obligation of your own free will, and swear you'll carry it out or die trying?"

"Sure," said Wes absently, not really paying attention to Pomander's words. His mind was still trying to grasp the concept of a swirling nothingness. Was that even possible? At that exact moment, a bestial roar erupted from the other side of the doorway. "Wait," he said, "did you say dragon?"

Pomander shoved him roughly through the doorway and slammed the door. With a gleam in his eye and a sinister chuckle, he started back down the long hall.

ₒᴼᴸᴼ ᴼᴸᴼₒ

Awareness returned to Ryan in a slow wash of pain. He struggled to sit up, causing his head to fall off. That's what it felt like, at least, as the pain overcame him and everything faded out again. When the wave passed, he put his hand to his temple and reassured himself that his head was, indeed, still attached. Much more worrisome to him, though, was the blood that covered his hand when he pulled it away. It took him a few moments to realize that the darkness around him was due to night having fallen while he was unconscious. Rain poured in torrents, and he was covered in blood and caked with mud. Comprehension dawned, and memory slowly returned.

I fell, he thought to himself. I hit my head on something. I must have been out for hours! He stood up quickly, and immediately wished that he hadn't. His knees buckled, and he sank halfway back to the ground before regaining his balance. He could tell both from his grogginess and the fact that he was still bleeding freely after all this time that he must be hurt badly.

There was something he needed to do, if only he could think of it. Where was Wes? The house! Wes had been about to go into that

34

house in the hollow! He turned his head quickly and again regretted it as nausea struck him. When his vision cleared, he could see the house silhouetted in flashes by the occasional lightning. There seemed to be a light on in a second story window, but other than that, all was dark and quiet, the only sound the rain and thunder, and the occasional frog braving the torrential downpour.

The light started thoughts racing through Ryan's head, dark thoughts that chilled him to the bone. Child molesters, serial killers, crazy murdering hermits squatting in abandoned, secluded houses. He had to get to Wes! The fog of confusion, though, was hard to work through. He struggled upright and started toward the structure, his feet squelching in the muck. He was having too much trouble concentrating, too much difficulty keeping his thoughts focused, as he took a few stumbling steps toward the shack and again fell to his knees. Every few seconds, his vision would fade out, and when it came back, he'd be a little closer to the house. Somehow, he found himself on the porch, lurched toward the door, raised his fist, and pounded. Every blow sent lightning bolts through his skull.

The door slowly creaked open, and Ryan fell inside. He was surprised that he was having so much trouble standing, seeing, concentrating. He hauled himself to his knees once again, trying to count how many times he had fallen to get this far, trying to shake his vision clear. Working his way back to his feet, he made his way past the entryway to the large sitting room. He felt a strange sensation, something bizarre perhaps emanating from the house itself, but it was so vague that he dismissed it from his mind.

"Wes?" His voice sounded like a bellow in his head, but to his ears it was a whisper. He tried again, louder.

"Wes! Are you in here?" He shuffled forward, single-minded now that he was inside.

"Who are you?" The voice came from the bottom of the staircase. Squinting in that direction, Ryan spied an odd little man in archaic clothing who was staring at him in obvious surprise.

"I'm... I... who are you? Where's Wes?" Ryan stood straighter and took a few halting steps toward the little man.

"How rude," said the man. "You didn't answer my question, and you're dripping blood all over the rug." He stared at Ryan reproachfully. "I am, umm, Pomander, and I'm afraid Wes is gone. Now, sir, as I said before, who are you?"

"Ryan. I'm Ryan." When Pomander said nothing, Ryan clarified. "Ryan Bellamy." Ryan's knees buckled for a moment, but he retained his balance. "I saw my son come in here. Where is he?" He felt a sudden surge of anger toward the little man. "Where's my son?" He lurched toward Pomander, intending to grab him and shake the answers he wanted out of him by force.

"Hmm," said Pomander, taking a step back. "A father's anger. That could be quite dangerous. Quite useful, too, I admit, but to be honest, I don't think you'll be around long enough to be either a danger or a use to me." He looked Ryan up and down as if sizing him up. "You realize you're not in the best condition at the moment, don't you? You're bleeding rather badly, and you can hardly stand. No, I don't think you'll be able to interfere at all, for good or ill. Regardless, your son is not here. He's running a little… errand for me at the moment, and I'd really rather you be kept out of it."

Ryan drew himself to his full height, angry now, the little man's callous words galvanizing him to action. He was by no means an aggressive man, avoiding confrontation at almost any cost, but not where his son's safety was concerned. "Tell me where he is." He took two steps forward, right up to Pomander, towering over the little man. "Tell me now, or take me to him. You do not want me any angrier than I already am, I promise you that!" He hoped Pomander didn't call his bluff. It was taking everything he had to stay upright, and he was sure even this tiny little man could take him easily.

"Spirit. You have it in abundance, don't you, my good man?" Pomander looked up at him, a gleam in his eye and no trace of fear. "That and bravado. You can't even stand, and you're threatening me with violence." He looked thoughtful for a moment. "You love your son a great deal, I can see that. I may be able to use you after all. I'm not sure what you'll be able to accomplish, even if you survive the trip. Confusion, if nothing else. Chaos is always an admirable goal! Wes has been there for quite some time, and will surely be well on his way to finishing my little task by now, if he's going to finish it at all." He waved his hand theatrically, and dizziness again overtook Ryan. When his vision cleared again, he found himself standing in a hallway with no apparent end, a doorway in front of him, and the little man nowhere in sight.

"What…?"

36

"Quiet," a sharp voice said in his head. "You are about to make a journey beyond anything you've known, with little chance of survival and even smaller chance of success. It will be difficult, and there will be danger to you, and to Wes. But if you want to have any chance at all, when you arrive, immediately tell whoever you meet that Pomander sent you, and ask for Diaticus. Your son is in danger. It's up to you to save him. Now, go."

The door in front of Ryan opened slowly, and he felt a hard shove against his back. Then a sensation of falling… falling…

Ryan fell to his knees in the dust, hot sun beating down on him. He rose shakily to his feet and looked around. He was in some kind of courtyard surrounded by a high wall. Directly across the broad court from him, a woman in strange clothing saw him and raced off around a corner with a cry of alarm. From the other direction, four very large men wearing what appeared to be some kind of armor approached at a run, spears lowered, charging. He held his hands palm out in front of him, unable to find words or think of anything else to do. Panic engulfed him as danger approached. Finally, he squeaked out, "Puh… Pomander sent me!" And then he collapsed into oblivion.

Chapter 4

Unexpected Talents

OR THE SECOND TIME, Ryan's vision cleared and he woke with no immediate memory of where he was or what had happened to him. This time, though, when he put fingertips to temple, they came away free of blood and pain. With that thought, memory suddenly returned, and he sat bolt upright with a shout.

"Wes!"

His unexpected cry roused the tall man seated in a high backed chair next to the bed. The man surged to his feet and sprang to Ryan's side, placing his hands on Ryan's shoulders and easing him back down in the bed.

"Ho, friend, be calm! Peace!" The man's voice was firm as he did his best to keep Ryan in the bed. Ryan struggled feebly for a moment, but only managed to get himself tangled in the bedding, and he finally let himself fall back, exhausted.

"You don't understand," he said weakly. "I have to find my son. I have to find Wes."

"Believe me, stranger, I understand, but things are not exactly as they seem." The big man walked to the door and leaned out, speaking briefly and quietly to someone outside, and then returned and settled himself back in his chair. The man was huge, easily seven feet tall, with a barrel chest and long blonde hair that hung past his shoulders. He was in his middle years, perhaps fifty, but he gave the impression of a much younger man. "I've called for the mage, and he should be here straightaway. First, though, I think introductions are in order. I am Luther Askadi, master at arms at High Keep and visiting here at the Collegium. And you are?"

Ryan ignored Luther's question and asked several of his own. "Where am I? What happened to me, why am I in this bed? Why am I so weak?" His mind was awhirl with more questions, but he couldn't put voice to any of them. He strained to remember how he'd gotten here, but all he could recapture was a vague memory of a door and an image of a little man that looked like a character out of a kids' book. The only thought that was strong enough to seize upon was that Wes was in some kind of danger.

"You're in Collegium Keep," Luther said patiently, adding after a moment, "in the kingdom of Canellin. As for what happened, we were rather hoping you would…"

"We were hoping you would enlighten us when you awoke," came a high pitched, creaking voice from the doorway. Ryan looked up to see a tall man, taller than Luther despite his stooped posture, entering the room. The man was rail-thin, almost emaciated, and was garbed in a long flowing robe of deep scarlet and a large, intricate golden pendant with some sort of sigil engraved on it. He was stooped over a long, twisted walking staff. Ryan watched in silence as the man shuffled over, pulling another chair next to the bed.

"I am Diaticus, First Wizard of the Conclave, Master of the Collegium of the Arts, and Lord of Collegium Keep," he said grandly, although a bit nasally. "And what is your name, good sir?"

Ryan swallowed hard. "Ryan. Ryan Bellamy. Sir." Ryan had no idea what was going on here, but this man exuded authority somehow. There was no way he'd find Wes if he ended up locked away somewhere out of sight. A 'sir' here and there didn't seem out of order.

Diaticus looked surprised at the suddenly respectful tone, and quickly waved his hand in dismissal. "No, no, friend, my apologies. I've been under a great deal of stress lately, and I suppose that tends to magnify my already world renowned pomposity." He smiled deprecatingly. "Please, call me Diaticus."

"Diaticus. All right." Ryan glanced around at the strange room, trying to grasp what was going on. "A wizard," he said, amazed. "And some kind of medieval warrior," he added, referring to Luther. "Could someone please tell me what's going on here? What did I fall into?" He shook his head as if trying to clear it. "Am I dreaming? Did I lose too much blood and pass out?"

"You did indeed lose quite a bit of blood, but I can assure you, this is no dream," said Diaticus. "I healed you."

"That's right. I hit my head. I fell down a hill and smacked my head against something, maybe a tree stump. I was trying to get to Wes!"

"Ah, yes, I had wondered how you came to be so gravely injured. That must have been quite some fall, stranger!" Diaticus smiled at Ryan warmly. "The only words we've been able to get out of you for the past three days were the names Pomander and Wes. We weren't able to ask you how you came to be here, and so badly hurt. When I heard you'd said Pomander sent you, I was afraid there might be trouble at the Gatehouse."

"Trouble? Gatehouse? I don't know anything about trouble, or any gatehouses." Ryan's eyes suddenly widened as something Diaticus had said dawned on him. "Three days! I have to get out of here and find Wes!"

"You know nothing of the Gatehouse? How is that possible, if Pomander sent you?" Diaticus' eyes narrowed suspiciously.

Ryan settled back, straining to remember. "Pomander… that weird little guy that was in the shack Wes went into? I remember. He… he sent me here somehow. Pushed me through a door, and suddenly I was in a courtyard." Ryan sounded confused.

"Did Pomander not explain all this to you?" Diaticus sounded incredulous.

"I don't know. He may have. I can't remember. He just said that Wes needed me."

"Ah, well, as to that… Wes is your son, I take it?" At Ryan's nod, Diaticus glanced away almost nervously. "Well, he may need you at that. I simply don't know for sure."

"What's that supposed to mean? Where's my son? Is he here?"

"No, not anymore. He left us almost two weeks ago."

Ryan stared at Diaticus, uncomprehending. "Two weeks? That's not possible!" Ryan was starting to get agitated. "I can't have been unconscious for more than a couple of hours, and you said I'd been here for three days. How can Wes have been gone for two weeks?"

"I understand your confusion, my friend. Your frame of reference is skewed, particularly in regard to time." Diaticus' voice settled into a lecturing tone. "Time flows differently between the worlds. A moment there could be a week here. Wes arrived here nearly two months ago, and left us two weeks ago."

Ryan's mind boggled. Two months? Impossible! "Time flows differently. Sure. This has to be a dream."

"Didn't Pomander explain any of this to you?"

"No, he didn't explain anything to me! He just shoved me through some weird swirly door and told me to find Wes!"

"I see," said Diaticus, puzzled. "You know nothing of the Gatehouse, you were gravely injured, and yet Pomander sent you through the doorway anyway. How odd."

"Everything about this is odd," muttered Ryan. "As far as I can remember, I was looking for my son in the woods a few hours ago, so we could have dinner with my parents. And now, I'm apparently insane!" He pounded the bed in frustration. "Where's my son? Where's Wes?"

"Well, it's a bit of a long story." Diaticus leaned forward and met Ryan's gaze. "You see, when Wes arrived here, he was nearly hysterical. Because of the manner of his arrival, which was quite similar to yours, and because he kept repeating the name Pomander, he was immediately brought to me…"

Ryan did his best to remain calm as he listened to Diaticus begin to relate the story of his first meeting with Wes…

⚬◑ ◐⚬

The day Wes had arrived, Diaticus had been hard at work penning dispatches to King Edward. Roving brigands had again been at work in the outlying townships, committing depravities on the defenseless populace, and the king needed to be kept informed. The scratching of quill on parchment was the only sound to be heard, until a soft knock on the door interrupted the mage's thoughts.

"Come," he called in his creaking voice.

The door opened to admit the sergeant of the guard, escorting a strangely dressed youth by a firm grip on the arm. The boy's face was ashen, and his eyes were wide. His gaze darted around the room, never resting in one place for more than an instant.

"Your pardon, my Lord," said the sergeant, "but this requires your attention. This lad appeared in the courtyard as if from nowhere, obviously by magical means. He's been babbling about gates and doorways, and told us someone named Pomander sent him. I brought him to you straightaway."

Diaticus looked from the guard to the frightened boy and back again. "Pomander, did you say?" The guard nodded. "Thank you, sergeant. Leave the boy with me and wait outside."

The guard nodded, releasing Wes and saluting with an arm across his chest. He turned on his heel and strode from the room. The boy seemed to shrink in on himself, confused and terrified. Diaticus rose and slowly walked around the desk, trying to look as reassuring as possible.

"It's all right, child," he said. "No one's going to hurt you. Please, sit." He gestured toward an overstuffed chair. The boy looked at the old wizard for a moment, and then fell heavily into the offered chair.

"They almost killed me," he said quietly.

"What? Who almost killed you?" The wizard made a discreet gesture behind his back, releasing a calming spell toward the boy.

"Those guys down there with the spears and the armor," replied the terrified youth numbly. "They were running at me full blast with their spears pointed at me, until I yelled that Pomander sent me. Then they brought me here."

Diaticus chuckled. "Imagine how they felt, child. A strangely clad boy, appearing from nowhere in a supposedly impregnable keep?" He gave the boy a wide grin. "You probably took ten years off their lives!"

The boy's agitation was starting to lessen perceptibly; the calming spell was obviously taking effect. He smiled back at Diaticus nervously.

"Yeah," he said, "I guess that'd freak me out, too."

"There, now, see? Just a misunderstanding." Diaticus' voice was calm, almost hypnotic. "Now, what are you called, boy?"

"Wes Bellamy."

"A worthy name, Wes Bellamy. Please, call me Diaticus." He returned to his seat behind the desk and regarded Wes from across the expanse of dark wood. "Now, Wes, please, tell me what has transpired, and how you came to be in my courtyard."

Wes began telling his story, hesitantly at first, and then it came rushing forth in a torrent. He told of finding the strange house in his grandparents' woods, the Gatehouse, the house that shouldn't have been there. He told of the fascinating items he had seen there, and even opened his pack and showed Diaticus the ornate sextant that he had inadvertently brought with him. He told of meeting Pomander, and of the little man's bizarre behavior. And, finally, he detailed the long trip down the endless hallway, his conversation with Pomander and the little man's cryptic instructions, and his stomach churning fall through nothingness. He looked almost relieved when the story was finally over.

"Interesting. You say that before today, you had never heard of Pomander, or the Gatehouse?"

"No, sir," said Wes. "Even when he was telling me all this, I just thought he was some crazy little man. I never imagined I'd end up… someplace like this."

"And you're certain he told you to defeat the dragon?"

"Yes. He said I'd be able to go home after I defeated the dragon and its minions."

"How strange." Diaticus was genuinely puzzled. He knew of Pomander, of course; he was well known to the high-ranked wizards of all the worlds, being the only wizard on any world who could travel between them without the aid of the doors. Indeed, Diaticus was proud that Pomander considered him his agent on this world. Why would Pomander send an untrained stripling on a quest, particularly to this world, after so long refusing to send a champion at all?

"Well, now that you've relaxed, Wes Bellamy," said Diaticus, his easy manner putting Wes further at ease, "I believe there is a puzzle here that must be worked out. You see, I believe you have been sent here in error."

Wes didn't respond.

"Understand, Wes, that I am quite familiar with Pomander and his duties, and he with our difficulties. But for years beyond counting, indeed, since before my own birth, Pomander has insisted that to send his own agent here would accomplish nothing but to sow confusion. You see, the Unnamed is not active here. The evil at work here is native to this world, although humanity is not.

"Long ago, our world was dying, some impending disaster that has been lost in the depths of history. Pomander's people came to us with an offer of aid. Pomander himself led the mages who journeyed to our world, conveying them through the Gatehouse. An immense exodus was undertaken, the Great Crossing, and thousands of people were saved from the catastrophe and brought here to settle. A few of our saviors remained here, helping us build a society to replace the one we'd left behind. Once we were self sufficient, those that saved us left us here to fend for ourselves. We respect and revere them for what they did for us. We've kept what memory we can of them alive as best we can. Indeed, such artifacts as they left behind are kept here at the

Wizard's Collegium and in the Tower of Lore in Karsenon, and are among the Kingdom's most valued possessions.

"However, this world was not ours. Dragons have existed here since long before the Crossing. None had ever troubled us here, though. Their domain was far away, on a continent halfway around the world. We kept up relations with them, and they would send us an occasional emissary, but there was never any strife between us. The dragons were, for the most part, relatively peaceful creatures. Don't misunderstand, they were dangerous predators, but they were also thinking beings. They had evolved a morality and society that mankind has never matched.

"Nearly two thousand years ago, a dragon appeared on that far off continent who rebelled against their rather rigid code of morality and ethics. It was a violent, evil creature, and very powerful. Its magical abilities and physical prowess were without peer. The other dragons tried to reason with the beast, but it was cunning, and unwilling to conform. Through subterfuge and subtle machinations, it was able to gain immense power, becoming known as the Great Dragon, its true name lost to history. Indeed, names have a great deal of power in the world of magic, and the dragon made certain its true name would be hidden in the annals of time. Eventually, the Great Dragon became unstoppable. Within two hundred years, it had done away with its brethren, becoming the last of its kind in the entire world.

"The beast caused little trouble in this part of the world at first, but over time, it began extending its territory until it encompassed its entire continent. It then began extending even further, crossing the Great Sea, and eventually arrived here, in Canellin, about eight hundred years ago." Diaticus shuddered. "The results were devastating. The other continents on this world are largely uninhabited, except for this one. The dragon for the first time met real resistance, and was not pleased. But it was determined. War was inevitable."

"War with a dragon? You couldn't just send people out to kill it?"

"That was tried, but with no success. You see, the Dragon has magical abilities that dwarf any human's on this world. Even I am no match for the sheer arcane might it can wield. After meeting humans in battle the first few times, the dragon decided to revise its methods. It began capturing humans, commoners, people who would not be terribly missed. Using its magics on them, it transformed them, causing them to become something between human and dragon." Diaticus rose and shuffled to the large bookshelf along one wall of the room, extracting a book and returning to the desk. He flipped through several pages, finally settling on one, and turned the book so Wes could see. On the page was a small painting of some kind of lizard creature towering over a warrior in plate mail. The creature was vaguely humanoid, covered in scales and wearing bits and pieces of armor and clothing. The face was long, the jaws extended, and the forehead sloped back sharply. The mouth was open to reveal rows of large, sharp teeth.

"That's… that used to be a person?" Wes was horrified.

"Yes, a normal man or woman, transformed by the Dragon's magic." Diaticus snapped the book shut sharply. "And the Dragon created hordes of them. Troops for its new army." He moved the book aside.

"So he invaded your country."

" 'It', child, not 'he'. Dragons have no gender. They lay… or rather, laid… eggs, which were germinated magically. The eggs were then hidden away until it was decided to allow them to hatch, usually one at a time. All it took was for the germinated egg to come into close proximity with a mature dragon, and the hatching began. We believe that is how they controlled their population so rigidly, and how the Great Dragon was able to destroy them in the end. It destroyed the hatching grounds.

"Be that as it may, the Great Dragon more than invaded. It devastated and desecrated everything it came in contact with, gaining more and more followers, more and more power, and creating hordes of soldiers in an attempt to overwhelm us. The war raged for over a hundred years before we were able to drive the dragon back. It retreated to a mountain cavern on the border of the conquered territory. We've never been able to retake that territory, but we've held the beast back. There are occasional skirmishes and flare-ups, of course, the most recent sparking a shorter war that lasted almost ten years. But for the most part, the last two hundred years have been quiet."

"Then… why am I here," asked Wes, "if not to save you from the Dragon? That's what Pomander said I was supposed to do." He pondered for a moment. "Why would I even be here for that? I don't know anything about alternate worlds, or magic, or the Unnamed! If your whole army's no match for the thing, how can you expect one kid to do anything at all?"

"Exactly my point! Not only are you woefully unprepared for the chore, but this is not the type of task Pomander would even choose for one of his agents, capable or otherwise! Let me ask you a question. Do you know the purpose of the Gatehouse, and Pomander's great task?"

"Yeah," said Wes, "I think. Sort of, I guess." He looked thoughtful, but didn't sound sure at all. "Pomander protects all the worlds from this evil guy called Crowley who works for some big bad guy called the Unnamed. When a world is in danger, he sends someone to mess up Crowley's plans and save the day."

"An incomplete assessment, but accurate as far as it goes." Diaticus rose and shuffled around the desk, taking the seat next to Wes, leaning forward to meet his eyes more closely. "The Gatehouse opens onto a multitude of worlds. Each world has a doorway that leads back to the Gatehouse. However, Crowley has control of a place that is something like the Gatehouse, in the realm of the Unnamed. No one on our side knows exactly how it might manifest, but it's safe to assume that it's similar to the Gatehouse. They also have the ability to travel to the multitude of worlds that their doorways can access, and those worlds have a doorway back to Crowley's realm. However, where things get interesting is when there is a world that intersects with both the Gatehouse and the realm of Crowley and the Unnamed. Such worlds need protection to keep the Unnamed from gaining a foothold and laying waste to entire universes, bringing them completely under the sway of evil." He paused to let that soak in, looking into Wes' eyes. "Ours, however, is not such a world."

Wes looked at Diaticus, perplexed. "What does that mean?"

"It means, the realm of the Unnamed has no intersection here in Canellin or anywhere on this world. It means that Crowley cannot come here. It means, in effect, that we are safe from the machinations of evil from beyond our plane." He looked at Wes meaningfully. "It means, lad, that there is no reason I can imagine that Pomander would send you here."

Wes merely stared at Diaticus. After a moment he rose, numb, and walked to the window that looked out over the courtyard. He surveyed the view, seeming to ponder things, and then turned to Diaticus.

46

"So Pomander has never sent anyone here to help you? No one from my world has ever been here?"

"Well, not exactly." Diaticus also rose and went to join Wes at the window. "Pomander has never sent anyone, but there have been visitations by people from the world of the Gatehouse. The fabric between the worlds sometimes grows thin, you see. Between one step and the next, someone from your world, where the Gatehouse lies, can find himself on any one of the thousands of worlds that the Gatehouse connects with. Oftentimes, they immediately find themselves back on their own world, and assume their minds were playing tricks on them. Sometimes, they find themselves trapped here for a time, a day, perhaps, or a week or even longer. Most find that when they return, only a few moments have passed, thanks to the differences in the way time flows between the worlds. Others, though, travel to those rare planes where time flows slower than it does on your world instead of faster. Those poor souls may find that the minutes or hours they spend there have equaled weeks, even years or decades, on your world." He looked away for a moment, pondering. "They may make it home, but not the home they knew. Everyone they knew may be dead and gone, and the world may be unrecognizable to them." He looked at the horrified expression on Wes' face. "Ah, lad, not to worry, this isn't a world like that. Time here flows much faster than it does in the Gatehouse."

"So you're saying that before too long, I'll sort of snap back to my world, and it'll be like I never left," said Wes with obvious relief.

"Oh, no, I'm afraid not, Wes!" Diaticus put his hand on Wes' arm in sympathy. "I'm sorry if my words misled you. No, you came here through the Gatehouse, and you must return there through the doorway on this world. It is the only known way back to your home. But I vow, lad, I will do everything in my power to find another path."

Wes looked at the old man for a moment, meeting his gaze, detecting something in the catch in his voice. As he regarded the wizard, he asked, "And where is the doorway?" His expression made it plain he already had some idea. A sad look settled on Diaticus' face.

"In the lair of the Great Dragon."

⚬⚬⚬

"Wait. There's no way home?" Ryan's voice was disturbed as he interrupted the wizard's long winded narrative.

"I said no such thing, friend. We don't know if there is another way home for you or not. We do know that there is a passage in the lair of the Great Dragon. I have been working tirelessly to solve that very problem." He looked at Ryan and asked curtly, "May I continue? There is much more to tell."

Ryan lapsed into silence, listening intently.

⚜ ⚜ ⚜

Diaticus saw to Wes' comfort by assigning him a guard to watch over him and see that he learned his way around, and partly to keep the lad company in his strange predicament. He then began poring through his magical texts seeking some hint as to a method of returning someone across the veil between the worlds. To his knowledge, only two beings in all creation could cross between realities without the use of one of the great doorways: Pomander, and the demon Crowley. Each had the power to travel anywhere their individual realms touched. But alas, it was beyond the skill of every other wizard Diaticus had ever heard of.

His search appeared to be fruitless, though, all of the magical texts he was able to decipher confirming that travel between the worlds was not possible without the doorways, or Pomander's magic. Diaticus didn't give up, even turning to several of the untranslated texts he'd collected over the years. He hoped to find some reference that would allow him to translate just the right passage that might give him a clue. But it was unlikely, particularly since he didn't know which of these untranslated books, if any, might hold the clue, and he couldn't read them in the first place. He went to bed that night discouraged.

The next morning, Diaticus had Wes brought to his study once again.

"Did you sleep well?" he inquired, looking at the boy's disheveled appearance. Wes was wearing the same clothes he had arrived in, wrinkled and unkempt.

"I guess," said Wes, sounding irritable.

"And your chambers were acceptable, your comfort was seen to?"

"Yeah. The guard you sent me with, Gideon, he was nice enough. He hung out with me for a while and made sure I was settled in."

Diaticus looked confused. "Lad, I must tell you, sometimes I have trouble comprehending your speech. I think I have puzzled out that last statement, though."

"I'm sorry, I didn't really think about it, but I guess it would be hard hearing me use expressions from back home. You probably don't know what hanging out is."

"It's not just that. You see, part of the problem is the language barrier, a problem of which I don't think you're aware."

"What language barrier? We're all speaking the same language."

"Yes and no. We are indeed speaking the same language, it's just not the language you think it is. I realized that during our conversation yesterday, and last night I confirmed my hypothesis while searching my texts for a way to get you home."

Wes suddenly snapped alert, hopeful.

"You found a way home?"

"No, lad, no, but I won't stop searching. No, what I found was more information on the Gatehouse and what it does to the travelers it sends."

"What do you mean, what it does to them? To me, I mean?" Wes sounded concerned.

"Nothing bad, my boy. Just adjustments it makes. One of the more minor ones is language." He held a parchment out to Wes. "Tell me, can you read this?"

Wes took the parchment, glancing at it, but all he saw were a bunch of squiggles and dots. He shook his head.

"I thought not," said Diaticus. "Then would it surprise you to know that that is the language we're speaking?"

"We're speaking English," said Wes, not understanding.

"We're speaking Trade, the most common tongue on this world. The Gatehouse adjusts."

Wes shook his head, then thought a moment. He opened his mouth and uttered a nonsense word that Diaticus missed completely.

"I'm sorry, what?"

"I just… I was testing a theory. I figured that there might be some words that couldn't be said in your language, like," and he spouted several more nonsense words, "and I guess I was right."

"What were you trying to say, if I might ask?"

"Mainly names of things I figure you don't have here, technology stuff." Wes considered for a moment, searching for the words to explain. "Let's see, one is a flying machine with spinning blades on the top of it that lift it in the air, another is a box that shows moving pictures on a glass in the front of it, and the last one was a machine that just about everybody on my world uses to travel around from place to place." He thought for a moment. "And you really didn't understand any of them? That second one, the box with the moving pictures, part of the word is 'vision', you didn't get that?"

"Not at all, lad, not a bit of it. But the word for 'vision' in Trade may not be at all similar to the word in your language."

"Weird. Cool." Wes smiled. "I wonder if I could switch back to English to talk to people, kind of like a secret code."

"I don't think so. But who would you share this secret code with, even if you could? No one here would understand a word of it."

"Good point," Wes said, embarrassed at having missed it.

"Be that as it may, lad, that's not the only reason I wanted to see you again." He motioned Wes to take a seat. "I have formulated a theory, based on the cryptic wording of a passage in a very ancient text. It spoke of the magical identifiers, sort of signatures, of beings who cross between the realms. If we can detect your signature, I may have a way in which we can contact Pomander."

"How?"

"A magical contact spell. It's all very complicated, child, but trust me, if I can detect your magical signature, which is unique to you and your world, I should be able to contact him."

That got Wes' attention. First, contacting Pomander might be the best chance he had of getting home, even though Wes didn't entirely trust the little man. But also, it would involve magic. Wes had always dreamed of experiencing real magic, the kind that only existed in books and stories where he was from.

"What do you need me to do?"

"I will be delving your aura magically. I need you to sit quietly and clear your mind. Can you do that?"

Wes nodded quickly and leaned back in his chair, trying to still his thoughts. It was difficult for him, especially as Diaticus placed both hands on the boy's temples and pressed gently. The old man began to move his fingertips forward, across Wes' forehead and back again.

"Still your mind, Wes. Empty it of all conscious thought."

Wes tried, but couldn't make himself think of nothing. How can a person think of nothing? Thinking of nothing is something, therefore you're not thinking of nothing. Blackness? No, that was something. Blank white? No, that just reminded him of paper, and that got him thinking about school and all the problems he'd had in that area. His mind kept bouncing over these seemingly random ideas as Diaticus worked.

"Still, Wes. Quiet your thoughts. Your mind must be still."

"I can't," said Wes in disgust. "My mind doesn't get still. How can you think about nothing?"

"Don't try to think about nothing, as you say, boy. It's not possible for the human brain. I don't need your mind to be a blank, just still." He lowered his fingertips from Wes' head. "Do you understand what I mean by that?"

"I don't think so, not really. How can my mind be still?"

"Well... is there anything that you do that you don't really have to think about to do it? Some task that you're so used to performing that you can do it on instinct?"

"I... maybe, yeah."

"Good, good. Then think of that activity, think of how you go about it, how you do it instinctively. Do you have that centered in your mind?"

"Yeah. Yeah, I have it." Wes closed his eyes, letting the stillness come. "It's there."

"Good. Now, in your mind, do it. Let the instinct take over, and do whatever it is that you do, let it flow on pure instinct without having to think. No conscious thought, just the instinct, let it happen without directing it." Diaticus' fingers were back against Wes' temples. "Let it flow. You're doing well." His fingers traced across Wes' forehead, back again, flowing through random patterns. He stopped speaking and let the magic flow through him, delving into Wes' makeup, the way the energy and matter that made up his body fit together, seeking the unique energy pattern that represented his world. He sensed it, gently pushing toward it, and finally, there it was. He traced his mind through the pattern, recreating it within himself.

"There, now. That's it." Diaticus removed his fingers from Wes' temples. "I have it." He smiled down at Wes, but the boy didn't respond. He wasn't moving, his eyes gently closed, a peaceful expression on his face. Diaticus shook his shoulder gently, and the boy's eyes snapped open.

"Sorry. I kind of got lost there for a minute, I guess."

Diaticus smiled down at him. "It's all right, Wes, though I must admit that once you found the stillness, you kept it solid much better than I could at twice your age. If I may ask, what was the instinct you latched onto?"

"Music," Wes said reverently. "Playing my trumpet."

"Interesting. And quite effective, I might add."

"Did you... did you find what you needed?"

"Indeed I did. Now if you would, please, make yourself comfortable while I consult my notes, and we can begin."

"Well... do you mind if I get up, walk around a little bit? Whatever you did, I'm feeling kind of tense."

"Certainly, child, just don't wander off."

"Okay," said Wes, and he rose and walked slowly across the room, his eyes taking in the contents as Diaticus returned to his desk.

Diaticus began consulting a large book he had laid open on his desk, the oldest and most powerful tome he owned that was intelligible to him. He pulled a sheet of parchment over that he'd been working on, comparing his notes to what he read on the page. It would be very complex, using the magical signature he'd replicated from within Wes to bridge the ether between the worlds to make contact.

"Diaticus," interrupted Wes' voice, "what are these?"

Diaticus looked up to see Wes pointing to the large bookshelf along one wall of the study.

"Spellbooks, boy, collected over many years of magical study."

"I figured that. I meant, why are these separate?"

Diaticus saw that he was pointing to about a dozen books off to the side of the rest.

"Ah, yes. Those are books that I have been unable to translate." He waved dismissively. "They're rumored to be some of the most powerful books of magic in existence, but they're all from other worlds. They're all in languages that have proven impossible to read for any in Canellin who have ever tried."

Diaticus went back to his studies, trying to ignore the interruption. He thought he might be making progress, nearing a breakthrough, when suddenly Wes' voice intruded again.

"You gotta' be kidding!"

Diaticus glanced up to see Wes removing a large book bound in some unfamiliar material from the shelf.

"Wes!" His voice was sharp. "Please, do not touch!"

Wes ignored him, pulling the book from the shelf.

"Magic 101," he said cryptically. "It says Magic 101!"

"It… what?" Diaticus stared in astonishment as Wes flopped the big book upen.

"The book's title is Magic 101: An Introduction to Magic Theory and Spellcasting. It's in English!" He read from a page near the beginning of the text. "'Gather your thoughts and draw in magical energy as discussed in Section 1.2. With your left hand, perform gesture 1.7 with a half twist to the right (see diagram) and recite the chant: diaso flickore mar semplium'. It's written like a textbook!"

"A… textbook?" Diaticus' eyes widened as it finally dawned on him what Wes was saying. He sprang to his feet. "Wes… you can read it? You can decipher this?"

"Sure," said Wes casually. "You can't?" He grinned at the old man's astonishment.

"Of course I can't!" Diaticus rushed to Wes' side. "What was that spell you just recited, boy, read it again, the full instructions."

"Let's see," said Wes, "it says here it's a simple mage light spell. Here's the diagram for the hand gesture, see?" Diaticus looked carefully. "It says to draw in your magical energy, make the gesture," he made the gesture with a flick of his wrist, and Diaticus repeated it, "and repeat the chant 'diaso flickore mar semplium'." Diaticus repeated the chant, and was delighted when an orb of pale luminescence appeared above his extended palm.

"Wonderful!" He glanced down at Wes and found his jaw dropping in astonishment. Hovering an inch above the boy's palm was the pale twin of Diaticus' mage light.

Wes merely blinked, his eyes wide.

⊷ॐ ॐ⊶

"You're telling me," said Ryan in disbelief, "that my son can do magic." He had been listening to the old wizard's long tale as patiently as he could, and had gotten caught up in the story. "He's a wizard?"

"Well, not exactly a wizard, though the potential is there. An untrained wizard. But it's much more than just magic, friend, as I explained to him. That particular magic book had thwarted me for years. Legend says it once belonged to Pomander himself!"

"So what?"

"That was Wes' reaction as well. Why should I be excited about that book, when I have so many others that I can read for myself far more easily? Why should I be excited about having cast such a simple spell?" Diaticus' expression grew intense. "Because, my friend, it was new magic! Of course I know how to make a magical light, but not that way! Our world has had no new magic for thousands of years. We have stagnated! But this book held the promise of an entirely new magic, performed in entirely new ways. And this was merely the first spell in a very large book! My mind could scarcely grasp the possibilities!"

"And Wes could do this new kind of magic." That was what Ryan's mind had so much trouble grasping.

"Yes indeed, which I believed held much promise. If he could teach me enough of this language, English, to be able to read the book, not only was I certain I could return him home, but I would be able to bring about a renaissance of magic upon this world." He shook his head sadly. "Unfortunately, that isn't the way things have worked out."

⁂

Over the next several weeks, Wes and Diaticus worked feverishly, learning spells from the great book. It seemed to come somewhat naturally to Wes, although his inattention to detail often led to unexpected results, but Diaticus usually required repeated instructions and demonstrations to acquire the new skills. He explained that it was a matter of forgetting old ways that he had used for hundreds of years. But they kept working, in the hope that someday, somehow, they would learn enough to send Wes home.

Wes' days had turned quite routine. He would join Diaticus in the mornings, where they would work on digging information out of the magical textbook. After the noon meal, Diaticus would spend his afternoon on the mundane responsibilities of maintaining order in the keep and overseeing the Wizard's Collegium nearby, while Wes spent his time with Gideon, the guard the wizard had assigned to him that first night. The grizzled old soldier had taken him under his wing. He was instructing Wes in horsemanship, swordplay, and other soldierly skills. Most of these things did not seem to suit Wes, except for the horsemanship, but Diaticus chose not to interfere. Wes obviously enjoyed his time with Gideon.

Before and after the evening meal, Wes would again be hard at work with Diaticus, deciphering more and more of the book. Wes seemed quite adept at this, attributing it to the fact that the book was organized very much like a textbook used on his world to teach schoolchildren.

A few weeks into this routine, Wes arrived for the morning's study looking quite disheveled, his clothing rumpled, dark circles under his eyes. Diaticus realized that the boy had been showing signs of exhaustion for some time. He had also begun to notice Wes becoming more and more irritable and morose with each passing day.

"You look dreadful, Wes. Have you been sleeping well? I could mix you something that would allow you to sleep through the night and wake feeling refreshed and energized, if you'd like."

"No thanks. I don't really like medicine." He slumped down in his usual chair across from Diaticus. "Besides, I'm sleeping fine. Gideon and I were up late last night. He's teaching me to play stones."

"Ah. Well, I suppose that's all right. Though I'm not sure I approve of him keeping you up all hours."

"Okay, Dad, I'll remember that," Wes said sarcastically.

Diaticus frowned for a moment at the boy's tone. "I see your point, boy. Still, I think I'll have a talk with Gideon myself."

"Whatever," replied Wes caustically.

Diaticus wasn't oblivious to Wes' attitude, but was unsure of what to do at this point.

"Wes... what's wrong, child? What can I do?" He looked at the boy earnestly, trying to emanate the same feeling of reassurance he had on that first day Wes had arrived.

"Nothing," said the boy sourly. "We're doing it already, I guess."

"We are, Wes, you've got to believe that."

"I know. It's just... it seems to be taking forever."

"We must go cautiously, Wes, I've explained that. Magic can be very dangerous for those just learning. I must guide you carefully through this, and it's made even more complex by the fact that you must guide me just as surely."

"I know. But..." Wes paused, considering his next words carefully. "What would be the chances of just going into the Dragon's lair and finding the door?"

Diaticus had been afraid that it would come to this.

"Very slim, Wes, very slim indeed," replied Diaticus. "The Dragon's power may have been broken during the last war, but that doesn't mean it is defeated. It still has a host of transformed troops at its disposal, as well as its own formidable magics. Not to mention its physical prowess." He shook his head. "No, Wes, nothing short of a direct assault by all the armies of Canellin could root the beast out of that mountain, and rooting it out would be the only way you'd ever get inside."

That should have been the end of it, but naturally, Wes was unable to let the idea go. Every day, he would ask more questions about the Dragon and its abilities, strengths, and weaknesses. He also seemed keenly interested in the doorway back to the Gatehouse, and how it could be recognized, where it might be in the lair. Diaticus answered these questions as truthfully as possible, all the while making sure Wes understood that it would be suicide to make the attempt. That, at least, seemed to get through to the boy, and he grew more irritable and ill-tempered with each passing day as hope of getting home dwindled in him.

One morning, a month after Wes' arrival, Diaticus went to join Wes in his study to begin another day of deciphering the book. He went to the bookshelf to retrieve the great tome, only to find it missing from its usual spot. In a near panic, he searched the study thoroughly, but there was no sign of it. He flung open his door just as a guard outside was raising his hand to knock.

"Quickly," he told the guard, "go to Wes' quarters and bring him here!"

"Sir, I've just come from there," replied the guard. "When Gideon didn't return to the barracks this morning, the guard captain sent me to check on him. There was no sign of him, or the boy."

⚬⚬⚬

"And that was more than two weeks ago," Diaticus said slowly. "Neither of them has been seen since."

"And you just let them go?" Ryan felt anger and fear rising in him simultaneously. "You didn't send anyone after them?" He levered himself up to a sitting position. "What's wrong with you people? He's just a kid!"

56

"Easy, friend," said Luther, who had been silent through Diaticus' long narrative. "It's not as simple as all that."

"What's not simple about it? You let my son run off with some strange man to get himself killed!"

Diaticus waved Luther to silence. Luther seemed about to speak anyway, then thought better of it and snapped his jaws shut.

"The very day that Wes and Gideon disappeared," he said quietly, "the Dragon broke its long silence and attacked several key points throughout the kingdom. We've had no one to send. The beast has invaded Canellin in numbers not seen since before the last Dragonwar. In most points, they have been driven back, but the beast knew where the attacks would have the most effect. It knew from where the true opposition would come." He took a deep breath. "The High Lord's Castle and Collegium Keep have been under siege since the day your son left us."

Chapter 5

Swords, Stones, and Tragedies

"**D**OWN, WES!" SHOUTED GIDEON, grabbing the boy by the nape of the neck and pulling him behind the rock face they were using for cover. It was a small rock outcrop with a cave at the back and a low wall of boulders and strewn rubble in front. As Wes' head dropped below the level of the wall, an arrow struck almost exactly where it had been to ricochet off and clatter to rest behind them. Gideon quickly rose and fired off a crossbow bolt down the slope, which glanced off the scaled hide of one of their assailants, staggering him slightly but failing to penetrate the thick natural armor. Gideon instantly dropped back behind the wall and began cranking back the string of his crossbow.

"This isn't happening," muttered Wes. "It's not happening. I'm not hiding behind a rock from a bunch of scaly monsters who want to have me for dinner!"

"Aye, lad, but tell them that," said Gideon grimly as he fitted another bolt to his bowstring. He rose and fired at another of the creatures, a nearer one this time. The creature let loose a strange, high-pitched roar of pain as the steel tip slipped between the scales in its shoulder joint and penetrated deeply. Gideon again began the task of reloading as the creatures fell back, leaving their wounded comrade to fend for itself. He rose again and fired another shot at its retreating back, the bolt catching the creature squarely in the spine and punching through the tough hide. The dragonman collapsed to the ground and twitched for a moment, then was still.

"Now might be a good time for some of that magic of yours, boy."

"Magic." Wes looked at the grizzled soldier blankly and then scrambled to his pack, digging for the book.

Gideon fired another shot down the slope, but the range was too great. The creatures below formed up into a group, ducking behind a boulder for cover.

"They're forming up for a charge, lad. I count six of the buggers left. I don't think I'll be able to drop more than two, maybe three, before they cross the wall." Gideon looked down at Wes calmly. "You might want to hurry yourself along."

"I'm looking, I'm looking," cried Wes, furiously turning pages in the great book.

"Here they come," said Gideon, loosing a bolt, reloading, loosing another. Two of the creatures dropped, shrieking. Then they were almost on the wall, and Gideon tossed aside the crossbow and drew his sword, preparing to fight in close quarters.

Wes suddenly leaped up, shouting, "Luz impenetra colderati!" As the last sound passed his lips, he flung his arms wide. The remaining creatures sprang toward the top of the wall as a flash of bluish light expanded from Wes' outstretched arms, encircling him and Gideon, forming a bubble of luminescence that solidified in the air around their position. The dragonmen recoiled from the barrier as if hitting a solid wall.

Gideon let out his breath, relieved.

"Very effective, lad." He glanced around for a moment, surveying Wes' handiwork. "I don't know if you've noticed, though, but the scaly beasts are out there, and they're still attacking. And we," he added as an afterthought, looking at the shield Wes had created that not only kept out the attackers, but effectively trapped Wes and Gideon, "don't really have anyplace to go."

"Working on it," snapped Wes, thumbing through the book quickly. He needed to find just the right spell…

"Work faster, lad," said Gideon as a slow moving arrow, its arc only partially deflected by the shield, sailed gently past his head. "They seem to have found a soft spot in your armor."

"Got it," Wes exclaimed, rising, the book held open in the crook of his left elbow. He made a strange thrusting, twisting gesture with his right hand, chanting, "Movare colloqum, vidala luanzir!"

A few sparks jumped up around the dragonmen, but that was all. Wes ducked down behind the rocks and read through the spell again. What had he done wrong?

"Faster, lad," said Gideon tersely.

Wes jumped up and made the twisting gesture again, this time moving his hand to the left. "Movare colloqum, vidala luanzir!"

The attacking dragonmen stopped their efforts, confused, as flashes of light began to dance across their scaled bodies. They began to shake uncontrollably, as if the ground beneath them were itself shaking, but there was no sound. Suddenly, all four of the beasts went rigid and, one after another, seemed to explode into thousands of tiny motes of flickering light which quickly faded into nothingness.

Gideon stood, staring at the spot where the dragonmen had been only moments before, and the protective barrier faded away. He peered down the slope to see that the three beasts he had managed to drop were also gone. He turned his attention to Wes, who was casually, smugly, returning the book to his pack.

"That was... impressive, boy," said Gideon breathlessly. "I've never seen a living thing destroyed so... so thoroughly before in my life. Look, there aren't even any burn marks on the stone!"

"I didn't kill them," said Wes absently. "I just sent them away."

"You mean they're still out there somewhere?" Gideon sprang into action, gathering their belongings and moving toward their horses. "We'd best be moving along quickly, then. They could be back, or they could have friends about."

"I don't think so," said Wes, but he dutifully began tying his pack to his horse's saddle. "The intent of the spell is as important as the incantation, according to the book. Every dragonman within ten miles just got transported far, far away." Wes absently picked up a smooth stone, examining it for a moment before slipping it into his pocket.

"How far?" asked Gideon anxiously.

"I don't really know for sure. The way I did it, it's kind of random. Just away from anyone or anything they could harm." Wes shrugged his shoulders indifferently, feeling incredibly pleased with himself.

⁓◌ℰ ℰ◌⁓

The dragonmen shuddered as reality seemed to bend around them, and suddenly the stone wall and barrier of light before them were gone. All was dark for an instant. Then their leader found himself scrambling with his clawed toes for footing, but there was none to be had. He felt a wrenching disorientation and realized dimly that he was falling. His slow mind worried for a moment at that, but dismissed it. He and his fellows were made of stern stuff. A fall any smaller than a high tower wouldn't harm him at all, and it would take much more height than the slope up which they'd charged to actually kill him. His tumbling through the air continued, though, far longer than it should have. For a moment, he found himself facing downward at a vast expanse of water rushing toward him. He had time for a moment of concern before he and his comrades struck the water with a force that expelled the air from their lungs. After all, dragonmen can't swim.

☙ ❧

That night, Wes sat beside their campfire with Magic 101 open across his lap. A magelight hovered by his left ear, providing enough illumination to read by. Gideon crouched nearby, a pair of rabbits skewered on the stick he held above the flames. As the rabbits began to sizzle, Gideon spoke.

"Wes," he said quietly, "that spell you used. The one that transported the dragonmen away. Could it not be used to send us to our destination?"

Wes looked up from the book and shook his head. "I thought about that right after I found the spell, before we ever ran into the dragonmen, but it doesn't work that way. If I've never been to a place, I can't send anything there. The spell just sort of flings whatever I'm trying to teleport out to someplace more or less random." He considered a bit more before speaking again. "I could send us back to Collegium Keep, I guess, or maybe any of the places we've been since we left, but not to someplace I've never seen, or anyplace between the worlds."

"Ah," said Gideon. "I suppose that makes sense, lad." He pulled out his dagger and poked at the roasting rabbits. Apparently deciding they weren't done cooking, he wiped his dagger on his trousers and returned the skewer to its place over the flames, propping it on a log.

"Shame, though," he said, pulling a whetstone from his pack and swiping his dagger against the rough edge with a slow rasp. "It would have made this journey more than a bit easier, not to mention shorter!"

Wes chuckled sheepishly. "I was actually more interested in making this journey unnecessary!" He shrugged. "I had hoped it could send me home, but it's not that kind of spell."

Gideon looked mildly uncomfortable for a moment, then smiled at Wes. He sniffed the air and smacked his lips. "I believe our dinner has finished burning, lad. Hungry?"

Wes tried to keep studying as he ate, but then decided to give it up for the night. There was so much to learn, and he wanted to know it all, but sometimes the enormity of the task overwhelmed him. He had probably studied harder in Canellin in the past weeks than he had in the past several years back home.

He was glad Gideon was with him. He didn't think he could have come this far, or even made the attempt, without the grizzled veteran's support. Gideon was a solid friend, the kind of man you could look to for loyalty and aid in your darkest hour. He was good company, too, his witty chat doing a great deal to put Wes at ease in their perilous situation. Aside from being a good companion, Gideon was a capable soldier. He was a big man, about six foot in height and broad shouldered, in excellent physical condition despite his years. His face might show lines of experience and age, and his beard might be speckled with gray, but he was certainly in better shape than most younger men Wes knew back home. Most importantly, the man would do anything to protect his friends, and Wes felt lucky to be counted among them.

"Gideon," said Wes around a mouthful of rabbit, "tell me about your sons."

Gideon stopped chewing and looked at Wes askance. "What about them, lad?"

"I heard the other guardsmen back at the keep talking about them a couple times, and I know they were heroes in the war, but you've never mentioned them." He looked up at the old soldier, wiping grease from his chin. "They died, didn't they? In the last Dragonwar?"

"Aye, lad, they died." Gideon's voice took on a somber tone. "And only one could be counted a hero."

"What happened?"

Gideon sighed. "It's a long story, lad, and it starts back in the village where I grew up, long ago when I was barely eighteen years old. I was a soldier in the Home Guard, newly married to the true love of my childhood. Her name was Alanna." Gideon's eyes lit up when he said the name. "A sweet girl of sixteen years. She loved me truly, and it was the happiest moment of my life when we kissed under the marriage altar… at least, until a few months later when Randall was born. A year later came Conner. They were hardy little boys, and quick to learn as they got older. Our little family grew closer as the years passed, and the bonds only seemed to get stronger." He swallowed hard. "But then came the Dragonwar."

"The boys were young when the war broke out, Randall just twelve and Conner eleven. I was called off with the rest of the guard to join the main army to battle the threat, leaving Alanna to tend the boys alone. She and my lads left our cottage and went to the country to stay with her parents and sister until my return. It was supposed to be a short, easy war, and we were to be back home by harvest.

"We marched to the border, where the fighting was most fierce, and I got my first taste of real battle. It was a sour taste, that I can tell you honestly, lad. Stories of war always seem full of glory and excitement, but that's not the way of it at all. It was also apparent almost from the start that this would be no short task." He shook his head. "Not short at all. I spent six years of that bloody war fighting along that border. I used to keep track of the number of times we gained and lost a particular piece of ground, but it was no use, it happened too often. I was a good soldier, though. I went where I was told, did as I was ordered, and battled my foes with all my strength. On more than one occasion, my unit was so depleted that we were absorbed into other commands. We were constantly being pushed back, giving ground to the enemy." His voice was heavy with emotion. "It was, at the time, the worst experience of my life."

"It sounds horrible," said Wes. "In books, it always sounds more… adventurous, I guess."

"Then the people writing about it have never actually seen a battlefield. People die. People you care about. After six years, I was the only man left alive from my original unit. The very last." Gideon bowed his head.

"Over the years, I had not gone unnoticed by my commanders. I had been steadily promoted, sometimes by the captains and generals who commanded us, and sometimes by battlefield necessity. Eventually, I was transferred to the King's Regiment with the rank of first lieutenant, and given command of my own platoon.

"One day a runner came in from one of our rear encampments with a message for me. My sons had ridden into the camp in the small hours of the morning, looking for me. I was overjoyed! I had received no news of them for months, no letters from home, and had not seen them at all since I left in the first year of the war. I immediately took to horse and practically flew to the rear camp.

"When I arrived, I almost didn't recognize the lads, but they knew me. Conner was embracing me almost before I dismounted, tears running down his face in a torrent. Randall was more reticent, standing back a bit and regarding me with a strange look. When I approached him, he forestalled me with a single dire pronouncement.

" 'Mother is dead,' he said."

"I couldn't speak, couldn't think. I placed my hands on his shoulders, but my legs would no longer support me. I fell to my knees, unable to grasp the sense of it." Gideon cleared his throat. "All I could say was, 'How?'"

"Conner was the one to explain, gently. The war had been going badly for several years now, particularly on the opposite border. It's hard to fight a two front war, and we were not having much success. The dragonmen had advanced far enough into our lands to overrun several towns and even a few of the smaller cities. My little village, near to the city of Chalanar, managed to last a good while, but eventually, it fell, as did the city. The little farm where my family had taken refuge… it was gone. Alanna's father and the boys had managed to flee, but not before Alanna, her sister Deanna, and their mother, Sinead, were slaughtered by the beasts."

Gideon stopped speaking, choked up for a moment.

"Gideon, I'm sorry. You don't have to tell me any more, it's okay."

"No, lad," Gideon replied. "It was many years ago, the pain's not as fresh as it once was." He wiped at his eyes. "It's still there, though." He cleared his throat and continued his tale.

"The lads were determined to join the fighting, and indeed, both were of an age for it. I petitioned my commanders to allow them to join my regiment, although not under my direct command. Reluctantly, it was agreed, so long as I did nothing to arrange any special treatment for them. Still, I was able to prevail upon their commanders to allow me to watch their progress. I made sure that the men who were training them were the best we had, ensuring that they'd learn the skills necessary to keep them alive. Both my lads were apt pupils, especially Conner, and were soon acquitting themselves well in battle.

"For three years, we fought, gaining ground, losing ground. The lads advanced through the ranks much as I had. Even quicker, in truth. Randall was a corporal for one of the most respected platoons in the regiment, and Conner... Conner had caught the interest of the highest general in our army, and thus the attention of the king as well. He was transferred into the King's Own Guard, an elite troop whose only purpose was to keep King Edward safe in battle. Our king was not a complacent one, and was often to be found in the thick of the fighting, and the King's Own were always right there with him.

"The time came for a final push, our last attempt to force the invaders back to their own territory. The war had turned in our favor in the last year, and we were optimistic that we could end it with one decisive stroke. The invaders had been contained in a corridor of troops with their only escape route being back to their own lands, and we had them outnumbered nearly three to one.

"Little did we know there were traitors among us."

Wes listened raptly to Gideon's words, unable to tear himself from the story.

"My platoon led the initial attack, with Randall's following to the east. The king came behind with a full regiment, spreading out and cutting off the invaders from pushing past us. The newly-named High Lord held back with the reserves. Ours, though, was the main thrust, pushing the dragonmen and the human mercenaries and thralls in their employ along the corridor we'd created.

"The assault went well at first, but no battle plan ever survives the first engagement with the enemy, so I'm told. The invaders turned and began striking back with more ferocity than we could have expected. I found myself back to back with Randall as both our platoons were nearly overrun, battling the beasts furiously. We were surrounded, swords rising and falling in terrible rhythm as we fought. Then, the sound of a battle horn rose over the ranks of the invaders, deep and ominous. The attackers seemed to halt, one and all. My son turned to me and spoke in the sudden quiet. 'I'm sorry for this,' he said without explanation. The next thing I knew, his arm lashed out, and I barely saw the hilt of his blade approaching before it struck my skull, and everything went black."

"He hit you?!" Wes was shocked. "Why? What happened?"

"I'm not really sure of all the details, but it became obvious that our army was being betrayed from within. Fully one third of our troops turned on us when that horn sounded. When I regained my senses, I found myself alone among the dead, behind the enemy line, the fighting far off in the wrong direction. I rushed toward the sound of battle, hoping beyond hope to find the king alive and pushing the traitors back with the invaders. It hadn't even dawned on me then that Randall was one of those traitors.

"I finally reached the line and found a melee. The battle raged all around me as I hacked my way through, desperate to find my king. Our troops were engaging men they had fought beside only hours before, as well as hordes of dragonmen. I forced my way inward, trying to get to the center of battle, where I knew I would find the king. When I finally got to high ground and could see the battle unfolding below me, I was horrified. There in the distance was the king's party, surrounded by dragonmen and turncoats, cut off from his troops. He and the few members of the King's Own that I could see were fighting a desperate battle just to stay alive. The turncoats... they were beginning to transform, becoming dragonmen themselves. Not a quick transformation, though. You could still see the faces of men you once knew, hear their battle cries as scales spread slowly across their flesh.

"Inside the ring of attackers, the king and five of his guard were holding their own, but barely. I spied Conner among them, a bloody wound in his side, fighting valiantly to protect the king. I began working my way through the carnage to reach them. By the time I got close enough, only Conner and King Edward were left, with four half-transformed men attacking them. I leaped into the fray, engaging one of the traitors while two struck at the king. I was back to back with Conner, who was facing his own attacker. After a few vicious blows, I was able to strike my opponent down, and I turned in time to see Conner run through the chest by a savage thrust. The traitor twisted his blade free and leaped at the king's unprotected back as Conner collapsed. Without thinking, I struck out, taking off the man's sword arm at the elbow. He turned to face me, roaring in pain, and I thrust my sword through his belly in a rage. Our gazes met, and a sob escaped me as I looked into the eyes of my oldest son."

"Your... Randall?" Wes was aghast, seeing tears running unashamedly down Gideon's cheeks. "You killed your son? He killed his brother?"

"Aye, lad, he did, and I did, though it wasn't a quick death for Randall. I had time to ask him why.

" 'Where were you when mother died,' he asked me with contempt, straining to get the words out through the pain. 'Where were you when we had to hide in a midden heap? The dragon promised me power, life everlasting. What have you ever given me?'

"I was a good soldier, though. I was always a good soldier. I had no time to waste on a traitor. My king had dispatched his opponents, but he was sorely wounded, and left with no defenders. We were also still trapped in the middle of a pitched battle.

"I fought that day at the side of my king. The battle raged for what seemed like days. Loyal troops joined us and split off several times throughout the day, but King Edward refused to quit the field of battle. Then, as the sun was sinking, the sound of trumpets reached us. Over the hill charged the high lord with his reserves, and more, he had gathered in the stragglers and broken regiments and even the walking wounded to swell his ranks to bursting. Their numbers turned the tide of the battle. Within an hour, the Dragon's forces were in full rout, pushed back into the corridor of troops we'd prepared for them. We expected them to turn and fight again, but their retreat continued on over the border as we harried them. Within a week, the war was over. We had won." He sighed again, brushing the wetness from his cheeks. "I had lost, but we had won. For my part in fighting alongside my king, I was offered a command in the capital. I couldn't bear it. I declined, and returned to my home. But it wasn't my home any longer."

Wes sat quietly for a few moments, unable to speak as he felt a tear sliding down his own cheek. He couldn't help but think of his own father, and what it would do to him if Wes wasn't able to return home. In some ways, Gideon reminded Wes of his father. Not in personality or appearance, of course, but some undefined sense of person. His loyalty, maybe, or his dedication to his sons.

"I'm sorry, Gideon. I didn't know. I knew they were dead, but not that way." He shook his head. "Not… like that."

"Lad, there's not a thing for you to be sorry about. It's good to remember them, warts and all, and my dear Alanna too. My family was everything to me, and the pain of their loss is still bitter, but I'd not lose the pain if it meant losing my memories of them." Gideon put his hand on Wes' shoulder and squeezed. "In truth, you remind me somewhat of my son, Conner."

Wes snorted. "I doubt that. It's probably just wishful thinking."

"No, Wes, it's there to see. You're polite, thoughtful, studious, brave... all the best qualities a young man should have."

Wes pulled out of Gideon's grasp, rising and stalking a few steps away. He leaned against a tree, purposely facing away from Gideon and gazing into the woods. Sudden irritation flared in him at being held up for comparison next to this golden boy from Gideon's memory.

"Is that what this is? You're here because you think I'm like your son?" Wes turned to face Gideon, his ire building. "You don't know me, Gideon. You know me here, but not back home, not the real me. Things are a mess back there! I've screwed things up so bad that I thought about not going back! I've messed up my Dad's life, destroyed my future, and made it impossible for anyone to like me!" He turned away quickly, swinging the side of his fist against the bark of the tree. "If anything," he said in disgust, "I'm more like Randall than Conner."

"Boy," said Gideon quietly, "don't ever say that again. Randall was my son, and I loved him dearly, but he betrayed his king and his entire race. He betrayed everything I ever believed in. Nothing you could have done on your world could be as bad as that."

"Shows what you know," said Wes.

"Indeed it does, lad," said Gideon. "Indeed it does."

Wes suddenly felt shame, realizing the words he'd just said to Gideon, his only real friend on this world.

"Gideon," he said tentatively, "I'm sorry."

"Aye, Wes, I know."

"I'll set wards tonight so you don't have to keep watch." He tried to make his tone friendly, to recapture the feeling they'd had before his outburst.

"You do that, lad," said Gideon in a neutral voice.

Wes opened his book to the section on wards, feeling once again lost in a strange world.

⚬⚭⚬

The next morning, Wes and Gideon rose with the sun and packed their horses to get an early start. Wes was silent, fearing to

68

speak and invite a confrontation over their argument of the night before. Gideon, too, seemed disinclined to break the silence. They rode out without a word ever being spoken.

As midday approached, the two travelers came upon a small, inviting lake nestled between two hills. There was a tree line to the south of the lake that looked like it might be a good place to stop for shade and a quick meal. Gideon called a halt and they both dismounted.

They left their horses packed except for the waterskins and some dried beef and biscuits. Wes took the waterskins to the edge of the lake without a word. This was a very practiced routine for them after two weeks of traveling together.

When Wes returned, Gideon was seated on a fallen log munching dried jerky and nibbling on a hard biscuit. Wes handed him a waterskin and retrieved his own meager ration. He took a seat for himself on a broad flat rock facing Gideon. After a moment, Gideon finally broke their long silence.

"Wes," he said, choosing his words with care, "why do you think you're so awful?"

Wes couldn't meet Gideon's gaze, so he kept his eyes lowered.

"Because I am," he replied. "Nothing I ever do is the right thing. I lie to my Dad, I don't do my homework, I get in trouble at school all the time. I don't do as I'm told, ever. I only do what I want to do, no matter what anyone else wants." Wes glanced up at Gideon, then lowered his eyes again. "I've ruined my life, my Dad's life, everything. No matter what I touch, it falls apart."

"I'm not sure I understand all that, but I can't find it in me to believe you're such a horrible person, lad. I've seen you every day since you came here. The boy I know isn't the boy you're describing. You are brave, hard working, and you have a spirit that hasn't been broken despite all that's happened to you in so short a time." Gideon paused, waiting for Wes to look up. When the boy met his gaze, he continued. "You've worked harder since you arrived here than any man I've ever known. Dawn to the wee hours, every day. I myself have worked with you on horsemanship and swordplay, and while you'll never be a swordsman, you have learned the other so quickly that it seems you've been sitting horseback your entire life. And your magic, lad! I've seen students at the Collegium in their fourth or fifth year that couldn't do half the things I've seen you do, and don't work a quarter as hard!"

"But I've had to do all that! I had no choice!" Wes clenched his fists, frustrated that Gideon couldn't seem to understand. "You just don't get it. The kid you're talking about, who works so hard and does the things he needs to do… that kid doesn't exist where I come from."

"Tell me, boy, what have you done that's so inexcusable? I truly can't imagine what it could be."

"I don't know, it's something that's hard to explain to someone who isn't from back home." Wes' fist was pumping up and down, striking the stone beneath him in rhythm with his words. "It's different back there. I have responsibilities, and I just don't meet them." He struggled to find the right words. "Back home, I'm supposed to go to school, study, get good reports from my teachers, do my chores, obey my father, you know… all of that. But I can't seem to make myself do any of it. I don't do anything, really. If it's not something that I want to do, or something fun, I just don't do it at all."

"I understand. So what you're saying is, you're a bad child because you act like a child." Gideon smiled to soften his words, showing Wes that he was merely teasing him.

"No, you're not getting it," said Wes, still frustrated. "Other kids do those things. Other kids get good grades, do as they're told, don't get in trouble." He shook his head yet again, sure that Gideon was not seeing his point. "Right before I came here, I got in trouble at school. There was this kid who was bothering me, and we got in a fight. He was threatening to hurt me, to beat me up. I knew he was all talk, but he had me pinned against a wall. I got him off me, but I broke his nose to do it. And then, I just went berserk! I went at the kid and started trying to beat him silly, trying to really hurt him, just because…" Wes paused, ashamed at what he was about to admit. "Just because he scared me."

"Fear is nothing to be ashamed of, Wes, especially when it's justified."

"Maybe so," replied Wes, "but I tried to hurt him. I was angry, and so I tried to hurt him. It got me kicked out of school. My Dad… he was so mad when he came to get me! He wouldn't even speak to me. I could tell that this was just the one thing that was too much, the straw that broke the camel's back."

Gideon looked at Wes with sympathy apparent in his eyes. "Wes, nothing you've said makes you a bad child. None of it even makes you an unusual child." He shook his head. "Truly, I believe you're a worthy person, despite your opinion on the matter."

"It's not opinion, Gideon," muttered Wes. "It's fact. My father nearly lost his job because of me. Where I come from, that's a big thing." He shook his head, turning his face away from Gideon in shame. "You just don't get it. Things are too messed up. It's all too far gone now to come back from."

Gideon reached out to Wes, lifting his chin until they were eye to eye.

"It sounds to me as if you simply want to be happy, Wes, and there's not a thing wrong with that. You just have to learn that sometimes, you have to weigh happiness against responsibility and decide which is more important. It's never too late, lad, and nothing but death is irrevocable."

Wes merely looked back at him, the pain in his eyes cutting Gideon to the bone. They rose, silent once again, packing the scraps of their meager meal and mounting. Wes tried to let Gideon's words sink in as they rode on.

∘৩৫ ৩৯৹

Ryan woke feeling tired, but he had regained more than enough strength to want to be out of bed. His conversations with Luther and Diaticus the day before had left him with more questions than answers, and he felt the urge to be doing something. He was still feeling the residual effects of his injury and the subsequent healing potions, but he was recovering quickly. He rummaged in the wardrobe, but could see no sign of his clothes. He was beginning to get irritated when there came a knock on the door of the chamber. He flung the door open, the blankets from the bed wrapped around him.

"Feeling better, I see," said Luther sardonically, stepping past Ryan into the room. "Although you're not exactly dressed for company, if I may say so."

Ryan felt color rise in his cheeks.

"My clothes aren't here." He gestured to the open wardrobe.

"Ah, yes. I'd say it's likely they were disposed of, from the amount of blood covering them when you arrived." Luther walked over to the wardrobe and removed a shirt and breeches. "However, Diaticus seems to have made sure to have replacements provided. Several, it appears."

Ryan looked at the outfit Luther held out to him and began shaking his head.

"No. No way." He took the garments from Luther's outstretched grasp. "I am not wearing these."

Luther laughed. "Ryan, my friend, while the weather is certainly warm enough for skin, there are ladies about. I'm afraid your only option is to wear them, or closet yourself in this room for the duration."

Ryan actually considered that for a moment, but the desire to be out and about won over embarrassment at the unusual garments.

"Fine. I'll be out in a minute."

Still laughing, Luther left the room.

Ryan struggled with the strange clothing. Apparently, the zipper had not been invented here, nor had the snap, and it took some doing to puzzle out the various ties and buttons designed to keep the clothing from falling down. Eventually, he exited the chamber, appropriately clothed. Luther grinned as he approached.

"Much better." He gestured for Ryan to follow him. "I thought you might like to see a bit more of the keep, especially after so long in a stuffy sick room."

"What I'd like is to go find my son," Ryan replied with heat, "instead of being a prisoner in some medieval castle out of a fairy tale."

"Perhaps we can discuss that as we walk," said Luther meaningfully, glancing toward the door to Ryan's chamber again and gesturing for him to follow. Ryan followed Luther's gaze, only then noticing the guard seated outside his door, dozing on duty. He didn't really understand, but it was obvious that Luther didn't want to discuss it here.

"Uhhh… sure. I guess I'll take the nickel tour."

Luther narrowed his eyes in confusion.

"I mean, lead on," said Ryan.

Luther led the way down the long corridor. They came to a narrow staircase which led down several flights, and finally out a side entrance. Ryan realized Luther was taking him through the rarely used servant's path out of the main keep and into the surrounding courtyard. Luther led him across the courtyard to a high, broad stair that led to the outer wall of the keep, looking out over the countryside. When they reached the top of the wall, Ryan looked out over the scene below them and froze.

"How... how many are there?"

"I'd say five or six thousand on this approach, and as many each at four more points around the wall," replied Luther. He leaned against the top of the barrier, looking down at the teeming masses of hideous scaled creatures below. "And twice as many encircling High Keep, the citadel of the High Lord. I was on my way here from High Keep when the attacks began. In one maneuver, and with ten times as many troops as we thought the beast had available, the Dragon has cut off the majority of the armies of Canellin. Between the High Lord and Diaticus, more than two thirds of our armies are bottled up and useless." He turned to face Ryan, his back to the wall. "And they just sit there." Luther spat on the cobblestones, disgusted. "Oh, there's an occasional skirmish, but no real attempts to take the walls. Their purpose here is not to conquer, but to contain." Luther shrugged, standing upright and motioning for Ryan to follow him down the stairs. "I just wanted you to see, to truly understand, the realities of our situation here. But for now, there's something far more important that I'd like to discover."

"What's that?" Ryan followed Luther across the courtyard to a large open area surrounded by a low fence and several racks that appeared to contain toy swords, spears, staves, and axes.

"What you might be capable of," replied Luther. He removed a wooden sword from the nearest rack and tossed it to Ryan.

"Wait, what is this?" Ryan looked at the weapon he'd caught from the air, realizing that it was no toy. It was stout, heavy, and blunted on the end. He held it up in one hand, looking at it without comprehension. "You can't mean what I think you mean. I'm not going to fight you! I've never held a sword in my life!"

"Of course not! In the first place, that's a practice weapon, it's not meant for fighting. In the second, my weapon of choice is the axe. Swords require far too much finesse." Luther waved his hand toward the side of the practice yard, and Ryan noticed for the first time a small girl standing there, a practice sword in her hand also. On second look, he realized that she was not a girl, but a young woman, perhaps twenty three, but she was tiny. She couldn't have been but an inch above five feet, and looked so willowy that she could have blown away in the breeze. Ryan found the grace to be insulted.

"Now come on, that's going a bit too far. I'm not some little kid!" He seemed to have forgotten that a moment ago, he hadn't wanted to cross blades with anyone, much less this girl.

"Of course not. Neither is Jiane. What exactly is your objection?"

"You mean other than the fact that I have about seven inches and a hundred pounds on her?" Ryan felt like he was stating the obvious.

"Trust me, friend, that won't make a bit of difference." Luther smiled mysteriously and motioned Jiane over. Ryan got a good look at her then. Lithe and lean, she moved with the grace of a tigress stalking her prey. Her long blonde hair was pulled back by a leather thong, revealing her smooth, delicate features and sparkling eyes. She strode confidently to where the two men stood and took up a position opposite Ryan with a mischievous smile. Finally, he shrugged, assuming what he thought was a fighting stance and raising his sword.

"All right, then," said Luther, "two touches or one fall for a point, three points wins. Ready?"

Ryan nodded, and Jiane just stood silent, her sword held negligently at her side.

Luther raised his hand, and then brought it down in a chopping motion. "Begin!"

Ryan slowly approached Jiane, his sword held out level with the ground. She watched his advance calmly, waiting. When he was within swords reach, her blade flashed up, knocking Ryan's aside, and she tapped him hard on the hip with the tip of the wooden sword. Ryan jumped back with a yelp, but Jiane merely lowered her blade to its earlier position. Ryan rubbed his hip where the sword had struck him, looking at the tiny woman with newfound respect. If nothing else, she was fast!

Ryan raised his blade and advanced again, sword outstretched as before. This time, though, he was ready for her, and when her blade leaped toward his, he used his own blade and superior strength to block her. He whipped the sword around awkwardly, aiming a blow at Jiane's arm, but by the time the point arrived, Jiane was no longer there. He yanked the sword back around, barely blocking her thrust, and before he knew it, his blade was on the ground and hers had struck his shoulder hard enough to stagger him.

"Point," said Luther.

Ryan stepped back, rubbing his shoulder to get feeling back into it. He gingerly reached down and retrieved his sword. Jiane looked at him appraisingly, a wicked smile on her face. This time she took a guard position, her sword held in front of her across her body.

Ryan advanced toward her once again, attempting to mimic her stance. He watched her closely, trying to detect any sign of the lightning fast movement she was capable of. Suddenly, she lunged forward, her sword thrust before her point first. Ryan twisted aside, narrowly avoiding the tip of her blade, and swung his own toward her leg as he stepped past her. She stepped to one side casually, flicking her blade back over her shoulder to tap Ryan gently on the side of the head.

Ryan was starting to get the idea he'd been had. He turned to face Jiane, who grinned at him and winked. He scowled back, but he was enjoying himself despite the embarrassment. Suddenly, he charged forward, hilt held firmly in both hands, the tip of his sword pointed firmly at Jiane's chest. Her sword swung up in a defensive move, again knocking his blade aside, and then whipped back to strike him solidly across the back of his knees. He retained his balance, but it was still the second touch.

"Yeah, yeah, I know, point," Ryan said before Luther could speak. The big man laughed aloud.

Ryan took a defensive posture, the sword held in one hand in front of him, his body angled to present the smallest target he could. Jiane regarded him for a moment, her sword at the ready, and then decided to take the offensive. She stepped forward and her sword shot out in a thrust toward his thigh. Without thinking, Ryan whipped his sword down almost gracefully in a circular motion in front of his body, knocking hers aside forcefully at the bottom of the arc. She immediately swept back into motion, her blade spinning high and thrusting toward his shoulder this time. Ryan's sword came up in a slightly different circular motion, deflecting her sword off to his right. Without a pause, her sword again flashed for Ryan's thigh, and was again blocked. He anticipated her next blow and had his sword inscribing the same upward arc that had deflected her so effectively before. Unfortunately, that's not where her next blow was aimed, as she twisted her body and whirled around Ryan, striking the backs of his knees from behind, causing his legs to buckle. He fell to the ground with a gasp as Luther yelled, "Point!"

Ryan lay on the ground facedown for a moment, out of breath. He rolled over to see Jiane standing over him, grinning from ear to ear.

She offered her hand to help him up, and he took it gratefully, smiling. Luther approached them, also grinning.

"Ryan, allow me to introduce my daughter, Jiane. Jiane, this is Ryan, our visitor from another world."

Jiane grasped Ryan's hand firmly as Ryan goggled.

"Daughter. I should have known!" Suddenly feeling gallant, he bent low over her hand and touched his lips to her fingers gently. "It's a pleasure to meet you, milady."

Jiane's laughter was the tone of silver bells. "And you as well, good sir," she said formally with a curtsy, which looked awkward in her boyish clothing.

"Just so you know, Ryan, you did far better than I expected," said Luther.

"Really? I couldn't tell!" Ryan laughed at himself.

"No, Ryan, you did well for someone untrained," said Jiane earnestly, agreeing with her father.

"Truly," said Luther. "You said you'd never held a blade before, but those few parries in that last exchange were almost perfectly executed. Where did you learn that?"

Ryan thought for a moment, unsure of that himself. It came to him so suddenly he had to laugh.

"Wax on, wax off!"

Luther looked back at Ryan, obviously not understanding.

"It's from a movie," said Ryan. "Wax on, wax off, you know?" Ryan chuckled as Luther shook his head. "Never mind. It's something I saw back home, just never with a sword."

"Well, it was performed quite well." Luther grinned. "You may have a knack for the blade. Had you been born here, you might have earned a blademaster's tassel by now."

"A tassel?" said Ryan, making a sour face. "I don't know if I'd wear one if I had one," he said with a grin.

"Oh, I'm certain you would. The blademaster's tassel is the dream of every child who ever wanted to be a soldier. It's a very prestigious rank."

Ryan returned his blade to the rack. "I'm still not sure I'd want one. You know, I played with toy swords as a kid, but I've never actually been in a fight with one. It was... illuminating."

Jiane had to see to her duties in the practice yard, as men began to gather around for the day's training session. Luther and Ryan bid her farewell and took their leave, crossing the courtyard toward the keep.

"To be honest with you," said Ryan, "I enjoyed that. I've always fantasized about something like this. I mean, all this. Coming to another world where magic is real and someone with wits and skill with a sword can fight evil and save the world. I know the reality of it is filled with real danger instead of the kind I've read about, but still, it's something I've always daydreamed about." His expression turned sour. "If not for Wes being lost out there somewhere, this might be a great adventure for me." He paused a step, and Luther stopped, regarding him. "I have to go after him, you know."

"Of course you do. There was never any doubt."

Ryan looked at Luther quizzically. "Then what was all that about, taking me up on the wall to see those… creatures?"

"You had to know what you'd be facing," replied Luther evenly. "You had to see that you couldn't just hare off on your own without a thought. You have to be prepared."

"Diaticus doesn't want me to go," said Ryan.

"You might be surprised, I think," said Luther. "Beyond his seeming fondness for Wes, I believe Diaticus wants that book back, and I think he believes you can get Wes to bring it to him."

"Maybe so," said Ryan, "but even if I could, what good would it do? We'd still be stuck here."

"But you'd be together, and as safe as anyone can be with what's coming."

"I suppose," replied Ryan without enthusiasm.

Luther spent the rest of the morning with Ryan, giving him more background on the history of this world, and the ins and outs of the society here. In a lot of ways, it was similar to the feudal systems that had once existed on Earth, although commoners were often able to break from their roles through farming or the merchant trades. The nobility still held much of the power, but the common man was gaining strides in great leaps and bounds. Some of this, according to Luther, was due to the progressive ideas of King Edward and the High Lord.

Ryan found all of this very interesting, but wasn't sure how useful it would be to him. His overriding desire, which colored every thought he had and every decision he made, was finding Wes. The thought of his son out there, alone in a strange world, terrified him.

The boy was reckless and headstrong in his own world, how much more so would he be here?

Just before the evening meal, a guard approached Ryan and Luther. As he reached them, he saluted, arm across his chest, and handed Luther a scrap of parchment.

"I fear I must bid you good evening, Ryan," said Luther regretfully. "I have duties to see to, and it seems you have been summoned immediately to see Diaticus. He's waiting in his study for you now." He turned to the soldier who had brought the note. "Dylan, Ryan is still unfamiliar with the Keep. Would you please see him to the wizard's study?"

"Yes, sir," said Dylan, saluting again and motioning for Ryan to follow.

Ryan felt a surge of hope when he heard that Diaticus wanted to see him. Perhaps the old wizard had found a way to get Wes back here! He hurried Dylan along, and by the time they reached the long corridor where the wizard's study lay, they were both practically running. Ryan burst through the wizard's door, breathing heavily.

"Heavens, Ryan, I didn't mean for you to run all the way here!" Diaticus seemed surprised.

"I thought… I mean, I hoped…" Ryan trailed off. Diaticus looked at him with sympathy.

"There's been no word of your son, I'm afraid," he said, understanding. "However, I may have hit upon another idea." He waved a page of parchment in the air before him and gestured at a small stack of similar pages on the desk. "One of the things Wes and I worked on before he left us was this. Each time he would translate a new spell for us, he would copy it down onto another page." He held the parchment out for Ryan to take. "Tell me, can you read this?"

Ryan scanned over the document and grinned.

"Barely," he said. "Wes isn't exactly known for his penmanship."

"As long as you can read it," said Diaticus, excitement in his voice. "You see, while Wes copied the spells, I linked with his mind in an attempt to learn them through him. It is an old technique, often used by a pupil who wishes to learn magic more thoroughly and directly from his teacher. But today, I had another notion." He smiled sheepishly. "It was so simple that I can't imagine why I didn't think of it before."

"What's your idea? Will it help us find Wes?"

"It's very possible. You see, I concentrated on learning the spells while linked to Wes. What if, I thought, I concentrated on learning the language itself?"

Ryan considered that for a moment. "But what good would that do, without the book?"

"The utmost good, both now and when the book is returned! That book may be our only hope of defeating the Dragon and getting you and your son back where you belong!"

Ryan considered the magician's words, unsure if he could put his trust in the man. After all, Diaticus had done nothing so far to try and find Wes. He realized that it wasn't fair to blame Diaticus for Wes' decision to leave the keep, but it was hard not to. In the end, though, it was concern for his son that won out.

"You really think this will help get Wes back?"

"My good man, if I'm correct, one of the last spells Wes copied out for me will enable me to place you at his side instantly."

Ryan didn't waste any more time considering. "Then do it."

Diaticus leaned back in his chair, a pleased smile on his lips. He closed his eyes, his breathing becoming steadily deeper. Ryan felt nothing, but after a moment, Diaticus spoke.

"Begin reading when you're ready."

Ryan scanned the page in his hand, reading quickly, as he always did. The text was very dry, but it was easy to understand. It was a simple set of instructions for casting a spell. He went over the page twice, then reached over to Diaticus' desk and grabbed a second page and read it through. Who would have imagined magic spells written out like instructions for a stereo?

"I can see it… I almost… it's there, just out of reach," Diaticus said, talking to himself. Ryan kept reading, sensing nothing of this link Diaticus spoke of. He read the page over four more times, and then reached toward the desk for another. Suddenly, Diaticus' eyes snapped open, and he swore aloud.

"I almost had it!" He shook his head in disgust.

"What went wrong?"

"I'm not sure," Diaticus replied. "I think… I believe the problem lies in the pages themselves. The parchment contains no magic in and of itself, and so my magical senses can't penetrate the text." His eyes lit up suddenly. "Come with me," he said quickly. "I have another notion."

Diaticus led Ryan out of the study and into the long corridor. They walked down the hallway, passing by door after door, until they finally reached the main staircase down into the entry hall. From there, they walked toward the kitchens, and then the passage veered off to the left. They came to a large, solid looking recessed door at the end of the passage. Diaticus waved his hand before the door with a strange gesture, and there was a loud click from the lock. The door swung open with a huge groan, as if the hinges hadn't been worked in a century.

"I intended to show this to Wes," said Diaticus, "but he left before the opportunity arose." He walked through the doorway and began to descend a narrow flight of stairs. Ryan paused at the doorway, and then followed reluctantly. Diaticus noticed his hesitation. "What's the matter?"

"I don't really like tight spaces," said Ryan. It hadn't been a problem for him in a long time, but when he looked down that narrow, unlit passage, claustrophobia seemed to grab at him.

"I understand. Please, though, bear with me." Diaticus kept walking, and Ryan forced himself to stay behind the man. "I am about to show you one of the most revered artifacts left from the first Dragonwar almost five thousand years ago. It is the only other artifact I know of in this world that is also from Pomander's home, at least we believe it to be, and the only other for certain that has any trace of your language connected to it at all. Of course," he added, "no one is sure what it says." He beckoned Ryan to hurry. "I often come down to simply look at it. I find it helps me collect my thoughts."

"So what is it?"

"You'll see in just a few moments," said Diaticus as they reached the bottom of the stairs and were faced by another massive door. Diaticus again waved his hand near the lock, which disengaged. He swung this door open as well, and they entered. As they did so, torches on the rough wall surrounding the chamber lit of their own accord. What was revealed in the sudden light was a large, natural seeming cavern of rough stone. It seemed to be a cave over which the keep had been built, rather than something that was carved out during the construction. Ryan let his attention wander around the periphery of the cave, until his gaze finally settled on the object in the center of the room. He had to force himself not to laugh outright at the absurdity of it.

80

"A sword," he said incredulously. "A sword in a stone." He couldn't stop himself, and a chuckle escaped.

"Yes," said Diaticus in a reverent tone. "It's called the Obsidian Blade, for obvious reasons. Few in this day know of its existence, and even fewer know its location." He strode forward, laying a caressing hand on the pommel of the great black blade embedded in the bedrock. "Legend has it that hundreds of years ago, during the first Dragonwar, the blade was wielded by an unknown warrior clad all in black armor. He appeared as if from nowhere at a time when all seemed lost, and his intervention proved to be the only obstacle to the Dragon's goal of enslaving the entire world. The enemy was finally defeated on the very spot where Collegium Keep now sits. After the enemy was routed, and it was certain that they would not return, the warrior struck the ground with the blade, and this cave opened up beneath him. With a mighty blow, he thrust the sword into the very bedrock. As the blade struck home and slid into the stone, a flash of light obscured the vision of the onlookers, and when they could finally see again, the warrior was nowhere to be found. All that was left was the sword, and the inscription." Diaticus sighed. "I often come here to reflect and meditate, talk things through with myself when I'm faced with a conundrum."

Ryan noticed for the first time the letters carved into the stone floor beneath the blade. He peered at the carving, reading intently.

"Well? Can you decipher it?"

"Yeah," said Ryan, stifling laughter. "It's just bad poetry! It says…"

"Stop! Don't speak, just read the words silently. When you finish, start again. Keep reading until I say enough."

Obediently, Ryan began reading the words as Diaticus concentrated. There seemed to be a hum in the air, and Ryan felt an uncomfortable itch behind his eyeballs. A sudden gasp from Diaticus broke his concentration, and the wizard began to speak.

"Excalibur's brother,
Obsidian Blade,
Born of the stars
Yet of the Earth made.

Bane of all evil, when
Wielded for right

81

In the hand of a stranger
In garb of a knight.

I will come to the aid
Of the warrior in need.
The mail, and the blade,
Bring heroic deeds.

To save all the worlds,
For this purpose forged,
From death, then destruction,
Then evil once more."

"That's it," exclaimed Ryan, astounded. "It worked!"

"Yes, it did," said Diaticus gleefully. "The words are really quite lovely!"

"You must be joking," said Ryan, laughing.

"Not at all! The poem flows nicely. However, what's best is that it fills me with hope!"

Ryan looked at Diaticus sideways. "Why is that?"

"Because, if I interpret this correctly, twice more the blade will be wielded in our defense. First from death, then from destruction, then evil. We can now look forward to the blade saving us not once, but twice more." He grinned at Ryan smugly, reaching out to caress the hilt of the blade again. Suddenly, his eyes widened. He turned to Ryan and spoke. "The warrior in need...

"Ryan! Quickly, come here," Diaticus said urgently, and Ryan did as he was told. "Ryan, you are in need!" Diaticus seemed more excited than Ryan had seen him in the short time since they'd met. "We are in need, this whole world! No one has ever been able to draw this blade, not since the day it was put here by the dark warrior." He motioned Ryan forward frantically. "Ryan... try! You must try! With this blade, you could save your son, save this whole world!"

Ryan looked around self-consciously, but he and Diaticus were alone in the chamber. "Are you sure about this?"

"Yes, yes, it all makes sense!" Diaticus urged him on. "Simply grasp the hilt with both hands and pull with all your strength!"

Ryan stepped up behind the sword, feeling more than a little foolish. He placed both his hands firmly on the hilt and bunched his

82

shoulders. There was a strange tingle from the sword's pommel, as if there were a small electric current running through it. He took that as a good sign that this might work after all. He squared himself, readying all the muscles in his arms, and counted to three. On three, he pulled upward with a mighty yank.

Chapter 6

In the Heat of Battle

DIATICUS SLAMMED OPEN THE DOOR to his study, rushing over to the long divan and brushing stray scrolls and books into the floor. Immediately behind him came two burly guardsmen, Ryan's prone form held between them, soft moans escaping between his clenched teeth.

"Here, lads, lay him here!" Gingerly, the two guardsmen deposited Ryan on the soft cushions, assisting him into a reclining position between his grunts of pain. "Thank you, men," said Diaticus, moving across the room and pouring some water for Ryan. "That will be all." He returned to Ryan, handing him the cup.

Ryan groaned as he tried to shift positions. "Pull the sword, Ryan," he said in a creaking imitation of Diaticus' voice. "You can save us, Ryan, pull the sword!" He turned his head to glare at the magician, who glared back indignantly.

"It made sense at the time," said Diaticus, taking a position near Ryan's head and placing his fingertips on the stricken man's temples. "There was no way I could foresee the sword reacting to you like that! Every king of Canellin in living memory, and a goodly number of royal champions, has tried to draw that sword. It's never reacted to anyone at all, in any way." Diaticus' fingers began tracing Ryan's forehead. "Rest silently for a moment. I'm delving your body for injuries." He closed his eyes and concentrated, then snapped them open a few seconds later. "Fortunately, my boy, the lightning appears to have done no serious damage. However, either your exertion in tugging at the blade's hilt, or your impact against the wall, have caused a serious strain to the muscles of your lower back." Diaticus tsk'ed at him. "You should have lifted with your knees."

Ryan couldn't help himself, bursting into peals of laughter that were hard to quell, despite the sharp pains they brought to his injured back. He groaned, his spine arching. Diaticus passed a hand over Ryan's eyes, mumbling something unintelligibly. Instantly, Ryan's pain vanished.

"You healed me again," said Ryan, relieved, as he began to sit up. "Thank you."

"I did no such thing," said Diaticus, pushing Ryan firmly back down on the cushions. "Wes' new magic may be capable of such things with a wave of his hand, but I'm limited to my potions, poultices, and compresses for healing. I've merely suppressed your ability to feel pain, a fairly simple trick of the mind." He took his seat, facing Ryan. "I'll prepare a draught for you tonight. You'll be right as rain by morning." Leaning forward, Diaticus changed the subject. "Tell me what happened when you tried to draw the sword."

"Tell you what? You were there, you saw it."

"I saw a flash of light, and I saw you flung across the cave. Tell me what happened."

Ryan thought about that for a moment. "I don't know. It was strange, really." He reviewed the incident in his mind. "The sword kind of tingled when I touched it. I figured that was a good sign." He shook his head, chuckling. "I'm guessing it wasn't. I tugged on the sword, and it was like there was a voice in my head. It said, 'It is not yet time'. That's when the lightning struck, and the next thing I remember, I was slamming against a cave wall twenty feet from where I started."

Diaticus sighed. "I had so hoped I was right. It seems the sword is not meant to save us in this time of danger."

"Well, the next time there's danger, have somebody else go pull on that sword." Ryan grimaced at the memory. "I'll leave heroics to people who are cut out for it." He shifted his position gingerly. "I think your little Jedi mind trick is wearing off."

Diaticus rose, solicitous. "I'll have you conveyed to your room and send a servant with the healing draught later. Get some rest, and you'll be fine by morning. I should have news for you tomorrow, after I've had a chanced to examine Wes' texts."

As far as his healing medicines, Diaticus was as good as his word, and Ryan was back on his feet and free of pain by morning. However, two days came and went with no news of Wes. Ryan never seemed to be able to see Diaticus when he wasn't busy with something or too occupied to deal with him. Luther was preoccupied with the defense of the keep, unable to spare the time to keep Ryan company. The horde encircling the castle had become more active, and there had been several very minor skirmishes, but the attackers still seemed to have little interest in taking the walls. No one else in the keep seemed to take much interest in the man from another world, except for Luther's daughter Jiane. She seemed to find his story intriguing, and went out of her way to spend time with him, in particular, teaching him the ways of the sword.

And so it was that Ryan found himself blade to blade with Jiane in the practice yard on the third morning after his attempt to draw the Obsidian Blade.

"You're going easy on me," Ryan said with a grin as he parried three quick blows.

"Would I do that?" Jiane's answering grin was mischievous. "Perhaps you're simply improving." She stepped forward, thrusting toward Ryan's chest, and he brought his sword up to block. Her swing changed direction with lightning quickness and swept his legs out from under him. "Or perhaps I am going easy on you!"

Ryan grimaced, but took Jiane's hand when she offered it to help him to his feet. "I appreciate you trying to spare my feelings, Jiane," Ryan said dryly, "but I'm trying to learn. I can't start to think I'm better than I really am if I'm going to be any use to Wes. What if I were face to face with one of those things out there, and I got overconfident?"

"Point taken," she replied, "but what man ever learned the sword by losing every time he faced an opponent? Besides, I must admit, I'm surprised at your progress. In half a week, you've gained more skill with a blade than I would have believed possible." She took their wooden blades and returned them to the weapons rack and retrieved her sword, buckling the belt around her waist.

"The Gatehouse adjusts," Ryan muttered, a sudden realization hitting him.

"What was that?"

"It's nothing," Ryan replied. "Just something Diaticus said when I first woke up." He walked out of the practice yard by Jiane's side. "Where are we going?"

86

"My father asked me to join him for the noon meal, and I was hoping to freshen up a bit beforehand. If you'd like to join us, I'm sure he won't mind."

"I'll do that. Just let me get back to my room and I'll change out of these sweaty clothes."

Without warning, the sound of a deep horn rang out over the walls, immediately followed by cries of alarm from the keep's defenders. Jiane instantly broke into a sprint toward the wall. Ryan followed, straining to keep up despite his longer stride, puffing with exertion. As they rounded the corner of the keep, the wall came into view, and the sight chilled Ryan to the bone. Dragonmen were swarming over the wall, engaging the defenders fiercely. Ryan skidded to a halt.

Jiane kept running, and Ryan realized her intent as she drew her sword. Without a thought, Ryan leaped into motion, following. Jiane didn't even seem to notice, sprinting up the stairs with her blade bared.

Ryan charged up the stairs moments later, distinctly slower, unsure of what he was going to accomplish but unwilling to let Jiane rush into danger alone. As he reached the top of the stairs, he froze in horror. Dead defenders seemed to litter the parapet, men that Ryan had seen over the past several days. He couldn't seem to move. He had never in his life laid eyes on the remains of a person killed in violence, and as his eyes locked on the dead man at his feet, paralysis gripped him.

"Watch out!" Jiane's shout penetrated his stupor, and he looked up to see a dragonman charging toward him, sword raised to strike. Ryan instinctively dived to the side, rolling against the wall with jarring force. He saw the dragonman's sword come down on top of the parapet where he'd stood only moments before, the blade embedding itself in the wooden railing. He scrambled to his feet, rushing the beast as it struggled to free the weapon, colliding with it with a crash. It staggered against the railing, tottering, and toppled over the wall to crash among the rushing attackers below. "Ryan! Here!" Ryan looked up in time to see Jiane grab a fallen defender's discarded sword and toss it toward him hilt first. He caught the hilt in midair and whirled, thrusting hard, taking the nearest dragonman through the throat. He looked in astonishment at the sword he held as the dragonman slid backward off the blade and fell to the flagstones, dead. He didn't have time to consider, as another dragonman topped the wall in front of him, and the battle began in earnest.

Ryan lost track of himself as the attack continued. The thrust and parry of battle was all he could afford to concentrate on as his blade rose and fell. He found himself losing his fear as the fighting continued, simply trusting in his sword and his strength. His muscles began to burn after a while, and the dragonmen kept coming, their dead littering the parapet at his feet. Ryan had no inkling of how many had fallen to his blade, but he knew the number was higher than he would have thought possible. The battle seemed to last for hours, but when the attackers finally retreated to their lines, the sun was still high in the sky. The hour was not much past noon. He found himself standing shoulder to shoulder with Jiane. Their blades were bloody and wet, and Jiane panted with exertion. Ryan was breathing heavily also, but no more so than the tiny swordswoman. He lowered his sword and surveyed the carnage surrounding them. Several soldiers were busy pulling up the attackers' scaling ladders to deny them their use for another attack, and others were busy gathering the wounded to safety in the main hall of the keep.

"Jiane," Ryan said, his voice trembling. He cleared his throat and tried again. "Are you all right?"

"I'm unharmed," Jiane replied, her voice also quivering. She laughed nervously, then stopped. "My first battle," she said tightly. "But you... you were amazing! Hardly a blademaster, but you fought as if possessed! How is it possible?"

"I think maybe I was." Ryan seemed disturbed by the thought.

"Jiane! Ryan!" Luther's voice penetrated their tension. "Jiane! Thank all the gods!" He ran up the stairs, his broad axe chipped in several places and dripping ichor. "When they told me you'd joined the battle, I feared the worst!" He took Jiane in his arms, crushing her to him, and then pushed her to arms length and began examining her for wounds.

"I'm fine, Father, please," she said, stepping back from her father's concerned examination.

"I know, I know," he said, brushing his fingers through her hair. He turned to face Ryan, a curious look in his eye. Ryan numbly laid the borrowed sword across his palms and offered it to Luther. "No, friend," the big man said with respect. "Keep it. You earned it today, from what I'm told." Ryan swallowed hard.

"I suppose I did," he said shakily. He looked at the blade, not sure what to do with it. Luther bent and retrieved a discarded scabbard that had been sliced from someone's belt in the melee. Taking the sword from Ryan's trembling hands, he wiped it clean on the hem of his tunic and slid it home, returning sword and scabbard to Ryan. He took it, still not sure what to do with it, and finally settled on slipping it behind his belt.

"I have to see Diaticus," he said firmly.

Luther gave him a surprised look. "He's tending the wounded in the Main Hall. I doubt he'll be able to spare the time."

"Still, I have to see him. It's important." Ryan's voice was hollow.

"As you wish, friend." Luther reached out and clasped Ryan's hand. "You fought well today by all accounts, Ryan. Will you join me later, after the evening meal? I believe there are things we should discuss."

Ryan nodded, then turned without another word and walked away on shaking legs.

୭ଚ ଚ⊱

Ryan found Diaticus ministering to the injured men that filled the Great Hall from wall to wall. The old wizard appeared harried as he handed out potions, examined injured men, and occasionally closed a pair of unseeing eyes with a look of sadness. Ryan realized that Diaticus knew these men. They weren't just nameless soldiers, they were his subjects, the defenders of his keep, and their loss was obviously painful for him. Wherever he went, though, cries of anguish faded. His so-called simple mind trick was finding plenty of use today.

"Diaticus," called Ryan as he approached the old magician. When Diaticus didn't respond, he stepped directly in front of him. "I need to speak with you."

Diaticus looked at Ryan in alarm. Ryan realized then that he was splattered with blood and ichor from the battle, although none of it was his.

"Ryan! Are you injured?" The old man stepped forward worriedly, grabbing Ryan and examining him for wounds.

"I'm fine, I'm not hurt," said Ryan, batting the man's hands away in annoyance. "I just need to speak with you."

Diaticus glanced around at the wounded men littering the floor. "It must wait, I fear. I have other obligations at the moment." Ryan gave him a determined look. "All right, we can take a moment to

89

speak, but it must wait at least a short time. Go to my study and rest there, I'll join you within the hour." Without another word, Diaticus stepped around Ryan and moved on to his next patient.

Ryan hesitated a moment more, considering demanding the wizard's immediate attention. But his good sense reasserted itself, and his realization that the men down here had a more immediate need of Diaticus' attention than he did, and he left the wizard to his ministrations. His mind was awhirl as he mounted the main staircase and worked his way toward Diaticus' study. He was planning a course of action that he knew Diaticus would object to, but he was determined to convince the man. He thought he understood what had happened out there on the wall, and if he was right, he was done waiting for the old wizard to find Wes.

Ryan reached the study with his decision firmly made. He was going to find his son, and he certainly wasn't going to let Diaticus, Luther, or anyone else stop him now. He used the time before Diaticus' arrival trying to work out how he was going to convince the old man. By the time Diaticus arrived, he was seething with impatience.

"I'm leaving," he blurted as soon as the old wizard walked through the door, and then grimaced. That wasn't how he'd intended to start this conversation.

Diaticus paused for a moment, sighing. "Come with me," he said quietly. "We can discuss it while I work. I'm afraid there are a goodly number of loyal soldiers who won't survive the night without healing draughts."

Ryan felt a sudden shame. Of course Diaticus would have work to do after today's battle! But Ryan could not abandon his plans now. "Fine, you work and I'll talk." He followed Diaticus through the door off his study into a small workroom. Diaticus shuffled over to a long table against the far wall and began gathering his potion making implements. Ryan moved to follow, but Diaticus raised a hand to halt him.

"My hearing is quite acute," he said sharply. "I have much to do. Please stay out from underfoot and speak your mind while I work."

Diaticus' tone rankled, but Ryan did as instructed, taking a position against the wall near the door. He was determined to make the wizard hear him, determined to make him understand.

90

"I'm going after my son, Diaticus. I have to." The wizard didn't respond, so Ryan continued. "You don't have to help me if you don't want to. No one does. I'll go alone if I have to." He swallowed heavily at the prospect. "You told me before that the Gatehouse adjusts us when we go through the doors. I think I saw that in action today on the wall. All of the sudden, I knew how to use a sword as well as any man up there, with only a few days training. That's what the Gatehouse gave me."

"Mhmm," responded Diaticus absently.

"Wes needs me. Even Pomander said so. He might be able to do magic here, but he's still just a kid. He's just a fifteen year old boy that's never had to be scared of monsters or dragons or men with swords in his entire life. He's just a kid, and he shouldn't have to do this alone." Ryan shook his head, emotion welling up inside him. "I'm going to find my son, and I'm going to help him finish this crazy quest of his and save your crazy kingdom, with or without your help."

Diaticus finally turned to face Ryan, arms folded across his chest. "Are you quite finished, my good man?" He seemed about to explode with suppressed anger. "Then let me explain this to you. You are going nowhere, for several very good reasons." Diaticus raised a finger. "One, you and Wes are both very special, very important to this world. You are the only people Pomander has ever sent through the Gatehouse. You may hold the key to saving us all." He held up a second finger. "Two, I can't risk the security of this keep, of this entire world, by letting you fall into the hands of the invaders. You and your son may have powers and abilities that we here can't fathom. I've already lost Wes, I won't risk you as well." He held up a third finger. "Three, I am the lord of this keep, granted title by King Gabriel, Edward's great great grandfather. My word here is law. I can hold you here, with or without your consent, until the white in your hair rivals mine. You will go nowhere, even if I have to place a guard on you every hour of every day." He lowered his fingers, re-crossing his arms. "I hope I've made myself perfectly clear." He stopped speaking, waiting for a reply. When none was forthcoming, he turned away from Ryan in dismissal and went back to work. "Please leave me now. There is much to be done."

Ryan stormed from the room, consumed with rage.

᪲᪲ ᪲᪲

Diaticus watched Ryan's retreating back, hating himself for what he'd just done. Not only was it unkind, it was unfair and, in his opinion, unnecessary. He looked down at the vial of healing potion he'd been mixing and grimaced in disgust. It had congealed to uselessness while he'd dealt with Ryan. In a sudden fit of pique, he grabbed the vial and flung it across the room to shatter against the wall, the slimy mess inside slowly dripping to the floor.

Reaching under the worktable, he retrieved a small globe of polished amber, perhaps five inches in diameter. He gently placed it in a stand on the tabletop and stared intently into its depths, concentrating hard. Within moments, smoky colors began to whirl around the surface of the globe, finally coalescing into the image of a weathered face.

"What is it?" asked the image of Pomander irritably.

"We need to talk about Ryan and Wes," Diaticus replied. "I don't agree with your course of action in this."

"It's not important for you to agree," the image replied. "If you wish to save your world, it is only important that you follow my instructions."

"But we're using them terribly! Surely, if you would explain to me why all this is necessary, I could convey it to Ryan and we could enlist their aid voluntarily."

"Enough. Maintaining this contact is difficult for me. I must accelerate my time reference whenever you feel the urge for a little chat. It is sufficient that you know that all is proceeding according to my plan. Your world will be saved, if you simply follow my orders." The image in the orb started to fade. "Just make sure Ryan doesn't leave the keep until I instruct. It is imperative that he not interfere with Wes' quest until the appropriate time." Pomander's voice and image faded into nothingness.

∾౷౷౷∾

Wes and Gideon rode through farmland that stretched as far as the eye could see. They had passed through the low hills south of the Keep and the forests that covered most of the middle of Canellin, and were finally in the breadbasket of the land. Wheat, beans, corn, and potatoes were the only attractions that could be found now. They had been traveling through farm country for almost three days, but had rarely been welcomed at the various small houses and farmsteads they had come upon. Between the dragonman attacks of a few weeks ago and an unexpected increase in the frequency of attacks by roving bands of brigands, the common folk of the countryside were understandably wary of strangers. One burly farmer had gone so far as to chase them off his land with a pitchfork. Gideon took all of this in stride, never once becoming angry as ragged folk flung insults and threats at the weary travelers, but Wes found himself chafing at the reception they were constantly receiving. He was weary of sleeping on the ground under the open sky, and would have welcomed even one night in a hayloft just to have a roof over his head.

It was more than just a matter of being tired, though. For the past few days, he had been having bouts of weakness. His magic wasn't obeying him, either. More of his spells were doing nothing when he tried them, or worse, going awry. He'd also been plagued with strange dreams in which Diaticus, Gideon, and even his father were slaughtered at the hands of hulking dragonmen or marauding men with vicious blades. He was always reassured to find when he awoke that Gideon was safe and sound within the camp's wards, and he thanked whatever gods ruled here that his father was back home in his quiet, peaceful world.

They reined in for the night, having yet again been turned away by a belligerent commoner who accused them of being rogues. Wes was seething with anger, but Gideon was unruffled.

"I don't understand how you can be so calm about this," the boy said to his companion as they began unpacking the horses. "These people are practically telling us that we're not worth helping. They're saying we're scum!"

Gideon looked at Wes with an amused expression. "Ah, lad, that's not what they're saying at all. These are the kind of folk I come from. What they're saying is, they're scared. Strangers have hurt them, or hurt their neighbors, and so strangers are kept at bay to keep it from happening again. You can bet that each time we've been refused lodging for a night, the man that refused us was ashamed of himself by morning once he realized we weren't coming back to kill or rob him." He shook his head sadly. "No, lad, these aren't bad folk at all, they're just frightened."

"I guess you're right," said Wes after a moment's thought, "but I'd still rather be sleeping in a hayloft tonight."

Gideon laughed. "It builds character, lad!" Wes smiled in response.

After setting up camp and picketing their horses, Gideon took out his hooks and line and headed down to the nearby pond to supplement their meager rations, and Wes sat down to his study of Magic 101. The spells had increased with difficulty as he worked his way along, but he had found that if he committed them to memory the casting became much easier. Once he had discovered this phenomenon, his pace through the text had slowed, but his facility with individual spells had increased dramatically. He was now able to produce much larger and brighter magelights, and his shield spell was nearly unbreakable. The wards he placed on the camp every night were so effective that everything from large animals to the tiniest insects were kept at bay. At least, they had been until the past few nights. However, the most recent section of the book was the one he wanted to study in more detail, and it wasn't even a spell. He read the passage again and then set about practicing faithfully.

As Gideon returned from the pond with a stringer of fish, he found Wes sitting in silence repeating an arcane gesture over and over again. Gideon set about cleaning and preparing the fish for roasting, every once in a while glancing at Wes curiously. After a while, his curiosity could no longer be contained.

"Lad," he said, chuckling, "I don't mean to be disrespectful of your art, but you look remarkably odd sitting there waving your hand about. What is it you're doing?"

"I'm trying to light a magelight," the boy said, again making the twisting gesture.

"I've seen you do that dozens of times. Doesn't it require some sort of magic words?"

"That's the way I learned it, yes," said Wes. "But remember when I told you that the intent was as important as the incantation?" At Gideon's nod, the boy continued. "Well, the book says that after mastering a spell and becoming completely adept at its execution, it should be possible to cast it with just the gesture, or even with just a thought. It says the mark of a skilled magician is the ability to cast a greater and greater number of spells without any words or gestures at all. More than that, it says a true master of magic can manipulate magical energy directly with no need for a spell, just by visualizing what he wants to happen. And this...well, it's the only spell I'm really what I'd consider adept at."

"That would certainly be impressive," said Gideon conversationally. "It almost seems like a true master would have the power of a god."

"Not really," replied Wes. "For one thing, Diaticus always said there was a limit to the amount of magical power a person can channel at one time without some magical aid, what they call a Catalyst Stone. Too much would burn the magician to a crisp. For another thing, according to the book, you can't create or destroy anything with magic, only change it. I'm not exactly sure what that means, but I think what it's saying is that I can't wave my hand and make something out of nothing. Isn't that something a god could do?"

"I suppose so, lad," said Gideon. "Still, it seems like a road to a great deal of power."

"Well," said Wes nervously, flashing his quick twisting gesture again, "I'll need a lot of power if I'm going to defeat a dragon." He grinned in delight as a ball of pale fire appeared above his open palm.

Gideon's eyes widened in alarm. "Defeat? Lad, the plan is for the dragon to never know we've been there!"

"Yeah. About that." The brave face Wes had been wearing slipped a bit, but he recovered quickly. "I've been giving that a lot of thought. I think there's a good chance the dragon didn't just happen to pick the only spot on this entire world with a door to the Gatehouse. That would just be too… coincidental." He closed his eyes tightly and rubbed his temple, the magelight above his other palm flickering. "I think the dragon is there because the doorway is there. I don't know why or how, but I think being at the mouth of a portal between the worlds must… I don't know… feed the dragon power somehow."

Gideon looked at Wes appraisingly. "And where is all this insight coming from?"

"I just sort of reasoned it out," Wes said. "Logically." He made his twisting gesture in reverse, and the magelight vanished. He brought it back just to prove to himself that it wasn't a fluke. "I figure sneaking through the door won't be an option. I'm going to have to defeat the dragon somehow. Besides, that's what Pomander said I was supposed to do."

Gideon gave a low whistle. "You're placing a great deal of trust in the words of a man you knew for less than an hour before he shoved you into danger!"

Wes frowned at the old soldier. "I know. Diaticus trusts him, though, and I guess I trust Diaticus. I just think he was wrong about my being here by accident."

"Maybe so, lad, but I still don't like the idea of facing the dragon by ourselves. Don't get me wrong, your magic is impressive, and you've been gaining skill by leaps and bounds, but I'd not enjoy trusting our lives to just that."

Wes shuddered, all attempts at a brave front abandoned for honesty. "Neither would I, Gideon." He put one hand on his forehead, massaging his sudden headache. "It's the scariest thing I've ever had to do. But I do have to."

"No, lad, you don't. We... I mean, you and I... there's always hope! Diaticus could find another way to get you home..."

"He won't, Gideon, don't you see?" Fear and frustration hit Wes all at once, as his head began to throb even harder. "Diaticus' magic is nothing! He's got mind tricks and potions and a few defensive spells, but no real power! The magic in this book is a hundred times more powerful than anything Diaticus can do, and there's nothing in here that can send someone between the worlds without a doorway. Believe me, I've looked!" He struggled to rein in his frustration. "It's not just getting home. There's more to it. I was sent here to do a job no one else can do, and it has to be done. If this world is going to survive, that dragon has to die."

Gideon stared at Wes, astonished. "Lad... I don't know what to say." He struggled to speak, but no more words would come. He clasped Wes' shoulder firmly, squeezing, and smiled down at the boy. Finally, he was able to put his thoughts into words. "That's probably the bravest, most selfless thing I've ever heard," he said, trying to choke back emotion. "I can't tell you how proud I am to hear you say those words." He gathered the boy into his arms, hugging him tightly.

"Gideon," grunted Wes, embarrassed. "It's nothing, Gideon. Just something I've been thinking about lately."

Gideon released him, still beaming. "No, boy," he said. "It's everything! It's the sentiment of a man grown, not that of a stripling youth!"

Wes didn't know what to say to that, so he blushed and sought after a way to change the subject.

"So, how long until we get to the Dragon's mountain?"

Gideon's grin lasted a few moments longer, and then he went back to cleaning his fish. "Hmm. Well, lad, we should be in Karsenon within another two days, three at the most. It's a big port city on the channel that divides the continent. From there, it's about three days by boat to cross the channel to Coveport, the main landing on the other side. Perhaps four days from there to the Great Escarpment, and another day at most to cross the Plateau to Dragon's Mount. Ten, twelve days, give or take. Make it an even two weeks if we have trouble hiring a ship in Karsenon." Gideon suddenly froze. "Port city," he said quietly. He started chuckling, then snorting, and finally howling with laughter.

"What's so funny?" Wes asked, confused.

"Oh, lad," Gideon guffawed. "I'm an oversized idiot! When I planned this journey, I was thinking like a soldier, an infantryman. Infantrymen walk where they're headed!" He buried his face in his hands, his hoots of laughter getting louder by the second as Wes looked on, bewildered. "Lad, I'm sorry, you don't see it. There's a town, Cybralta it's called, on the shore of Crater Bay. We could have hired a boat there. It's five days by fast boat from Cybralta to Karsenon! We've traveled overland for weeks, circling around the bay and through the center of the kingdom, when we could have been in Karsenon in five days! Lad, we'd be at the Dragon's lair by now!" He couldn't contain himself, and roared with laughter.

Wes stared at Gideon, aghast. After a moment, his face split into a grin, and then he started laughing himself. They both giggled and chortled like children for several minutes before Wes was finally able to get himself under control.

"It's all right, Gideon," said Wes finally through his laughter. "Really, it's okay! It's better this way. I needed the extra time to study. I'm not ready to face the dragon yet."

"As you say, lad," still grinning wryly. "Still and all, I'd be just as pleased to get this all over with and get you back where you belong."

"I'll drink to that," replied Wes, grinning back at the grizzled old soldier. His grin faded after only a moment. "Karsenon. We're going to Karsenon."

"Yes, lad. It's the only place we'll have even a chance of finding passage across the channel."

"Diaticus mentioned something about Karsenon. About the Tower of Lore. It's got the largest collection of artifacts from the

Crossing in the world!" Wes quickly began paging through his book, settling on a page near the end. "It's a shot," he said to himself.

"A what?"

"A shot. A chance!" Wes turned the book to show Gideon the page. There was a large illustration of a round gemstone set into a bright gold setting, four points leading off the setting to a square of thin metal bar. "This is a Catalyst Stone. It's a conduit for power. With this stone, a magician can hold and control a hundred times, maybe a thousand times, more power than he can alone! It just mentions it here, it doesn't say how to use one, but I bet I could figure it out."

Gideon looked at the illustration, considering. "And you think there's one of these stones in the Tower of Lore in Karsenon?"

"I don't know. Diaticus mentioned Catalyst Stones, and the Tower of Lore. But if there is, and I can get it, it could make the difference in a fight with the dragon. I don't have enough control over my magic. With this...with this, I could do almost anything!"

"Well, then." Gideon rubbed his hand over his chin. "I suppose that's something we should look into."

⚬⚬⚬

Ryan struggled to rise. He had been walking through this desolate wasteland for days in agony, frightened and alone. His horse had died beneath him a week ago. He'd had no food for four days, and no water for two, but the mountain was growing larger in his view, and his determination refused to wane. He trudged on, his steps weak and leaden, his only thought to find his son. He struggled up one hill, down another, each movement a battle in itself, his mind dulled by the monotony. But still he persevered, concentrating on the singular task of putting one foot in front of the other.

Topping a rise, Ryan beheld the most wondrous sight he could have imagined. There below him was Wes, walking unconcerned toward his destination, toward inevitable danger. Ryan rushed forward, scrambling down the hill and calling out to his son.

"Wes! Wes!" The boy stopped, turning, and even from that distance, Ryan could see his son's face light up with joy.

"Dad?" Wes' voice was incredulous. "Dad!" The boy began running toward him, dropping his packs and ignoring everything else.

At that very instant, a troop of dragonmen crested the hill opposite Ryan, coming their way.

"Wes, run!" Ryan's thoughts flew away in a panic, his mind latching onto the one thing he could grasp: saving his son. He quickened his pace, sprinting toward the frightened boy, determined to get Wes to safety.

Wes looked back over his shoulder, seeing the creatures advancing from behind him, and screamed in terror. He turned back to Ryan, pushing himself harder, racing desperately toward his father.

"Hurry, Wes," cried Ryan, speeding up, trying to get to his son, get him to the shelter of the rocks, to somehow find safety for him.

Twenty feet from Ryan, Wes suddenly staggered with a shocked look. He kept moving, but Ryan could see that something was wrong. As the boy moved forward, he staggered again, and then again, finally falling to his knees just a few feet from Ryan and looking up at him accusingly. His eyes seemed to roll back, and he slumped face first into the dust at Ryan's feet, three arrows planted in the boy's spine. Ryan could clearly see the dragonman directly behind, nearly fifty yards away, bow still held up at the ready.

"NOOOOOOOO!" Ryan's wail was wrenched from his very soul, the agony unbearable. He scrambled to Wes' side, dropping to his knees and gathering the boy's limp form into his arms. "No," he said weakly, sobs wracking his body as tears streamed from his eyes to be soaked up by the dry ground beneath him. "God, please, no!" He looked up slowly to see a hulking form standing over him, and a blade descending toward his unprotected face.

"No!" Ryan cried, sitting bolt upright, his sweat soaked blankets clinging to him like clammy fingers. He shuddered, cringing, and buried his face in his hands. "Just a dream," he muttered quietly to himself. Throwing the covers from him, he climbed out of the bed.

After haphazardly throwing on some clothes and splashing some water on his face, Ryan left his quarters, his boots tossed over his shoulder. He crept out past his snoring guard, careful not to wake the man. He padded silently down the hallway in his stocking feet, making his way toward the kitchens. The normal chaos of a kitchen meant to feed a keep of this size was subdued so late at night, but there were still people about banking fires, kneading dough, and stirring huge bubbling stock pots. Ryan grabbed the elbow of a passing man in servant's livery.

"Excuse me," Ryan said, "but I need something to drink."

The servant bowed low and spoke in a respectful tone. "Certainly, milord. There be water in the jug there, and chilled punch in the pitcher on the counter. Or would milord be wanting some warm lamb's milk to settle him for the night?"

Ryan shook his head. "No, I was hoping you might have something... a little stronger?"

The man got a twinkle in his eye. "Ah, of a certainty, milord! I've just the thing ye be wanting! Wait here, I'll fix you up." The man walked away with a jaunty step, returning only moments later with a stoppered bottle in his fist. "Cybraltan Whiskey, milord," he said with a grin, "twelve years old this past winter. Me brother runs a distillery over near Cybralta, and he gifted this to me this past Name Day."

"Oh, no, that's yours," said Ryan quickly. "It was a present. I can't accept that."

"Nay, milord, I insist. 'Twould be lost on me humble palate." He smiled as he handed Ryan the bottle. "Besides, milord... well, I'm rather fond of your lad. The little rogue could often be found down here of an evening trying to wheedle something sweet from the kitchen maids. Consider the bottle a gift, milord." The man handed the bottle to Ryan.

Ryan looked at the bottle thoughtfully. "Thank you. I didn't know anyone around here knew Wes except for Diaticus."

"Nay, milord, your lad was well known about the keep, especially among the servants. He made quite an impression, I'll tell you. The boy was incorrigible!" The man said it with a grin, showing his fondness for Wes with his tone.

"I'm glad he found some friends here." Ryan reached out his hand, and the man shook it firmly. "What's your name?"

"Anton Mallory, milord."

"Well, Anton, thanks for the whiskey, and thank you for being a friend to Wes." Ryan turned to walk away, and then reconsidered. "Hey, Anton. Why don't you join me for a drink?"

"I couldn't, milord. I'm the night cook, and me watch here don't end for another hour. Mayhap another time, eh?" With that, Anton turned and went back to his duties running the kitchen.

Ryan left the kitchens, wandering aimlessly through the keep. He held the bottle tightly, imagining Wes living in this dusty old building. The boy had probably loved every minute of it. This place was like something out of one of the books he and Wes loved to read.

After a thought, Ryan admitted to himself that he, too, would have found this to be an incredible place to live. But not now, not this way.

After only a few days in this place, Ryan didn't really know his way around yet. He continued to wander, the bottle of whiskey still unopened. He probably wouldn't even bother. He had never been much of a drinker, but for some reason it was comforting just holding the bottle in his fist. He felt as if his world were coming apart. Wes was out there somewhere, heading into danger. Ryan couldn't help but dwell on images of Wes being slaughtered by monsters or roasting alive in the Dragon's flames.

After wandering for a time, Ryan looked up and realized where he'd unconsciously arrived. Before him was a massive door, the door to the sword chamber. He reached out for the latch, and was surprised to find that it was unlocked. He looked around to see if anyone was watching, but he was alone in the hall. Shrugging to himself, he pulled the huge door open and started down the stairs.

⊷⊶

Jiane walked into the kitchen, looking around. She was trying to find Ryan, and the night maid had seen him coming in the direction of the kitchens. Jiane finally saw who she wanted and called out.

"Anton!" The man looked up and spied her across the kitchen, grinning, and walked her way dodging the scullions who darted in and out with their loads. Anton was a tall, lanky man who nearly reached Jiane's father's height, and he had a wry, mischievous grin that he used to full effect. The man was by no means handsome, but he had a charm about him that won people over quickly. She had known Anton since she was a tiny girl at High Keep, and he a roguish young lad with a dry sense of humor, and she counted him as a true and trusted friend. He had many useful skills besides being a cook. He was a very good infighter, and quite a capable tracker as well. It was commonly known that Jiane's father, Luther, relied heavily on spies to gather information for him, and Jiane had suspected for years that Anton was among them. When Anton left High Keep for this assignment at the Collegium, she had more than anyone regretted his going. She had always been much more at home among the servants than with the nobility of which she was technically a member. Anton had been her confidante and co-conspirator on more than one occasion for her childhood escapades. She had for years suspected that there was more

101

to him than even she knew, but whatever it was, she let the man have his secrets.

"Lady Jiane, what a pleasure it is to be seein' ye," Anton said, smiling as he approached.

"And you, Anton," Jiane said. "I'm hoping you can help me tonight. I'm looking for our guest, Ryan. I was told he was heading in this direction. Have you seen him?"

"Aye, milady, he was here not quite an hour past seeking something to fortify him for the night. I sent him off with a fine bottle of spirits."

"And did you see which way he went?"

"He went off down the south corridor, milady. May I ask, what's so important at this hour o' the night?"

"It's not that important, Anton," she said evasively. "I just wanted to speak with him."

"Now, milady, I think I know ye' better than that. Somethin's afoot. Yer father was down here not two hours afore Lord Ryan, asking after Diaticus himself, and now ye're down here asking yer own questions." He laid a finger alongside his nose, grinning conspiratorially. "Ye know I can be trusted, milady."

"Yes, Anton, I know you can, but truly, there's nothing afoot that I know of besides my own plans. I have no idea what my father is up to."

"Perhaps not, milady, but I'd wager ye know what ye're up to yerself."

Jiane grinned in spite of herself. "Fine. I'm going to offer Ryan my services."

"What services might those be, milady?" Anton winked at her, and she suddenly realized that the man knew exactly what she had in mind.

"I'm going to offer him my sword arm and myself as a guide to go and find his son. I can't believe that no one here has done so yet, not least of all my father."

"The thought has crossed the mind of a few, so I've heard, milady," said Anton. "Mayhap those with the courage have just been awaitin' someone with a good lead to follow." He bowed to her, low and graceful. "Milady Jiane, 'twould be my pleasure to assist you in finding Lord Ryan."

102

Ryan crept down the stairs, glad his boots still hung over his shoulder. When he'd started down, he'd simply thought the sword chamber would be as good a place as any to be alone with his thoughts. But as he had trudged down the stairway, clutching his bottle and trying to push away his morbid thoughts, he heard a voice below. He almost turned back then, especially when he recognized the voice as belonging to Diaticus, the person he least wanted to encounter. Curiosity won out, though, and he continued, keeping to the shadows. He reached the bottom of the stair and peered out silently.

"It doesn't make any sense," the wizard was muttering to himself. "Why would he want me to keep them apart? What purpose could be served by forcing the boy to take it all on alone?" He began pacing around the sword, dry washing his hands as he went. "The man has been acting strangely of late. Sending an untrained child here, after so long refusing to send a representative at all. Worse, sending a half dead man through without giving him even a hint of what's really going on!" He paused, an almost angry expression crossing his face. "Not that I know what's going on any more than Ryan does." As Diaticus reached a point in his pacing where his back was to him, Ryan slipped around the corner and out into the room. He kept to the shadows, making sure to stay out of Diaticus' line of sight, until he reached a small alcove that was completely in shadow. All the while, Diaticus kept up his rambling monologue. "The more I ponder, the less sense all of this makes. And the sword! Why did the sword react so to Ryan?" He shook his head, sighing. "Something is amiss here. Something is wrong with Pomander, or the Gatehouse. But I can't risk it! I can't take the chance that going against his instructions might doom us all!" The old wizard sighed heavily. "There's nothing to be done but wait." With a final look at the sword and another shake of his head, Diaticus turned and strode from the cave, never even knowing of Ryan's presence.

Ryan stepped from his shadowy alcove, stunned beyond words. He looked nervously to where Diaticus had exited the cave, scratching his head in confusion. He couldn't for the life of him figure out what all that had been about. Diaticus was following instructions from someone? Pomander, apparently? Instructions to keep Ryan and Wes apart? It was too much to take in! Ryan thought he should feel anger stirring at all of this, but he was just too confused by this development to capture the emotion. He pulled the stopper from his bottle and tipped it back, almost choking as the fiery liquid hit the back of his throat. It was true that he wasn't much of a drinker, but that first swallow made him certain that the liquor they made here was more potent than anything back home. Gasping, he raised the bottle to his lips for another drink.

"Amazing what a person can learn when no one knows he's about," came a deep voice from the shadows. This time, Ryan did choke, sending a spray of whiskey in the direction of the great sword as he gasped and tried to catch his breath.

"Luther!" Ryan wiped his mouth on the back of his sleeve as the big warrior stepped out of his own shadowy corner and walked toward him. "You almost scared me to death! What are you doing down here?"

"The same as you, I expect, at least in part," replied Luther casually. He reached out his hand for the bottle, gently taking it from Ryan's hand and tipping it back for a long pull. He started to speak, then looked in wonder at the bottle in his hand. He tipped it back again for an even longer drink, smacking his lips appreciatively when he finally lowered it. "Good stuff," he said finally. "Where'd you happen to get it?"

"A servant in the kitchens. Anton. He said his brother ran a distillery and sent it to him as a gift."

"Ah, yes. Anton. He said his brother runs a distillery?" Luther laughed. "Anton's brother is a scoundrel in Karsenon who's twice been convicted of thievery and sentenced to lose a hand, and somehow managed to talk his way out of it. No, I expect Anton nicked this fine bottle from Diaticus' larder." He took another long drink and handed the bottle back to Ryan, his expression turning serious. "You heard much of what I heard. Have you any thoughts on what we just witnessed?"

"I don't really know," said Ryan, taking another drink. The liquid seemed to go down smoother this time. "It seems like Diaticus has been lying to me since I got here, but it almost seemed as if he wasn't exactly happy about it."

"That's the way it seemed to me as well," said Luther thoughtfully. "I've taken a keen interest in the wizard's late night wanderings since I arrived at the keep, just after the invasion began. I believe he's been in contact with your friend Pomander since the day Wes arrived."

"He's not my friend," said Ryan coldly.

"I expect not." Luther held out his hand, and Ryan gave him the bottle. "The situation renders down rather simply, though. Diaticus has been taking instruction from someone even he is not sure can be trusted, which means Diaticus himself cannot be trusted. Steps must be taken to halt whatever plan the two of them have brewed." He tipped back the bottle, emptying nearly half the remaining contents in one swallow.

"To hell with their plans!" exclaimed Ryan. "My concern is finding my son and getting him home. Whatever Diaticus and Pomander have planned, they can do it without us." He looked toward the sword in anger, as if drawing strength from it. "Even if it means finding a quiet corner of this world and living out our lives here."

"I believe for the moment, our concerns are in alignment. Wes must be found and brought to safety, if for no other reason than to keep him out of the hands of the invaders." He looked deep into Ryan's eyes. "And believe it or not, friend, I also feel a bit of a moral obligation to see you reunited with your boy. Whenever you're ready to find him, just say the word."

Ryan considered for a moment. Was he truly ready for this? What could he hope to accomplish? But it didn't really matter. Ready or not, Wes needed him, and he had to do whatever it took to be there for his son. He'd never be able to live with himself if he didn't at least try.

"It's about time," came a woman's voice from the shadows on the stair. "I can't believe you've let him wait this long to ask, Father."

Ryan and Luther both started at the words, turning to the stair to see Anton and Jiane stepping out of the shadows.

"It seems it's the night for eavesdropping," Luther said wryly.

"I was looking for Ryan, father. I was going to offer him my sword in his service, to help him find his boy." She smiled at her father. "It seems you've beaten me to it, though."

"I don't know that you're ready for something like this," began Luther, but Jiane interrupted him.

"I'm as ready as I need to be, and far more so than you were when you first went to war." She glared at her father, daring him to forbid her in this. "Besides, you need me. An extra person won't slow you down, but an extra sword might make the difference in battle."

"That's as may be, daughter." He looked at her for a moment, then shook his head, giving in. "We'll be traveling quickly to catch them. Pack lightly."

"Pardon me," said Anton quietly. "Milords, milady, I don't mean ta' be stickin' me nose in where it's unwanted, but if ye be plannin' on goin' after the lad, I'd like to offer me services as well." He looked at them one after another hopefully. "I know me way around a fight, and I've got a few skills you may be needin' on the road. I believe I'll be joinin' ye in yer journey."

Ryan cleared his throat. "I... uh, that is... I'm not sure we'll be needing a cook where we're going."

Anton grinned back at him. "Sure'n a lesser man'd be offended by that, milord," he said with a chuckle, and a wink for Luther.

"Ryan," said Luther, stifling a grin, "allow me to introduce Anton Jacobson, spymaster for the High Lord of Canellin. He may not look like much, but looks can be deceiving." He gave Anton a hard look. "I can only presume he's on assignment here at the High Lord's direction. I'm not privy to everything that the High Lord does."

Anton seemed momentarily startled by Luther's words, but then he shrugged. "As ye' say, milord," he replied. "But if I'm not mistaken, me duties here can wait, don't ye think?"

Ryan looked Anton up and down, digesting this new information. "Well, then," he said finally. "I apologize, Anton. You're more than welcome to travel with us."

"Much obliged, milord," he said, still grinning. "But one way or t'other, I wasn't gonna' take no for an answer."

⚬⚬ ⚬⚬

The next night found Ryan creeping out of his room in the small hours once again, as planned. He quickly padded to the door in his stocking feet and gently cracked it open. The guard outside was snoring soundly, this time assisted by a bottle of brandy supplied by Anton. Ryan crept out the door and down the stairs, moving with decided purpose through the passageways until he came to the great iron bound door which had been conveniently left open yet again.

Ryan was almost afraid that Luther would not be waiting. But there he was, standing a few feet from the sword, a lumpy bundle at his feet. When he spied Ryan approaching, he kicked the bundle toward him.

"Time to change," he said peremptorily.

Ryan glanced around, but no one else appeared to be in the chamber with them. He knelt and untied the bundle, revealing a mail shirt and helm, a pair of sturdy leather gloves, and the tabard and wide sword belt worn by soldiers in the Keep's guard. He slid the mail shirt on over his tunic, and Luther assisted him in adjusting the tabard and belt, tucking the gloves behind the belt firmly. Finally, he placed the helmet upon his head.

"It'll do," Luther said critically after Ryan was appropriately attired.

"I hope so," said Ryan. "This stuff is heavy, and I feel like an idiot."

"Ah, but you look like a sergeant, and that's what's important. And you'll thank me for the mail after our first skirmish, that I'll warrant." Luther picked up his pack and motioned for Ryan to do the same.

"How are we going to get out of the Keep?" Ryan asked.

"Just follow me and keep silent." Luther stepped to the wall and removed a torch from a sconce. Then he walked to the alcove where he'd hidden himself the night before, stepped into it and seemed to vanish. Curious, Ryan followed. Just inside the alcove was a narrow crevice leading downward. Once Luther had stepped around the stone, he and his torch had been completely hidden from sight. Ryan followed the crevice down a few dozen steps to where it exited into a small passage. Luther was waiting for him there.

"Great," said Ryan. "Why does it always have to be caves? I had no idea this was here."

"Not many do, outside the Guard and Diaticus. There are tunnels down here that stretch for miles. We've been using them to slip out past the dragonmen and scout the countryside or send dispatches." Luther began walking down the passage, which widened with every step. "Anton and Jiane slipped out ahead of us from the stables with mounts and supplies. We'll meet them on the road."

Ryan and Luther walked for what seemed like hours. Luther's steps were confident and sure, which gave Ryan some comfort that he knew where they were going. They finally reached a broad passageway, broad enough for several horses to be led side by side if need be, and Luther turned left into it. Here he halted.

"We'll be coming upon a guardpost in a few minutes," said Luther quietly, "so do your best not to look startled, and hold your tongue. They're unlikely to try and deny me exit, but I'd bet they have instructions to keep you inside. Keep your helmet low and try to look like a soldier." He turned and led on.

Not more than five minutes later, they were stopped by a voice that seemed to issue from nowhere.

"Halt and identify."

"Luther Askadi and Sergeant MacGowan," Luther replied.

"Code of the hour?" The voice sounded bored.

"Coriander."

"Advance and be recognized."

Luther resumed his confident stride, Ryan following apprehensively. Ten steps down the passage, a soldier appeared in front of them, spear held across his chest.

"Lord Luther," said the man, saluting.

"At ease, corporal. We're bound for the east passage with dispatches for High Keep."

"Aye, sir," replied the corporal. "All's quiet to the east. We have two patrols out tonight in that direction, and one to the north. West and south are out of bounds. There are dragonmen scattered throughout the hills in both directions."

"Thank you, corporal. I don't foresee any problems. Dismissed."

The man saluted once again, and melted back into the shadows. Ryan and Luther continued on past several bends in the passage before Luther finally spoke again. "All right, we'll be coming to a fork in the passage soon. We'll be taking the left fork, out the west tunnel."

"I thought you said we were heading east?"

"When trying to avoid notice, confusion is your friend," replied Luther with a grin. "We're headed west, to Cybralta." They continued walking for another eternity, finally arriving at the fork in the passage and veering to the left.

As they continued walking, Ryan decided it was time to ask the question that had plagued him since they'd discussed their plan the night before. "Luther," he asked, "how are we going to find them? Wes has been gone for nearly a month. How are we going to catch up to him?"

108

"We're going to count on the habits of an old soldier," Luther replied cryptically.

"I don't understand."

"Wes left in the company of a soldier named Gideon. The man served under me during the Great War." Luther smiled slyly. "Gideon was in the infantry. Infantrymen walk everywhere they need to go. I'm hoping he stays true to his training."

"What good does that do us?"

"Friend, it's several hundred leagues to Dragon Mountain going overland. I don't plan on riding all of that on horseback, or we'll never catch them. Less than a day's ride west of Collegium Keep is a town called Cybralta on the shores of Crater Bay. It's five days by boat to Karsenon, a port city where one can cross the channel to Coveport easily. That should put us only a week or so behind them. With luck and hard riding, we'll catch them up before they reach the Plateau. If we can do that, there'll be plenty of time to turn them back before they reach the mountain."

"And what if this Gideon guy didn't take the overland route?" asked Ryan.

"Then they're probably walking into the dragon's lair as we speak, and whatever we do will be for naught."

৵৹ ৶৹

Diaticus sat staring into his amber orb, watching Ryan and Luther make good their escape. He had a tense moment when the guard confronted them, and breathed a sigh of relief as they were cleared through with little fuss. He watched them travel through the tunnels and exit into the countryside to the west of the keep, meeting up with Jiane and a peasant on the main road. Satisfied, he replaced the orb under the work table.

He hoped he was following the right course. Going against Pomander's wishes could be disastrous, but he refused to believe that keeping Ryan from his son was in any way helpful to their situation. Pomander's behavior in their communications had been too strange, too distant. Something was wrong, something beyond Diaticus' understanding. The Pomander he knew would never make such outrageous demands. He would never insist that his plans were the only option. Pomander had always been the type of man who welcomed discussion and even disagreement. Lately, the little wizard seemed almost sinister in his behavior.

It was too late now to change his mind, but he felt certain that he'd taken the proper action. Diaticus knew, deep in his bones, that Ryan should be with Wes. He left the workroom with a sigh and walked to the window of his study. Looking out over the walls, he imagined he could see the travelers out on the road, beginning a quest to save a young boy in dire peril, and perhaps an entire kingdom as well.

"Godspeed, my friends," he said softly.

Chapter 7

The Great Stone Caper

GIDEON AND WES RODE THROUGH THE GATES of the walled city of Karsenon, carefully weaving through the milling crowds. Wes had never seen so many people huddled together in one place in his life. Throngs crowded the walkways and thoroughfares driving wagons, pushing carts, or with just the clothes on their backs. They all wore identical expressions of hopelessness and loss. There were beggars and urchins everywhere, but almost no one paid them any heed. Wes was astounded to see ragged, dirty children, most far younger than himself, working their way through the throng with their hands held out in supplication. Occasionally, someone would toss a coin to the cobblestones, causing a scramble from the children and adults alike. More often than not, those piteous faces earned them a cuff or kick from the passersby. The urchins would merely stumble away, their chins held to their chests, looking with hollow eyes for someone's generosity.

"Is it always like this?" Wes asked Gideon.

"Not usually this bad. Most of these are refugees from the surrounding countryside. They came here for safety, probably after finding their farms or homes destroyed by the passing armies." Gideon looked about him in pity.

"It's awful!" exclaimed Wes. "Somebody should do something! This isn't right."

"And who is there to fix it, lad? The king and the high lord are occupied just now dealing with an invasion, and I'd wager the lord here is overwhelmed just trying to keep these hordes fed." He shook his head sadly. "As for us, lad, we're on our way to do what we can for these folk. That's all we can do."

"Still," said Wes, "it's not right. Nobody should have to live like this."

"That's the Gods' own truth, lad." Gideon maneuvered his mount around a group of child beggars, and Wes saw him surreptitiously drop a handful of copper coins to the pavement. He sighed as the children began scrambling, fighting over the booty. "There's plenty of daylight left. With any luck, we'll get to the docks and be able to hire a ship before nightfall. The sooner we're gone from this place, the better."

Wes reined in his horse quickly. "What about the Tower of Lore? The Catalyst Stone?"

Gideon sighed. "Lad, I just don't like the idea. First, we don't even know if the stone is there. Second, we have no way of getting it if it is."

"We could ask the lord here for it. Tell him what we're planning."

"And you think he's likely to believe us?" Gideon shook his head ruefully. "Lord Joachim is a bit of a cagey man. I've seen him before, when he was visiting the Collegium to consult with Diaticus. He seemed rather full of himself. A blademaster with no great love of magic, and a particular dislike of Diaticus, from what I could tell. No matter what we tell the man, I can't see him allowing us to take a Crossing artifact with us."

"So we steal it." Wes shrugged.

"Again, an idea I'm not fond of." Gideon looked to Wes, seeing the boy's shoulder's slump in defeat. "All right, lad. If we can't find a ship to carry us across the channel today, we'll look this tower over. No promises, though."

"That's all I'm asking," said Wes, satisfied.

The two travelers made their way through the crowded streets slowly, steering their mounts around the milling throngs with care. As they neared the city center, Wes marveled at the architecture surrounding them. He had seen skyscrapers before, but the buildings here were both tall and ornate, and they got larger and more elaborate as they neared the prosperous areas of the city. He couldn't imagine how these people, with the technology they had, were able to construct such marvels.

"Gideon," he asked curiously, "how many people live here?"

"Usually forty or fifty thousand, I'd say, and crowded at that. Likely more than half again that number now. More than this city was meant to hold, that's certain."

112

They passed through the city center, working their way toward the docks. Karsenon was a prosperous port city, and its docks were impressive even from a distance. As they neared, Wes found it difficult to tear his eyes from the immense ships tied to the massive wharves. He looked at the great vessels with a mixture of awe and fear. The largest boat he'd ever been on was his grandfather's little aluminum fishing boat, and the deepest water no more than fifteen feet. He said as much to Gideon as they approached the waterfront.

"What's to fear about a boat, lad? As long as the deck stays between me and the water, I'll be satisfied."

"Sure, but what if we end up in the water?"

"Can you swim?" Wes nodded, and Gideon continued. "Well, then, what's to be frightened of? How deep it is? It makes no difference. What matter how much water is under you, as long as there's none above?"

Wes laughed, realizing he was being silly. But he couldn't completely suppress his trepidation as they approached the churning water.

Gideon led the way down the docks, apparently trying to decide which vessel to approach. He finally chose a huge ship with three decks, four masts, and an intricate arrangement of sails. He strode toward the side of the ship, but could see no way to board. Looking around, he finally shrugged and cupped his hands around his mouth.

"Ho, the ship! Permission to come aboard!"

A head popped up from behind the boat's broad railing, then ducked back down. A few moments later, the same head popped up again, and the man stretched out his arm, pointing down at Wes and Gideon. Another man stepped up to the railing, his clothing of a much finer cut than the deckhand's, obviously an officer. He looked down at Wes and Gideon impassively.

"State your business!" he called gruffly.

"Two travelers seeking passage across the channel. Permission to come aboard and discuss terms?"

"Denied! We've no room for passengers, and no need. Begone!" The man turned rudely and walked out of sight behind the railing. Gideon shrugged, taking the denial with equanimity. As the day wore on into early evening, and they continued to receive the same reception at all of the larger vessels, his patience was sorely tested. They continued to try many of the huge ships, always walking away disappointed after a chilly reception. After more than an hour of wandering the docks, they wound up nearly back where they started and no further toward their goal.

"Perhaps we'll have more luck if we head back to the street and work our way down to one of the other wharves," Gideon said in frustration. "I can't think of anything else to do."

"Beggin' yer pardon, friends, but I can't help but wonder what ye be tryin' to do," said a creaky voice off to their left. Wes looked that direction and saw that the voice issued from the deck of an equally creaky ship, smaller than the ones on which they'd been inquiring, but still larger than the landing boats they'd seen rowing back and forth between the truly great ships out in the bay. Standing relaxed on the deck was an old man, his clothing finely cut but well worn, his weathered face regarding them curiously. "Ye've been crossin' these docks fer quite some time, and I can't figure out yer plan. Yer tryin' to git across the channel, aye?"

"Yes," replied Gideon, "But the captains of these fine vessels don't seem to be interested in paying passengers."

"It's not that they dislike payin' passengers, me boy, it's that they're not headed where yer goin'! Ye've walked past twenty ships or more that make the channel crossin' ta' beg passage on cargo ships headed out to sea!" The old man cackled. "Why would men with ships as grand as those bother runnin' em acrost here? They leave such smaller tasks ta' the local vessels, lads."

"And I suppose yours is such a vessel?"

"Well, as to that, I make me livin' with the net, but I'm not the kind that'd refuse a couple o' payin' passengers if they's wantin' to git acrost. Trigg's me name, and I do be sailin' with the sun day after tomorrow, if yer still wantin' ta' go."

Gideon sighed. It was clear to Wes that he didn't trust this man's creaky ship, but it was the only offer they'd had. He frowned down at the dock, and then looked back up at the weathered man. "How much will the passage cost?"

"A silver coin from each of ye would do it, fer certain. We'll be draggin' the nets behind us as we go, so I don't need ta' rob ye blind just ta' drop ye off on t'other side!" The man winked at them shrewdly.

Gideon looked around them once again, and finally agreed. "When can we leave?"

"I'll be shovin' off not long after sunrise, on the eighth bell, day after tomorrow. If yer here when I do, that's when we leave. I'll have ye acrost by evenin' two or three days followin'."

Shrugging, Gideon said, "It will have to do. We'll be here before the eighth bell." He turned his horse back toward the street and rode away, Wes spurring his mount to follow.

"So what now? We've got to stay two nights. Can we at least take a look at this Tower of Lore place?"

"Aye, lad, I suppose we might as well. We'll get a room at a decent inn first." Gideon looked around at the multitudes crammed into the city. "If there's one to be had."

The first inn they came to was full to capacity. The innkeeper suggested an inn further down the street, but it was also full. The innkeeper there irritably pointed out the wooden placard hanging from a nail next to the entrance depicting a bed with a red X across it. Exploring the other inns in the area revealed that they all had the same placard next to the door, and they rode on.

Night began to fall as they wandered through the city, yet the crowds seemed as thick as ever. Wes realized that most of them would likely have no place to stay, just like them. Indeed, many were already slipping into alleys or shadowed doorways and laying out bedrolls, or just stretching out on the pavement. He was beginning to suspect that they would have to do the same.

They had wandered into a seedier quarter of town, the buildings smaller and showing more wear. Night was falling quickly. They rode their horses wearily down the narrow street, looking for another inn at which to inquire.

"There's another," said Gideon.

Wes looked up to see the sign hanging over a door halfway down the block. He couldn't read the script, of course, but the painted sign clearly showed the figure of a woman hanging from a gallows. The Hanged Woman, maybe. Inns in this town had some very odd names. As they approached the establishment, Wes could clearly see the sign hanging next to the door, the red X visible, and he let out a sigh.

"I think we're going to end up sleeping on the sidewalk tonight," he said in resignation. Just then, the double doors on the front of the building slammed open, and a scruffy man came crashing and tumbling to the pavement in front of their horses. Behind the man came a huge shape, advancing menacingly. Gideon quickly reached back for his sword, and Wes began to prepare a spell, wondering how a dragonman had gotten so far inside the city undetected. However, when the shape came into the light, it was revealed to be a very tall, very round woman carrying saddlebags and a large pack. She flung her burden into the street after the prone man.

"Next time, make sure ye've the coin ta' pay fer yer lodgin'!" Her voice was higher than Wes had expected from such an imposing figure. The man she'd tossed through the door scrambled for his belongings and fled down the street. The woman turned to go back inside with a great harrumph, then reached back out in afterthought and flipped the sign around to the side showing an empty bed. Gideon quickly called out to her.

"Pardon me, madam. I presume you now have a vacant room?" He smiled ingratiatingly. Wes still marveled at how Gideon seemed to be able to switch from the rough country guardsman to the educated soldier so easily.

The woman looked the two of them over carefully, taking in their looks and demeanor. Despite their travel-worn appearance, their clothes were of a much finer cut than most of the rabble that flowed through the streets, and unlike most, they were on horseback.

"Aye, milord, but I think ye may be on the wrong side o' town. My establishment's not fer the likes o' you." She jerked her thumb in the direction from which they'd come. "They's places back that a' way more befittin' men of yer station. Just a mile or two off." With that, the imposing woman turned away once again, dismissing the two travelers from her mind.

"You're mistaken on two points, madam," Gideon called after her. "Firstly, I'm no lord, just a common soldier traveling with his son. And secondly, I believe that you may have the only room available in this entire bloody town!"

Gideon realized his mistake as soon as the woman halted in her tracks. She turned to him, a mercenary gleam in squinted eyes.

"In that case, soldier, it'll be three silver a night. Each." She gave Gideon a wicked grin.

"Highway robbery!" exclaimed Gideon, his eyes widening. "I'll not pay more than five coppers for both of us!"

"Times be hard, and prices steep, Captain. I could take two silver each, or ye c'n try yer luck someplace else."

Grumbling, Gideon dismounted, grabbing his saddlebags. "Two silvers a night each for the room and a good meal. Agreed?"

"Agreed," said the woman firmly, and whistled shrilly. A scruffy boy of about nine years ran from around the corner of the building and grabbed Wes' reins out of his hands, reaching down to grab Gideon's where they trailed on the ground. Gideon unpacked his blanket and bedroll while Wes dismounted. When both of the horses were unpacked, the stable boy quickly led them back the way he'd come. Gideon and Wes started toward the entrance, only to be halted gruffly by the huge woman.

"I'll have me coin in advance," she said with a stern look, and Gideon bristled.

"Half now, half when we leave," he said curtly. The woman frowned, then nodded and held out her hand. Gideon reached into his pouch and retrieved four silver marks, depositing them on her outstretched palm.

"And we'll take our supper in our room within the hour," the man said.

The innkeeper shot him a look of displeasure. "As ye say, Captain."

"Sergeant, madam."

"As ye say," the woman repeated. "If ye be needin' anything in the night, come down to the common room and ask fer Rosalinda. I'll make sure yer taken care of." She stalked inside, leading them up a narrow staircase to a small door, opening it gruffly and then stalking off down the hall.

"What an unpleasant woman," Gideon said when she was out of earshot. He and Wes stepped inside the small room.

Wes looked around uncomfortably, noting the austerity of the chamber. A small washstand stood in the corner next to the window, and a chamber pot in the opposite corner. A narrow bed, hardly more than a cot, ran along the near wall. The only other stick of furniture in the room was a high backed wooden chair set against the wall.

"Well, I guess I'll be sleeping on the floor tonight," he said, disappointed. "Better than laying on the ground. We can go look that tower over in the morning."

"No, lad, you take the cot," said Gideon. "An old soldier's used to sleeping rough."

Wes smiled up at his friend gratefully. Dropping his packs beside the cot, Wes flopped down and stretched out on it. He reached down to his backpack and pulled out the book, propping it on his knees while Gideon set about sharpening his sword. Presently, there came a knock on the door, and a serving maid entered bearing a tray and platter of steaming roast and cheese with a loaf of bread. Gideon took the platter and slipped the girl a copper coin, and she smiled shyly at him before leaving. He set the platter on the cot near Wes' feet, pulled his chair over, and began cutting the bread. When Wes didn't stir, the old soldier glanced up to find the boy's eyes closed, his breathing steady. Gideon grinned.

"Lad!" he said sharply, chuckling when Wes jerked in surprise. "Wake up, boy, supper's arrived." Wes' eyes opened slowly as he sat up. He saw the trencher of meat at his feet, and his eyes widened.

"Wow," he said, abashed. "I'm sorry, I don't know what happened. How long was I asleep?"

"A few minutes at most, else I'd have let you get your rest. I thought you might like to fill your belly before sleep takes you for the night."

"Yeah," said the boy absently, laying the book aside. He selected a slice of bread and topped it with a small portion of meat and cheese. "I don't know what it is, Gideon. I'm exhausted! I have been for days now."

"It's nothing to worry about. We've been on the road for weeks, with only the occasional hayloft for a bed. It's not what you're used to. Believe me, it took years of soldiering before I grew accustomed to sleeping under the sky."

"I don't know if that's it or not. I've been feeling… I don't know. Weak, I guess. And a little sick."

Gideon reached up and felt the boy's forehead in concern. "I had noticed your appetite was a little off. I marked it down to worry more than anything else. You don't feel feverish, though." He looked into Wes' eyes, checking for discoloration. "Your color's good. I don't think you've anything to worry about."

"You're probably right," said Wes wearily, nibbling at his impromptu sandwich. After just a few bites, he set it aside. "I'm not very hungry. I think I'm just going to go to sleep. We have a lot to do tomorrow."

Gideon sighed. "Well, the food'll be here in the morning when you wake, so suit yourself. Rest well."

"Sure," replied Wes around a yawn. "Just wake me up when we need to leave, okay?" He laid his head on the pillow and was asleep almost before the blanket settled around him.

Gideon smiled, taking the platter from the foot of the bed. He spent a bit more time filling his own belly, and then put the half empty platter on the washstand. In truth, he was nearly as tired as Wes. He spread his bedroll on the floor and stretched out, using his pack for a pillow.

੭ତ ୨ୡ

Wes came awake upon hearing a loud crash, followed by several thumps and sounds of a struggle. He sat up and ignited a magelight without thinking. Revealed in the sudden brightness was Gideon, wrestling with a small form that was shrouded in a dark cloak. The unexpected light seemed to startle Gideon's assailant, giving the old soldier an opportunity to grab a flailing arm and twist it around behind the intruder's back.

"What's going on?" cried Wes, sleep still clouding his thoughts.

"It seems we have a visitor," said Gideon, grunting as his captive propelled an elbow back into his ribcage. He increased the pressure on the other arm, and the struggles subsided. "He came in through the window and decided I was a bundle of rags to tread on. Clumsiest thief I've ever come across," the man muttered in disgust.

"Please, don't hurt me!" The voice was high pitched and feminine, and filled with terror. "I was hungry, is all!"

"He's a girl!" exclaimed Wes in surprise, and Gideon released the girl, shocked. She scrambled away from him and pressed her back against the wall, sizing them up. She eyed the door, then the window, as if weighing her chances of escaping through each.

"Don't try it, girl," said Gideon, moving between the girl and the window as Wes moved between her and the door. "You won't get out that way. You're going to the town watch." Gideon's voice was harsh and unforgiving.

"No! Please! I'll do anything!" The girl's eyes grew wide as she looked for an avenue of escape. "Please, don't call the watch! They'll take my hand!"

"What do you mean, take your hand?" asked Wes.

"Thievery is usually punished in these parts by lopping off the offender's right hand," put in Gideon matter-of-factly, and Wes' jaw

119

dropped. "It's no more than she deserves, boy, and she knew the penalty before she crept into our window," he said upon seeing Wes' astonishment.

"Please," said their captive weakly. "Please, don't call the watch." She stepped toward Gideon with an exaggerated swaying of her hips, her hand stretched out in invitation. "I can make it worth your while."

"None of that, girl," said Gideon quickly, grabbing her by the wrist and shoving her bodily into their hard wooden chair. "What are you, eleven? Twelve years at most? Too young by far for such ideas."

"Sixteen," she replied with venom, "and better that than the watch." She rubbed her wrist where Gideon had grabbed her.

"That should have been your thought before you crept into an honest traveler's room with mischief in mind," Gideon replied. He started for the door, apparently meaning to call for the authorities.

Wes looked at the pathetic girl in sympathy. Sitting there, her cloak thrown back, he could see she was rail thin. Her cheeks were sunken and smudged with dirt, her hair matted, and her eyes full of fear. The girl's skin was pale, her eyes slightly slanted, and her dark hair hung limply over her shoulders. There was something else, though... a strange maturity, and a mixture of determination and strength.

"Gideon, wait," said Wes. Gideon paused, his hand on the door latch. Before Wes could go on, all three of the room's occupants were startled by a sudden pounding at the chamber door. Gideon tripped the latch and flung the door wide.

"What's all the ruckus?" demanded Madam Rosalind angrily, pushing her way inside the cramped room.

Gideon looked to Wes, then back to the innkeeper with a sigh. "'Twas nothing, madam. Just an unexpected visitor. All's well."

The imposing woman looked at the girl in surprise, and then turned a cold glare on Wes and Gideon, coming quickly to the wrong conclusion.

"Yer business is yer own," she said. "Keep down the noise, and send her out the back way when yer finished with 'er. And if ye don't mind, I expect the room to be available again after the morning."

"Madam," said Gideon archly, "you have the wrong idea, of that I can assure you. And as for the room, the agreement was for two nights, and that is how long we intend to stay. Now if you don't mind,

120

we'd like some privacy to chat with our friend here." He looked meaningfully at the door, and the huge innkeeper turned on her heel and stalked from the room, slamming the door so hard that the floor shook.

"I truly dislike that woman," said Gideon with distaste, but Wes wasn't listening.

"What's your name?" he asked the girl softly.

"Elarie," the girl said bitterly. "Milord," she added as a sarcastic afterthought.

"Not Milord. I'm Wes, and this is Gideon." Gideon crossed his arms over his barrel chest and regarded the girl impassively. "What were you doing sneaking in our window?"

Elarie regarded Wes curiously, as if trying to decide what tack to take with the boy, and Gideon spoke up.

"Truth now, girl," he said. "Your life's in the boy's hands, but don't try to sweet talk your way out of this. I'll not allow him to be gulled by a pretty face."

Elarie surged to her feet in outrage, her temper obviously getting the better of her. "Fine, you great lout! I meant to steal you blind and leave you paupers! It's what I do, and how I make my way, and I won't make any apologies to you lot for it!"

"No one's asking you to," said Wes, hiding a grin behind his hand.

"I might," muttered Gideon, and Wes waved him to silence. Gideon subsided. Wes wasn't sure why the big man was following his lead, but he wasn't about to question it now.

"Personally," he said to Elarie, "I think it's kind of cool. Are you a good thief?"

"One of the best in the city," she boasted, puffing out her chest.

"Hence the tripping and the crashing and the thumping," said Gideon wryly, laughing outright.

"Most people don't sleep directly under their chamber window, dolt." She glared as Gideon's grin broadened. "I've been practicing the art since I was a child, and only caught once in ten years. And I managed to get away, at that!"

"Twice," Wes interjected.

"What?" said Elarie.

"You've been caught twice now, and you haven't gotten away this time."

"Yet," the girl replied with a twinkle in her eye.

"You don't look all that prosperous for such a master thief," said Gideon.

"Time's are bad, mil… Gideon." Elarie straightened in her chair. "Food's scarce, and gold and silver are hard to come by. I'll admit, I've missed a meal or two, but I'm no worse off than most, and better off than a good many."

"She should go to the watch, Wes. You can't trust what she says, and she'd as soon slit our throats as have this little chat." Gideon gave the girl a hard look.

Elarie glared back at Gideon, steel in her gaze. "I've never taken a life nor harmed another human being," she said. "Thieving is my trade, not murder." She looked back and forth at the two of them, and finally shook her head disgustedly at her situation. "Do as you will with me, but you'll have to clout me or kill me if you call the watch. I'm as good as dead if they take me, anyway." She squared her shoulders, looking at them defiantly.

Gideon made as if to open the door, but Wes stopped him.

"Give her some money," he said to the man.

"What?" Gideon exclaimed. "What are you talking about, lad? Why would I give her money?"

"Because she needs it, and where we're going, we won't," Wes replied. "I saw you drop the coins for the kids in the square, Gideon. We both know you won't be turning her over to the watch any more than you would me."

Gideon scowled at Wes, and then reached into his pouch, drawing out a handful of coppers and pressing them into the girl's hand. As she spirited them into the pockets of her cloak, Wes saw several glints of silver.

"You're not going to turn me over to the watch?" She looked from one to the other of them, still not sure what would happen next.

"He was never going to," said Wes with a grin. "You have to know him, I guess."

"But don't try me a second time, lass. I'm not a very forgiving soul." He scowled at her and cracked his knuckles.

"But the money's not a handout. We have a small chore we need some help with." Wes winked at Elarie. "I think you may be the perfect person for the job."

Elarie's eyes narrowed. "What kind of a job?"

122

"We need your expertise and advice to acquire something we need desperately."

"Honest travelers, indeed," the girl replied with a snort. "And where exactly is this item you need?"

"The Tower of Lore," replied Wes, and Elarie's face blanched.

"I think not," she replied. "And I think I'll be leaving now. You won't be seeing me again." Without warning, the girl sprang past Gideon and dived out the window, disappearing from sight. Gideon rushed to the sill, Wes close behind him, and both peered into the empty alley three stories below. There was no sign of the girl anywhere.

"Perhaps she was a better thief than we thought," said Gideon in amazement. "I can't recall ever seeing anyone move like that!"

"You wouldn't really have let them cut off her hand, would you?"

"Of course not, boy. It's a brutal law, and it should be abolished. The King's Justice is much more refined, it just rarely stretches as far south as this." He patted Wes on the shoulder reassuringly. "I did hope frightening the girl would show her the folly of her path, though. She didn't seem much swayed."

"No, she didn't," said Wes. "Did you believe her story?"

"Not a word of it, lad!" Gideon replied, chuckling softly.

"Me neither," Wes said with a grin. "She was kind of pretty, though," he added, and Gideon guffawed, clapping the boy on the back again.

"Get back to sleep, you little rogue! We've things to do in the morning." He closed the shutters, still grinning.

৵৹৹ ৹৹৵

Elarie crouched on the ledge above the window as she listened to Wes and Gideon's conversation, balancing on tiptoe with one hand on the gutter. She had been amused to see them peering down at the street below. As soon as she'd dived out the window, she'd caught the gutter and swung herself up to her present perch, but those two had been too shocked by her sudden escape to notice. Listening to them talk about her was quite entertaining, but when they finally closed the shutters, she scaled the gutter and crept to where she'd hidden her packs, well back on the inn's flat roof.

So, they hadn't believed her story. That stung a bit. Some of it was even true! She checked her packs, making sure the night's take was safe. Not as much coin as she'd have liked, as usual of late, not more than a hundred silver and half that in gold. But there was plenty of merchandise to be fenced in the morning. She tied the packs securely about her person. They were ungainly, but she was more than agile enough for the climb down from the roof, even with the extra burden.

Still, how could she have been so clumsy? Even after treading on the big man, how could she have stumbled so? Chalk it up to exhaustion, she mused. She had been working all night, every night, for almost a month. Wartime was profitable. Her cache had grown so much that she was considering getting out of the business once the present troubles were past. But then, what would she do with the rest of her life?

A life she'd feared she might lose tonight. She had been totally at their mercy until the man, Gideon, had released his hold on her. After that, she knew she could have escaped at any time, but those two had intrigued her. But then, why had the boy insisted on letting her go? He could have had no clue that she could have escaped whenever she liked. He had truly wanted her to be free, and had thought that he was providing that freedom. Why the offer of work, why the handful of coins? Did they really think to hire her for a job? They'd had her dead to rights, in their eyes. As far as they'd known, they could have made an end of her right then and there. But the man had been intent only on scaring her, that had been obvious from the beginning of his little charade.

Elarie continued on her way, working down the darkened streets toward her hideout to stash her haul. She froze in her tracks as a sphere of azure light appeared from nowhere in the street twenty paces ahead of her. She backed away, looking about in alarm. She had no idea what the light was, but she wanted nothing to do with it. She turned to flee, and the ball of light suddenly streaked into motion, flying toward her with definite purpose. Before she'd taken two steps, the light struck, and she stiffened. The light faded, leaving a blue nimbus surrounding her. That, too, faded quickly, and she shook her head in confusion.

Perhaps... perhaps she would come back in the daylight. Just to keep an eye on them, keep them out of trouble. Maybe pass the word to the pickpockets and beggars that these two had done her a kindness, and were not to be molested.

What was she thinking? A boy shows her a tiny kindness, and she goes soft? Still, perhaps a trip back in daylight. Just to be certain.

৵৹৫ ৺৵৹

Elarie crept along the shadowed alley, careful to keep her quarry in sight. She felt a strange urge to find out what these two were up to. Whatever their ultimate goal, it was obvious they were delving into the world of shady dealings. The problem was with their execution. These two were the most clumsy and transparent amateurs she'd ever seen! So far, she'd used her influence to warn off four pickpockets and a pair of cutthroats, not to mention arranging distractions for the members of the city watch who'd taken too close an interest in the suspicious behavior of the inept pair. She'd owe a few minor debts after today, that was certain.

To be fair, they probably thought they were being inconspicuous. But the first and finest lesson in becoming a master of the criminal arts was that inconspicuous didn't always mean sneaking about and trying to avoid being seen. Until a thief became adept at being invisible in the shadows, a convincing front and a trustworthy face were vital. The best way for a budding thief to enter the heavily guarded home of her mark, if it must be done in daylight, was to make it seem as if she were supposed to be there. March brashly up to the door with a delivery for the household cook, or a message for the eyes of the master of the house alone. Once entrance was gained, the time for skulking and creeping through shadows would begin.

Elarie froze. Her quarry had stopped at the head of the alley, back in the shadows a bit, and were peering across the square to the Tower of Lore with quite a bit too much interest. Elarie strained her ears to hear their conversation.

"So how do we get in?" asked Wes in a whisper.

"I have no idea," replied Gideon. "I'm a soldier, boy, not a professional sneak. Are you sure you need the blasted stone? Or that it's even in there?"

"It's in there," said Wes. "I'm sure of it. And as for needing it, or if I can even use it if I find it, I have no idea. But we're in for a fight when we get where we're going, and I'll take any advantage I can get."

The two fell silent, staring across the square at the imposing tower. Elarie wracked her brain, trying to figure out what they were up to. She'd found herself unable to think of much else besides these two since their encounter the previous night. The young one, Wes, apparently needed some stone from the Tower of Lore. What kinds of stones would be there that these two would think was important? Magical stones, obviously, or perhaps a very valuable jewel from the Crossing. No, these two weren't the type to be stealing gold or jewelry. Perhaps the boy was a mage. Who could tell? Elarie moved forward in the shadows, her feet making no sound on the cobblestones. She was within a few feet of the two now, but they had no inkling of her presence.

"Do you think we could climb it?" Wes' voice sounded dubious to Elarie.

"Not likely." Gideon shook his head. "Oh, it could be done, but not without being seen. This square is lit at night, as are the walls of the tower. We'd be easy pickings for any pimply faced guard cadet with a crossbow."

Wes turned and angrily kicked the wall behind him. "Why couldn't we just ask that guy you told me about, that Lord Joachim, to give it to us? He's in charge around here. Maybe he'd listen to reason."

"Not likely. From all I know, Joachim is a petty man, drunk on power, and not all that pleasant to deal with. All the same, no lord worth his salt would give us something so valuable on just our word, and we can't count on Diaticus' name helping." Gideon looked around, apparently considering their options. "It'll have to be stealth. We'll try it tonight. Perhaps climbing the tower is the best chance after all."

"Don't be an idiot," said Elarie, unable to contain herself. Gideon and Wes whirled in surprise, hands going to their weapons. Elarie continued, unperturbed by their reaction. "A thousand thieves have tried climbing that tower to get at the fabled wealth inside, and only one has ever succeeded. And that one barely escaped with her life, and no booty to speak of."

Wes and Gideon relaxed visibly as they recognized the girl.

"And what business is it of yours, girl? You chose not to join us on this venture. Go away, we have work to do." Gideon's voice was gruff but amused.

126

"If I go away, you two will continue this foolishness and find yourselves dead or in the thieves' cells below the council building. I'm fairly certain neither of you would enjoy that." Elarie spat in disgust. "Whatever it is you want from that tower, it's not worth your lives. Give it up before you get yourselves hurt. Amateurs have no business with the Tower of Lore."

"Our business is our own, little girl," Gideon said with a growl. "Interfere at your own risk."

"Gideon, wait," said Wes. "I want to hear what she has to say."

"Finally, a voice of reason," said Elarie. She opened her mouth to speak, but then turned away and muttered to herself. "Gods, why am I getting involved in this? It's not good for me." She looked back to Wes and Gideon and began again, taking on a lecturing tone. "That's the most heavily guarded treasure trove in the entire kingdom. Between the magical traps and protections and the guards and more mundane security measures, no thief has ever managed to escape there with so much as a pebble from the rooftop garden. If you've a need for some valuable artifacts, I'll show you many less dangerous marks. But give up this foolishness."

"Magical protections won't be a problem," said Wes confidently. "And neither will the guards. Once we get in, getting what we need and getting out without getting caught won't be a problem. But getting in is what has us stalled right now."

"So you think you can handle the magic. What makes you so sure you can handle the guards? And the traps? You seem pretty sure of yourself."

"Trust me. I've got magic of my own. I can handle the magical traps, and I can keep us from being found by the guards inside. It's the guards outside, and all over the square, that I won't be able to handle on my own."

Elarie looked at Wes for a few moments. "You can neutralize the magic inside? And keep the guards from finding you?" Wes nodded. "Your magic is that strong?" He nodded again. "And how do you plan to get out?"

"Magic again. Trust me on this. Once Gideon and I get in and find what we need, we'll be back in our room at the inn before you can blink."

The young thief considered for a moment. Could it be true? Could this little magician have the secret to escaping the Tower of

Lore? If so, then these two might actually have a chance! She looked from one to the other, and then made up her mind.

"Come with me." Without another word, she turned and strode off down the dark alley. After a few moments, she heard two pairs of boots begin to follow.

"Where are we going?" came Wes' voice.

"Somewhere quiet, so I can tell you how this will go. If you want my help, you'll do as I say."

ᴑᴐ ᴐᴀ

"This is the place," Elarie said. Gideon and Wes halted and looked around nervously. Darkness had settled about the town. They'd spent much of the day at the inn as Elarie explained her plan, and she'd returned to them there after the sun had set. The three found themselves now in yet another seedy area, this one without even the benefit of street lamps. The only light was the occasional torch in front of a run-down tavern or inn.

"Are you sure about this?" asked Wes.

"Of course I'm sure. This is the way in." She bent down to the cobblestones, fumbling for a moment in the darkness. After a while, she let out a quick "Ah!" of delight, and grasped the hidden handle on the sewer grate. With a twist and a metallic click, the grate came free. She pulled it up easily on silent hinges.

"But we're at least a mile from the tower!" said Wes. "This is crazy!"

"It's not crazy," replied Elarie. "Thieves have been operating in this city for generations. Trust me, we know what we're doing by now. The best way to get in and out of anyplace is through the sewers. It's dirty work, but it'll keep you alive."

"That I get," said Wes. "But why so far from the tower?"

"Because there are only so many entrances that have been rigged like this, and this is the one nearest where we want to go." She gave a shrug. "Now, are you ready to go?"

"I guess I am," said Wes reluctantly.

"Buck up, lad," said Gideon. "As the girl says, it may be dirty work, but it'll keep us alive and get us your bloody stone."

"You were the one who didn't want to trust her a couple hours ago," said Wes sullenly.

128

"And I don't trust her now, which shouldn't be a surprise to either of you. But if you're so dead set on trying for this bauble, she's our best bet."

"Fine. So we go." Wes turned to Elarie. "Lead the way."

With a diffident shrug, Elarie led the way through the grate. There was a rusted iron ladder attached to the wall, and she scrambled down it quickly while the others struggled to follow. "Pull the catch back on the grate before you come down. We don't want anyone finding it open." A soft clang told her Gideon had done as she asked, and she settled in to wait.

By the time the pair of bunglers joined her, Elarie's eyes had adjusted to the dark. She peered down the sewer tunnel to where it branched. "We go that way," she said confidently.

"I'll give us some light," said Wes, raising his hand to cast his spell.

"No! If there's a light down here, it'll be seen every time we pass under a grate. Let your eyes adjust. You'll find that the grates above let in enough light for us to see by." Wes sheepishly returned his hand to his side.

"I hate wandering in the dark," he said. Elarie gave him a reproving look. "Fine, whatever, we'll do things your way."

"Good. Once you've got your stone, you can take over with that magical escape plan of yours. Until then, I'm in charge, and you'll follow my directions. Now, if you can see well enough, let's go." Elarie turned and strode off down the ledge next to the smelly river under the city. Giving the stream of sewage a distasteful glance, Wes followed, Gideon taking up the rear.

They trudged along under the city for more than half an hour, Elarie leading them confidently through every bend and turn. Finally, in a spot that looked much like every other they'd passed, she stopped.

"This is it. That grate above us leads into the lower sub-level of the tower. From there, we can make our way up and start looking for your stone." She motioned Gideon to her and had him hoist her up. Standing on the big man's shoulders, she was just able to grab hold of an iron hook next to the grate. Carefully reaching into her pack with her free hand, she took out a length of knotted rope with a hoop on one end. Fixing the hoop over the hook, she dropped the rope. She quickly braced her feet against a knot near the top and pushed against the grate, lifting it just enough for her to squeeze under. As the two below began climbing the rope, she heaved the grate aside to give them room to enter the building. They scrambled up to join her, and Gideon replaced the grate.

"Now quiet time begins," she whispered. "Sounds often travel in strange ways through stone buildings." Gideon and Wes nodded, and she continued. "There's a hatchway over here that leads to a chimney. It's not much used these days, but it's intact. We'll climb up the chimney to the main floor and then go from there. It's likely your stone is on one of the upper levels, but we can't be sure. We'll start at the bottom and work our way up."

Squirming up the narrow chimney wasn't as difficult as it sounded. The walls were close enough to allow Wes and Elarie to brace their hands and knees on one side and their backs on the other, working their way up at a crawl. Gideon had the most trouble, unable to bend himself enough to make the climb the way his smaller companions did. He finally managed to pull himself up through sheer strength, using only his hands braced on opposite walls. After he heaved himself out of the chimney onto the ground floor of the tower, all three breathed a sigh of relief.

"All right," whispered Elarie. "Here's where the fun begins. In a moment, we'll begin searching. Both of you remember, step only where I step, and touch nothing unless I've examined it first. There are traps in here that would boggle the mind." She gave Wes a glance. "And now it's time for a little of your magic, boy. This place is likely crawling with guards, how many I haven't a clue. You must do something to make us unseen. Also, there are likely magical safeguards I know nothing about and won't be able to detect. Those will be your responsibility as well."

"No problem," he replied with a hiss. "As for the traps and stuff, I've already cast a spell on myself that'll let me see them. I'll extend it to include you and Gideon. And for the guards, I've got a new one I'm going to try. It's a Cloak of Shadows. It doesn't exactly hide us or make us invisible, but it should do the trick. It'll make us… I'm not sure how to explain. Unobtrusive. The guards won't notice us, even if they see us."

Elarie looked at Wes closely. "And you're sure this spell of yours will work?"

"Every spell I've tried so far has worked," bragged Wes with a smirk. "Eventually. But I've practiced these. Trust me."

"I hate when people say that to me," said Elarie with a grimace. "As you will. Cast your charms and let's get on with this."

Wes closed his eyes and concentrated, spreading his arms wide. He muttered something under his breath, and Gideon gasped. Elarie managed to stifle her own exclamation, but only barely. What she saw was incredible. Throughout the room were shining glyphs, arcane markings on seemingly random items. They shone clearly to her eyes, some a faint shine, some an intense pulsing glow.

"Did it work? Do you see it?" Wes' eyes were still shut tight.

"Yes," breathed Elarie. "It's incredible! I had no idea there would be so many!" Under her breath, she muttered, "It must have been pure luck last time."

"What was that?" said Wes.

"Never mind. Why are some brighter than others?"

"I don't know," replied the young mage. "Maybe it indicates which are stronger or more sensitive. Or more dangerous. But even if it does, I don't know how it judges it. The brightest ones might be the fairly tame ones, and the dim ones might be the most deadly. The only safe thing is to not touch anything that's glowing."

"That was the route I figured on going, myself," said Gideon. "And even that's going to be hard."

"Don't worry about it. We can see them, we can avoid them. As for the regular alarms and traps, just keep close to me and follow my footsteps. Now, about this shadow cloak..." She looked at Wes expectantly.

"Right," said Wes. He again closed his eyes and concentrated hard. Elarie could barely hear his whisper as he chanted under his breath, but the gestures he made with his hands were almost like a dance. They were also very hard to discern; it seemed every time her gaze locked on Wes' twitching fingers or flowing wrists, her eyes slid away of their own volition. After a few moments, the spell was finished, and Wes gave her a wink and a nod.

"All right. Let's hope it works." With that, Elarie started forward, slowly but with supreme confidence in her abilities, looking back only occasionally to make sure the others were following as instructed.

The search of the lower floors took much less time than she expected, but Wes and Gideon were chomping at the bit thanks to her cautious pace. She also thought Wes might have caught a glimpse of her tipping an occasional item into her pack. At first he seemed amused by her casual thievery, but after a few times he seemed to grow more irritated. What did he expect? She wasn't doing this out of the goodness of her heart, after all. It seemed only fair that she gain some profit from this venture, and with the advantage of being able to see which items were magicked, she knew what she could safely pocket.

After searching the bottom four levels of the tower, Elarie called a halt. While the search was going quicker than she'd expected, the pace was still slow enough that they'd never finish the rest of the building before dawn. She also couldn't help notice that as the night wore on, Wes seemed more and more fatigued, far more than she'd expect from their creeping about.

"What's the problem?" she asked him, planting her fists on her hips.

"I don't know," he replied wearily. "I'm just exhausted all the sudden. It's happened before." Wes shook his head, blinking his eyes to clear them. "I think it's the magic. I've got two spells going right now, and neither one of them's simple. They both take a lot of energy, and it's harder to do than I thought."

"Bloody hell," muttered Elarie. "What about our magical way out? Are you going to be able to manage that, or are we in serious trouble here?"

"I think I can handle it," said Wes. "I've done the spell a few times before, and it's not that hard. But I'll have to release the others before I can do it."

"We won't need the others by the time we're ready for it," Elarie replied. "But I think, to be safe, we should hurry ourselves along. I intended us to search every floor, but we'll have to try another way. The likeliest place for the stone you talked about, if it's truly a magical artifact, will be the top floor. I say we just go straight there and hope I'm right."

Wes yawned, then looked aghast. "I think that's probably a good idea. I was almost falling asleep there while you were talking. I just didn't know it would be this hard!"

They made their way to the spiral staircase that worked itself around the outside wall of the tower and headed straight to the top level. On the way up, they passed several guards. The first few didn't notice them at all, just as Wes had promised. As they neared the top of the stair, they encountered one last guard. He walked past them, indifferent, and then stopped a few steps below them. He slowly

132

turned, and the three froze in their tracks. The guard looked directly at Elarie for a moment, his eyes widening, then he blinked in confusion and scratched his head. With a shrug, he turned and proceeded down the stairs. All three waited till his bootsteps faded before letting out their breath.

"Wow," said Wes.

"If that means 'that was close,' I'll second it," said Elarie. "It looks like your magic's fading. I think we should either hurry ourselves up, or get ourselves out of here!"

"Considering we haven't got what we came for yet, and your pack's bulging with treasures, I think we'll continue along for a bit," said Gideon with a grin. "You haven't yet earned your passage out of here, lass."

"You haven't been caught in any traps yet, have you?" she replied. "I'd say I've earned my way. But I said I'd help you find the stone, and that's what I mean to do."

"Maybe there is honor among thieves," said Wes wryly.

"Maybe, maybe not," replied Elarie. "Either way, let's get going." They trudged up the last few stairs to the top of the staircase. Before them was a massive arched door with a large, intricate iron lock. To Elarie's eyes, the lock glowed with a faint but sinister looking arcane sigil. As she watched, though, the mark faded from view.

"Umm… Wes, that lock was glowing a moment ago, and it's not now. Tell me that means the spell's faded from it. Please?"

"I can still see the mark," replied Wes. "Gideon?"

"Nay, lad, it's gone. I think we may have a problem."

"No, it's fine," said Wes quickly. "It'll be fine. I can still see the magic on stuff. I must have just let it slip off you two. I can tell you what I see. It'll work."

"Fine," hissed Elarie. "I just want it on record here that I vote we go, now! Even if I could see the mark, it wouldn't do any good! I can't pick a lock that's been magicked!"

"I've got an idea for that," said Wes. "Keep a lookout down the stairs, and let's hope there's nobody on the other side of this door. I'm going to have to let down the cloak." Gideon obediently kept a close watch down the staircase while Wes examined the magicked lock. Elarie watched as he concentrated, his brow furrowed.

"You have no idea how to get past that lock, do you?" she asked, her voice an accusation.

"Give me a minute," said Wes. Suddenly, his eyes lit up with a sudden idea. He stared hard at the lock, making more bizarre gestures in the dark and muttering to himself. Elarie wasn't sure what he was saying, but it sounded like a spell. She almost yelped in alarm when the lock started to glow red. She watched as the heavy iron melted and then dripped from the door in sizzling globs. With a smug grin, Wes gripped the door handle and twisted firmly before Elarie could stop him. The gong of an immense bell, a single strike, nearly threw them to the floor.

"That's done it, you dolt!" cried Elarie, her hands over her ears. "The guards will be here in minutes! Seconds, maybe! Get us out of here!"

"Not yet! I've got to get the stone!" Wes rushed through the door.

"No, lad! We're discovered, and we must go now!" Gideon followed Wes into the room, Elarie on his heels. The young thief slammed the door and began looking around desperately.

"Gideon, help me block the door. We can buy a little time that way, but Wes, you have to hurry!" Gideon leaped to her side and began looking for something to drag in front of the door. They manhandled a large cabinet from one side to brace in front of the entrance and turned to find Wes furiously searching the large room.

"I've got to find it," panted Wes. "It's got to be here somewhere!" Wes was furiously throwing open cabinets and dumping chests onto the floor. "Help me look!" he shouted.

"Wes, we have to leave," said Gideon. "We can't stay here any longer!"

"No!" cried the boy, his voice desperate. "I need the stone! We can't leave without it!"

"Listen to me, Wes! The stone isn't here, and even if it is, we don't have time to find it!" As if to drive home Gideon's words, there was a sudden banging on the door to the chamber.

"You gave me your word, boy," said Elarie. "You said you could get us out if I got us in. I won't be caught again!"

Wes looked from Elarie to Gideon and back again. He blinked his eyes as if to clear his thoughts, and then his shoulders slumped.

"You're right," he said. "I'm being stupid. It was a long shot at best." The sound of something large and heavy slamming into the door startled Wes so badly that he jumped. "All right! Okay, I get it!"

134

Motioning for Elarie and Gideon to move to the opposite side of the room, Wes began the preparations for his spell. There was a slight shimmer in the air when he finished the chant, but that was all. The pounding outside increased, nearly deafening.

"Umm, Wes, I don't mean to complain, but could you please hurry a bit more?" Elarie flinched at every bang and bump.

"It's not... it didn't work," said Wes. His eyes betrayed his exhaustion, and his posture was that of a defeated man. "I think I'll have to send us out one at a time. Elarie, come over here with me. Gideon, stay there." Elarie joined Wes, who again made his strange twisting gestures and chanted his spell. "Movare colloqum, vidala luanzir!" The shimmering began around Gideon, and sparks began to dance. By the time they'd engulfed him in their tornado of brilliance, his eyes were wide with fear. And just like that, he was gone.

"Your turn," Wes said to the girl. The pounding outside had grown into a regular rhythm, now accompanied by the sound of wood splintering. Elarie moved to where Gideon had stood, waiting for her trip to safety.

"Here we go," said Wes. As he raised his hands to begin the spell, there was a loud crash and the doors to the cabinet blocking the entrance fell open. Wes turned, startled, but the makeshift blockage still held the heavy door shut. He resumed his spell, but stopped in mid-gesture, turning back toward the cabinet.

"Wes! What are you waiting for? Get me out of here!" Elarie's frustration was evident. "You gave me your word!"

"The stone," said Wes quietly.

"Forget the stone!"

"No, look," he said quickly, rushing to the open cabinet and reaching inside. "The stone!" He turned triumphantly. Dangling from his hand by a thin chain was a purplish stone in an ornate gold setting. Elarie let out a gasp at the beauty of the thing. Another boom from the doorway was accompanied by the sound of men's voices shouting. "Here!" shouted Wes, tossing the stone across the room to Elarie. She caught it deftly, quickly putting it in her pouch. Without another word, Wes threw up his arms once more. "Movare colloqum, vidala luanzir!" As the sparks began to flow up Elarie's legs, a resounding crash came from the doorway, and the huge cabinet fell inward. Guardsmen began to force their way through the breach, grabbing at the boy. As the spinning lights worked their way up her body, Elarie saw Wes fall from a savage punch, his eyes shut, and then...

And then, she was somewhere else.

᪥

"Douse him," said the slender man. The man's hair was long and dark, and somewhat greasy, and his face had a definite pallor to it. He was dressed in a very fine velvet doublet of dark blue. Obediently, the burly guard next to him upended a bucket over the prone boy lying on the hard table. The boy spluttered and coughed, sitting up and shaking his head groggily.

"Welcome back, thief," said the slender man in a sneering voice. "I tell you true, I do not much care for being awakened in the small hours to deal with your kind."

The boy blinked, squinting his eyes, and then rubbed the large knot on the back of his head. "Where am I?"

"You're in my dungeon, boy. You'll answer my questions truthfully, and things may go easy for you once you're moved to the thieves' cells. I want to know who you are, what you were trying to steal from the tower, and I want an explanation for the blue fire my men saw when they captured you."

"Who are you?" asked Wes, still groggy.

"I am Lord Joachim Roderick DiMornay, governor of Karsenon. Answer my questions. What were you trying to steal, and why? What was the blue flame?"

The boy cleared his throat, shivering from the cold. "W-Wes," he said. "My name is Wes."

"And the blue flame?"

"It was...I mean..." Wes spluttered again, and then looked up at the man with frightened eyes. "I'm on a mission. You have to let me go."

"Ah, a mission," replied Joachim with a snort. "And I'm to let you go. Certainly, boy. And do you need any funds for your mission? Shall I assign soldiers to help you? Don't be foolish, child! You go nowhere until and unless I say! What was the blue flame? Tell me true, and I may let you keep your hand!"

"You don't understand," replied Wes. "It's important! It's..." He shook his head. "It's...um...Diaticus sent me."

136

"I'm certain he did," laughed Joachim. "And you probably have the blessing of the King as well! Be serious, boy, and answer my questions truthfully."

"It's true, I'm a mage! I can prove it!" The boy seemed more sure of himself now. "The blue flame was a spell. I can show you!"

"And what does the spell do?"

"Nothing bad, I promise. It won't hurt you, or anyone." The boy raised his arms, but Joachim moved faster. His gloved fist drove the boy's head backward, almost knocking him to the floor.

"I think not, boy," said Joachim. "I have no love of magery, and certainly no trust for you. Your time is short. Use the next few minutes to consider your words carefully, for when I return, I'll not be so kindly." With that, Joachim turned on his heel and strode from the cell.

"See that he tries no tricks," he said to the guardsman outside the door. "Archers trained on him from the alcoves. He's to die if he makes any move to escape."

"Aye, milord." The guard made a discreet gesture, and two more burly men bearing crossbows took up positions, their weapons aimed through the cell's arrow slits.

"Milord," came a high pitched voice, and Joachim looked up in surprise. A very short, effeminate man approached, drywashing his hands. "I'm sorry to disturb you, milord, but I fear this cannot wait until morning."

"What is it, Jessup?" Joachim said in annoyance.

"A message, milord. From across the channel."

Joachim's head snapped up, his eyes narrowed. "Quiet!" He glanced around nervously, and then led Jessup into a vacant cell. "Who sent it?" he asked angrily.

"Dunham, milord. It's marked urgent." Jessup held out the sealed message, and Joachim snatched it from his hand. Breaking the wax seal, he opened it to reveal his nephew's nearly illegible scrawl.

"That dolt," he said after reading the message. "He has fifteen bands of marauders at his disposal, and he's unable to keep independent rogues out of my territory!" Joachim crumpled the note angrily. "Ready my ship. We leave in two days. I've got to get over there and get this under control. Think up some excuse for cover."

"Aye, milord. I'll see to it." Jessup bowed low and left the cell, leaving the dungeon with quick, short steps. Joachim brushed his fingers through his stringy hair and sighed. This was not something he needed right now!

Ah, well, there was nothing for it. For the moment, he had more entertaining things to see to. He smiled a sinister smile and walked back toward the cell where Wes was being kept. With a wave to the guard and a quick order to keep the archers trained on the boy, he flung open the door.

ை௲ ௲ை

As the door to the cell closed, Wes let out a deep breath. He needed to think, to concentrate. This was a mess he wasn't sure he could get out of. The man's punch had made him see stars. He looked around the stark cell, hoping to see some way to escape, but there was nothing. It was going to have to be magic.

That might be a problem, though. The magic hadn't behaved in the tower, and he couldn't feel it anywhere now. Without the magic, he was trapped. He took a deep breath and crossed his legs, settling into a meditative pose.

Wes relaxed his mind as best he could, allowing his thoughts to float. His practices with Diaticus served him well, and his mind drifted away, his inner self seeking those tendrils of magic that only a mage could feel. It was like walking through mud, though. It was there, just out of reach, but it kept slipping through his grasp. He opened his eyes irritably, took a deep breath and tried again.

There it was, still just out of reach. The magic didn't seem to want to obey him. Chalk it up to his bump on the head, or the strange fatigue he'd been feeling lately, but the magic seemed to dance away from him every time he reached for it. He stretched his mind farther, closer and closer...yes! There it was! The magic flowed into Wes, filling him, revitalizing him. He felt the surge of power rush into him, and he knew he'd make it out of this.

The door to the cell suddenly burst open.

"Shall we continue our conversation, child?" Joachim said with a sneer.

Wes looked up at him, the fear gone from his eyes.

"Are you going to let me go, or not?" Wes asked, and Joachim laughed.

138

"Of course not, boy! You've committed a crime! There's something strange about these events, though, and I want to know what it is."

"You know what?" said Wes. "I'm feeling much better now. I've been sort of testing the waters since you left, and I think I've decided to leave now."

Joachim laughed again. "And how do you plan to do that, boy?"

Wes fixed Joachim with a scowl of hatred. He quickly raised his arms before Joachim could cross the distance, and made his twisting gestures. "Movare colloqum, vidala luanzir!" The sparks began immediately, flowing upward from the floor to engulf his body. Joachim stared in shock.

"What is that?" he shouted. "What are you doing, boy?"

Wes grinned at the man. "Bye!" he said with a short laugh.

"Archers! Fire!"

Wes looked up in alarm as two arrows flew toward him from the shadows. And then the sparks obscured his vision, and he was gone. The shafts thunked into the wall and fell to the floor. Joachim stared impotently at the vacant cell.

"A wizard," he breathed. "This may complicate matters."

⋘ ⋙

With a soft pop, Wes found himself seated on the hard cot in the room he and Gideon shared at the Hanged Woman. Gideon and Elarie both whirled from the window at his arrival, their faces astonished.

"Hi, guys," he said with a smirk. "Miss me?"

"Wes!" cried Elarie, leaping across the small room and engulfing the boy in a powerful hug. As if realizing what she was doing, she jerked herself back and stepped away. Gideon approached more sedately, but he was unable to hide the relief on his face.

"Gods, lad, you had us scared," he said. "What happened?"

"I had a little run-in with the authorities," Wes replied calmly. "It's a good thing we're leaving. I think Lord Joachim may be a little ticked off at me."

"Well, you've made it back just in time. I was about to send word to Captain Trigg to leave without us, and mount a rescue!"

Gideon laughed. "Thank all the gods, you made it out." At that moment, the town bells rang seven.

"Uh oh," said Wes. "We've got an hour to get to the docks."

"Aye, that we do," replied Gideon as he grabbed their packs and threw them over his shoulder. "Not to worry, we'll make it. I'd already had the horses saddled to come rescue a certain wayward mage!" He laughed again and slapped Wes on the back.

"Elarie," said Wes quickly as Gideon gathered their belongings. "Thank you for your help here. We could never have done it without you. I wish we could repay you somehow."

"Don't worry about it," she said with a grin. "I think my trip to the tower was profitable enough to make up for it." She winked at him and then reached into her pack. She pulled out the Catalyst Stone and placed it in his hands. "I hope this was worth it."

"It was," he replied. "If I can get this thing to work, then it definitely was." Wes smiled back at her, and then turned to place the stone in his pouch. When he turned back, the girl was gone. He glanced around the room, and then grinned in spite of himself.

"Come, lad," said Gideon. "We must hurry if we're to make our ship."

Most of the vagabonds who had taken their sleep on the sidewalks were gone, and the crowds seemed thinner than they had before. Their trip to the wharf was uneventful, which was just as well in Wes' mind. They rode their horses all the way to Captain Trigg's gangplank and dismounted.

"I guess we're in time to catch the boat after all," said Wes.

"Ship, boy, ship! Don't let the captain catch you calling his vessel a boat. He's liable to toss you overboard."

While this ship was smaller than the monstrous vessels Gideon had been trying to book passage on, it was still large enough to make Wes nervous. There was a hold belowdecks for their horses, and a flat causeway led up to it from the docks. Two deckhands trotted down and led the nervous beasts across the causeway to the hold while Wes and Gideon mounted the plank and climbed toward the ship. Captain Trigg was waiting for them on the deck.

"Permission to come aboard, Captain," said Gideon as they reached the top.

"Permission granted," said Trigg, and the two stepped onto the gently rolling ship. "And right on time!" He gave them a wink and held out his hand for his payment. Gideon sighed and reached yet again into his pouch, pressing the coins into the Captain's hand.

"Captain," said Wes in an agitated voice, "how long will the crossing take?"

"With a good wind, I'll have ye on the shore by evening two nights hence," replied the Captain. "If we has ta' tack agin' the wind, it'll take a mite longer, but not more'n four days in all."

"That will be fine, Captain. Where are the boy and I to bed down for the trip?"

"Ah, seein' as how yer payin' passengers an' all, I'd be happy ta' show ye to me own cabin, and I'll bunk in the wardroom below the wheelhouse. Will that suit?"

"I'm sure it will do fine, Captain," said Gideon. "Is there any news from across the channel? With the invasion, what can we expect when we land?"

"All's quiet over there. I just sailed in from Coveport three nights ago. There's nary a dragonman left on t'other side." The Captain again gave them that sly wink.

"That's good news," replied Gideon. "We'll stow our gear in your cabin, then, and let you get underway."

Trigg beamed at them with his crooked smile. "Right this way, milords. The Spray Dancer is at yer service."

Chapter 8

Riding the Maelstrom

RYAN STOOD ON THE DECK OF THE HUGE SHIP, his stomach lurching with each swell. He'd been seasick for the entire voyage thus far. Two days without being able to keep a single bite down, and yet he still felt the urge to run for the rail every time the ship crested a wave.

The ship was more massive than anything Ryan could have imagined. He still wasn't sure how Luther had managed to procure their passage. When they'd arrived in Cybralta, the big man had left him, Jiane, and Anton at an inn near the gate and crossed town to the docks by himself. He'd returned less than an hour later with the news that he'd arranged passage for them on a ship of the King's Fleet.

"She's called the King's Wind. I'll warn you now, don't remark on the name to the captain or crew. It seems none of them could see the humor when I asked when the King's Wind would be breaking for the open seas." Luther said this with a wink and a grin. To his chagrin, it took Ryan more than a minute to get the joke.

When they'd arrived at the docks, Ryan had been awed by the sheer size and power of the vessel. As long as most of the barges he'd seen traveling down the river back home, and that was saying something. The crew consisted of crisp military men, all in uniform down to the lowest deckhand, and smartly uniformed at that. It was a far cry from the smaller private vessels he had seen at the dock when they boarded. But somehow, Luther had managed to convince a captain in the King's Navy to bear them in a chase halfway around the kingdom to find a lost child. Apparently, he held more clout as master at arms for the High Lord than Ryan had thought.

"Still feeling delicate?" asked a musical voice from behind him.

"That's an understatement," he replied miserably as Jiane joined him at the rail. "I feel like my insides are trying to claw their way out. And I'm tempted to let them."

"Here," she said, handing him a small pouch. "Chew this. It should help."

Ryan took the pouch and sniffed at the contents. "Mint?"

"Laced with one of Diaticus' powders. Chew a pinch whenever you feel nauseous. It'll help you get your sea legs." She flashed that amazing smile.

"Thanks," he said, taking a pinch of the ground leaves and placing it between his teeth. "Why didn't you give me this two days ago?"

"Because I'd have had to explain to my father why I brought it along," she replied with a chuckle, taking a pinch for herself. "I do my best to keep my feminine frailties from his notice."

"Oh, but it's okay for me to be a frail old woman," said Ryan, laughing. The powder was already doing its work, and the mint was really quite pleasant to chew.

"Many things that are acceptable for others are less so for the daughter of Luther Askadi," she said with a grimace. "It's the way of the world. The way of my world, at least."

Ryan smiled at her in understanding and then went back to gazing at the waves. She stood silently at his side, also contemplating the vast ocean that stretched out before them under the night sky.

"Jiane," Ryan said after a while, "what are our chances of finding them?"

The tiny swordswoman turned and regarded him, her hair glowing in the moonlight. "Oh, we'll find them all right, have no fear of that. Between my father and Anton, they'll track them down." She shook her head, her expression turning serious. "No, the question you should ask yourself is, what will you do when we find them?"

"That's easy. I paddle Wes' behind for getting himself mixed up in this, and then I drag him back to the Collegium so Diaticus can find us a way home."

"And if the wizard fails?" asked Jiane.

"I don't know. I guess we find a nice, quiet, safe little corner of this world and live out the rest of our lives. Someplace far from dragons and monsters."

"If the dragon isn't defeated, there may be no safe corner of the world." Jiane's voice was soft. "And once it's finished with this world, what's to stop it from using the portal to travel to another world, even your world, and doing the same thing? And another, and another?"

Ryan looked away, shamefaced. "Listen, I know what you're saying. But I'm one man, and Wes is just a teenage boy. What are we supposed to do?" He turned to face her, an unreadable expression on his face. "If it were just me, and I thought I could help, I would. But this is my son we're talking about! His safety... his life... is the most important thing in the world to me. It was bad enough when all I had to worry about was him mouthing off to the school bully, or crossing the street without looking, or getting hooked on drugs. But a dragon?" He shook his head. "He's not thinking straight if he thinks I'm going to stand around while he does something this stupid."

"It seems to me your son has made a very informed decision. He wants desperately to get home to a father he misses. Diaticus could offer him no assurances. The portal in the dragon's lair may just be his best hope of getting back to your world." Jiane turned to face Ryan directly. "It may have been impetuous. It may even have been stupid. But it may just have been the only decision he could have made. Perhaps you should hear his reasoning before 'paddling his behind'."

Ryan looked back out at the swelling waves, pondering Jiane's words. The problem was, she made sense. Ryan had mulled it over quite a bit on his own, and it seemed Wes' course was the only one with a real chance of getting him home. The chance of success was slim, but it was more of a chance than he'd have waiting around for the wizard to come up with a plan. Knowing Wes, he couldn't imagine the boy sitting on his thumbs waiting for a rescue that might never come. Still, the idea of his son facing off against a dragon was one he didn't care to contemplate long.

"Jiane," he said, changing the subject. "Why don't you wear the blademaster's tassel? You've definitely got the skills for it."

Jiane's good mood seemed to dissipate as she turned around, propping her elbows on the railing behind her. "It's unlikely I'll ever achieve the tassel," she said bitterly. "I'm a woman. For a person to be named a blademaster, he... and I stress 'he'... must exhibit his skill before nine recognized masters. These nine must judge the person worthy, and the decision must be unanimous. That's the way it's done in these civilized times. What nine men would grant that honor to a mere woman?" She spat on the deck.

144

"I don't think you'd have a problem proving your worth where I come from," he said honestly. "Then again, most people don't go around wearing swords there, either." He gave her a broad grin, and she returned it. "You said, 'in these civilized times'. I take it things weren't always so civilized?"

"In olden days, if you bested a blademaster in single combat, you earned his tassel, his sword, and the title." She winked at him. "It's considered impolite in this day and age to go about challenging people to duels to the death simply to earn an article of clothing. Besides, there are less than a hundred blademasters left in the world, and almost all are in service to the king. It's bad form to kill your allies."

"I suppose that's true," said Ryan wryly. "Still, I'd say the king has at least one more blademaster in his service than he thinks he does."

Jiane's face lit up at the compliment. "I thank you for the sentiment, Ryan." She stood upright, stretching. "I believe I'll go below and see what Father and Anton are up to. You should get some rest. We should be reaching the channel crossing in three or four days, and you'll want to be at your best." She walked away across the pitching deck.

"Jiane," called Ryan, and the young woman turned. "Thanks for everything."

She smiled again and nodded, then turned away, leaving him to his thoughts.

✺ ✺

Wes stood alone on the deck, reveling in the sensation of being on the ocean. He couldn't believe now that he'd been frightened of the whole concept just this morning! Within half an hour of leaving the harbor, a pod of dolphins had begun pacing the ship. Dolphins! They had stayed with them for several hours before finally breaking off as Trigg cast out his nets. Breathing in the cool, salty air, Wes smiled in pleasure.

"Tis something, isn't it, boy?" came a voice from behind him.

"It certainly is, Captain," Wes replied without turning. "I wish I could be out here forever."

"I do know the feelin'," the captain said with a grin, joining the boy at the rail. "Seafarin' must be in yer blood, as it is mine. Me father

145

was a seaman, ye know. He was a deckhand, never made it to Officer's Row, but the sea was his life. His fondest desire was to own his own vessel. I do believe it an honor ta' carry on in his name now that he's gone."

"My dad's never even been on a boat like this, so far as I know," said Wes.

"Well, ye've got the bug for sure, wherever ye got it from," said Trigg with a crooked grin. "But it's not all loungin' on deck an' smellin' the salt air, ye know. Come along to the wheelhouse when yer of a mind, an' I'll show ye some o' the art that makes a sailor inta' a captain."

"I'll do that, Captain," replied Wes with a grin. "Thanks."

"None necessary, boy. Showin' off me skills is a guilty pleasure!" Trigg clapped Wes on the back jovially, then turned and walked aft toward the wheelhouse.

Wes wondered what his father was doing right then. He almost felt guilty for enjoying this experience. Was his father worried? Wes had no idea how long he'd been gone from his own world. Hours? Days? Diaticus had not been very specific about the time differential between Canellin and home, merely assuring him that Canellin ran faster. Surely, though, he'd been gone long enough for his father to miss him and start to panic, and he was sorry for that.

With a sigh, Wes turned away from the railing and made his way aft toward the cabin he shared with Gideon. Upon entering, he was greeted by a low moan.

"Still not feeling so hot, I guess," the boy remarked with a grin.

Gideon lay on the long, narrow cot, his face an almost ashen green. He looked up at the boy piteously, then rolled over and retched noisily into a bucket kept next to the bed for just that purpose.

"You have no idea, Wes," said the man. "Now you see another reason infantrymen prefer to walk where we need to go."

"Are you sure you can last three more nights of this?" asked Wes, concerned.

"There's really not much choice, is there? It's either cross or go back, and I didn't drag you all this way to turn around now." Gideon hiccupped, his eyes widening, but was able to keep from needing the bucket again. "But if I survive this, boy, I may just have to find a nice place over there to settle down and get old. Better that than enduring this again."

146

Wes laughed. "Don't worry, Gideon. When this is all over, I'll do my best to send you home by magic. That, at least, I think I can handle."

"Bless you, child," replied Gideon feebly.

Wes grabbed his battered backpack and slung it over his shoulder. "I'm going up to the wheelhouse," he said. "Captain Trigg wants to show me a few things about sailing, and I have some questions I want to ask him." He turned and left the cabin.

"Careful you don't fall overboard," called Gideon after him, but the boy was already gone.

Wes arrived in the wheelhouse to find Captain Trigg bent over a large map that was pinned to the table. Trigg looked up as Wes topped the stairs, smiling his crooked smile.

"Ah, boy, ye came. Good, good!" Trigg gave Wes his familiar wink. "Take a look at the chart, I'll show ye where we be."

Wes joined the captain next to the table. The map covered the entire surface, showing the channel they were crossing in fine detail.

"Here's Karsenon," said the captain, tapping a spot on the map. "And here be Coveport," he said, tapping a spot across the channel to the south and east of Karsenon. "And here," he said, tapping a point less than a third of the way between the two spots, "be where we ride the waves this very moment."

"And how do you figure that out?" Wes asked curiously. "The shore's out of sight, so there's nothing to tell you there. All we can see are the stars and the waves. I'm guessing you're using the stars?"

"'Tis a complex bit o' cipherin' involvin' measurement o' angles and such for things in the night sky."

"I understand a little bit of it," said the boy hesitantly, reaching into his backpack. "I was hoping you could maybe teach me a little bit about this," he said, pulling out the sextant he had inadvertently brought from the display in the Gatehouse.

"Ah! I knew seafarin' ran in yer blood, boy," exclaimed the captain, delighted. "'Tis a fine instrument ye've got there. I use somethin' much like it, only mine's of a much ruder design." He pointed to the railing, and Wes saw a spyglass mounted there. There was a sliver of metal suspended out in front of it for a counterweight, and a stick marked with numbers in the unreadable script of Canellin. Wes looked at the device for a moment, noting the similarities to the one he held.

"I see, I think. You get the same results with that as you would with this. But what exactly do you do with it?"

"It's not all that difficult, boy. Come over here to the rail and I'll explain it to ye."

Once at the rail, Wes went to hand the sextant to Trigg, but the captain declined.

"No, no," he said. "Ye see them markin's along the curve there? I hope ye c'n read 'em, 'cause I can't make head nor tail of 'em."

"Sure, I can read it. Just tell me what to do."

"All right, boy. Stand here and face north. No, no, boy, north! Look at the compass!" Wes righted himself, and Trigg nodded. "Good. Now, follow my finger. See that bright star a span above the horizon?" Wes looked where the captain pointed and nodded. "That's the North Star. She don't hardly move a'tall, so she's a good one to do yer sightin' on. Look through yer lens, there. Do ye see the half mirrored glass? Put the horizon right on the line where the silverin' stops. When ye've got 'er centered, move the crosspiece there till the North Star's reflected dead center on the horizon line. See, it'll reflect off this little mirror at the top o' the crosspiece. Got it? Now flip the clamp on the crosspiece ta' lock 'er in place, and read me off the number ye see there."

Wes followed Trigg's instructions, calling out several different numbers and measurements, which the captain dutifully scratched onto a small paper.

"Fine, boy, close enough. Well done! Now come back to the chart." Wes followed the captain back to the table. Trigg flipped open a large reference book and rifled through the pages. "Now, I find the reference on me trusty tables that match up with yer measurements, an' it gives me a new number. Look along both sides o' the map and ye'll see numbers marked. Find the numbers from the table."

"Um… I can't. I don't know the numbers you use."

"No matter, I'll find 'em for ye. They're here, and here, see, straight opposite each other." Trigg tapped two points off the east and west sides of the map. He brought a straight edged ruler up so that it crossed both points. "Now, we take a bit o' charcoal for markin', and we trace a line between the points. That be our latitude line. Tells us how many degrees we be either from the North Pole or the equator. Got that?" Wes nodded again mutely. "Now, boy, here's where it gets complicated. How's yer cipherin'?"

148

"Not that great, especially since I don't know your numbers." Wes looked crestfallen.

"Not ta' worry. I'll do the cipherin', and just tell ya' what I'm about as I go. First thing we do is go back ta' the railin'. This time, we're goin' ta' sight the moon instead o' the North Star. See that group o' nine stars there, a bit away from the moon? Yer goin' ta' sight them stars and lay yer horizon marker along the edge o' the moon. Move the crosspiece again an' bring the stars down ta' the horizon line. That way ye c'n measure the angle between 'em." Wes sighted carefully. After a few moments, he called off his angle measurement.

"Now what we has ta' do is consult the book," said Trigg, flipping through the pages of the reference manual. "This here book's a navigator's almanac. It's got charts an' tables and all sorts o' things a seafarin' man might find useful. What I do is look up the measurement ya' just gave me, an' then check the chronometer. It's set accurate fer the time at zero longitude. That gives me a set o' numbers that I use ta' calculate a new measurement. It's a difficult bit o' cipherin', but I've been at it a long while, so I c'n pretty much do it without half tryin'." Trigg consulted the almanac and jotted some notes on a bit of scrap parchment. He quickly ran through a complex formula and came up with a new number. "Now I've got our figure, and I just drop it onto the map same as I did yer angle a while ago. Only this time, I use the markin's on the north and south ends o' the chart." He again brought out his straight edge and laid it across the map, drawing in a vertical line that intersected the previous mark. "That line's called the longitude. It tells us what line we're on east to west. And where the two cross, that's where we be sittin'! An' that's all there is to it, boy. 'Tisn't all that complicated, but not so simple, either."

"Wow," said Wes, amazed at the captain's skill. "How did anyone ever figure all that stuff out?"

Captain Trigg laughed. "Don't ask me, boy! I just do as I've been taught. It takes a bigger mind than mine ta' hold the whys and wherefores!"

"Same here," replied Wes with a grin. A sudden gust of wind came up from the west, rustling the map. Trigg's head snapped up and he sniffed the air.

"Storm comin'," he told Wes quickly. "Ye'd best get below. Tell Schaeffer ta' come on up ta' the wheelhouse as ye go, if ye don't mind."

"No need, Cap'n," called the first mate as he topped the stairs. "I smelled it myself and came up straightaway."

"Good lad. Wes, ye'd best be goin' now."

"How bad a storm are we talking about here?" asked Wes in alarm. For a response, Captain Trigg took him by the shoulders and turned him to face west, off the stern of the ship. The line of clear night sky terminated abruptly a few short miles behind them, giving way to a mass of swirling black clouds that advanced at breakneck speed. The darkness was punctuated every so often by flashes of light, creating a coruscating effect in the clouds.

"Bad enough, boy, and sprung up out of nowhere. Not ta' worry, though, we'll weather it fine. But best ye stay below and care fer yer friend 'til she blows over."

Wes nodded numbly and turned, walking as casually as he could down the stairs to the deck. He felt his pace picking up despite his desire to walk calmly. By the time he was belowdecks, he was practically running, and he thundered into the cabin with a crash.

"Gideon! Wake up! Storm!" Wes' voice was an unintentional shout. He raced across the small cabin and sealed the porthole shut as Gideon sat up with a moan.

"What? A storm?" Gideon shook the sleep from his eyes. "How bad?"

"Bad. But Trigg says he can handle it."

"Wonderful. Just what we needed." The big man fell back onto the cot. "If he says he can handle it, all we can do is trust in him." He rolled over with a long suffering sigh. "Wake me if we survive."

◦⊙◖ ◗⊙◦

"That's a big one, Cap'n. Think maybe we should head for shore and buckle down for it?" Schaeffer looked at the big map, noting their current position. "We haven't gone all that far south. Three or four hours due north should put us right up to the beach. We can drop anchor and ride this one out."

"I be thinkin' we ain't got three hours," said Trigg. "That monster's movin' up on us quick like." The captain scratched his chin, then shook his head. "No, our only course is ta' head east on the storm's line an' hope she passes over us fast. Rouse all hands an' haul in the nets. We've a busy night ahead." Schaeffer nodded and pounded his way down the stairs, calling all hands as he did so.

The seas began to grow more and more violent as the storm approached, the ship bounding across the waves like a stone on a pond. Schaeffer deployed the men as needed, under Trigg's watchful eye. His first mate knew his job, as did the small crew. A ship like this could carry twenty, perhaps thirty crewmembers, but Trigg preferred to run light. Less space for bunks meant more space for cargo, both legal and less than legal. Times like these, he wished he had the extra hands. As the ship tossed and men scurried around the deck under the first mate's adept command, Trigg kept one eye on the approaching storm front.

"Eyes front, buckos!" he shouted. "She's almost on us!" And with just that much warning, the storm crashed over them in a torrent.

Captain Trigg grasped the table for support as the howling wind tore at him. A part of him cried out to rush down to the deck and help the beleaguered men, but he knew that his place was here in the wheelhouse overseeing the mayhem. The charts had been carefully put away in their watertight tubes, and every loose object in the wheelhouse had been either stowed or lashed down. All that was left for him to do was keep a steady course and an eye open in case he needed to shout orders to the crewmen scurrying around the deck. They needed his confidence and his steadiness now more than they needed his aged fingers trying to tie off lines. His fingers might be aged, but his eyes were sharp, and he spotted a need almost immediately.

"Schaeffer! Get a body on that secondary line or we'll lose the riggin'!"

"Aye, Cap'n," came the first mate's faint reply, and a deckhand ran to the loose rope. Once it was securely tied off, the man went back to whatever task Schaeffer had originally assigned him. They were a good crew, Trigg knew that. He knew that if any motley bunch of roughnecks could get through this, they could. The thought didn't make his bowels unclench as the ship listed from side to side, though.

"Schaeffer! Get that mains'l down and lower the boom, blast ye! Drop cloth!"

"Working on it, Cap'n," called the mate calmly.

Trigg yanked the wheel as a sudden lurch pulled it roughly from his grasp. It was going to be a long night.

Wes huddled belowdecks with Gideon, doing his best to keep the terror at bay. The storm had raged all night and through the next day. They were now well into the evening on the second night, and it still showed no sign of letting up. The crew had been noticeably absent from the lower decks, except for a couple of visits, one by the Captain and one by the first mate, just a pair of hasty conversations to update them on the status of the ship and to check to see that they were weathering the storm well enough below. The mate had made a point of assuring them that their horses were secure.

Wes felt the ship begin to lurch upward yet again and braced himself for the inevitable drop. Up the ship rose, almost as if it could take to the sky. Soon enough, though, it began to fall, and Wes experienced a moment of weightlessness. Then there was a jarring crash, and the ship's timbers groaned under the strain. Gideon grunted at the impact.

"How's your knee?" asked the boy with concern.

"Serviceable. Hurts like the dickens, though!" Gideon had injured himself the night before when he'd been flung out of bed by the lurching of the ship. Wes had almost laughed until he'd seen the angry purple bruise on the man's knee, and the swelling beginning. "At least my stomach's settled," added Gideon with a grimace, and Wes chuckled quietly. Gideon looked at him sourly. "What's so funny?"

"Twelve hours when the ship barely rolled at all, and you puke up half your body weight. As soon as the tossing and bouncing starts, you're fine!" Wes laughed out loud at that.

"Yes, well, I've never claimed consistency as a virtue," replied Gideon sarcastically. He frowned at the boy, but after a moment, he shook his head and smiled. "I'm sorry, lad. I'm irritable, is all. I've never liked the sea."

"I don't really like it very much right now, either," said Wes as the ship began to lift again. When it finally reached the pinnacle of its rise, the feeling of weightlessness returned and they fell for what seemed like forever. When the impact came, the bulkhead seemed to press inward and outward at the same time. The noise of the timbers was deafening. Suddenly, the porthole slammed open, and a torrent of water rushed in the small window. It was hard to tell if it was simply sea spray, or if the lower deck were submerged in the water. Wes

152

leaped to his feet and rushed to the opening, slamming the metal cover shut.

"That's it! I've had enough!" cried the boy in frustration. "I'm going above! It's time to tell the captain to get us to shore, now! The ship can't take this much more!"

"Calmly, Wes! Trigg knows his business! If he says the ship can take it, it can take it!" Gideon laid a restraining hand on Wes' shoulder.

"Fine," said the boy, jerking away from Gideon. "I can't take it, then!" He banged out the door and staggered down the short passageway as the ship continued to lurch. With an oath, Gideon struggled to his feet to follow, but his knee gave way underneath him and he almost fell. Grabbing his sheathed sword, he used it as a cane and staggered down the passage after Wes.

What Wes saw when he reached the deck was a scene of utter mayhem. The foresail had torn away, leaving only tattered cloth and tangled lines. Its mast had cracked two thirds of the way from the top, and the remaining shaft threatened to fall at any moment. Crewmen darted this way and that performing any number of tasks unfamiliar to Wes. Every time the ship lurched, salty spray washed over the deck, making the footing treacherous and threatening to wash men over the side, but the crew persevered. The roar of the wind was deafening, and it was a moment before Wes realized Gideon was shouting at him.

"...to get below, boy! We can't do anything up here but get ourselves killed!"

Wes shook his head, not even bothering to try and make himself heard. He staggered across the rolling deck and mounted the stair toward the wheelhouse. When he finally made it to the top, he found Trigg straining at the wheel, his muscles heaving as he struggled to keep the ship on a more or less straight course.

"Captain!" shouted Wes. "We have to get out of this! Get us to shore! Put us on land!"

"An' how do ye propose we do that, boy?" the captain shouted back hoarsely. "The compass is all off kilter, an she won't point north! There be no sky ta' sight with, an we're all turned around ever which way! I don't even know where the shore be from here, or which side we be closer to!"

"Cap'n!" came a faint cry from down on the deck. "Rocks ahead!" Schaeffer's voice, normally calm and composed, held a trace of panic. That, more than anything else, chilled Wes' blood. "Hard a'port!"

"How far?" bellowed Trigg as he spun the great wheel, desperately trying to turn the ponderous vessel.

"Two hundred yards and closing!"

Trigg hauled harder at the wheel.

"Brace yerselves!" he shouted to Wes and Gideon. "We won't be able ta' make this turn!"

Just then, a wave crashed over the wheelhouse, and Wes and Gideon were smashed to the deck. Wes looked up to see Trigg flung over the railing like a rag doll, the wheel spinning freely.

"Captain!" shouted the boy. Without pausing to think, he made a twisting gesture with his right hand, acting purely on instinct. The boat lurched as it began a slow spin, out of control with no one to man the great wheel. Wes and Gideon slid toward the railing. Wes righted himself, grabbing the railing for leverage, and Gideon clutched at the wheel's support beam. Wes peered out into the murky night, desperately hoping his spell had done as it should.

"There!" he cried, pointing out over the water to a pale blue light that could barely be seen through the crashing waves. He shaped his hand into a grasping claw and then swept it toward the deck below. The crew froze, watching in amazement as a glowing orb sped into sight, the astonished Trigg safe inside it. The orb gently lowered itself to the heaving deck.

Trigg wasted no time questioning providence. He immediately began shouting toward the wheelhouse, pushing against the sides of the orb and trying to force his way out.

"The rocks!" he shouted desperately. "Take the wheel, blast ye! The rocks!"

Wes turned quickly to look off the starboard side. A massive rock spire rose up menacingly from the churning water just a few hundred feet away. Again without thinking, the boy whirled and waved both arms toward Trigg, drawing the magic outward. The orb of light surrounding the captain began to expand, creeping out across the deck of the storm tossed vessel. Divining Wes' purpose, Gideon urged him on, grabbing the freely spinning wheel.

"Faster, Wes. You can do it, but you have to hurry!" Gideon hauled on the wheel, and the ship began to gradually turn to port. "Just a few seconds more, lad! Hurry!"

154

"This isn't as easy as it looks!" Wes had both hands at his temples, his eyes closed, concentrating as hard as he could on making the shield grow. The expanding wall reached the wheelhouse and washed over them, cutting off the wind abruptly. The sudden silence was intense. The shield continued to expand, passing over the stern rail just as it made contact with the huge rock formation. Rather than smash to bits, the timbers groaned, cushioned by the shield, and the vessel again listed far to the side. For a moment, it seemed as if it would capsize, but it quickly tipped back upright with a crash and rebounded from the rocks without apparent damage. All was calm inside the glowing shield, but the storm still raged outside.

"I never saw the like," breathed Trigg softly from the deck below, clearly audible in the sudden silence. "I don't know how ye did it, but ye've saved us, boy!"

"Not yet," said Wes, his voice strained. "I'm not sure how long I can hold this shield. You guys better figure something out, or we're going to…" Wes trailed off with a strangled cry. Lightning struck the shield, dancing over its surface in a shower of sparks. Bolt after bolt lanced down from the sky, over and over, striking the shield and driving Wes to his knees. The storm raged, but now it seemed concentrated on their location, almost as if it were trying to break through Wes' glowing dome. Wes collapsed to the deck and began to tremble violently with each lightning strike, his heels thumping against the hardwood in a sharp staccato. The shield held, but it was taking a terrible toll on the boy.

Gideon struggled to Wes' side, unsure of what to do. He grabbed him across the chest and held him to the floor, cradling the boy's head with his other arm. Trigg bounded up the stairs and looked around for something to do, some way to help, but he was out of his depth. Then, as suddenly as it began, it was over. The lightning tapered off with a few more desultory bolts, and the wind outside the shield died away. The clouds above parted, and within moments, the storm had nearly dissipated. A light rain fell against the glowing dome over the ship. Wes' trembling subsided, and his eyes rolled back in his head as his body went limp. Then the shield popped like an errant soap bubble, and the gentle downpour fell to the deck unobstructed.

"I never saw the like," repeated Trigg, and then wiped the water from his face roughly.

"Wha… what happened?" asked Wes, struggling in vain to sit up against Gideon's grip.

"Easy, Wes. You did it!" Gideon pointed up to the clearing sky. "You made the storm go away!"

"I couldn't have," said the boy, giving up his attempt to sit up. "The lightning... it hurt me. It was like it was striking inside my head. It was all I could do to hold up the shield!" Wes lay back in Gideon's arms, exhausted.

Gideon shrugged. "Whatever you did, lad, the storm's gone."

"Aye, it's gone," said Trigg, banging his fist on the rail. "An' I c'n tell ye exactly where we be now without even lookin' at me charts! Blast!"

"What's wrong, Captain? That's good news!" Gideon stood, lifting Wes up in his arms, the boy limp and barely awake.

"See them rocks out there? Them's the Dragon's Teeth. We're clear t'other end o' the channel from where we was headed!" Captain Trigg swore bitterly. "Shape we're in, it'll take us four, five days ta' limp in ta' Coveport, if we c'n make 'er at all!" He stalked over to the top of the stair and bellowed down to the deck below. "Schaeffer! Get the men started on basic repairs! We need ta' set course for Coveport!"

⤜◈ ◈⤛

Joachim leisurely sipped his drink at the Inn of the Flowering Oak in Coveport, waiting for his guardsman to return. Four soldiers stood unobtrusively about the inn, giving the lord his privacy but keeping an eye out for danger. Not that there was likely to be any danger in this disgustingly sedate little town.

"Milord," came Jared's voice, and Joachim turned in his seat to face the young soldier.

"Finally," said Joachim irritably. "What have you learned?"

"Milord, the boy has not been through Coveport, of that I'm sure. The sketch is a good one, and the description reliable. He has not been seen."

Joachim cursed quietly. "Perhaps they met with trouble on the crossing. Or perhaps the information I received in Karsenon was wrong, and they never boarded a ship. No matter. The boy is secondary." He got up to leave, not bothering to pay for his drink. He turned on his heel and strode from the inn arrogantly, his guardsmen following behind. When his horse was brought to him, he issued orders to his men. "Corporal, take the men and travel on to Briarton.

I will meet you there in a few days. I must meet privately with several of my suppliers. Prepare lodgings for us at the inn. Tell Lysander, the innkeeper, that we'll be along to conduct some business in town."

"But milord, that will leave you unprotected!" exclaimed the corporal. "At least take Jared and Devon with you."

"Impossible, corporal. My private business dealings are to remain private. You and the men will travel on to Briarton."

"Sir, listen to reason! If not them, at least allow me to accompany you. You can trust my discretion."

Joachim fumed. The last thing he needed was a dutiful guardsman trailing along with him. But to refuse might arouse too much suspicion, which he must avoid at all costs. The corporal may have to meet with an unfortunate accident along the trail.

"Fine, corporal. You alone, though."

"Thank you, sir," replied the corporal gratefully. He gave the orders to the other soldiers, and then he and Joachim rode out of Coveport at a canter.

Chapter 9

Hide and Seek

JIANE AND RYAN FACED OFF ON THE DECK of the King's Wind, their swords held at the ready. They had found that Ryan's skill, discovered in the heat of battle, had remained with him after the battle's end. But Jiane could still best him, so she had decided that he should train with her in the hope that his artificially acquired abilities could be honed further. Ryan was certain that her real motive was simply to have someone to spar with. Much to her surprise, and his, he did improve each time they crossed swords. He looked forward to these matches, both as something to do during the tedious voyage, and because he had come to the conclusion that the ability to fight might be the difference between life and death for Wes. Luther stood to one side, observing the dance of blades with interest.

Ryan moved forward lightly, his sword thrusting at the young woman's midsection, and then he changed direction with a spin as she brought her sword in line to block. Jiane managed to whip her sword into position and ward off his savage blow, but he spun again in the opposite direction. Again she managed to block him, and they traded blows furiously for nearly a minute before backing off to catch their breath.

"I wouldn't have believed it if I hadn't sparred with you that first day," said Jiane appreciatively. "It's like you're a different man! Give me six months, and I'll have you wearing a blademaster's tassel!" She lunged forward, her sword flashing in an overhead arc.

"I don't really have six months to spare right now," he said with a grin, easily parrying her attack and thrusting back at her quickly. "It almost seems like cheating, though. I didn't exactly come by this naturally." He slashed with a quick cut that nearly scored on Jiane's thigh. She danced backward a step, and then whirled her hilt around to catch Ryan across the ribcage with the flat of her blade.

"You're not a blademaster yet, it seems," she said with a silvery laugh.

"That's becoming painfully obvious the more I practice with you," said Ryan, rubbing at his bruised ribs.

"Shall we have another go?" the girl asked, raising her sword.

Ryan shook his head as he spotted Captain Bartleby approaching. "I think the good Captain might have some news for us," he said, as Bartleby began speaking to Luther in a quiet voice. The two men spoke briefly, and then Luther beckoned for Ryan and Jiane to join them.

"We have a decision to make," said Luther. "Or rather, you do, Ryan. Do we make port at Karsenon, or continue straight on across the channel to Coveport?"

"I don't know," said Ryan in surprise. "Why ask me?"

"It's your son we're trying to catch," said Luther. "You should be the one to weigh the options."

"Which do you suggest?" Ryan asked. "You said they'd have to stop in Karsenon. I don't suppose they'll still be there?"

"Both have their merits," replied Luther. "Anton and I have been discussing it at length. He feels our quarry has most likely been to Karsenon and gone already, and we know they'll have to pass through Coveport to reach the Escarpment. However, Bartleby here tells me that hiring a private ship to make the channel crossing is near impossible since the invasion."

"Most crews are leery of encountering ships full of dragonmen out on the open water," put in the Captain. "There have also been freak storms in the channel of late. The only people crossing these days are fishermen and smugglers."

"So there's a chance your boy might not have been able to find a ship to ferry them over yet. We could find him sitting on his thumbs in Karsenon, just waiting for you to arrive." Luther shrugged. "I'd say it's about an even chance. Anton disagrees. He thinks your son and Gideon have been resourceful and lucky just in slipping away from the Collegium, and if they've made it this far, there's no reason to think their luck's gone sour. He thinks they're likely landing at Coveport as we speak, if they haven't already."

Ryan considered his options, hating having to be the one to make the decision. "How long will it take us to find out if they're in Karsenon, assuming they've already gotten that far?"

"I'm certain a little ferreting at the wharf will tell us what we need to know," replied Luther confidently. "It would set us back a day, perhaps less. And the King's Wind can make the crossing faster than any ship they're likely to have hired, or so Bartleby assures me."

Ryan sighed. "I hate to waste a day. But, if they're still in Karsenon, I don't want to sail by and miss them. If they're gone already, we should only be a few days behind them, and we can make up the time in the crossing." He shrugged his shoulders. "I say we take the chance and stop at Karsenon."

"I agree," said Luther, nodding. "How long till we dock, Captain?"

"We should be in sight of the city as soon as we round the cape," replied Captain Bartleby. "Another four hours, give or take."

"Then we should prepare for going ashore," said Luther, dismissing the man. Bartleby saluted and strode off across the deck. Ryan and Jiane followed Luther below to get themselves ready to disembark.

⟨ೋ☘ ☘ೋ⟩

Just under four hours later, as promised, the King's Wind pulled up to the dock at Karsenon. Ryan, Luther, Jiane, and Anton huddled in a group on deck as they waited for the ship to be tied off and the gangplank lowered.

"We'll split up once we go ashore," Luther was saying. "Anton and I will each take part of the wharf and ask around. Jiane, you and Ryan stay together and go into the city to make your own inquiries. We'll meet back here at sundown. If anyone finds any information before then, have Bartleby send a runner to find the others." He looked at each of them in turn, his gaze finally settling on Ryan. "Agreed?"

Ryan nodded, and the others followed suit. As soon as the boards of the gangplank thudded to the dock, Luther trotted purposefully down and began making his way along the pier.

"He seems almost as eager to find Wes as I am," Ryan said to Jiane as they followed Anton down to the dock. When they reached

160

the bottom, Anton bid them goodbye and walked off in the opposite direction.

"I think he's very impressed with what he's heard of your boy, as am I," replied Jiane. "It's not every youth could show the courage your son has, however rash his actions might have been." She shrugged. "Then again, it could just be the thrill of the chase. Father chafes at being cooped up in a musty keep. Being in the field again, for whatever reason, probably thrills him to no end."

"Whatever his reasons, I'm glad for his help, and yours. And Anton's," Ryan added as an afterthought.

"Don't discount Anton," Jiane said. "He's been all around the kingdom in his young life. He has skills which may surprise you."

"Maybe so. I just hope he's wrong this time, and we find Wes here safe and sound."

Ryan and Jiane strolled up the dock toward the city, making discreet inquiries as they walked. Ryan had no idea where to go or how to go about searching for his son, but Jiane seemed to know what she was doing, and he followed her lead. Every once in a while, the young woman would stop and speak quietly to someone they passed by; a vendor running a stall selling sweetmeats, or a beggar huddling by the side of the cobbled streets. She would flash her dazzling smile, speak softly, and perhaps a coin would change hands. More often than not, she was answered with a shake of a head. Occasionally, there was a nod, or a finger pointing off in one direction or another. They were being directed toward more run down areas of the city, but they seemed to be narrowing down a general location, and Ryan's pulse raced. From the answers they were getting, Wes had almost definitely been here.

"Excuse me, little one," he heard Jiane saying to a small girl dressed in rags. Ryan felt a pang of sympathy when he looked at the little girl. Her clothing was tattered and draped about her, obscuring her form, and her face was covered in soot and grime. She looked up at them with imploring eyes when she heard Jiane's voice.

"We're looking for someone, and wondered if you might have seen them. An old soldier, gray at the temples, traveling with a young boy of perhaps fifteen summers. About so tall, probably well-dressed?" Jiane indicated Wes' height with one hand, and produced a small silver coin and held it between the first two fingers of the other. The girl regarded them suspiciously for a moment, and then pointed over Ryan's shoulder.

"That them, missus?" she said.

Ryan's heart leaped into his throat, and he whirled to look where the girl pointed. Behind him walked a small boy, no more than nine years old, with a stooped old man. The man limped along with a stout staff as a walking stick, and the boy's dark hair hung past his shoulders in stringy ringlets. Ryan brushed his hand through his own hair and swallowed hard, turning back to the beggar child.

"No," Jiane was saying, "the boy we're looking for has dark blonde hair, cut short. Ryan, have you still got that portrait? What did you call it?" She thought for a moment, searching for the unfamiliar English word. "A foldocrat?"

"What?" said Ryan. "Oh! Yeah! Photograph!" He reached into the pocket of his cloak, fishing for his wallet. He pulled out Wes' school picture and held it up in front of the girl. "This is the boy we're looking for," he said. The girl squinted her eyes as she peered at the picture.

"I've never seen him before, milord," the girl said. For some reason, several other children had gathered around while they talked, and they all marveled at the photograph. "Why are you looking for him?" the beggar girl asked. Ryan started to answer, but Jiane interrupted.

"He has something of value that belongs to a friend of ours, and our friend would like it returned," she said. She gave the girl the silver coin. "If you see him, you can find us on the King's Wind, tied up at the west dock."

"I seen 'im," said an older boy, stepping forward. "Him an' a soldier took a room at the Hanged Woman on Broad Street." The boy held out his hand in expectation.

Jiane looked quickly at Ryan, and then back at the boy. "And where is Broad Street?" she asked.

"Two streets down that way. Turn left and go half a mile. It's on the left."

Ryan didn't hesitate. He sprinted away in the direction the boy indicated as Jiane hurriedly pulled a gold coin from her pouch and tossed it to the boy. Then she turned and pelted off down the street after Ryan.

When Jiane and Ryan were out of sight, the beggar girl rounded on the boy angrily and punched him hard in the shoulder.

"Ow! What was that for?" he exclaimed, indignant.

"Walter! What were you thinking, telling them that? Now they know where he stayed!"

"I was thinkin' I'd get a bit of silver, but I got gold instead!" he said, holding up his prize for her to see. "And what's wrong with that?"

"Dolt! If I'd wanted them to know where he stayed, I'd have told them myself!" She punched the boy in the shoulder again.

"Guess that's why I got a gold piece and you got a silver mark," Walter replied with a sneer. He turned angrily and strode off down the street.

Elarie watched the boy go in disgust, wondering how she could possibly get a warning to Wes now that he'd already left the city. She didn't understand why, but she still felt a connection to the strange young man, even though he was long gone with his grizzled friend. He had been in her thoughts almost constantly. It was almost as if she could feel him out there somewhere, scared and far out of his depth. Elarie couldn't help but wonder why she was so intent on getting him a warning in the first place, why he refused to be put out of her mind, but she dismissed that thought almost as soon as it came and turned to follow the man and woman to the Hanged Woman.

⚬⚬⚬

Jiane caught up with Ryan just after he had rounded the corner onto Broad Street. He was leaning against a signpost trying to catch his breath when Jiane stepped up behind him.

"Ryan? Are you well?" Jiane put her hand on Ryan's back and looked at him with concern.

"Fine… just… winded…" said Ryan, panting. "Not in… the best… shape… for running."

"Come, you'll catch your breath better if we're moving." She took his arm and started down the narrow street. "The Hanged Woman should be but a few streets down."

Ryan followed along, Jiane's arm in his. He was amazed by how fast his breathing was returning to normal. Fresh air and exercise were starting to show on him.

"Jiane," he said suddenly, "why did you lie to those kids back there?"

"Because I knew what you were going to tell them, and every one of them would have refused us any information at all," she replied.

163

"Most of those children are likely orphans or runaways. The orphans have lived on the street for most of their lives, hardly able to comprehend the idea of a loving parent. The runaways... well, they probably escaped their parents for very good reasons. Either way, runaway or orphan, none of those children could have imagined a father searching half a continent out of love for his son." She shook her head sadly. "They'd have assumed a sinister motive and hidden any information they might have held. By giving them a motive, even one that seemed like it might not be in Wes' best interest, we've brought it into the realm of their understanding. They understand thievery because it's part of their world." She gestured to a group of ragtag children on the other side of the street. "None of these children would pass information about one of their own, but a stranger, a boy whose life doesn't affect theirs... well, he'd be fair game."

Ryan was thoughtful for a moment. "Fair enough," he said. "I hadn't really given it that much thought. Even if I had, I doubt I'd have come up with the same conclusion. But you got results when I didn't even know where to start. Thank you."

"It's just a matter of me knowing the ways of this world, and you being a stranger," she said with a shrug. "It's no great magic or skill."

"Still, I don't know where I'd be without you and your father, and even Anton. I owe you all more than I can ever repay."

Jiane looked at Ryan with a quizzical expression. "Are we friends?" she asked, seemingly out of nowhere.

"What?" said Ryan, glancing at her sideways. "What kind of question is that?"

"A fair one. On my part, I consider you a friend, and I know my father does as well. So the question stands, are we friends?"

"Jiane... it's not..." Ryan didn't know quite how to reply. "You and Luther are my only friends in this world." He shook his head. "That's not right. You're more than that. There's not a single person on this world or mine, outside of family, who would do what you two have done for me, and for Wes. I've known the two of you for what, two weeks? I'd trust either of you with my life, and I'd give my life to save yours. So yeah, I'd say we're friends."

Jiane considered her next words carefully. "That's more than I expected for answer," she replied. "But the point I was trying to make is what you've just said. Friends help one another, without question

164

and without thought of reward. It's not necessary to thank friends every time they give some small measure of aid."

Ryan blushed. "I just feel like I owe you so much. Where I come from, it's polite to thank someone when you're grateful for their help."

"The same holds true here," she said. "But the words may lose their meaning if uttered too often. If you feel gratitude, thank me when this adventure is all over. You may find that when that day comes, it is I who owe you thanks." She looked up and stopped walking. "We're here."

"What?" asked Ryan, missing her meaning.

"The Hanged Woman," she replied, and Ryan followed her gaze to the sign above the door on their left. As soon as his mind registered the meaning of the picture, a woman hanging from a gallows, he rushed to the door and banged it open. Jiane followed him inside, stopping next to him in the common room. She leaned close to speak quietly into his ear.

"You're distraught, Ryan. Don't do anything rash, and let me do the talking."

Ryan nodded mutely as he scanned the crowded common room for any sign of his son. Jiane turned and walked to the counter, and when he didn't see Wes, Ryan followed.

"Excuse me, madam," Jiane said to the hulking woman drying tankards behind the bar. "We were wondering if you could help us. We're looking for someone."

"Doubt I'll be able ta' help ye, lass," the woman said crossly. "As ye can surely see, I've more patrons than I knows what ta' do with. These days, all the faces mix together." The woman turned her head and spat loudly onto the floor. "I'd barely know me own husband if he come up an' planted a kiss right on me lips."

"I'd hope that'd be enough for ye ta' rec'onize me, Rosalinda," said a short, skinny man pouring drinks at the opposite end of the bar. "Get me a stool ta' stand on, an' we'll try 'er out!" The man cackled outrageously.

"Hush up, Morry, else I'll brain ya' one." The woman raised the tankard in warning, and Morry merely laughed louder. Jiane again flashed her magic smile, which usually refreshed the foggiest memories and loosened the tightest jaws. The big woman behind the bar was unmoved.

"Yes, well, if you'd just hear us out," said Jiane. "This man is searching for his son. The boy's been missing for several weeks, and his father is understandably quite worried for him. He was last seen traveling in the company of an old soldier by the name of Gideon." She turned to Ryan. "Show her the portrait." Ryan wordlessly laid the photo of Wes on the counter.

Madam Rosalinda picked up the photograph, marveling at it. "Amazin'," she said, awed. "The little paintin' is very well done," she said. "Almost like ye could reach in an' grab 'im!" She examined the picture in great detail and then laid it on the countertop. "I seen 'im, all right."

"Where is he?" Ryan asked urgently, and Jiane waved him to silence. She removed a gold coin from her pouch and laid it on the counter.

"Pray, madam, could you tell us how to find them? Our gratitude would be immeasurable."

The big woman pushed the photograph back across the counter and palmed the coin in one smooth movement.

"Afraid I was right, an' I won't be able ta' help ye much," she said with a shrug. "They took a room four, five nights ago maybe. Stayed two nights, an' good riddance. They caused a bit o' ruckus in the night, 's why I recollect 'em. I told 'em ta' get themselves gone early."

"Do you know where they went after that? Are they still in the city?" Ryan's voice was frantic.

"Simmer down! They was headed fer the docks ta' catch a ship last time I seen 'em."

"Thank you, madam," said Jiane politely. "You've been a great help." She took Ryan by the arm, and they turned to go.

"Why's the lad so popular?"

Jiane stopped, turning back to the woman. "What do you mean?"

"City watch was here askin' after a boy fittin' the description o' the one ye're lookin' for, 'bout two days ago. My thinkin' is it's somethin' to do with the theft at the Tower of Lore the night before they left. Lord Joachim himself put out the word that he was to be found, tho' the portrait they showed around wasn't as fine as yers."

166

Ryan and Jiane looked at each other in surprise. "Thank you again for your help, madam," said Jiane, and they turned once again to go.

"If it was me, I'd get the boy away from the rogue he's with," the innkeeper called after them. "Him an' his lecherous doin's is no good influence fer a child, I tell ya' true!" Ryan began to turn back to again ask what she meant, but Jiane steered him firmly to the door.

"What an odious woman," said Jiane when they were safely back on the street. "It's a wonder anyone puts up with her long enough to sleep under her roof!"

Ryan was thoughtful as they retraced their path toward the docks. He had a new worry, one he hadn't considered before, but it nagged at him.

"What kind of man is Gideon?" he asked Jiane after a while.

"I've never met him," she replied. "But my father speaks highly of him. They fought alongside one another in the Great War." She glanced at Ryan as they continued to walk. "You're concerned about what that woman said as we were leaving?"

"Well... yeah, shouldn't I be?" he said. "They've been alone together for what, a month now? I just assumed he was a good guy, you know, and that he'd take care of Wes, especially after the way Luther and Diaticus talked about him. Now... I just don't know. And why would the watch be looking for them?"

"Don't let her words get to you. She seemed the type to jump to wrong-headed conclusions." She gave Ryan's arm a reassuring squeeze. "Besides, everything I've heard about the fellow suggests he's an honorable man." Jiane shrugged. "As for the watch, who can say? That's something we'll have to ask them once we find them."

Ryan looked off at nothing. "I hope you're right about Gideon, or he and I are going to have some harsh words when we meet."

As they approached the docks, Jiane and Ryan saw a man in the uniform of the King's Wind sprinting in their direction. He skidded to a halt when he spotted them.

"My apologies," the man said quickly. "I thought to have to search farther afield to find you. Your companions have returned with news, and we shove off as soon as you're aboard." Ryan and Jiane looked at each other in surprise, and quickened their pace toward the ship. Anton was waiting for them when they reached the top of the gangplank.

"Yer pardon, milord, Lady Jiane. Lord Luther and Captain Bartleby are waitin' in the captain's ready room ta' conference with ye." He turned to go, and they followed, Ryan anxious to find out what they had learned. As they went, the crew busied themselves untying lines and getting the ship underway.

On arriving in the spacious conference room, they found Luther and Bartleby examining a map of the southern half of Canellin. Luther looked up when they entered and smiled warmly.

"Good news and bad, I'm afraid," he said. "They've been and gone already, but we found out when, and what ship they took."

"We found where they stayed," said Ryan. "And it looks like they left four or five days ago."

"Five," said Luther with certainty. "They took passage on a small fishing vessel. According to Bartleby, it's unlikely the ship could have made the crossing in less than three days. He assures me that the King's Wind can do it in two or less. We'll be landing here, in Coveport," he said, pointing to a spot on the map across the channel and east of their present location. "It's almost certain Wes and Gideon will have passed through there. We'll be able to find out their direction from the watch at whichever gate they left from. I'm going to predict due south. Gideon's a military man, and he'll have taken the most direct route to the Escarpment. They'll travel the South Road through this grouping of villages, and end up here, in Cliffton," he said, tapping the map. "It's near to the main pass up the Escarpment. That should only take them three or four days, all told, from the time they land to the time they reach the cliffs." He jabbed the map at a point between Coveport and Cliffton. "They should be right here, about two days shy of Cliffton." He smiled again as he looked at Ryan. "We'll be three, maybe four days behind them when we make Coveport. If we travel light and hard, we should be able to catch them within sight of Dragon Mountain." He grinned. "A week, Ryan. It'll be close, but we'll have him back in your care within a week."

Ryan grinned back. "He's alive and well. That's what matters right now." He sighed. "He's alive."

⚬ⲝⳍ ⳍⲝⲟ

Elarie crouched behind a barrel of fresh water as the two sailors went about their task of lashing down the provisions in the cargo hold.

She couldn't believe what she was doing! All of this, for a boy she didn't really even know!

Stupid, she thought to herself. Stupid, insane, and inexcusable! Stowing away on a ship of the King's Fleet! What was she thinking? She shook her head in disbelief at her own actions. And where is my escape route if I'm discovered? Where do I run to on the open sea? She chewed a fingernail nervously as the two sailors came nearer to her position. After they had finished securing the barrels, luckily without peering behind them, they left the hold, laughing at some shared joke. Elarie almost fainted with relief. She carefully climbed out from her hiding place, listening intently for the sound of boots. No sound came but the creaking of the timbers, and she let out a heavy sigh.

Without pausing to thank her good fortune, the girl explored the cargo hold. It was large and spacious, with plenty of shadowy alcoves and other nooks and crannies that she could use to hide herself. Unfortunately, other than the huge cargo bay doors in the deck above, there was only one exit. Not an ideal situation, unless one wanted to find oneself trapped with no escape. Still, she spent a couple of hours searching the walls and floors for some other means to exit the hold, to no avail. Her heart sinking, she sat down on a crate to think.

What was it she was trying to accomplish, anyway? To get a warning to Wes? To save the boy from these people who apparently meant him ill? Yes, that was part of it, but it couldn't be the whole of it. There was something about the boy, something she'd sensed. He could be trusted. Not only could he be trusted, but he should be trusted, and aided in whatever he was about. She didn't know why she felt these things, but she kept finding herself acting on the feelings without thinking. She even imagined she could sense him, off to the south.

Elarie sighed, climbing to her feet. There was nothing to be done for it now. The ship was long underway, and she was well and truly committed. Her only course was to follow her initial plan, nebulous though it was. She had to find out what these people wanted with Wes, and somehow get to him before they did. That meant leaving the relative safety of the cargo hold. With a deep breath, she crept to the door.

Gently cracking the door open, Elarie peeked out into the narrow passage beyond. No one seemed to be about, and so she poked her head out further. The passageway ended dead to the left of the door, but ten or twelve steps to the right was a narrow staircase leading up to the next deck. She quietly crept up the stairs, again pausing and peeking out carefully. Slipping into the passageway and slinking along the curved wall brought her to a wide doorway. She could hear voices inside, and the clanking of pots and pans, and determined it to be the galley. She crept past the closed door and down to the next passage.

For nearly an hour she continued in that manner, creeping from door to door, passage to passage, and eavesdropping for the familiar voices of the man and woman she'd met in Karsenon. More than once she'd come close to discovery, but her skills served her in good stead. Slipping into shadow whenever anyone came near, and even once darting rashly into an open cabin, she had managed to search three full decks without detection. She began to think her luck might hold on this crazy adventure.

And then she rounded a corner and nearly collided with a uniformed man.

"Hey!" he exclaimed upon seeing the girl. "What are...?"

Elarie didn't wait around to engage in conversation. She turned around and sprinted back the way she'd come. When the sailor got over his startlement, he tore after her with a shout of "Stowaway!" The unfortunate thief could hear boots thudding on the deck as the man's cries alerted more of the crew to her presence. She saw another man ahead of her, rushing down the stairs in her direction, and she quickly darted into a narrow passage to her left. Boots thudded behind her, and she saw shadows approaching around the corner ahead, so she did the only thing she could think to do. She skidded to a halt and dashed through the door of the nearest cabin.

❦

Ryan, Luther, and Anton looked up as one when the door to their small cabin banged open. Luther was on his feet in an instant, dagger in hand, and Anton followed almost immediately. Ryan also rose, unsure of what was happening. The girl who had caused all this commotion stopped in her tracks, her eyes wide. She backed into the corner of the cramped cabin, a dagger appearing in her hand as if from nowhere, her eyes darting to the corridor outside where the thunder of boots grew steadily louder. Her face was fearful and her expression feral as she crouched into an attack position.

"Whoa, hold on," Ryan said, stepping toward the girl just as three crewmen burst through the open door. There were now six grown men and one frightened little girl in a cabin that had been cramped with just three occupants. As soon as the crewmen made it inside, the man in the lead lunged for the girl. Without thinking, Ryan shoved himself between them.

"I said hold on!" he exclaimed when the man bumped up against him. He shoved the crewman backward to keep both of them from crushing the frightened girl. "What's going on here?" He turned to regard the girl in the corner. "Who are you?" he asked her sternly.

"You'll not take me," she snarled. "And you won't hurt Wes if I can help it!"

"Hurt Wes? Nobody wants to hurt Wes, and nobody's going to hurt you either!" He looked hard at the girl for a moment. "Wait, I know you. You're the girl we talked to on the street in Karsenon!" He gawked at her, bewildered. "You look… different. What are you doing here?"

"I followed you," she said, clutching her dagger. "You're after Wes. Why?"

"I think things are a bit too crowded in here," said Luther. "Gentlemen, if you'd please excuse us? And could one of you send for Lady Jiane straightaway?" He shooed the men out the door without waiting for a reply. Despite his calm tone and seeming indifference to the girl and her knife, she clutched the dagger so tight her knuckles whitened.

"I would never hurt Wes," said Ryan soothingly, his hands held out to show they were empty. "He's my son. I'm trying to save him."

Her dagger point dropped a fraction, and she regarded him through narrowed eyes. "Save him from what?" she asked suspiciously.

"He ran away just before the invasion," said Ryan. "He's got it in his mind to go on this insane quest. He's in danger, and I've got to find him."

"Lass," put in Anton, "Wes is a good lad, but he's lost his way. 'Tis certain the child doesn't understand the risk he's taking."

"What's this insane quest?" the girl asked defiantly.

"He's gone to kill the Great Dragon," Ryan said quietly.

The girl's eyes grew even wider, and the dagger dropped from her numb fingers.

"I knew it," she breathed. "I knew there was more to him. He's special. That dolt! He's sure to get himself killed!" She leaned back against the wall and slid to the floor, exhausted, as Jiane entered the room and looked at her curiously.

❧ ❧ ❧

An hour later, Jiane returned to the men's cabin, a satisfied smile on her face. She had taken the girl to her own cabin to have a quiet conversation after she'd arrived on the scene.

"A very resourceful child," she said upon her return. "I slipped her one of Diaticus' sleeping draughts as we talked. The poor girl has hardly slept in days."

"So what's this all about?" asked Ryan. "What does she know about Wes?"

"Her name is Elarie. If even half of what she says is true, she's one of the preeminent thieves in all of Canellin. I'm inclined to believe she has some skill in that area, considering she secreted herself aboard a crowded naval vessel at a bustling dock in broad daylight." Jiane sounded impressed.

"But why did she do it?" asked Ryan again.

"Apparently, she encountered your son and Gideon in Karsenon. She was rather vague on the details, but I gather she was attempting to abscond with their belongings." Jiane grinned impishly. "She was caught, and had a conversation with them before making what was, from her description, an incredible escape. Apparently, though, Wes made quite an impression on her. She followed them the next day and discovered some plan of theirs to steal an artifact from the Tower of Lore. She helped them with their heist, and they parted ways." Her eyes twinkled. "But she seems rather enamored of your son. She found herself shadowing them to the docks just to make certain they arrived unmolested. She describes the next several days as a blur. She couldn't sleep for worry over the boy, all out of proportion to their short acquaintance. It almost seems as if she's been bewitched."

"You mean Wes cast a spell on her?" Ryan sounded confused. "Why would he do that?"

172

"I can't imagine," said Jiane with a wink, "although she is very pretty, don't you think? Then again, perhaps it wasn't Wes at all. Perhaps it wasn't even magic. It could be that your son's natural charm merely overwhelmed the girl." She laughed at her jest.

"Very funny," said Ryan.

"The question is what to do with the girl now," said Luther. "I'm tempted to remand her to the good Captain's custody and be done with it."

"She was quite insistent on coming along, believing she could aid in our search," said Jiane.

"Absolutely not!" exclaimed Luther. "She'll only slow us down, and as you said, she's a thief. She can't be trusted."

"On the contrary," said Jiane stiffly, "where Wes is concerned, I believe her trustworthiness is unquestionable. And she has skills which may prove useful." She turned toward Ryan with a grin. "And I've saved the best for last. She says she can feel Wes. Sense him. She can't pinpoint his location, but she can feel we're getting closer to him. She says it started a day or two after he left, and it seems to be the source of her obsession with your son."

Ryan stared at the young woman, his jaw dropping. "Can she tell... is he okay?"

"All she can say for certain is that he's alive, and that we're getting closer," replied Jiane in an apologetic tone.

Ryan looked at Jiane, and then at Luther. "She's coming with us," he said firmly.

"I suppose she is, at that," replied Luther with a sour grimace.

Chapter 10

The Dragon's Thrall

AT THE VERY MOMENT THAT JIANE was singing the praises of the thief, Elarie, the Spray Dancer was pulling up to the dock at Coveport. The small crew had been busy over the previous days making impromptu repairs, and though she was still heavily damaged, Trigg had coaxed every bit of speed out of his beleaguered ship. Despite his lack of sailing skill and his injured knee, Gideon had helped out when and where he could, even though the best he could usually offer was a strong back or a steadying hand, and they had made the journey from the Dragon's Teeth in three days instead of the Captain's prediction of five.

Wes and Gideon stood on deck with Trigg while their horses were unloaded. As they prepared to disembark, the captain held out his hand to shake first Gideon's, and then Wes'.

"Thank you for all your help, Captain," said Wes quietly. He was still somewhat weakened from his magical exertions during the storm, and had been suffering from chronic headaches since awakening from his exhausted sleep. "I wish we could do something more to repay you."

"Ye saved me ship from certain destruction, boy, an' me an' me crew from a watery grave." Captain Trigg grinned his crooked grin. "I'd say it's me that owes the debt." He turned to Gideon and pressed two gold coins into the old soldier's hand.

"No, Captain," said Gideon. "You earned every bit of it on this trip."

"I insist, man! Without the boy's mumbo jumbo, and yer strong back these last days, we'd have never made port. Ye've earned yer passage, and more beside!"

Gideon took the coins gratefully. "I thank you, Captain," he said sincerely. He and Wes walked down the gangplank to their waiting mounts, Gideon limping only slightly. His knee had healed well over the days on the ship, the bruise fading to a sickly yellow and the swelling abating completely.

Wes' own knees wobbled as he stepped onto the steady pier. After five days aboard ship, his balance was off without the roll of the deck. He and Gideon packed their belongings on their horses, and Gideon set about looking the mounts over to check their condition. He looked at their eyes and teeth, examining them for signs of sickness, and then lifted each hoof in turn.

"Where do we go from here?" asked Wes.

"First we find a smithy," said Gideon. "The horses are in need of some attention. It'd be best for them not to go lame between here and the dragon's lair. They'll need to be re-shod."

"And then?"

"South, boy. Always south until we reach the mountain." Gideon took the reins of his mount and led the way down the dock, Wes leading his own horse behind.

Coveport was a drastically different experience than Karsenon. For one thing, the population was about a quarter that of the great city, even though Coveport sprawled out over a larger area. There were no crowds clogging the streets, no homeless vagabonds to wade through. While there were often children to be seen running along the sidewalks, their eyes were bright, and they frolicked and played rather than accosting the travelers for coin. It was more than just less people over more area, though. The folk Wes passed were smiling and friendly, usually giving a nod to the two as they led their mounts down the cobbled streets.

"This place is a lot different than Karsenon," remarked Wes after a while. "You'd think it'd be the other way around, with the dragon so close here."

"That's one of the reasons things are the way they are," replied Gideon. "After the Great War, most people were skittish about living on this side of the channel. The folk that stayed were brave and hardy. They were prepared for the danger, and they worked hard to not only make this place safe, but to make it prosper. But there's been no danger from the dragon for years, and these good people have more than prospered for their decision to stay." He tipped his hat to a smiling man who hurried down the broad street with a heavy sack of produce on his back. "Even the latest troubles seem to have bypassed the town, from what Trigg told me. The dragonmen launched their invasion from far east of the Dragon's Teeth, and their ships never even came in sight of Coveport."

"It sounds like they've been pretty lucky."

"Aye, lad, that they have," said Gideon. "And if we succeed in what we're about, these people should continue to thrive. It's a worthy goal, and worth striving for."

They continued down the street in silence for a while, and Wes concentrated on enjoying the peace of the sprawling town. Being here put him in mind of the wood behind his grandparents' house, despite the buildings and the smiling people that occasionally passed by. It wasn't the solitude of the wood that he was reminded of, but the sense of peace and safety that he felt when he walked among those trees. This was a town of good people, and a place where a weary traveler might find some comfort.

Gideon spotted a sign hanging above an open workshop, and he and Wes led their mounts to the rail out front. They left their horses there with the smith, with assurances that they'd be freshly shod within a couple of hours. The weary travelers went across the street to an inn marked with a flowering tree to have a good meal.

"I like this place," said Wes around a forkful of potatoes once they'd been served. "The town, I mean. It'd be a nice place to live."

Gideon shook his head vigorously. "Visit, perhaps. I prefer the life of a soldier. It's all I've known, and all I know how to do. I enjoy the peace and quiet, but give me a troop of raw recruits to train any day."

Wes nodded, and they finished their meal and sat back to relax.

"Gideon," said Wes, "what will you do when this is all over? I mean, after the dragon's gone, if we succeed?"

"I'll return to my duties. And likely take a reprimand for this little misadventure," he said wryly. "I may take a holiday first and visit my old home, where my wife and I lived. I haven't been back there since the year after the Great War ended. I find that I suddenly miss the place."

"That sounds nice." Wes was thoughtful for a moment. "When this is all over," he said after a while, "and the dragon's gone... that is, if something happens and we win, but I can't get home..."
Wes cut off, unsure how to continue. "I'm not a little kid, but I know

176

I'm not exactly grown, either. And I don't want to end up like those other kids, the ones back in Karsenon."

"You'll make it home, Wes. One way or another, you'll find a way." Gideon reached across the table and squeezed the boy's arm with a reassuring smile. "You'll see your father soon."

"Yeah," said Wes, "but if I don't…" he trailed off again.

"There'll always be a place for you wherever I am, lad. That I can promise."

Wes looked up at Gideon gratefully, then cleared his throat.

"We should probably go see about the horses and get back on the road," he said.

"That we should, boy," said Gideon, rising. "Come along."

Their horses were indeed ready, and they mounted up, refreshed by their short break. Their ride through Coveport was uneventful, and Wes looked back regretfully as they passed through the south gate and on into the countryside. He turned away from the peaceful town, steeling his resolve to face the rest of their journey.

෨ඐ ඐ෨

"Milord, are you certain we're in the right place?" Corporal McKee's tone was dubious.

"Yes, corporal, I'm certain," replied Joachim curtly. "This is the place." The two men pulled their mounts into the run-down yard, and Joachim dismounted. "Wait here, corporal, and keep watch."

"Aye, sir," said McKee doubtfully.

Joachim entered the pitiful farmhouse and closed the door. He was greeted by a very large, very dangerous looking man in patched and worn clothing.

"Lucas. Where are Dunham and Cassidy?" Joachim's greeting was blunt.

"In the cellar, boss, waiting for you." The big man spoke with a slow country drawl.

"Good. We have things we need to attend to. Meantime, do you see that soldier out in the yard?" At Lucas' nod, Joachim continued. "Kill him."

Lucas grinned and unlimbered his crossbow. As Joachim made his way to the cellar, the twang of the bowstring and thunk of the bolt eased his mind.

"Dunham!" he shouted when he reached the bottom of the stairs. "I left you in charge here for a reason, you halfwit!"

At the sound of his name, a tall, lanky fellow looked up in alarm.

"Now, boss," he said, sniveling. "It's not like that! They won't listen to me! They won't follow my orders!"

"Of course they won't," replied Joachim. "They're not scared of you. I should have left Lucas or Cassidy in charge." Joachim considered. "In fact, Cassidy, you're promoted. Keep the rogues on track and doing what they're supposed to be doing. I want this side of the channel crawling in fear and suspicion. I want them too disorganized to even think for themselves!"

"Sure, boss," said Cassidy.

"Are they gathered, then? All at the cave?"

"They said they would be, boss," said Dunham.

"Good. Cassidy, gather Lucas and come with me. We'll hike down to the cave and give them the good news ourselves. Dunham, stay here and tend to our mounts. We'll return in a day or two. We've a lot to discuss." He turned to leave, Cassidy following. "Oh, and Dunham," he said in afterthought. "There's a body in the yard. Dispose of it." And he strode away without another word.

⊷⊶ ⊰⊱

"Lazy, good for nothing lout!" shouted Gideon as he swung down from his mount. The horse had begun to falter in late afternoon, and by early evening it was obvious the gelding was going lame. The poor beast was favoring its right front hoof a great deal, and Gideon had finally called a halt.

"Who's a lout?" asked Wes.

"The smith back in Coveport," replied Gideon. "If we were back there, I'd rap his skull for shoddy workmanship." He bent down and lifted the gelding's leg to examine the hoof. To his chagrin, there was a rock jammed firmly between the hoof and the shoe. It was likely only happenstance, and no fault of the smith. Still, it was an irritating development. He pulled his dagger and pried at the small gravel chip with the point, but the stone refused to come loose. Twisting the blade further up under the shoe, he pulled sharply and let out a groan when

178

the rearmost nail sheared cleanly off. The pebble dropped freely to the ground, but now the shoe hung loose.

"Blast! That's done it," he said angrily. "I owe the smith an apology. Now it's my own fault." He sighed and let the horse's leg drop. "We'll have to camp tonight, and ride double till we can find a village where we can get the nails pulled and the shoe replaced."

"It's okay, Gideon," said Wes. "This looks like as good a spot as any to camp. And I'm not really in that much of a hurry to get to the mountain." He smiled. "A few days walking through some quiet country doesn't sound so bad." He bent down and picked up the gravel chip and rolled it around in his palm.

"It'll do for a campsite," he said. "Not as if we have much choice."

"I'm tired anyway," said Wes. "I don't think I've quite recovered from the boat ride." Wes unpacked his gear wearily and pulled off his backpack. Gideon unsaddled the horses while Wes gathered firewood. By the time Gideon finished picketing their mounts, Wes had a fire burning and was chewing some dried beef, his book of magic open on his knees.

"How go the studies?" asked Gideon.

"Slow but steady," replied Wes, rubbing his eyes. "There are a couple of spells I want to work on a bit more before I try them out, but I'm getting better at the ones I've memorized." To demonstrate, Wes flicked his hand and a magelight appeared. Then he swept his arm in an arc, and almost instantly the familiar glowing dome snapped into being.

"Impressive," said Gideon. "How strong is it?" he asked, remembering a dragonman's arrow sailing slowly past his ear.

"You could hack at it for hours, and you'd break your sword before you broke my shield," Wes said with a boastful grin. "And I've already set the wards for tonight. I can do those now without any words or gestures. I laid them while I gathered the firewood."

"Well done," said Gideon sincerely. "The magelight and wards are certainly practical, and I can see the shield will be of use when we face the dragon. But have you found anything yet that will be of any use in fighting the beast? Have you puzzled out how to use the stone?"

"A couple of things, yeah," replied the boy. "But those are the ones I want to study more before I try them. The book says offensive magic can be tricky, and they're dangerous for the mage as well as the enemy. As for the stone..." Wes shook his head. "I'm not sure what I'm doing wrong. I can't get anything out of it at all."

"Better safe than sorry," said Gideon. "However, we're within a week's journey of the dragon's mountain. I'd concentrate quite a bit on those offensive spells and making the stone work."

"I am, believe me," Wes replied. Suddenly, a wave of dizziness struck him, and he swayed where he stood. Quickly, he doused the magelight and released the shield to stop any further drain of mystical energy. "Whoa," he said. "Tried to do too much at once, I guess." He shook his head to clear the cobwebs. "I think I'll turn in early. I'm awfully tired all the sudden."

"As you say, lad. Rest well. We'll need to get an early start in the morning if we're going to find a smith to rectify my stupidity."

"I'll be ready," said Wes. "Just wake me when it's time to pack."

❧❦ ❦❧

Gideon roused Wes at false dawn the next morning. They packed their belongings and mounted, Wes behind Gideon on their sole healthy horse, the reins of their other mount tied securely to their saddle's pommel. Their progress was slow, but by the time the sun began to crest over the horizon they were riding through a stretch of neglected farmland a considerable distance from their previous night's campsite. As they continued past the overgrown fields, a rundown shack came into view with a half-burned barn next to it. They could see a man trudging back and forth, ferrying heavy sacks and the occasional chest from the barn to the shack.

"Ho, friend," called Gideon, and the man looked up in surprise. He dropped the sack he was carrying and ran to the barn, emerging immediately with a rusted pitchfork held menacingly.

"Don't ya' come any closer, now!" the man shouted. He was tall and lanky, and very scruffy looking. His clothes were patched and worn, and he looked as if he hadn't bathed in a good long while.

"Peace, man!" shouted Gideon, holding up his empty hands as he guided their mount closer with his knees. "We've a horse gone lame, and are seeking a smith!"

"No smithy 'round these parts," the man shouted back. "They's one up the road in Briarton. Day or two's walk." The man

180

looked at them for a moment, considering, then lowered his makeshift weapon. "But maybe I can help ya' out. Got a horse I can sell."

Gideon halted their mount about ten feet from the man.

"We'd prefer just to have the shoe fixed," he said. "How far is the village?"

"Ah, come now, mister, won't ya' even take a look at the merchandise?" said the man in a sniveling voice, and Gideon sighed.

"I suppose it can't hurt," he said, motioning for Wes to dismount. After the boy was on the ground, Gideon climbed down as well and handed the reins to him. "Where's this nag you're so eager to be rid of?" he asked irritably.

"Ya' wound me, mister," said the scruffy man with a mercenary twinkle in his eye as he dry washed his hands. He turned quickly and scurried into the burnt out barn. Within a few moments, he returned, a set of reins in his hands and a tall horse prancing behind.

"Gods," Gideon said softly, stunned. "What a magnificent animal!" The stallion's back stood higher than the lanky peasant's head. Its coat was a glossy black, as was its silky mane. On its back was a brightly polished black saddle worked in silver. The scruffy man cackled as Gideon marveled at the sight of the beautiful stallion.

"Not too good at horse tradin', are ya', mister? You's supposed ta' tell me ya' wouldn't pay a copper for such a swaybacked nag!"

Gideon eyed the scruffy man suspiciously. "Where could you have come by such a beast?" He asked with narrowed eyes. "Who did you steal him from?"

"Again ya' wound me!" exclaimed the man. "I come by him honest, that I'll swear!"

"Then where?" repeated Gideon.

"It's a sad story, mister," the man said. "A few nights back, a man rode inta' my yard here, wounded so as like ta' drop dead on the spot. Said he'd been set on by bandits in the woods what killed his guards an' stole his wagon full o' goods bound for Cliffton. I took 'im inside, an' by mornin', blamed if he wasn't stone cold!" The scruffy man shrugged. "Buried 'im over by the north field," he said, pointing to a mound of freshly turned soil. "Didn't know what ta' do with his animal. Not likely too many'd believe I come by 'im honest!" He winked. "An' then along comes you, needin' a horse, an' I find we're in a position ta' do each other a favor!"

Gideon looked at the man dubiously, but his gaze kept returning to the splendid stallion. Finally, he sighed.

"And how much were you thinking to charge for this favor?" he asked in resignation.

"Oh, I don't know. Bein' providence an' all, say... seven gold? An' your lame animal?"

Gideon's eyes widened, and Wes thought he would refuse. Without a word, the old soldier dipped his hand into his pouch and counted out seven gold for the disreputable fellow. The peasant cackled gleefully. Gideon walked to his old gelding and removed his saddlebags, throwing them behind the saddle of the great stallion.

"Thank ya', mister. I hope he brings ya' better fortune than he did his last master!" The man turned away, cackling still, and led Gideon's former mount into the barn. Gideon patted the stallion's neck, smiling, and then swung up into the silver worked saddle.

"Are you sure about this, Gideon?" said Wes worriedly.

"Lad, the saddle's worth ten times the gold I gave him, and the animal itself is worth ten of my gelding."

"That's what I mean! Didn't the guy seem kind of... I don't know, shady to you?"

"He was nervous, boy. It's the common reaction when peasants are confronted by their betters. But his story rings true. That's exactly the kind of dilemma a peasant might find himself in."

"If you say so," replied Wes dubiously, and Gideon laughed.

"Boy, trust me. You need to give common folk more credit! If you treat them well, you'll find most people are honest enough at the core." He kicked his new mount to a canter, and Wes followed him down the dusty road, still feeling that Gideon might have been a bit gullible.

❦

"You did what?" shouted Joachim furiously.

"Easy, boss! It's okay, I'll get it back!"

"You imbecile!" Joachim snatched off his fine, wide-brimmed hat and began beating the scruffy man about the head and shoulders with it. "That stallion cost me near a thousand gold, and you traded it for seven gold and a common gelding? What were you thinking, Dunham?"

"Boss! It's okay! I got a plan!" said Dunham, cringing back from Joachim's assault. "I seen which way they headed! We can track 'em and get your horse back, and the gold they carry! An' another horse besides!"

Joachim ceased his abuse of Dunham as Cassidy and Lucas snickered behind their hands. The finely dressed man wiped his hand through his hair, replacing his hat upon his head. He brushed an invisible piece of lint from his expensive coat, turning away from Dunham.

"You don't get to make plans anymore, you idiot. Leave that to me." He clenched his fists in frustration. "The paltry funds two common travelers would carry aren't worth this effort, much less the risk of losing my mount!"

"I'm sorry, boss," said Dunham miserably. "I'll get the horse back for ya', I promise. Ya' don't have ta' lift a finger!"

"Oh, no," said Joachim, whirling on the man. "You'd get my stallion back and find some other customers before you returned him to me!" He shook his head firmly. "Why did I ever think you could handle this? No, we'll do this my way. Besides, these two sound familiar, by your description. Especially the boy. Either way, I'll be suitably mounted again by sunrise, and they'll be in shallow graves." He turned and stalked from the shack in a fury.

"You've stepped in it now," said Cassidy with a grin. "I'm surprised he didn't run you through on the spot!"

"He wouldn't do that! He's my uncle!"

"If my nephew had risked losing me a thousand gold," chimed in Lucas, "he'd join those fellows in that shallow grave!" Dunham cringed visibly, and Lucas and Cassidy exited the shack shaking with mirth. After taking a moment to regain his composure, Dunham followed.

"Dunham!" shouted Joachim gruffly. "Saddle me one of the wagon horses! They've got a three hour start on us, and I plan to catch them tonight!" A few short minutes later, the men were mounted and on their way.

Joachim fumed as they followed the uneven road. This was irritation he didn't need! Getting personally involved in one of Dunham's idiotic schemes was likely to expose him. It was vital that his disguise be maintained. It certainly wouldn't do for those in power to discover his connection to the increase in brigandry throughout the kingdom. Still, it was a fine horse, and he wanted it back. He fingered the wide gold tassel that hung over his shoulder irritably. And if these were the two he sought… well, things might go easier on Dunham if he'd had the good fortune to discover the thieving boy, even if it had been pure chance.

The party followed the dusty road for a considerable time until Cassidy, in the lead, motioned for a halt. Night had fallen several hours ago, and it was likely that their prey had made camp some time past. It was nearing midnight now, and the sky was pitch black.

"They left the road here, boss," said the burly tough in a quiet voice. "The tracks lead off through the field here. Hours old, by the look. I'd say late afternoon, early evening. My guess, they rode a ways into the woods across the field there to camp. Guess they're not much in a hurry."

"Can you follow them through the woods in the dark?" asked Joachim, also keeping his voice low to stop it from carrying in the still night.

"Like they was tied to me on a string," Cassidy said with a feral grin. "They're not exactly tryin' to hide. I'm betting we're within a mile of 'em right now."

"Good," said Joachim, dismounting. "Hobble the horses. We'll go the rest of the way on foot and come on them in their sleep." He glanced at Dunham irritably. "You'd best hope my property is safe," he said, "else I'll turn your skin inside out to dry in the sun." He waved Cassidy forward. "You're point. Find them, but hold well back."

Cassidy nodded and started across the open field toward the woods, Dunham and Lucas following close behind, Joachim taking up the rear.

๑๏๏ ๑๏๑

The rasp of Gideon's stone was almost soothing as he ran it down the length of his sword blade, and Wes' eyelids grew heavier with each stroke. The boy sat with 'Magic 101' propped open on his knees, studying a particularly difficult spell. It was late in the evening, past midnight, and he was fighting to stay awake. With one last swipe of the stone, Gideon finished his task and wiped his blade clean. He slid it into the scabbard with a thunk.

"It's getting late," said the soldier as he tossed a few more branches onto the fire. "We'd best put our blankets to use if we want to make an early start of it."

184

"Not quite yet," replied Wes. "I've almost got this figured out. I think I'm just about ready to try this spell."

"What kind of spell?" asked Gideon.

"It's one of those offensive spells I told you about. It's tricky, but I think I've got it."

"You're tired, lad," said Gideon, concerned. "You said those spells could be dangerous to you. Hadn't you best wait till you're rested?"

"No," said the boy, setting the book aside and climbing to his feet. "I'm ready now, and I really want to see this one in action. It'll just take me a couple of minutes to get myself prepared. The spell takes a lot of power, so I've got to draw in some energy and get my mind focused. I'm also going to try focusing it through the Catalyst Stone, see if I can figure out how to work the thing."

Gideon looked at Wes dubiously. "As you say," he said with a shrug. "You're the mage. Let's see this spell."

"Okay," replied Wes. "Just give me a minute to get it going." He closed his eyes and concentrated hard, his fingers tracing intricate patterns in the night air. The Catalyst Stone sat on a stump in front of the boy, glittering in the firelight.

Off in the woods, perhaps fifty yards from where Wes stood, Joachim and his cronies huddled together. Joachim gestured for the others to pay attention. With quick hand signals, he laid out his plan, and the others nodded silently. Cassidy and Lucas rose and started creeping toward the campsite about ten paces apart from each other, their spiked cudgels held low. Dunham followed a few paces behind and between them, drawing a dagger in each hand. Joachim held well back, following at a safer distance.

Back at the camp, Wes finished the intricate pattern his hands were drawing in the air. "Okay, Gideon," he said, "here it goes. You should probably stand off to the side a bit."

Gideon quickly moved to one side, his eyes never straying from the boy's strained face. "Are you certain you want to do this right now, Wes? What could it hurt to wait till morning?" The visible strain the boy was showing was doing nothing to ease the old soldier's mind.

"It's fine, Gideon," said Wes in a waspish tone. "Just stand over there and watch."

Gideon sighed and nodded, crossing his arms. "All right, then, lad. Have at it."

Wes took a ready stance, legs spread, bracing himself firmly. His hands flashed in a final pattern of gestures, and then his right arm whipped forward in a sidearm throwing motion. A ball of flame about a foot in diameter flew from his curled fingers, expanding rapidly and passing inches above the Catalyst Stone. Within moments it had grown to enormous size, and Gideon's eyes widened as he realized he hadn't moved far enough away. With a gasp, he dived to one side, and he missed being burned by a scant margin as he rolled. The heat of the flames still scorched his eyebrows as the ball of flame passed by him and into the woods.

Gideon scrambled to his feet, staring in awe down the huge swath of burnt forest left in the wake of the flames. Where the flames had passed, trees and undergrowth had been completely incinerated, leaving nothing but gray ash coating the forest floor. Gideon turned toward Wes with a low whistle.

"I'd say that was pretty effective," he said, impressed.

"I… I don't understand," said Wes shakily. "The book said it was supposed to be a small fireball." And then the boy's eyes rolled back in his head, and he collapsed to the ground in a crumpled heap.

⚬ℰ ℰ⚬

Cassidy and Lucas froze as they saw the enormous ball of fire approaching, scorching everything in its path to ash. Dunham turned and tried to run, and Lucas and Cassidy both tried to leap out of the way, but it was too late. Joachim watched in horror as his men were engulfed in white hot flame, and then he too tried to dive to the side. The outer edge of the fireball brushed against him, and he let out a scream of agony that was completely obscured by the roar of the flame's passage. His left arm blackened instantly, and the flesh on the left side of his face began to blister as he felt himself slipping away.

Suddenly, Joachim found himself… elsewhere. He was confused, and he wasn't sure if he was awake at all. There was no pain. It seemed as if there should be pain. He looked down at his left hand and saw the blackened ruin that was there. Yes, he thought to himself, that should certainly hurt. His mind seemed detached from the entire concept. He looked around, trying to place his surroundings, but they were completely unfamiliar, and he grew even more confused. He was in a large cave, standing at the edge of a great chasm which gave off a dull red glow.

:*You have failed me*,: said a voice in his mind, and he started. That was familiar!

"Great master," he cried, "how have I failed you?"

:*You had them in your grasp and you let them escape*,: said the voice, and the memory came back. Tracking the travelers to retrieve his stallion. Creeping through the woods in the still of the night. The flames, and the pain.

"Great Master," he said, dropping to his knees. "Forgive me, Great Master! I had no way of knowing! The failure was through no fault of my own!"

:*To which you owe your continued existence*,: said the voice without pity. :*You have been very useful to me, Joachim. Your trusted position within the kingdom has furthered my plans well, and you have sown confusion among the humans to great effect. But you must now take on a far more important task. The boy must be stopped.*:

"The boy, Master?" Joachim's voice quavered.

:*The boy! The cause of your pain*!: An image came into Joachim's mind of a young boy with straw colored hair, the thief from the tower, flinging a fireball into the forest to incinerate his men. Suddenly, the blistering pain returned.

"The boy! I see him, Master, the boy!" The pain faded slightly.

:*He must not reach this place*,: said the voice. :*You must stop him.*: A strange sensation filled Joachim, as if liquid fire were being poured over his body, but the pain faded almost instantly. The sensation spread down his arm and into his hand, and he watched as the blackened claw filled out and became more firm, the cracked skin becoming supple. The hand was still black and charred, and he could still feel the blisters on his face, but the flesh was whole. His body was filled with energy and strength.

"Great Master," he said, "you've given me a wondrous gift!"

:*It is no gift*,: said the voice. :*It is a tool you will use in my service. Stop the boy, and you will receive power and riches beyond your imagining. Fail in this, and you will die.*:

Without warning, Joachim's vision began to swim, and he fell backward onto the ground. His eyes snapped open to behold the pale light of false dawn. He sat up quickly, astonished to find himself still in the woods, not far from the ashes of the fireball's passage. He looked down at his hand and saw the blackened flesh, but the hand still held the powerful gift of the Great Dragon. He felt stronger than he ever had in his life.

Not a dream then, he thought to himself. Somehow the Great Dragon had transported him to its lair, even if only in spirit. Dream or no, the result was the same, and the task laid before him no less important to his well-being. He stood and began walking along the burnt swath.

A glint of metal caught his eye, and he stooped to pick it up curiously. It was a dagger, the blade warped and melted from the extreme heat. Peering closely at the gnarled hilt, he could see bits of bone fused with the metal. Poor Dunham. He'd been an idiot, but he'd been Joachim's sister's only son. Despite his threats and abuse, Joachim wouldn't have wished this on the half-wit. Shaking his head sadly, he tossed the dagger aside and continued on his way down the burnt path.

When he reached the campsite, his quarry was long gone. The camp was strewn with debris and forgotten belongings, signs of a hasty departure. Two bedrolls lay near the remains of the fire, and a saddlebag sat on the ground, its contents spilled and left behind. A sudden sound caused him to turn, and he spied a saddle horse hobbled some short distance off among the trees. A hasty departure indeed, and hours past. Probably not long after the fireball.

Searching the campsite proved fruitless. He found no sign as to why his quarry would leave in such a hurry, nor why they'd left one of their mounts behind. He could plainly see their path, though. Giving up his search, he walked to where the forgotten horse stood and mounted, spurring the animal off in the direction of their tracks.

෯෧ ෧෯

Gideon rode toward the village at full gallop, Wes' limp form laid across the saddle in front of him. The hour was early, but there was a grizzled sentry seated next to the road into the village, a spear propped across his knees. The old man perked up as Gideon drew near.

"A healer!" cried Gideon, reining in the black stallion. "Is there a healer in the village?" The old man took one look at Gideon's burden and nodded.

188

"Aye, near enough to a healer," he said. "Old Mindalee. She lives in a hut just over to the other end of the main square. She's an herb woman, but she knows her potions and poultices."

Without a word, Gideon kicked the stallion to a gallop and headed for the square. When he spotted the herb woman's rude hut, he rode right up to the door, kicking it with a booted heel.

"Mindalee! Healer Mindalee! Your help, please!"

"Keep yer shirt on," came a quavering voice from inside the hut, and the door creaked open slowly. An ancient looking woman stepped outside as Gideon backed the lathered stallion away from the door. "What's all this ruckus?" she asked.

"I have a sick boy here who needs attention," said Gideon urgently, and the old woman snapped to attention. "I've ridden all night to get here. Will you help?"

The old woman moved forward with a sure step and laid a wrinkled hand on Wes' forehead. "He's burning up with fever," she said. "Quickly, lower him down, let's get him inside." Gideon lifted Wes down into the woman's surprisingly strong arms, and she turned and rushed inside with a quick step that belied her apparent age. Gideon dismounted and entered behind her.

"What happened to him?" she called back over her shoulder in a clear voice, all trace of her former country accent gone. She carried Wes into a back room, and Gideon followed.

"He's a mage," replied Gideon. "A mage in training. He was showing me a spell last night, and after he cast it, he just collapsed. I've tried to rouse him, but he won't wake."

"A mage?" she said in surprise. "Who's his master?"

"Diaticus of Collegium Keep was training him for a while. He's been studying on his own lately, though. He was trying to use a magic stone to amplify the spell. It seems to have been too much for him."

"Unbelievable," she said in disgust. "Wait in the other room. I need to examine him, and I need privacy."

"I'll stay," said Gideon firmly.

"You'll wait in the other room or I'll thwap you, you lout! Do as I say!"

Gideon stared at the crone in defiance for a moment, but she showed no sign of backing down. Grumbling to himself, he walked back into the main room. He found a seat and settled down to wait.

Mindalee entered the room just a few minutes later, shaking her head and clucking to herself.

"What's wrong with him?" asked Gideon.

"I give 'im a potion ta' bring down the fever an' help him sleep comfortable," she said.

"You can let go of the act," said Gideon wearily. "I'm sure it'll grow as tiresome for you as it already has for me."

Mindalee gave the man a hard look, and then straightened from her stooped posture. "How did you know?" she asked.

"Your speech changed when you saw the boy, and you moved like a younger woman when you carried him inside. And the paste you used to make your wrinkles is flaking off."

"I'll have to be more careful in the future," she said. "No one trusts an herb woman who doesn't act like she's older than dirt."

"I don't care a whit about your little charade. Just tell me what's wrong with Wes."

"There's really no name for it," she said, taking the chair opposite his. "It's something that happens to those with the power, although usually not so young. I'm guessing he's been using more magic than he should without more training. I've never seen it strike anyone so hard before." She sighed. "And you say his master is Diaticus?"

"Sort of," replied Gideon. "You know him?"

"That I do. I studied with him for a few years when I was younger, until he was sure I didn't have any real talent for the mind magic he teaches. My skills lie in herbs and potions." She shook her head. "Masters usually guide their apprentices through this. It's unthinkable that Diaticus would let a student out of his sight before he'd passed through the sickness."

"You're saying Diaticus knew this would happen?" said Gideon incredulously. "I thought it was just the stone he used."

"He had to have known. He knows everything there is to know about magic in this world." She looked Gideon directly in the eye. "I've seen him guide students through the sickness with my own eyes. Yes, he knew this would happen. As for the stone, it had nothing to do with it. Even if the boy knew how it was used, it would do him no good. The stone can't be used by a mage alone. Another person, a catalyst, must be the channel for the stone and amplify the magic pouring into the sorcerer." She shrugged. "Even at that, there's been no one capable of using a Catalyst Stone for over a thousand years."

Gideon stared at her in disbelief. "He knew. All along, the craven old charlatan knew."

Mindalee gave Gideon a sympathetic look. "It's done, and there's no going back. I've done what I can for the boy. It's up to him now. If he makes it through today and tonight, he should recover."

Gideon put his head in his hands for a moment, aghast. Then without a word, he went into the sickroom and settled into the chair beside the narrow cot to wait.

Chapter 11

Long Arm of the Law

THE KING'S WIND PULLED INTO COVEPORT AT midmorning, tying up to the dock next to a small fishing vessel that was undergoing repairs. Ryan waited on deck with Luther while Anton and Jiane packed their belongings to prepare to disembark. As they stood there by the railing, Captain Bartleby joined them.

"How's the girl?" he asked.

"She'll be fine," replied Luther. "Just some night terrors. I don't think she likes the sea very much."

"Not everyone does," said Bartleby in a tone that said he couldn't understand the sentiment. "I'm afraid we must part ways here, my Lord. My duties require me to travel east of the Dragon's Teeth and patrol for dragonman vessels. I wish I could help you continue your search, but my place is on the open water."

"You've done well by us, Captain, and it won't be forgotten," said Luther, shaking the man's hand firmly. "I'll see that you're rewarded one day very soon."

Bartleby beamed at the big man. "No reward is necessary, my Lord. I've simply done my duty for the kingdom." With that, the captain saluted and strode off across the deck, leaving the two men to themselves.

"You know it wasn't night terrors that Elarie was having last night," said Ryan once Bartleby was gone. "And I'd be willing to bet Bartleby knows that, too."

"Aye, that's true. But how was I to explain to Bartleby that the girl sensed that your son was ill or injured, and panicked in the night? We want as few people as possible to know the truth behind our search."

"I know. It's just got me worried."

"Of course it does. But the girl says Wes is alive, just not well at the moment." Luther sighed. "I wish she could be more specific about these feelings she's getting. For all we know, the boy could have the sniffles."

"I wish it were something as silly as that," said Ryan. "But I don't think it's anything that simple, and I know you don't either."

"True. But there's no use dwelling on it. Our goal is still the same, and we won't find your boy any sooner just because we're worried he might be sick or injured."

Ryan nodded in agreement. "I've been meaning to ask you something, Luther," he said suddenly. "The crew's been treating you like you're an admiral, and Bartleby calls you 'my Lord' and Jiane 'my Lady'. I thought you were the master at arms for High Keep, but they treat you like a nobleman."

"Well, technically, I am," said Luther with a grimace. "It's an empty title, really, granted for my part in the Great War. My duties are still the same. I recruit and train soldiers so the High Lord will have an army to field in service to the king." He shrugged. "I don't use my title much, but it comes in handy when one wants to commandeer a ship of the King's Fleet."

"We ready ta' get off this tub?" came Anton's voice as he approached with Jiane and Elarie from the aft deck. "I do have an urge ta' set me heels on dry land!"

"They're lowering the plank now," replied Luther, "and the horses have already been offloaded."

"An' not soon enough for me," said Anton with a grin.

Once the party was ashore, Bartleby wasted no time getting underway again. He shouted a final farewell as the huge ship pulled away from the dock, and the grateful passengers raised their arms in salute.

"All right," said Luther, taking charge. "Let's ride into town and make some inquiries. We should be able to determine their route in short order."

"If ye don't mind, milord, I've conceived myself a curiosity as ta' what happened ta' that little fishin' boat over there. Think I'll go an' have a chat with her captain."

"We don't have time for side trips, Anton. We need to find out if they've been here and how far we are behind them." Luther turned to go.

"Aye, we do, milord, that's the truth. An' I have a hunch on the matter, if ye'll allow."

Luther turned, exasperated. "I've learned to trust your hunches, Anton, but I hate to waste the time. Do you truly think it's important?"

"I do," replied Anton. "Won't take me but a few minutes. Ye can ride on, an' I'll catch up."

"Fine," said Luther. "Don't be overlong about it. I want to be on our way as soon as we know for sure which way to go. There's plenty of daylight left for riding." Anton nodded and headed off down the dock, and the others mounted up to ride toward town.

"Our first order of business is to buy this young lady a horse," said Jiane. "We won't make good time at all if we have to ride double."

"You don't need to do that," said Elarie indignantly. "I can make my own way. Let me down and I'll get my own horse."

"I don't think so," said Jiane with a grin. "While I applaud your self-reliance, I distrust your methods. I'd hate to ride out of town with cries of 'Stop, thief!' echoing after us." The others laughed aloud at the young thief's crestfallen look.

It took them no time at all to find a horse trader; the man had a stall set up at the end of the dock to cater to travelers. While Luther bargained with the horse trader over a placid mare, Anton returned from his side trip with a huge grin splitting his face.

"They've been and gone, just two days past," he said, and Ryan's heart leapt.

"Two days?" he exclaimed. "Are you sure? How did we gain so much on them?"

"Aye, it was them, no doubt," replied Anton. "An' it seems yer boy's a hero. Seems they was aboard the fishin' boat back there, an' was set on by a vicious storm. Blew 'em clear ta' the Dragon's Teeth. Wes' magic first saved the captain, then the whole blamed ship! They made port two days ago an' rode out through the South Gate."

"Two days!" said Ryan again. "I can't believe we're so close!"

"I told you we'd catch them up," said Luther, approaching with the mare trailing behind him. "You, young lady, owe me eleven silver marks." He handed Elarie the reins, winking at her. "I'll expect prompt payment."

"Put it on my account," she said dryly and mounted. With a wink of her own, she spurred her mount to a gallop. The others

194

looked at each other for a moment, and Ryan smiled. They kicked their mounts into pursuit, and rode together out the South Gate.

⊸⊙⦿ ⦿⊙⊶

Joachim's left arm was swathed in strips of linen. He'd torn them from a shirt that he found in the saddlebag of the horse he'd acquired, and his face was nearly half covered by a bandage that obscured his strange-looking scars. He had thought hard to come up with a story to explain his condition, and had finally settled on one that would also explain any questions he might ask about travelers passing through the various villages between him and Cliffton. He had been surprised that the tracks he followed led far off the main road, until he realized that they were headed toward the nearest village, Briarton. A stroke of luck! He was still unsure why his quarry would head for the village instead of following the straightest route to Cliffton, but the tracks were plain. Perhaps they'd decided to spend a night in an inn before going to the Escarpment. Whatever the reason, he hoped to use his familiarity with the village to some advantage. He headed into Briarton with his story firmly in mind.

He rode directly to the village inn, assuming a pained posture as he approached. He coached himself to give the impression of a gravely injured man. Dismounting, he affected an exaggerated limp and walked through the door. The innkeeper looked up as he entered, recognizing him immediately.

"Lord Joachim!" the man cried, rushing around the counter to take Joachim by the arm. He led the burnt man to a stout bench. "You look awful! What's happened to you?"

"Waylaid, friend Lysander," said Joachim feebly. "My party took shelter in an abandoned barn two nights ago, and we were set upon in the night by brigands. They slit my corporal's throat before we even knew they were there. I took four of the six scoundrels I saw with my blade, and my nephew Dunham gutted one with his dagger before he took a crossbow bolt to the chest. I'm ashamed to say that I was felled from behind by a youth with an axe handle. They took my prized stallion and put the barn to the torch, leaving me for dead."

"Awful!" said Lysander. "A noble such as yourself being set upon in such a crude manner! And your magnificent stallion, lost! What an injustice!" The innkeeper fussed over Joachim for a few moments, and then went to draw him a mug of cool ale. "You just

195

settle yourself here, Lord Joachim," he said when he returned. "I'll run and fetch the herb woman."

As Lysander turned to leave, Joachim grabbed him firmly by the arm. "That won't be necessary," he said quickly. He certainly didn't want his wounds examined! "As you can see, I've treated my injuries satisfactorily, and I have no need of the herb woman. Besides, I have an iron constitution. I'll be fine in a day or two.'""

Lysander looked doubtful. "As you say, my Lord. Your other four guardsmen arrived several days ago. Shall I fetch them for you?"

"Presently, my good man," Joachim replied. He released Lysander's arm and gestured for the man to sit. "What I am truly in need of is information. I've tracked the scoundrels since escaping the blaze, and their trail led straight here. That stallion is a valuable animal, and a good and faithful companion to me as well. I'll travel clear to Dragon Mountain to get him back, if that's what it takes. And to avenge my poor nephew, of course." The innkeeper nodded sympathetically, and Joachim continued. "Pray tell me, have there been any travelers through here in the past day or two? Particularly a man in soldier's livery, no doubt a disguise, and a stripling youth with straw colored hair, fourteen or fifteen summers in age?"

Lysander's face lit up in recognition. "Oh, what good fortune! I heard old Finney telling the tale just last night in the taproom! He was on watch at the road yesterday morning, and a soldier rode into town with a youth tossed across his saddle, shouting for a healer. Finney sent them on to the herb woman's hut straight away. And from what I've been told, they abide there still!"

Joachim forced himself not to leap for joy, but his heart raced. They were still in the village! He schooled himself to maintain his image as a weak, injured man. But oh, to have succeeded so quickly! His rewards would be unparalleled! He began to formulate a plan that would do away with the boy, recover his stallion, and still protect his guise as a trusted merchant lord.

"Lysander," he said with a smile, "I wonder if you'd do me the favor of finding the constable and bringing him here?"

⚬⚭⚬

Gideon dozed fitfully as he sat in the hard chair next to the sickbed. His back ached from sitting too long, and his head drooped till his chin touched his chest. He started, coming half awake, and rubbed his eyes.

"Gideon?" said a weak voice from the cot. "Where are we?"

Gideon's eyes snapped open and he looked at Wes. "You're awake! Thank the gods!" He turned toward the door and shouted. "Mindalee! He's awake!"

"Don't shout," said Wes, wincing.

"Sorry, lad. I'm just happy you're alive! You've been sleeping the sleep of the dead since two nights ago. How do you feel?"

"My head hurts," said Wes. "What happened?"

"You collapsed after you threw the fireball, boy. Do you remember?"

"No. Fireball? The last thing I remember is setting up camp."

Gideon swore. "It all comes down to Diaticus, lad. And me. I should never have trusted the man!" He sighed. "I have a confession to make, Wes. Please don't judge me too harshly."

Wes looked at Gideon in confusion. "Judge you? I don't understand. What's Diaticus got to do with anything?"

"There's something I… that is…" Gideon trailed off, not sure how to explain.

"Spit it out already," said Wes, and Gideon sighed again.

"Diaticus came to me about a week after you were placed in my charge," he said almost timidly. His voice had lost its normal casual tone, and his words were almost formal. "He could see you were growing fond of me, and he wanted to encourage that. He told me of your magic, and how you came from another world on a quest to slay the Great Dragon. He said it was your destiny." He shook his head in disgust. "I believe the old wizard played me as false as he played you. He asked me to continue in my friendship with you, and that as a friend, I should guide you toward making this journey. He told me it was the only way you'd ever find your way home again." Gideon buried his face in his hands, ashamed. "But he knew, lad. He knew that this sickness would come on you. Maybe he believed you'd have time to reach the dragon before it took you, or maybe he didn't think it would be as bad as it was. Regardless, I followed his direction and steered you on this course. When it comes down to it, this is my own fault. I was gulled by that… that charlatan!"

Gideon looked back at Wes, and the hurt in the boy's eyes was like a blade in the old soldier's gut. He reached out to his young friend, but Wes jerked away.

197

"He wanted me to do this? I thought he was trying to stop me! And he told you to convince me I had to go?" Wes looked at Gideon in hurt disbelief. "And you did! Every time I brought up the dragon, you treated it like I was being brave and courageous, like it was something I had to do! And all along, this has been some kind of scheme just to get me to do what Diaticus wanted all along! You pretended to be my friend just to get what you wanted!"

"No, lad, it wasn't like that," said Gideon. "I never..."

"Shut up! Just shut up!" Wes' face twisted into an image of hatred and betrayal. "You don't get to apologize! You don't get to explain! You used me!" The boy didn't even try to restrain his sudden fury. "You and Diaticus! All my life, grown ups have been pushing and pulling me to do what they wanted, and punishing me for doing what I want. And you're no different! I thought you were my friend!"

"I am your friend, Wes! I would die before I let harm come to you!"

"You'd die to make sure I killed the dragon and saved your little kingdom," said Wes with a bitter sneer. "It had nothing to do with being my friend. It had nothing to do with me at all, just getting rid of the dragon." He clenched his fists in rage. "Get out, Gideon. You're like everybody else. You just want to use me. Use me up." Gideon sat there, unable to move, unable to speak. "Get out! I don't want to look at you."

Gideon stood, trembling, and backed toward the door. "I... I'm sorry, lad. I only did what I thought was right, for you and for the kingdom." He turned away, his guts clenching. Without another word, he opened the door and left the room.

"That'll be far enough, friend," said a deep voice as Gideon entered the main room of the hut. "I'll ask you to stand fast. This doesn't need to get rough."

Four burly men stood near the entrance, two with crossbows trained on Gideon. The third man had his arm around Mindalee's neck from behind, a beefy hand clamped tightly over her mouth, and the fourth, the one who had spoken, stood directly in front of the door with his arms crossed.

"What's the meaning of this?" said Gideon, moving back a step with the thought of gaining some room to maneuver.

"Simmer down, friend, and don't try anything foolish. I assume the boy's in the back room?" The man stepped forward, gesturing toward the door Gideon had just come through. Gideon tensed, reaching for his dagger.

"I warned you," said the man almost sadly. "Take him down, boys." Gideon barely heard the twang of the crossbow before a blunted bolt struck him squarely in the temple, and he dropped like a puppet with its strings cut.

▪ ▪ ▪

Gideon moaned as he snapped to consciousness, his head throbbing. He rolled onto his belly and felt a cold, straw-covered stone floor beneath him. He struggled to his hands and knees and shook his aching head.

"Oh, good," said a sarcastic voice from somewhere slightly above him. "The hero's awake."

"Wes?" he said softly. "Is that you?" Gideon felt with his hands and found a wall in front of him. He levered himself into a sitting position, his back against it, and looked up to see Wes sitting on the small room's only cot, the dim light of the moon through a tiny window the only illumination. "What happened? Who were they?"

"The long arm of the law," said Wes bitterly. "The local constable."

"Oh, no. Word of the theft moved faster than we did, then."

"I don't think it's about the stone. Apparently, we waylaid some guy on the road, killed four people, and stole a rare and valuable black stallion." Wes leaned forward and glared at Gideon. "They're going to hang us for murder," he spat. "I told you that guy was shady, but you wouldn't listen. They found the stallion right outside the old woman's hut, and they told me that whoever it was said we were the ones who attacked him."

"But that's not true," said Gideon. "We never waylaid anyone! If anything, that peasant is the one who robbed the man!"

"He probably never saw who did it," said Wes. "He just saw that we were the ones with his horse and decided we were guilty. It doesn't really matter, it's our word against his."

The sound of a heavy latch being lifted interrupted their conversation. The door swung open silently on well-oiled hinges, allowing blinding light into the room, and Gideon shielded his eyes.

"Ah, good, you're awake," said the constable. "Come along, friend, we need to have a chat." Gideon felt rough hands lift him, and he was shoved out of the cell. He was held by two rough guards as the constable led the way down a short hall.

"So, friend," said the constable as they entered another small stone room, "it's time we talked." The two men shoved Gideon into a hard wooden chair, and the constable frowned. "That'll be all, boys," he said almost irritably. "See to your duties." The two men shot Gideon dagger-filled glances as they strode from the room, cracking their knuckles. "And leave the boy alone," called the constable after them. "I'll not have him mistreated!" When they were gone, the man took the seat across from Gideon. "My guards can get a little carried away sometimes," he said apologetically. "I'm Constable Willis, and I assume from my conversation with the boy that you're Gideon. Care to share your story?"

"I'm not sure I have a story," said Gideon slowly. "I don't really understand what's going on here."

"It's quite simple. You're accused of robbing the Tower of Lore in Karsenon, murdering four men in the employ of Lord Joachim, and running off with a horse that's worth more gold than the entire village sees in a year. Jog your memory any?"

"That's not what happened," said Gideon firmly. "I bought that horse off a peasant about two days' ride north of here." He began to relate the story of the scruffy peasant and his dead traveler. Willis listened attentively, nodding here and there, and when the story was done, he sat back in his chair with a sigh.

"And the tower?"

"Ah...well, as to that..." Gideon struggled for a story.

"Don't bother. Thievery in Karsenon is no business of mine. For the rest, it's much the same story the boy told," said the constable wearily. "I must say, it's quite a tale. And your description of the peasant, well, it certainly doesn't sound like your accuser." He pursed his lips thoughtfully. "I'm sorry to say, I believe you, and I believe the boy."

"You do?" said Gideon, incredulous. "But that's good!"

"Afraid it's not so simple," said Willis. "Lord Joachim is fairly well liked and respected around these parts, though I've never much trusted him. But he does a great deal of business here, and has the ear of the merchants. He and his men rode off for the High Judge's manor right after we brought you in, so as to bring him here to try you. Jasper's a good man, but he idolizes Lord Joachim. I'm to meet them

200

before dawn at the village inn, and I'm afraid it's very likely you and the boy will hang shortly thereafter."

Chapter 12

Jailbreak

RYAN SURVEYED THE VILLAGE DUBIOUSLY as they grew nearer. It was small, without even the standard wall he'd grown accustomed to seeing around every settlement of any size since coming to this world. It looked like a peaceful enough place, but it was several miles off the main road to Cliffton.

"Are you sure they came this way?" he asked Anton. "Why would they go so far off the main road?"

"Aye, I'm positive," said Anton. "All the tracks out of the camp led here." He shrugged. "Mayhap they was tired o' sleepin' on the ground and wanted a proper bed for once. Who can say? But this is the way they come, of that I'm sure."

Ryan wasn't sure what to make of Anton taking charge of the chase. He'd expressed his doubts to Luther, but the big man had simply grinned.

"There are some tasks that should be undertaken by the group, and some that should be left to those best suited to them. And trust me, Anton is best suited to this task."

"We'll find the local inn and inquire there," said Luther. "If they passed through here, we'll know soon enough."

They rode into the village, moving their horses at a slow walk. The road led past the usual animal pens and storage buildings and the occasional shop, curving around toward a main square. Just off the square they found the inn. Tying their horses to the hitching post out front, they walked inside, Luther in the lead. The common room was noisy and crowded, the country folk boisterous in their merrymaking. Luther led them to an empty table near the back of the room and summoned the innkeeper over with a crook of his finger.

"Good evening, friend," said the innkeeper with a broad smile. "What can I get for you? Ale, wine? If you plan to eat, it'll be a while. We've got more of a crowd tonight than we planned for, and the cook had to run off to Cully the butcher for more cuts to roast."

"Ale will be fine," said Luther, and then glanced at Elarie. "Watered wine for the girl. I take it you're not usually this blessed with patronage?"

"Oh, no, almost never," said the innkeeper gleefully. "Tomorrow's a big day. Constable Willis captured a couple of the murdering brigands that have been plaguing us these past weeks, and like as not they'll be a hanging on the morrow! The High Judge should arrive in the morning for the trial." The man turned and went off to fetch their drinks.

"If the locals are this rowdy for a hanging, I'd hate to see a witch burning," said Jiane with a grin.

"Ah, lassie, you'd likely be the one they was comin' ta' see," said Anton with a snort, and Jiane punched his shoulder playfully. Presently, the innkeeper returned with a tray and set their drinks in front of them with a flourish. Luther handed the man a few coppers.

"Thank you kindly, good sir," said the man with a grin. "If there's anything else you need, just give a shout for Lysander and I'll be right over."

"Actually," said Luther, "You could give us some information. We've been tracking someone, and their trail led us here. Would you happen to know if there have been any travelers through here recently? A grizzled veteran and a youth with straw colored hair?"

The innkeeper's smile vanished, and his voice took on a less than friendly tone. "Friends of yours?" he asked suspiciously, and Luther blinked in surprise.

"Not exactly," said Luther, and Jiane chimed in with her dazzling smile.

"They have something in their possession that belongs to a friend of ours, and he'd like it returned," she said, repeating the lie she'd told the beggar children in Karsenon.

"Ah, I see," said the innkeeper shrewdly, his grin returning. "That doesn't surprise me. It seems you're too late, though. They've already been caught." He winked at Jiane conspiratorially. "They're the ones that are to hang tomorrow!"

"What?" exclaimed Ryan, starting to rise. Anton's firm grip on his shoulder pushed him back down in his chair.

"Not to worry, sir," said the innkeeper. "If they had your friend's property in their possession, it'll doubtless be in the care of Constable Willis now, and I'm sure he'll see it returned."

"Aye," said Anton, returning the man's grin, "I'm sure he will at that. Tell me, how did he manage to catch 'em? They're a cagey pair. I can't imagine a village constable havin' the wherewithal ta' corner 'em."

"A stroke of good fortune, really," replied Lysander. "The young one took ill and like to died. His accomplice took him to old Mindalee, and she fixed him up. But while he was still in his sickbed, the noble lord they'd robbed rode into town and made his report to the constable. They'd killed his guards and footmen and stolen his horse, which was what they rode into town on! The constable found them still in the herb woman's hut, Lord Joachim's fine stallion tied right outside for the world to see!" The innkeeper laughed gleefully. "If you folks will excuse me, I have other patrons to see to. Just shout if you need anything!" The man turned and walked away to another table in the busy common room.

"Let's go," said Ryan urgently. "We've got to find them and get them out of there!"

"Easy, Ryan," said Luther calmly. "Anton's got the right of it. We can't let on we're other than victims of the highwaymen they think they've captured, or we'll be in the frying pan with them." He took a swallow of his ale. "Finish your drink as if nothing's wrong, and then we'll go see this Mindalee and find out the truth of it all."

It was all Ryan could do not to leap up and storm out of the inn, but Luther was right, and so he tried to appear calm as he gulped down his ale. He waited impatiently for the others to finish, and when they finally set their empty mugs down, he practically jumped out of his chair. Luther gave him a stern look, and then they all filed calmly out of the inn.

Mindalee's hut wasn't hard to find. They walked their horses around the square until they saw a crude sign with a couple of herbs and a potion bottle painted on it. Anton hobbled the horses, and Luther knocked on the door. When no answer came, he knocked again, louder.

"I'm comin'," came a creaky voice from inside. "Hold yer horses!" A moment later, the door cracked open slightly. "What d'ye want?"

"Information," said Luther curtly. "We want to know what transpired with the two strangers you sheltered here."

"Constable took 'em," she replied just as curtly. "Go ask him!" She tried to slam the door, but Luther's strong hand kept it from closing all the way.

"Madam," he said, "those two scoundrels have something that…"

"No," said Ryan. "Somebody's going to have to hear the truth sometime, Luther. Ma'am, the boy who was sick is my son. We've been looking for him for weeks. He's not a thief or a murderer, he's just a kid." He looked at her imploringly. "Can you help us?"

Mindalee looked Ryan up and down appraisingly. "Your son, you say?" She peered out down the street in both directions. "All right, get inside here, quickly. All of you, inside." She flung open the door and Ryan and the others filed in.

"Ma'am," said Ryan, "I know there's evidence against them, but…"

"Yes, yes, they're innocent, I know. I think the constable probably does, too. I've been warning folks about that snake Joachim for years now, but no one ever pays any attention. He's charmed them, one and all." She spat on the dirt floor. "I tried to tell them the boy was a mage in training, but they wouldn't listen. And there's nothing Willis can do until the High Judge gets here tomorrow morning, and by that time, Lord Joachim will have that idiot convinced it's a sacred duty to hang them."

"Then we'll just have to get them free before he gets here," said Luther confidently.

"It won't be easy," said Mindalee. "They're in the jail under the constable's barracks outside town. There'll be guards, and Willis isn't likely to let them free on your word, no matter how he feels about it."

"I can get them out," said Elarie quietly, and all eyes turned to the girl. "Don't look so surprised," she said indignantly. "If I can get out of the thieves' cells at Karsenon, I can handle some backwoods jail in a country village."

"That's as may be, girl, but I'd rather not risk you coming to more harm than you already have on this misadventure," said Luther.

"I'd listen to her, Father," said Jiane. "Who else here has any experience with a jailbreak?"

"I may've spent a night or two behind cell bars in me younger days," said Anton with a shrug.

"And I had my share of run-ins with the law in my own misspent youth," said Luther.

"Stop it, both of you," said Ryan irritably. "Just stop it. Wes is sitting in a cell not a mile from here, and you two are competing to see who can get caught first trying to break him out. Luther, less than an hour ago, you told me you have to let people take on the tasks they're best suited to, even if you feel like it should be you taking the risk." He turned to Elarie. "You're sure you can get him out?"

"Without half trying," replied the girl confidently.

"Then you're the one to do it," said Ryan firmly, and he turned back to Luther. "Why bring a master thief along if you're not going to use her?"

Luther blinked, clearing his throat. "As you say, Ryan. You're right, of course."

"Of course I am," said Ryan. "I've been taking lessons. Now, Ma'am," he said, turning to face Mindalee, "how do we get to this jail?"

◦๏ᱫ ᱫ๏◦

"When do you plan on speaking to me again, boy?" said Gideon. After several hours of silence and numerous attempts at conversation, Gideon had decided to simply talk, whether Wes answered or not. "We're going to be down here 'til the lord arrives, and it'll be rough going trying to convince him of our innocence if he only hears the story from one of us."

"It'll be pretty tough anyway, considering you were riding that guy's horse," said Wes with a sneer. "Between that, and this guy being old buddies with what's his name, Joachim, I'm surprised they haven't strung us up already."

"From what Constable Willis says, Judge Jasper is a fair and honorable man," said Gideon by way of reassurance. "Even if he's enamored of Lord Joachim, he'll listen to reason."

"He also says he's not that bright, and is more than enamored. He idolizes Joachim just because he's a noble and wears a blademaster's tassel," replied Wes. "Thank you so much for getting me into all this. And remind me to thank Diaticus, too, when I see him. Right before I turn him into a toad."

Gideon's face blanched. "You can do that?"

Wes laughed bitterly. "Right now I don't even think I could light a magelight," he said. "I can't feel any magic at all, I'm so weak."

"I wondered why you hadn't simply magicked us out of here," said Gideon. "I didn't realize the sickness had sapped your power."

"Even if I didn't still feel sick, I haven't got any spells memorized that I can see being any help. Well, except for the translocation spell, and I'm way too weak for that one."

"Perhaps you'll be well enough by morning," said Gideon hopefully.

"We'll see," said Wes with a sigh. "I kind of doubt it, though." He narrowed his eyes and looked at Gideon angrily. After a moment, his expression softened. "I'm sorry, Gideon. I don't mean to...that is..." He trailed off, then began again. "You were only following orders. I mean, when you took me out of the Keep."

"Aye, lad, I was. But that doesn't change anything that's happened between us. I didn't do it only because I was ordered to." He shrugged. "I did it because I truly thought it was the right thing to do, and because you asked it of me."

"I know. I overreacted. I was just, I don't know… I wasn't thinking straight. My brain was all fuzzy when I woke up. I hope you can forgive me."

Gideon opened his mouth to speak, but stopped when he noticed a shadow move in front of the narrow window, blocking the moonlight. At first he thought it was one of the guards making his rounds, but the shape was wrong. What's more, the shadow didn't move away. He peered up at the grate curiously, and almost jumped out of his skin when the dark shape hissed at him.

"Psst! Wake up in there!" Wes was on his feet in an instant, jumping up on the cot to look out the tiny window.

"Elarie!" he exclaimed, and then cringed, looking toward the door of their cell. When it didn't burst open, he and Gideon both let out a relieved breath. "Elarie," he said in a much lower voice, "what are you doing here?" The young thief lay prone on the ground outside, peering down into their cell under the barracks.

"I'm here to get you out, you dolt. Now move back!" Wes did as she said, and with two quick movements, she removed the lock from the outside of the grate. She grasped the bottom edge firmly and glanced around to see if anyone was coming, and then she lifted the grate with a quick motion to minimize any creak of the hinges. With no small effort, she slithered through the tiny opening and into the cell.

"Whew!" she said quietly once her feet were on the floor. "It's a safe bet neither of you will be going out that way!" Walking toward the door, she pulled out a pair of slender pointed tools to get to work on the latch.

"Wait!" hissed Gideon urgently. "There's a guard on the other side!"

Elarie froze, one of the tools halfway to the lock. "That complicates matters," she muttered in consternation. She turned to Wes. "Can't you..." She paused, looking at the boy meaningfully, and waggled her fingers at him.

"What, you mean magic?" said Wes. "No, I..." He sighed and looked down at the girl. "I'm weak," he replied. "I can't do any of the spells I've memorized. If I had my book, there's maybe something I could try, but they took it."

"Wonderful." she said in exasperation. "What could you do if you had it?"

"I'm not sure," said the boy. "There's a spell in there towards the beginning that I didn't bother memorizing because it didn't seem all that useful. It doesn't take much power, but I can't remember the words. If I could, then maybe I could make the guard go to sleep."

Elarie considered for a moment. "Wait here," she said and quickly slithered back out the window.

"Oh, sure, like we're going to go out for a snack or something while she's gone," said Wes sarcastically, and Gideon snorted.

Elarie crouched outside the cell, listening intently for the guard. She didn't know how long it would take him to get back around to this side of the building, so she certainly couldn't stay where she was. Quickly and silently, she scaled the wall to the roof. Creeping quietly across the tiles, she positioned herself just above one of the broad windows that opened into the barracks. Lying flat on her stomach, she quickly popped her head down and back up, hopefully too fast for anyone to notice. She closed her eyes and concentrated, recreating the room in her mind from her quick glance, a useful trick she'd learned early in her career. There! Directly across from the window she'd peeped into was another window, a broad table positioned next to it. Wes and Gideon's possessions were scattered on the table, and Wes' backpack lay near the open window. She rose and crept the twenty paces across the flat roof. Positioning herself directly above the opening, she sat on the ledge, her back to the open air. She crooked

208

her ankle around a drainpipe and let herself fall backward, hoping neither of the guards she'd seen inside happened to be looking that way. As she tipped backward, she let her upper body swing into the open window and hooked Wes' backpack with one hand. Reversing her momentum, she used all the strength in her thighs and abdomen to swing herself back into her position on the ledge. Untangling her ankle, she listened for any sign that she'd been seen, but there were no cries of alarm. She crept back across the roof and dropped to the grass, quickly shoving the backpack in through the tiny grate and twisting herself in behind it.

"What do you have in this thing, rocks?" she asked Wes as she handed him the backpack. The boy colored slightly.

"A few," he said, and she stared at him wonderingly. "It's kind of a habit," he said quickly. "I collect rocks from places I've been, and I've been a lot of places lately."

"Rocks," said Elarie in disbelief. "Brilliant. From now on, you carry it. Just tell me you keep your blasted book in there, too!" Wes quickly unzipped the bag and pulled out 'Magic 101', grinning at the girl. He climbed up onto the cot and held the book up to the moonlight, flipping through the first few pages.

"Here it is," he whispered. He read through the page several times, practicing the hand movements. "It shouldn't be too hard." He climbed down from the cot and moved closer to the door. "Okay, stand back, but be ready. I'm not sure I have enough power to cast even a spell this simple." He drew very close to the door and stood with his back to his companions. "Duermen lago adamanti," he chanted quietly. His hands moved in a caressing motion, as if he were gently stroking something. "Duermen lago adamanti," he said again. He repeated the chant several times, all the while making the caressing motion with his hands. On the fifth repetition, they heard a soft thump from the other side of the door, followed by quiet snores.

"Okay," he said to Elarie, "I think that did it. But be quiet! It's supposed to be an impenetrable sleeping spell, but I'm not sure how well it worked."

Elarie nodded and went to work on the door. Within seconds, the lock clicked, and the door swung inward silently.

"Nice," said Wes with an appreciative grin. Elarie winked.

"I picked harder locks when I was six," she said softly, stepping out through the cell door. The guard outside was lying prone on the floor, snoring soundly, his cudgel lying under limp fingers. "There are two more guards upstairs, and one walking about outside. Can you put them to sleep too?"

"I can try," said Wes. He stepped past the snoring guard. Gideon paused on his way by and knelt, gently pulling the sleeping man's cudgel from under his hand. The man never moved, and they crept on up the stairs.

When they reached the top, Elarie motioned for them to halt and pressed her ear to the door. She listened for a few moments and then gestured Wes closer. She leaned close to his ear and whispered.

"There are two more of them up there. One is pacing back and forth about twenty feet to the left of the door, and the other is sitting on a bench a few paces straight out from it. I can hear him whittling. I think they need a nap."

Wes nodded and moved as close to the door as he could. He repeated the spell, his hands moving rhythmically, and this time they heard the snores begin after only his third time through. Elarie signaled him to stop and then pressed her ear back to the door. After a moment she cracked the door open a hair and peeped out.

"All right, they're asleep. Move quickly, but be as quiet as you can. There's still another guard about somewhere." She pushed the door open and they all crept into the barracks section on tiptoe. "Gideon, you go gather up Wes' things and yours. Wes and I will try to pinpoint the last guard so he can join his friends in slumber." Gideon nodded and hurried to the table, quickly gathering up their belongings. Elarie and Wes quietly moved toward the front door. As Elarie was preparing to press her ear against the door, it suddenly swung open, and she staggered back with a startled oath. Frozen half inside the doorway was a huge man with gapped teeth, his eyes widening in shock. He recovered quickly, and moved forward with a snarl, his cudgel raised to strike at them. Without warning, another cudgel flew over Wes' shoulder and rapped the man solidly on the forehead. His head snapped back, and he teetered for a moment and then fell over backward with a crash. Elarie and Wes cringed, but the snoring guards never twitched a muscle.

Wes turned to Gideon, who was still next to the table across the room, his arm outstretched from throwing the club. "Thanks," the boy said quietly, breathing a sigh of relief.

"I told you before, I'll not allow anyone to harm you," said the old soldier.

210

"I'll remember that next time," replied Wes, his eyes sparkling in amusement. "Let's get our stuff and let's get out of here."

"Yes, let's," said Elarie. "I told the others I was just going to scout the situation. Won't they be surprised!" She led the way out the door and to the paddock. "We'll need to liberate a pair of horses for you," she said. "We don't have enough for all of us." She quickly opened the gate and grabbed the reins of two horses, already saddled and ready to go.

"Wait a minute, Elarie," said Wes. "What others?"

"Luther, Anton, Jiane, and Ryan," she said. "They're waiting off in the woods about a quarter mile that way."

"Lord Luther is here?" said Gideon in surprise. "And he's brought his daughter?"

"Yes, they've been trying to catch up to you for weeks. Now come on!" She started off toward the woods. Wes ran to catch up with her.

"Elarie, wait!" he said. "I'm not so sure I want to be caught up with. For all we know, they're out to stop me and take me back to the Collegium."

"Nonsense," said Elarie. "They're here to help. Your father said…"

"My what?" said Wes suddenly.

"Your father, you ninny. Ryan. He's waiting with the others." She pointed toward the woods.

Wes looked from Elarie to the woods and back again, and he snapped his mouth shut. Without another word, he took off running, tearing through the woods. After a minute or two, he saw vague, dark shapes moving around among the trees ahead of him.

"Dad!" he cried, and the shapes ceased their movement. One of them turned, and his face was illuminated clearly in the moonlight. Wes' heart leapt with joy.

"Wes?" said Ryan when he saw the boy coming toward him. He stared for a moment, a smile slowly growing, and then he stepped forward with his arms outstretched. Wes hit him like he'd been fired from a cannon, and they wrapped their arms around each other and fell to their knees, laughing.

"Oh my God, Dad, I didn't think I was ever going to see you again!" said Wes, tears streaming down his cheeks. "How did you get here?"

"It's a long story, but you shouldn't have worried," said Ryan, his own cheeks more than a little damp. "Did you really think something as silly as a parallel universe would keep me from finding you?" He squeezed the boy tightly. A moment later, Elarie and Gideon entered the clearing, leading the horses they'd acquired.

"See, Gideon?" said Elarie. "I told you, nothing to worry about!" But Gideon wasn't listening to her.

"Lord Luther," he said, saluting. "When this is over, I'll submit myself at High Keep for court martial on charges of desertion and dereliction of duty," he said humbly.

"Nonsense, man," said Luther in surprise. "You've done your duty to the kingdom, nothing more and nothing less." He returned the salute respectfully.

"Thank you, High Lord," said Gideon with a bow. Luther grimaced and glanced at Ryan, motioning Gideon to silence. "If I may ask," continued Gideon, oblivious, "what happens now?"

"That hasn't really been decided yet," replied Luther, "but I'd say our immediate need is to get as far from here as possible before we all hang. Mount up!"

Ryan and Wes untangled themselves, and Wes took the reins Elarie offered him and mounted. Ryan took his own reins from Luther and looked at the big man with a curious expression.

"High Lord?" he said with a tilted eyebrow.

"I'll explain later," said Luther with a sigh, mounting his own horse. Wasting no more time, they rode off into the night.

Chapter 13

Always On My Mind

HIGH JUDGE JASPER REINED IN near the paddock, looking over the barracks with a frown of distaste. The yard was quiet, the rays of the sun just beginning to shine through the trees with the coming of dawn. No one seemed to be about. No one came to take his reins or take charge of his mount, and he frowned even deeper.

"Constable Willis," he said, "it seems your men are rather slothful this morning. Be a good man and run inside to rouse them. I'd like to see that my horse is being tended before we begin this unpleasant business."

"As you wish, milord," said Willis sourly. Gods, this puffed up popinjay couldn't do a thing for himself, it seemed. Willis dismounted and crossed the broad yard to the barracks door.

"This yard is in deplorable condition," said Jasper disapprovingly to Joachim. "I'd not like to have to stable my stallion here overlong."

"Indeed, good sir," said Joachim ingratiatingly. "I'd as soon finish this business quickly and be on my way myself. I'm so pleased that you came so soon. I'd like to see the scoundrels pay, and pay dearly. I've suffered terrible losses, both financial and personal, and must begin the onerous task of rebuilding."

"Have no fear, old friend," put in the High Judge. "Once you've identified the rogues in my presence, your task is done and you may go as you please, if that is your wish. I'll not insist you stay for the trial and execution." Jasper smiled at Joachim ingratiatingly.

"Oh, no, my friend," said Joachim. "If it please you, I'd like to stay and see this to the finish. I'll gain some small satisfaction seeing the scoundrels swing for their crimes. Justice for my poor nephew and my loyal guardsmen."

"Of course," replied Jasper. "It's only right that you see justice done with your own eyes."

"Milord! High Judge!" Willis' shout came from the barracks entrance. "The prisoners have escaped!"

Joachim dismounted quickly and sprang to Willis' side, belatedly remembering he was supposed to be gravely injured. He affected a pained expression and limped toward the door. "What are you saying, man? How could they have escaped?" He pushed past the constable and limped into the barracks. His eyes fell on the unconscious man on the floor near the door, a prominent goose egg on his forehead, and then moved to the snoring men further back into the room.

"I don't know, milord," said Willis. "My men are sleeping as if drugged and won't rouse."

"Disgraceful!" exclaimed Joachim. "Gross dereliction of duty!" He turned to the constable. "I trust you'll see these men disciplined for their incompetence. It seems only one of your men took his duties seriously, and he allowed himself to be overpowered. I won't have it!" He leaned closer to Willis. "And you and I will have a conversation very soon about your continued employment."

Willis had had enough. He leaned right back, nose to nose with the overbearing lord. "We can have that conversation if you'd like, milord," he said through gritted teeth, "but allow me to remind you that I was elected by the good people of this parish. My continuing employment has little to do with your pleasure or displeasure. You're a visitor here, and might not be familiar with our ways. We're a free people, and not subject to your or any other noble's rule save the king's." He turned away and began again to try and wake the sleeping guards. "As soon as I can rouse my men, we'll set out on the trail of the prisoners."

"Oh, no," said Joachim with a snarl. "You and your men have already proven your prowess. I'll take my own men and track them down. And mark me, your little peasant council will hear of your impertinence, as will the High Lord as soon as I'm able to set pen to parchment."

Willis was unruffled. "As you say, milord. There's pen and parchment in the cabinet by the desk, and an ink jar in the inkwell."

Joachim seethed with anger, staring into the constable's eyes with hatred. "I haven't the time right now to see to your discipline," he said, turning away from Willis' unwavering gaze. "I've a pair of murdering thieves to catch." He strode from the barracks and slammed the door behind him.

"As you say, you overweening jackass," muttered Willis, and went about the task of rousing his men.

"Mount up!" shouted Joachim unnecessarily as he returned to the paddock. His four guardsmen had remained in their saddles throughout his exchange with the constable. "Jared," he said, nodding to one of the guardsmen, "scout the surrounding woods and find their trail. We'll have them in custody by nightfall, mark my words!" He mounted his fine steed and turned to the judge. "My apologies, High Judge Jasper," he said with a bow. "It seems your esteemed constable has allowed the prisoners to escape. Please, take your ease while my men and I round up the miscreants. Jared! The trail, if you please!"

"Aye, milord," said the soldier, trotting his mount toward the nearby woods.

◈◈◈

Ryan rode beside his son, following the others at a slight distance. They'd been riding all night, and Luther seemed intent on riding through the day as well. The sun had risen an hour earlier, and the morning light sparkled off the dew. Once they had cleared the woods and entered the open grassland beyond, Jiane had motioned to the others to pull ahead, giving Ryan and Wes a bit of privacy. They'd had little chance to talk since their reunion, barely enough to share some of their adventures and experiences since arriving in Canellin. Wes had seemed to delight in telling his father some tales, particularly his theft of the magic stone and escape from the authorities. Ryan had been suitably impressed.

Wes had in turn been astounded by Ryan's appearance. His father had dropped some weight since he'd last seen him, and seemed to have filled out a bit across the chest and arms. Ryan had grinned when Wes had mentioned his altered physique, and simply commented that regular exercise and clean air were doing him a world of good. He didn't approach Luther's stature or physique, by any means, but it seemed Canellin was good for him. Wes, too, was filling out a bit. He hadn't noticed before, but he did once it was brought to his attention. He had put on a few pounds of muscle since beginning this journey. They had talked in this way for a short time, but now, even with Jiane's

215

courtesy, they continued on in silence, simply enjoying having finally found one another. It was Wes who eventually decided to speak again.

"Dad," he said hesitantly, "I'm sorry."

Ryan looked at the boy in surprise. "Sorry for what?" he asked.

"For everything. Being such a pain. Mouthing off. Getting in trouble at school. It's just..." Wes paused, taking a deep breath. "It's just that everyone always seems to be pushing me to do what they want me to do, and I just get mad and do what I want. It's been the same way here, but I didn't know it until a little while ago. But I guess I was kind of a jerk back home. It's not fair to you. I'm sorry I've made your life miserable."

Ryan felt a catch in his throat as he opened his mouth to speak. "Wes," he said, "you've never made me miserable in my entire life. You've made me mad plenty of times, but miserable isn't even close to how I feel. You're the greatest thing that's ever happened to me."

"C'mon, Dad," said Wes. "If not for me, you'd still be safe back home. You wouldn't have to stress about whether I was doing what I'm supposed to do, whether I've got my homework done, whether I'm getting in trouble. If not for me, you'd have a completely different life." Wes turned away, looking off across the grass. "You could have finished college, or become a singer or a writer like you always said you used to dream about. You could do anything you wanted. You'd be a lot better off without me."

Ryan chuckled, and Wes was momentarily stung by the reaction. He opened his mouth to say so, and Ryan quickly spoke. "You don't know me half as well as you think, son," he said. "If I'd never met your mom or had you, would I have finished college?" He shrugged. "Probably not. Sure, taking care of you made it harder, especially when it was just the two of us. But before you came along, I was a screwup. I wasn't doing well in school long before I met your mother. Becoming your father gave me the sense of responsibility I'd been missing up to that point. And as for singing," he continued, rolling his eyes. "Well, I used to be good, but I was never great. I mean, not professional great. Singing was something that I loved to do, and still do, especially with you. But doing it for a living? That was a pipe dream, son, and I knew it even way back then. The best thing I ever got from my music was being able to share it with you. And in the end, you're way better on trumpet than I ever was as a singer." He looked at Wes, who was still avoiding his gaze. "But none of that really matters. Even supposing you're right, and I could have done those things if not for you, I wouldn't trade it. I'd never give up that moment."

Wes looked up, confused. "What moment?"

"That moment," repeated Ryan, shaking his head and searching for the words. "It's hard to explain. It was that moment in the delivery room when the doctor laid you in my arms, and you looked up at me with those bright blue eyes, and your little conehead was resting in the crook of my arm. That moment. From the first second you looked into my eyes, I was yours. Suddenly, giving you a better life was far more important than anything I'd ever wanted for myself. Because giving you a better life would make my world better than I'd ever imagined it could be."

Wes shook his head, trying to absorb what his father was telling him. "Then why are we always fighting?" he said. "If you want to give me a better life, why not just let me do what I want and be happy, without you and everybody else always pushing and pulling me all the time?"

Ryan laughed. "Giving you a better life doesn't mean giving you everything you want, Wes." Ryan shook his head ruefully. "Lord knows I wish it did. But sometimes it means specifically not giving you what you want. Sure, you'd be happy enough now, but what about the future, when it's time for you to make your own way in the world? Giving you a better life means raising you to know right from wrong, giving you opportunities I never had, and seeing that you grow up to be a responsible, well-adjusted, happy person. And it means making sure you learn to balance that happiness against your responsibilities."

"Now you sound like Gideon," said Wes with a sour look. "But I get it. It's just hard when there's so much stuff that I want to do that you won't let me, and there's so much stuff you want me to do that I hate doing."

"You know," said Ryan with a grin, "if you did more of those things that you hate without giving me so much lip about them, you'd probably get to do more of those things you wish you could."

Wes shrugged. "Yeah, I guess. I just haven't made things very easy on you, and I wanted you to know that I'm sorry. For real, this time." He gazed up at his father and gave him a tentative smile. Then his expression changed, and he narrowed his eyes. "What do you mean, conehead?" Ryan laughed and reached out to tousle the boy's hair.

"Ask your mom sometime. Her first words when she saw you, all drugged up from the delivery, were, 'My God, he's a conehead!'" Wes joined Ryan in laughter. After a while, Ryan's face grew serious. "The question now, though, is where do we go from here?" He looked at Wes questioningly.

"Yeah, about that," said Wes. He looked up at his father with a look that conveyed both nervousness and defiance. "I know you came after me to take me back to Diaticus, but you can't," he said in a rush. Wes' knees trembled as he spoke. "I'm not trying to start a fight with you or anything, but I can't go back there. I don't trust Diaticus anymore. I don't think he was ever really trying to find a way to send me home."

"I think you're right," said Ryan, "but I don't think he had a choice." Ryan quickly related the story of overhearing Diaticus talking to himself in the sword chamber. "I think he was pushed into it by Pomander," he concluded.

"Even so," said Wes, "I don't want to put myself back where I have to rely on him again. Besides, I kind of have a responsibility here. Pomander sent me here to get rid of the dragon, and that's what I plan to do, even if I don't really trust him or Diaticus anymore."

Ryan sighed, and Wes prepared himself for the inevitable argument. "You know what, son?" said Ryan. "I've been thinking about this since we started after you. Before that, actually." He turned his head, regarding his son carefully. Wes' face was determined, but there was more than that. The boy had changed in his time in Canellin. He had grown. And it was in that moment that Ryan made the decision he'd been debating since he'd arrived. "I just want to go home," he said. "And it seems to me there's a perfectly good doorway that's a lot closer than Diaticus and the Collegium." He reached over again and tousled Wes' hair. "It's kind of scary to think about, but I don't think we have much choice. What say you and me go kill ourselves a dragon?"

⁂

Around midmorning, Luther called a halt. The travelers were tired, and their mounts were laboring. A half hour's rest was definitely in order. As they all reined in, Luther motioned for everyone to gather round.

218

"We again have a decision to make," he said. "We've accomplished the goal we set out to do, at least as far as we've ever discussed. From here on in, it's up to Wes and Ryan. Do we go on, or do we return to the Collegium?"

"That decision's been made already," said Ryan, and Luther raised his eyebrows. "We were only waiting for a chance to talk it over with the rest of you. Wes intends to go on, and as much as I'd rather turn tail and run away, I won't stand in his way, and I won't let him do this without me. This may be our best chance to go home. We'll be heading to the dragon's lair." He looked around at the group. "We appreciate all you've done for us, and we'd certainly be grateful for any further help. But I won't ask any of you to take more risk than you already have."

"I knew when this began where the trip would end," said Gideon. "I'll be coming along."

Wes grinned at the big man. "Still want to be the hero who saved the kingdom?"

"I want to be the man who kept his word to his friend," said Gideon, scowling at the boy. "I'll not abandon you now, just because you've found your father. I'll be at your side till the end of this."

"Relax," said Wes. "I was just kidding."

"Whatever your reasons, I'll be happy to have you along," said Ryan. "Wes told me about what happened between you two, and about Diaticus. But you saved my son's life, and you've kept him as safe as you could on this trip. You're welcome to ride with us."

"I believe you're confused about something, Ryan," said Luther. "No one is intending to go back. Jiane, Anton, and I discussed it amongst ourselves. Our intent was to go on to the dragon's lair, whatever your choice. We're too close now, and the need too great. With or without your boy, we have to go on. Our only concern was how to see you two to safety if you chose to go back."

"That's no problem," said Wes. "My magic's coming back pretty quickly now. I don't know if I could send someone all the way to the Collegium, but I think I could send someone to Karsenon, maybe further."

"That could certainly prove useful if the need arises," said Luther, impressed. "Your magic is truly that strong?"

"Stronger, usually," replied the boy with a grin.

"If we're all agreed, I think I have me a suggestion ta' put forward," said Anton. "I been discussin' with Gideon here about all the obstacles what's been put in yer way. The rest of us've had a pretty easy trip of it, but it seems ta' me as if somethin' doesn't want the boy ta' get ta' where he's goin. I'm thinkin' it might serve us best ta' put a bit more sneak inta' our travels. I say we avoid Cliffton and the main pass there altogether. We should head out east o'er the grasslands an' find another way up the Escarpment."

"That might not be a bad idea," said Luther. "Particularly with Gideon and the boy wanted for murder. We'd likely beat any news to Cliffton, but we can't count on it."

"We'll go wherever you think best," said Ryan. "You know the land better than either of us. I'd certainly rather have a quiet trip and save the excitement for the end."

"It's settled, then," said Luther. "Anton, have you a route in mind?"

"Aye, milord, I think I can get us up the Escarpment with none the wiser."

"We'll be guided by your wisdom, then," said Luther with a broad smile.

Their decision made, Jiane passed around the waterskins and dried beef. They relaxed for a few minutes, and then mounted and resumed their journey. Elarie rode up alongside Wes, looking as if she wanted to speak, but held her tongue. Wes looked at his father meaningfully. After a few moments, Ryan took the hint.

"I believe there are some things I need to go over with Luther and Anton. Elarie, could you keep Wes company while I ride ahead?"

"I'd be happy to," she said with a relieved smile, and Ryan smiled at her as he guided his mount ahead next to Luther.

"So," said Wes when his father was out of earshot, "what about you? Are you okay with all this? Going to Dragon Mountain, I mean?"

"I don't really know," she said. "I'm still trying to take it all in. Everything's been a blur since I left you that morning in Karsenon."

"You don't have to, you know," Wes replied. "You can turn around and go back to your old life."

"I don't think I can," she said. "It's not that simple." The girl fell silent, looking troubled.

"Elarie," said Wes finally, "thank you so much for getting us out of the jail. I thought for sure we were going to die, but you saved us."

220

"I mislike jails as a general rule," she said with a grin, "and a gallows has always been my greatest fear. 'Twas only right to keep you from it if I could."

Wes smiled shyly at her. "How did you get there, though? Why were you trailing us?"

"That's... well, it's what I wanted to talk to you about," she said. "I need to know what you've done to me."

Wes looked at the girl in shock. "Done to you? I didn't do anything! We just talked! What do you mean?"

"There must be more than that," she replied, her voice almost desperate. "Since the moment you magicked me back to the inn, you've plagued my thoughts. I found myself doing things I'd never have done in my right mind." She shook her head. "Since before that, even. I've been risking my own neck out of worry for you. The morning you sailed, I trailed you clear to the docks, warning off cutpurses and thieves and even the beggar children. I made it known among the lower elements of the city that you had done me a service, and weren't to be molested. That alone was a risk to me. But that's not the worst of it!" She looked at the boy accusingly. "I couldn't sleep! I couldn't think! Your face was constantly in my mind. I could feel you, off somewhere in danger, and it like to drove me insane! When Jiane and your father were asking around about you in Karsenon, I was suspicious, and lied to them about having ever seen you. And then, when they found your inn and your route, I couldn't stop myself. I followed them to their ship and stowed away. I don't have any idea what I could have done if they had been enemies! When I found they were trying to help you, I couldn't stop myself from offering to help them any way I could." She sighed, exasperated. "And if you think I'm just a flighty little girl who's smitten with you, I'll instruct you better. Something's been done to me to chain me to you, and I want to know what."

Wes was dumbstruck by the girl's outburst. He shook his head, confused, trying to understand what Elarie was saying. "Honest, Elarie, I haven't done anything to you. I promise!"

"Someone has," said the girl bitterly. "Even now, I find myself worried about you and whether you'll survive this, and I'm right here beside you!"

Wes considered for a moment, slowing his mount. "It does sound strange," he said. "Our first meeting at the inn was short, and there wasn't any magic involved at all. And the things after that, in the

Tower of Lore... I can't believe they'd have this kind of effect on you." He looked the young thief in the eyes and thought hard. "Listen, I can maybe do something for you, if you'll trust me. It'll involve magic, though. Will you trust me?"

"I can't help but trust you," said the girl with a nervous laugh. "That's part of my problem!"

"Okay," said Wes. "I'm not sure I can do this on the back of a horse, though. I'm not sure I can do it at all, I've never tried it! But here, take my reins and guide my horse." He passed Elarie the reins of his mount, and she took them doubtfully. "Now give me your hand," he said.

"That'll be a bit difficult," said Elarie, holding up both hands to display Wes' reins in one and her own in the other. Wes chuckled.

"Yeah, that won't really work, will it? We'll have to wait till our next rest break."

"No, we won't," said Elarie, adamant. "Not to put too much weight on you over this matter, but I'd as soon have it resolved now, if I can." She turned toward the others. "Jiane! Could you please join us?" The swordswoman turned at Elarie's call and then wheeled her mount to ride back to the pair. Elarie explained the situation.

"I understand," said Jiane with a smile. She took a position on the opposite side of Wes from the girl. "Pass me the boy's reins," she said, holding out one hand. "I'll support him from this side if he gets too distracted." Elarie passed the reins back to Wes, who handed them to the swordswoman. Elarie held out her free hand to Wes hesitantly, and he took it with a reassuring smile.

"Okay," said the boy, "I've never done this before, but I've read about it. You don't need to do anything except hold on to my hand. You can talk to Jiane if you want, and you can pay attention to riding. I'll be trying to feel any magical intrusions or spells laid on you. Are you ready?" Elarie nodded. "All right, here goes." Wes closed his eyes, trying to follow his recollection of the instructions he'd read. It was complex, because this wasn't exactly a spell. It was more along the lines of the meditation exercises and techniques used to draw in magical power in preparation for a spell. He allowed his consciousness to flow down his arm and out through his fingertips, into Elarie's tiny hand. He pushed his mind further, gently, finding his way along the pathways within the girl, feeling for any trace of magic. Idly, he wondered how this must feel to Elarie, having someone rooting around

222

inside her head, but he supposed she probably didn't feel a thing. He traced his way all through the girl's body from her toes to her scalp, and then turned his attention to the more metaphysical side of the coin. He found the girl's consciousness and tried to explore it as unobtrusively as possible. There was something there! It was faint, fluttering just outside of the girl's conscious mind. Wes pushed himself toward it, unsure of what he was really doing, and there it was. He envisioned it in his mind's eye as a blue glow surrounding the girl's thoughts. He felt around its periphery, trying to figure out what it could possibly be. It seemed to be influencing the girl in subtle ways, but from what he could tell, it wasn't harming her. If anything, it seemed as if there was a benevolent intent behind whatever this was. Holding himself still in her mind, he allowed part of himself to slide back into his own head.

"I've found something," he said quietly. "It's faint, but it's there. It doesn't seem like it's dangerous, but it's definitely touching your mind."

"Get it out," said Elarie tensely. "Whatever it is, I want it gone. It's not part of me."

"I don't know if I can," replied Wes. "I'll try." He slid back along the path he'd created, following back to the place he'd marked in her mind. The blue glow was there, its tendrils gently caressing the girl's consciousness. Wes reached forward with phantom fingers and began to pluck at the tendrils with extreme care. There was little resistance at first; the glowing tendrils merely pulled away and then moved to another point and began their caressing anew. Wes began to pull the tendrils back and hold them in place, pushing them away from the girl's mind firmly. The glow seemed to intensify, pushing back against Wes' efforts, and he began to work hard to remove all of the groping tendrils from her mind. He pushed the glow back and contained it, forming it into a ball which tried hard to press back into Elarie's consciousness. Firmly, he shoved the ball away, and after a brief struggle, it sprang from the girl and was gone. Wes was suddenly snapped back into his own mind as Elarie screamed. His eyes opened wide to behold the girl leaned back precariously, nearly falling out of the saddle, his grip on her hand the only thing keeping her erect. Her own eyes seemed to be rolled back in her head, and Wes could clearly see the blue glow yanking away from her, pulling out of her body and speeding away a few hundred feet before seeming to dissipate. Once it

was gone, the girl slumped forward in her saddle. Jiane dropped Wes'
reins and moved around to support Elarie.

⁂

"So, High Lord," said Ryan sarcastically as he rode up next to
Luther, "am I supposed to bow and call you 'milord' now?" He
frowned at the big man, and Luther sighed.

"It's not what you think, Ryan," said Luther. "I never meant to
deceive you." He paused, scratching his head. "Well, no, I suppose I
did, but it wasn't from any sinister motive."

"Why the disguise, then? What would it matter to me if you
were the High Lord, or his master at arms?"

"It wasn't just you, Ryan, although I suppose you're right.
Nearly everyone at the Collegium knew my identity once the
dragonmen arrived." He shrugged. "It was just easier to keep up the
subterfuge. I've never truly been comfortable as High Lord. I come
from peasant stock, you know. I wasn't born to the nobility, nor did I
ever seek it out. It was thrust on me as a so-called 'reward' for my role
in the Great War." The big man looked uncomfortable. "When I
leave High Keep in any official capacity, I'm surrounded by retainers
and guardsmen and courtiers, all vying for my favor because of my
nearness to the throne. I can't avoid that. When I received word from
Diaticus about your son's arrival, my chamberlain began the task of
arranging my entourage for a trip to the Collegium. It would have
taken days, maybe even weeks, to make all the preparations he wanted.
I chose not to wait, particularly not for those puffed up pretenders he
would have had surrounding me. I've found that if I am to travel the
land unhindered, it's easier to do so as Luther the soldier than Luther
the High Lord. And when you arrived, I decided that I would have an
easier time of earning your trust if I were a simple master at arms." He
shrugged apologetically. "It gave me rank to explain why so many were
deferential to me, but it made me a man to you, not another official
trying to manipulate you. There were countless times I could have told
you. When I arranged our passage on Bartleby's ship. When we were
leaving the Collegium. But you must understand, Ryan, I count you as
a friend, and there are few enough of those for someone in my
position. By that time, I was afraid that you'd see my deceit as
betrayal."

224

"I understand why you'd hide out when you were traveling, I guess," said Ryan, "but honestly, what possible difference did you think it would make with me? High Lord or master at arms, you're Luther, the guy who offered to help me find my son."

"I suppose it wouldn't have made much difference at that," said Luther. "I was simply so used to the deception by then that I…" Luther was interrupted by a scream of pure terror from behind them. Without another word, he wheeled his horse and rode back toward Wes, Elarie, and Jiane.

⁓◎ ◎⁓

"What did you do?" cried Jiane as she wrapped one arm around Elarie's limp shoulders.

"I don't know," said Wes in a panic. "I didn't mean to hurt her! I found whatever the thing was that was messing with her head, and I pushed it out! Didn't you see it?"

"I saw nothing," said Jiane, gently brushing back the girl's hair. "You were holding her hand, and then she screamed and collapsed." She leaned close to the young thief's ear and whispered. "Elarie, can you hear me? Say something, girl!"

"I'm all right," said Elarie softly, straightening in her saddle. "It's all right, he didn't hurt me. It just… that was the strangest sensation I've ever felt! It terrified me for a moment, that's all."

"What's happening?" said Luther, reaching the little group. The others were close behind him, and all had weapons in hand.

"It's all right, really!" exclaimed Elarie quickly. "I didn't mean to frighten everyone, it just startled me!"

"Elarie had something in her head that was affecting her mind," said Wes. "Some kind of spell. I got rid of it, but it must have been fighting harder than I thought to keep hold."

"Who put it there?" asked Luther.

"I have no idea. It didn't seem to be hurting her, but it was definitely up to something. I think it's what was giving her the ability to feel where I was."

Luther and the others looked at each other with grim expressions. "This bodes ill," said the High Lord. "I don't like the idea of an unknown player having had a hidden hand in this game."

"What's done is done, Father," said Jiane. "Whatever it was, it's gone now. Our only course is to continue on and hope we haven't

225

been compromised beyond repair." She turned to Wes. "It is gone, isn't it?"

"Yeah," said Wes. "I saw it fade away after I pushed it out of her."

Jiane nodded. "Then I say we ride on." The others reluctantly agreed, and they resumed their journey. Elarie now rode forward to join the others, falling in beside Gideon, and Ryan dropped back again to ride next to his son.

Their direction was now almost due east. At length, they came to a narrow creek and waded the horses across. They continued to ride, crossing through a narrow strip of trees and onto a larger, broader stretch of grassland several hours later. To the south, the Escarpment came into view, stretching far along the horizon, a dull gray and brown color against the green brown of the tall grass. Anton waved them all to a halt.

"If me memory hasn't fled, I'm thinkin' we turn a tad more south than east here. Cliffton's off a few hours to the south an' west. We should reach the Escarpment well east o' the city. We can worry about makin' the ascent once we're face to face with the cliffs."

"How far?" asked Wes.

"We'll reach the cliffs by nightfall or earlier. They don't look like much now, laddie, but just ye wait till ye're standin' there lookin' up at 'em."

"Nightfall," said Wes. "And once we get over the cliffs, we're less than a day from the mountain." His voice held a note of fear and resignation.

"Aye, laddie. We're nearin' the end." Anton clapped the boy on the shoulder, and the group spurred their mounts back to the trail.

⚬ର୧ ୨ଵ⚬

Joachim fumed as he rode along behind his guardsmen, berating himself for his own stupidity. He should have done the task himself, and his guise as Lord of Karsenon be damned. Now he found himself saddled with men he hadn't wanted to bring in the first place, tracking the boy through the countryside instead of reveling in his promised rewards. What was worse, he had discovered something disturbing as they rode, when his bandages had slipped slightly from his wrist. Green and red flecks shone brightly on the blackened flesh.

226

It had taken him some time to determine what they were, and when he had, his blood had chilled. Tiny scales growing into the flesh. His body seemed to be changing far more than he'd expected from the dragon's 'gift'.

And their quarry seemed to have acquired new companions. Instead of just two sets of tracks, they were following six, perhaps seven horses. He had no idea who the newcomers might be, but he was certain they would complicate his plans. It was all becoming far too complicated, far too quickly.

"Milord!" called Jared riding casually toward them from his position out ahead. "They've changed direction on us!" He reined in his mount and waited for the rest of the party to catch up.

"Changed direction to where?" called Joachim.

"They were heading east here across the grassland. About a mile off in that direction, they crossed a little creek and turned back to the southeast." The young soldier scratched his head. "It looks like they're not going to double back toward Cliffton after all, milord. They still seem to be headed for the Escarpment, but not any of the well known passes."

"That makes no sense," said Devon, who led the guardsmen since Corporal McKee's unfortunate demise. "Not even brigands would chance having their hideout in the barrens atop the plateau. It's far too close to the dragon's territory."

Jared rode closer to his companions. "Unless they're not simple brigands," he said. "There have been mutterings of late that the outbreaks of brigandry since the invasion have been perpetrated by men sworn to the dragon's service."

Joachim smiled inwardly. An excellent excuse for following the boy all the way to Dragon Mountain, if need be! "Murderers and dragonsworn to boot," he said vehemently. "The theft of the stone takes on a far more sinister meaning. If that is the case, we're doubly obligated to bring them to justice!"

"We certainly are, my lord," said Devon. "And if they've an enclave in dragon territory, it's certain our best course would be to apprehend them before they reach the Escarpment."

"That's good sense," said Joachim in agreement. "Jared, get yourself back on their trail. We're barely half a day from the cliffs, and despite the gains we've made, they've still got a few hours lead on us. We must make the best time we can without losing the trail."

"Aye, milord," said Jared, and he rode off at a canter.

227

Chapter 14

Blades, Masters, and Blademasters

THE ESCARPMENT ROSE ABOVE THEM, over a thousand feet high, the cliffs curving to the horizon in both directions. The face was nearly vertical, a sheer expanse of rock that seemed to have no end. Ryan stared at the massive formation in awe.

"How are we supposed to get up that?" he asked Luther incredulously. "And how are we supposed to get the horses up?"

"Ask Anton," was Luther's reply. "He's the one that suggested we bypass Cliffton and the known passes."

"Aye, milord, that I did," said Anton with a cheery smile. "An' if ye'll be so kind as ta' indulge me, I'll soon show ye why." He turned his mount and rode slowly along the cliff face to the east. Jiane kept glancing north, away from the cliffs, but Ryan couldn't tell what it is she was trying to see.

"Ah, there 'tis," said Anton suddenly, spurring his horse forward. He led the party to a narrow cleft in the rock face, barely wide enough for two horses to enter side by side. "I found this here path the last time ye sent me down this a'way, milord. Found it a mite useful for avoidin' pryin' eyes."

"Excellent work, Anton," said Luther. "How long will it take to reach the top this way?"

"Three, maybe four hours," said Anton. "They's quite a few twists an' turns ta' wind our way around, but she's a pretty easy climb. We'll come out on a rise atop the plateau an' be able ta' work our way down onta' the flats without too much trouble."

"Night will be falling in an hour or so," said Luther. "We'll camp here and start the climb in the morning."

"I don't think that's going to be an option, Father," said Jiane, shielding her eyes and peering off to the northwest. "Riders approaching."

Luther turned and looked in the direction she pointed. "How far off?" he asked.

"They'll be upon us in less than half an hour if they can keep this pace. They've seen us, though, that's certain. The flat grassland out there doesn't really give much cover."

"Can you tell who they are?" asked Ryan. "Are they dragonmen?"

"No," she replied. "They're wearing livery, or some of them are. I'd say it's pursuit from Briarton."

"Blast!" Luther spat. "There's no help for it now. Anton, can we lose them in the pass?"

"Aye, I think it can be managed, milord. They's plenty o' switchbacks an' false trails up there."

"Lead the way, then," he said in resignation. "Everyone stay close. We don't want to get separated." They filed into the narrow gap with Anton riding in front.

The pass through the Escarpment was steep and narrow, climbing upward steadily. They came to the first switchback and turned sharply almost a hundred eighty degrees. The cliff walls rose up around them, leaving them just a thin strip of sky above to light their way. Following the steep trail, they climbed for almost an hour, and finally came to a broad ledge that passed out over the area they'd covered, affording them a clear view down into the narrow passages they'd already negotiated.

"Persistent devils, aren't they?" said Gideon, looking down to see their pursuers passing through the first switchback. "They don't seem of a mind to let us go if they're willing to follow into the dragon's territory."

"It seems you two made quite the impression on them," said Elarie with a grin. "Perhaps it was your miraculous escape from their impregnable dungeon."

"Oh, crap!" exclaimed Wes. "That's the guy!"

"What guy?" asked Ryan.

"The guy with the bandages, see?" Wes pointed toward a man near the rear of the group below. "That's Lord Joachim! He's the guy who had me in the dungeon in Karsenon!"

"Well," said Luther nonchalantly, "that confirms who they are, at least. Anton, how soon before we can start to try and lose them?"

"Just up here a ways, milord. The passage splits in a fork. We'll ride down the wrong fork a ways an' lay a trail, then double back an' take the proper one. I'll drag me bedroll behind us until we hit the next switchback an' clear our tracks a mite." He looked up at the darkening sky. "Night'll fall before they get that far, an' between that an' the rocky ground, we should be able ta' throw 'em off the trail for a while."

They reached the fork and followed Anton's instructions. After doubling back to the correct trail, the lanky man pulled out his blankets and began following behind them. He dragged the blankets along their path, every once in a while tossing a handful of dust and gravel onto the cleared ground to make it appear undisturbed. To Wes' eye, it looked like no one had been that way in years. When they rounded the next switchback, Anton mounted and rode back to the head of the party.

"Not as convincin' as I'd like, but hopefully it'll be enough ta' throw 'em off," he said. "We'll do the same at the next fork, an' not at the one after. It ought ta' confuse their tracker somethin' fierce!"

And so they repeated the procedure at the next branch, and then rode straight on through the third. They continued on in this way, Anton randomly choosing which forks they'd lay false trails in and even dragging his blankets and tossing his dust on a couple of the switchbacks they didn't take to add more confusion for their pursuers. Their progress was slowed by the constant laying of false trails, and the darkness had become almost absolute, but none of them was willing to risk allowing Wes to light a magelight. Near midnight, Anton signaled a halt.

"It's near enough a straight shot up to the top from here," he said. "We'll come out atop the rise an' have a gentle slope down a couple hundred feet to the plateau. Once we hit the flats, we should be able ta' put some quick distance between us an' them, an' I think I'll be able ta' confuse our trail enough that they'll lose it altogether."

The party rode up the last passage, the cliff walls growing ever shorter as they went. The narrow passage exited onto a wide plateau that led down to the flats below in either direction. Anton rode his horse out of the narrow pass and then froze, the others steering their mounts to stop alongside him in a row.

230

"Gods above," breathed Gideon, gazing down to the rocky land laid out before them.

"What are they?" asked Wes, peering out at thousands of points of light dotting the broad plain below. The lights flickered in place, but they stretched from horizon to horizon.

"Campfires," said Luther quietly. "That's an army down there. Thousands, maybe hundreds of thousands."

"An army," said Wes slowly, looking out across the plain to the huge cone known as Dragon Mountain. "Between us and the dragon. Perfect." He couldn't tear himself from the awesome sight. "An army of dragonmen?"

"Aye," said Anton. "Not much else they could be this side o' the cliffs."

"There have ten times the numbers they threw at us during the Great War," said Luther. "That's what the invasion was about. They meant to bottle up the armies of Canellin so this horde could sweep down and annihilate the common folk. Then, when all that was left was a demoralized army less than a quarter their numbers, they could destroy us with half a thought."

"How are we going to get past them?" asked Wes.

"More importantly, how are we going to get word back to the kingdom?" said Luther. "If these beasts make their move, Edward will have no warning. He needs to mobilize every able-bodied man in the kingdom!"

"I think we have a more immediate concern," said Jiane, lowering her voice and pointing down the long slope. "We have more company." The others followed her pointing finger down the slope and into the darkness below. They could make out hulking shapes moving around on the flat, working their way around to the slanting path. Jiane lowered her voice even further. "Dragonmen," she said. "Twenty or more. I don't think they've seen us yet."

"Quickly," said Luther, "back to the passage!" At that moment, a crossbow bolt arced over his head and struck Ryan's helm with a huge clang, knocking it from the surprised man's head. He ducked low over his mount's neck and danced the animal further back into the shadows.

"Too late," Ryan said, shaking his head to clear the ringing from his ears. "I think Jiane was mistaken." His voice was tight.

"Move!" shouted Luther. "We've a better chance in the passages! Even if we can't lose them, it's too narrow for them to come at us in a group and swarm us under!" They turned their mounts and headed back into the pass, Luther holding back to make sure everyone entered and then rushing in behind.

"What's the plan, milord?" shouted Anton.

"Head for the first switchback, and then down to the fork! We'll try to lose them up the opposite path!" They galloped down to the fork at a dangerous pace and wheeled their mounts into the path they'd skipped before. Anton wheeled his horse and reined in.

"Are ye sure about this, milord? The path here's narrow, an' it dead ends around the next bend. If they don't take yer bait, we'll be trapped."

"With any luck, they'll pass right by," replied Luther. "The mouth of the tunnel is well back from the connecting path, and they'll find it hard to see from that direction." He shrugged. "If not, we'll have the advantage that only two or three can come at us at once."

"As ye say, milord," said Anton dubiously. "I'm not fond o' the idea o' not havin' an escape route."

"It'll have to do," said Luther. "Keep the horses quiet, everyone, and keep your lips sealed."

The party crouched in the darkness, doing their best to keep their horses calm and themselves silent. A few minutes later, dim shapes could be seen passing by the mouth of the tunnel far up the slope. The clank of mismatched armor and the stamp of heavy boots created a cacophony in the silence. The dragonmen passed by, and Anton waited several more minutes to ensure they were gone. Then he crept back up to the main path and listened. After a few moments, he motioned the others forward.

"Seems the beasts found somethin' else ta' occupy 'em," he said. "There was some shoutin' below, an' then sounds o' steel on steel. Looks like they run inta' the fellows what was chasin' us."

"Then let's get out of here while they're occupied," said Luther, turning his horse back upslope, and the others moved to follow. Wes held back, looking down the passage worriedly.

"Wes, come on," said Ryan urgently. "We've got to get out of here!"

"They'll be slaughtered, Dad," said Wes. "Chasing us or not, they're people, and they're fighting monsters. We have to help them." He turned and spurred his horse quickly down the sloping passage.

232

"Get back here, you little fool!" hissed Luther, trying to keep his voice low. Wes ignored him, and Gideon was already moving to follow.

"He's right, Luther," said Ryan reluctantly. "What kind of people are we if we don't help?"

"The kind with a pulse!" said Luther, but Ryan was already leaping his mount after his son's, and Elarie was close on his heels.

"Blasted fools, one and all," said Luther.

"Shame on you, Father," said Jiane, working her mount past Luther's to get room to follow Ryan down the slope.

"Button it, girl," Luther growled. "I'm not about to let them go without me." And Luther, Jiane, and Anton heeled their mounts down the slope after their comrades.

༄ ༄

Joachim reined in his stallion as he called a halt, cocking his head to one side to listen.

"What is it, my lord?" Jared asked, and Joachim held his hand up for silence.

"Listen," he said softly, and the others strained their ears. In the distance far ahead came the clank of metal on stone and the sounds of heavy footsteps. "There!" whispered Joachim. "They're coming closer! I don't know why, but our quarry seems to have changed direction." He motioned to the three guardsmen in the lead to ride on. "Proceed slowly and with caution," he advised. "If we come upon them unprepared, we can take them in the darkness." He followed, and Jared took up a position at the rear.

They crept their mounts forward slowly, keeping their eyes and ears alert as the sounds of clanking armor and booted feet grew louder. They had traveled only a few minutes when the men on point rounded a bend and let out shouts of alarm.

"Dragonmen, milord, approaching from above! Twenty or more!" Joachim halted his mount, holding up a hand to halt Jared as well. After a moment, he and Jared continued on slowly around the bend. When his men came into sight, he could see the steel of their bared blades in the moonlight that filtered down from above. Several hundred paces up the pass was a party of dragonmen, snarling with bloodlust as they fought to be the first to reach the men below.

"Beware!" shouted Devon as Jared and Joachim rounded the bend behind him. He swung down from his horse and drew his sword as he rushed forward ahead of the other soldiers. They also dismounted, stepping out several paces past their horses to get more room to maneuver. The passageway was wide enough at this point for two men to stand abreast, but the hulking dragonmen could send only one of their number forward at a time. The savage creatures fell on them with howls of rage, and the soldiers waded into battle with their swords flailing.

The first two attackers fell easily at the hands of the guardsmen. A third monster fell quickly to Devon's blade, and the shape of the battle was established. A dragonman would rush forward down the slope to engage the men while their compatriots snarled and pushed for their turn. There was no room for finesse or fancy swordwork. It was merely hack, slash, and dodge in the desperate hope that the blades of the men were more sure than those wielded by the beasts. As Devon dodged a vicious slash and drove his blade through the dragonman's chest, another of the guardsmen went down, his neck sliced open ear to ear. The other stepped forward to block the creatures' further advance.

"Well, boy," said Joachim idly, "it's likely we'll get to wet our blades 'ere long. Are you up to the task?"

"I've never seen battle," said the young man nervously, "but Corporal McKee has seen all of his guardsmen well trained. I'll acquit myself well, milord, of that I assure you."

"Now's your chance," said Joachim as another soldier fell to an attacker's blade. "It seems there's another hole in the line needing plugged."

Jared leapt forward, his blade at the ready, and began the methodical work of killing dragonmen.

✦✦✦

Wes rounded a bend and brought his horse to a skidding halt. Not far ahead was the next switchback, the snarling dragonmen gathered there in a mass, struggling to push themselves forward. From around the corner came the sounds of battle and the cries of men. Wes swung down from his horse just as Gideon reached his side, Ryan

234

close on his heels. With a simple gesture, he flung a magelight out over the heads of the monsters to light the battle.

"Stay back, son," said Ryan. "You'll only be in our way."

"Wait!" cried Wes. "Jump in when I give the signal, but for now just wait!" Wes stepped forward and began making arcane gestures, concentrating hard. Gideon dismounted and pulled Ryan down off his horse as well.

"We'd best take cover," he said quickly. "I recognize this one." He moved off to one side behind Wes, taking cover behind a rocky spur. Ryan looked at him for a moment, and then decided it might be prudent to follow the man's advice. He crouched behind Gideon, peeking out to see what it was Wes was doing.

Wes was oblivious to the actions of the men behind him. He completed his gestures and chanted the words to the spell, his arm flashing forward in a familiar throwing motion. A fireball appeared, streaking toward the backs of the crazed dragonmen, expanding as it went. Though it was more controlled than his last attempt, the ball of flame was no less effective. It burned through two dragonmen in quick succession and caromed off the wall of the pass, once again moving through their ranks. Wherever it struck, dragonmen howled in pain and fury. As the ball of fire began to fade, Wes turned back to Gideon and Ryan. By that time, Luther and Jiane had also reached them, with Elarie and Anton close behind.

"Okay," Wes said quickly. "It'll only last a few more seconds, and then you can jump in. Be careful, Dad, please!"

Ryan nodded and crouched, waiting for the fireball to fade away. When it was finally gone, he and Gideon leapt forward, followed closely by Jiane and Luther. The pass was just wide enough for the four of them to engage the creatures without hindering one another.

The enemies' numbers had been thinned by the passage of Wes' fiery attack, more than a third of them either destroyed outright or too wounded to fight, but they still outnumbered the humans two to one. The attack from behind confused the creatures, as did the magelight hovering far above them, giving an advantage to Wes' party and their pursuers below. The battle lasted for just a few short minutes until finally, the last two attackers fell, one from Ryan's thrusting blade and the other from a wicked slash from Joachim's slender sword. The two men stood facing each other for a moment, panting, and then lowered their weapons. From the shadows, Luther stared at the tall man, waiting to see what his reaction would be. A lone guardsman remained alive, blood dripping from a deep wound to his thigh.

"Who are you, and what is your purpose here?" said the man haughtily after he caught his breath.

"I'm Ryan Bellamy," replied Ryan, a note of sarcasm in his voice, "and I guess my purpose was to help save your butts. But to answer your real question, we're trying to get to Dragon Mountain."

"And I'm certain your motives are the most noble kind." Joachim snorted. "The boy, and that man there, are murderous thieves. Do you know the sort you're consorting with? They robbed my tower, killed my men, and stole my horse. Stand aside, and you and the rest of your party may go about your business."

"But milord," said the remaining guardsman, hobbling forward on his wounded leg, "they aided us in battle. Why would they do such a thing if..."

"How dare you!" snarled Joachim venomously. "You question my honor?"

"No, of course not," said the injured man. "But their actions aren't those of guilty men. Is it not possible that you've made a mistake?"

"There's no mistake, Jared," said Joachim firmly, "These scoundrels have much to answer for."

Anton's sudden laughter brought Joachim up short. "Not ta' put too fine a point on it, milord," he said between chuckles, "but ye do realize ye be outnumbered more'n three ta' one, don't ye?"

Joachim rounded on the man, his face reddening in anger. "How dare you speak so to me, you filthy peasant!" he said. "I'll have you know..."

"Joachim Roderick DiMornay!" said Luther suddenly, interrupting the lord's outburst. "That'll be quite enough, you overbearing toad!"

Joachim again whirled, this time in Luther's direction, a reply ready on his tongue, but when he saw Luther's face, he bit back his words with his eyes wide. "M-m-my lord Luther!" he said instead. "What are you...?" He let his words trail off, and after another moment's hesitation, he dropped to one knee with his sword point first in the ground before him. "Forgive me, High Lord," he said. "Had I but known that you had already apprehended these louts, I'd not have bothered with the pursuit. However, as they have stolen something entrusted to my care, I'd ask that you remand them to…"

"Shut up, you overstuffed popinjay," said Luther disgustedly. "And get up! We don't have time for this foolishness! I didn't apprehend them, you dolt, I helped them escape!" Elarie shot Luther a hard look and cleared her throat. "With a little help," said the big man with a wink for the girl. "The theft of the stone was necessary to their task, and as for the rest, they're innocent of your charges. You've made a mistake."

"Innocent! They're murdering rogues!" Joachim's eyes grew wild.

Wes stepped forward to speak. "Listen, mister," he said, mustering all the courtesy he was able, "you made a mistake, that's all. It wasn't us who attacked you. I haven't seen you since the night in the dungeon!"

Joachim growled at the boy, and Wes flinched reflexively. Without warning, the Lord of Karsenon's bandaged hand shot forward and grabbed Wes' tunic, pulling the startled boy roughly to him. A dagger appeared in the man's hand, the point going immediately to Wes' throat.

"Stay back!" shouted Joachim. Ryan took two steps toward him, but the dagger's point dug into the soft flesh of Wes' neck, drawing blood. "Stay back, I say!" The suddenly deranged lord held Wes between him and the others, backing away slowly.

"Joachim, what are you doing?" said Luther in shock. "Stand down immediately!"

With a savage growl, Joachim picked Wes up and threw him over his shoulder, his strength surprising. Heturned on his heel, sprinting down the slope. Ryan immediately ran after them, Jiane a few short steps behind. The tiny woman quickly outdistanced him as they chased after the crazed Lord of Karsenon.

∽◉ ◉∽

Wes was rigid in Joachim's grip, terror filling him. The mad dash was terrifying enough with no light to see by, but the man's dagger was what had frozen Wes' muscles. With each step the point jabbed him in the side where Joachim gripped him, and his struggles had only made it worse. There was no hope of fighting the iron grip. Wes knew he was going to die.

The bandaged man came to a fork in the pass and veered to the left. He sprinted down the narrow passage, muttering to himself all the while.

"The great master will reward me for this," said Joachim in a maniacal whisper. "Your death will bring me power beyond imagining, boy!" He laughed hysterically. His laughter cut off when they rounded a bend in the passage and came face to face with a sheer wall. Skidding to a halt, he began looking about for some avenue of escape, but there was none to be found. He flung Wes roughly to the ground. Wes scrambled to his feet, but Joachim grabbed him from behind.

"Here is as good a place as any," said Joachim with a hysterical giggle. "Once my blade finds your heart, I'll have my reward, and no one will stand against me!" He raised the dagger to strike, and Wes' vision went white. Panicked, the boy did the only thing he could think of. He drove his head back into Joachim's nose with all the strength he had in him, and just as with the bully Cameron, there was a satisfying crunch.

Joachim roared with pain and anger as he staggered backward, his grip on Wes loosening. Wes fell to the ground and scrambled back as far as he could, away from the cursing man. He turned and started to rise, and barely ducked in time as a small form hurtled over his prone body to collide with the Joachim. Wes rolled onto his back and tossed a magelight into the air to see what was happening.

Jiane and Joachim were struggling on the ground, each trying to gain advantage over the other. Joachim's face was bloody, his nose crushed, and his bandaged hand clawed at the small woman's face. Wes scrambled to his feet.

"Jiane! Move!" Wes drew back his arm and chanted his spell, casting a fireball at Joachim.

"No! Not again!" shouted Joachim, terror in his voice. He leaped away and narrowly avoided the blistering flames. Wes' fear and anger seemed to strengthen his spell, and the fireball struck the sheer wall of the pass with an enormous crash that shook the very rocks themselves. Wes was thrown from his feet, as were Joachim and Jiane. Shouts from the passage behind told Wes that the others were feeling the effects as well as they approached. Jiane and the Joachim were struggling to their feet and preparing to fling themselves at one another again when Wes felt the floor tilt precariously. The pass suddenly gave way beneath them, and Wes felt himself falling. His head struck

238

something hard, blurring his vision. He landed on a sharply sloped ledge and slid down several more feet as the walls of the pass collapsed inward, cutting off all light from the sky above. When Wes finally slid to a halt, he flung out his arm and cast another magelight.

Jiane was struggling to her feet not ten paces from where Wes had landed. Blood flowed freely from a gash on her forehead. Not far beyond her, Joachim rose from a crouch, seemingly uninjured other than his crushed nose. The bandages on his face had torn away in the fall. Wes was disgusted to see red and green scales glittering on his blackened and blistered skin. Slowly, the man drew his sword.

"Your death was going to be quick, boy," he said with a sinister hiss. "A single dagger stroke would have ended it all. But now I intend to pull every bit of pleasure I can from flaying the skin from your bones."

Wes skittered backward, trying to gather his will for a spell, but his thoughts were scattered and incoherent. The blow to his head seemed to have jumbled his wits. He backed up against the rocky debris from the passage's collapse, his heart racing.

"You'll not lay a hand on the boy," said Jiane, stepping in front of Joachim with her blade bared.

"Don't be ridiculous, girl," said Joachim with a cold sneer. "This is no mindless dragonman you face, but a recognized blademaster. It's not your head I want. It's the boy's."

"Your tassel doesn't impress me," said Jiane calmly. "I'll not allow any harm to come to him."

"As you wish," said Joachim. He raised his sword and darted forward with a killing stroke. Jiane parried it easily, responding with a slash toward Joachim's thigh. He blocked it in surprise, dancing back out of reach, and then leapt forward with an overhand blow. Jiane again blocked his blade easily, returning a strike of her own.

"I'll not let you have him," said Jiane. "This boy is worth a thousand of you."

"This boy," said Joachim, "is a worthless piece of meat." He lunged forward, his sword scoring a minor cut on Jiane's thigh and drawing first blood. Jiane didn't react at all to the slight injury. The small woman responded with a return cut on his wrist, and he stumbled back in surprise.

Wes heard a scrabbling noise behind him, and faint voices calling his name and Jiane's.

"Dad! Is that you? Where are you?"

"Wes! It's me!" came the faint reply. "Are you okay?"

"No!" shouted Wes. "Jiane's fighting him! You have to help her!"

"We're trying!" replied Ryan, barely heard through the pile of debris, and the scrabbling sounds increased.

"Hurry, Dad!" shouted Wes, and turned back to the battle behind him. Jiane and Joachim's blades flickered like lightning, their every motion fluid and graceful. Both of them were marked with ribbons of scarlet where the opponent's blade had scored. It really was very much like watching a dance, these two masters trading furious blows and savage slashes under the mystical light.

"What's this about, man?" asked Jiane as she dodged a vicious swipe. "Listen to reason. The boy has done nothing to you."

"It's not about what the boy has done," said Joachim, panting. "It's what he is. My master wants him dead."

Jiane swung an overhand strike at the lord's unprotected head, and Joachim twisted aside easily. The blow slid through the air where he'd stood, and Jiane spun just in time to deflect a return thrust. "What master? Who would want Wes dead?"

"My master, and one day yours as well. The Great Dragon will rule over this entire world, and I will be rewarded for my hand in his triumph!" Joachim's eyes were wild, almost feverish.

"Your master," Jiane said in sudden understanding. "You're a thrall to the dragon. A traitor to your own race." She surged forward with a flurry of blows, her blade darting in and out, trying to penetrate the Joachim's defense. Joachim managed to deflect all her blows, but his speed was fading as Jiane's attack continued.

"Leave over, girl," he snarled, again dropping back out of the little swordwswoman's reach. "Give me the boy, and I may let you live. You've great skill with a blade. Join me, join my master! Share in the rewards of the Great Dragon's inevitable triumph!" His voice had a maniacal, desperate tone.

"I don't think it's a matter of letting me live," said Jiane calmly, with no trace of the tension Joachim's voice held. "It's a matter of whether you die from a thrust through the heart or by having your head struck from your body. It all depends on which attack you choose to make next."

Joachim roared wordlessly, leaping forward, his sword cleaving a long arc through the air in front of him. Jiane smoothly sidestepped

240

the blow and spun full circle, her sword lashing out in a long stroke to slice cleanly through the raving man's neck.

"The head it is, then," said Jiane. Joachim fell to his knees, his head toppling from his shoulders to roll across the floor as his body collapsed in a heap.

Wes looked from where Joachim's head had come to rest and back to Jiane, fighting to find his voice.

"That was incredible," he said finally.

"It was stupid," said Jiane, dropping to a crouch with a wince. "It took me too long to take his measure. Perhaps the blow I took when I fell…" She trailed off, her arms trembling. "I've never killed a human being before," she said. "It's not like killing dragonmen. It's more…" The woman lowered her head, her shoulders shuddering.

"I don't think he was completely human," said Wes, looking again at the head lying on the rocky ground. "And he was kind of crazy at the end, too."

"Wes!" came Ryan's voice, much louder now. "Can you hear me, son? What's happening?"

"It's okay!" shouted Wes. "We're okay!" He turned and scrambled higher onto the piled debris and started tossing stones aside. After a moment, Jiane took a deep breath and rose to help him. Within a few minutes, they had cleared away enough of the loose stones to reveal a small opening, and Ryan's face appeared. Wes exclaimed with relief. With just a little more work, enough rock was cleared for Ryan and Luther to squeeze through. Ryan grabbed Wes in a fierce embrace.

"I thought I'd lost you again," said Ryan tearfully.

"You would have, if not for Jiane," replied Wes, returning the embrace.

"Come on," said Ryan as he released the boy. "The others are waiting back there. We lost all but two of the horses, but we made it through all right. Joachim's man is hurt, but he's alive."

"My horse?" said Wes. "Oh, no. And the soldier's hurt?" Suddenly, his eyes grew wide. "My backpack! Is the book safe?"

"It's fine, it's okay, your horse made it. Your packs are still on its back." He gestured to the opening in the pile. "Come on, let's go."

"Wait, Ryan," said Luther. "Jiane, was he truly a blademaster?" he asked.

"Without doubt, father. He was the best I've seen."

241

"Other than yourself, obviously," Luther replied with a chuckle. "You do realize that his tassel is rightfully yours, as is his weapon. You may rightfully call yourself a blademaster now."

Jiane started, her eyes widening. She looked from her father to the headless corpse, and then spat on the body with disgust. "I want nothing this man's taint has touched," she said.

"I thought not, lass," said Luther. "But you've proven your title beyond doubt. I'll see that a blademaster's tassel is conferred to you as soon as we return home." Jiane frowned up at her father. "You've earned it and more, daughter. And no one can deny it to you now."

"It's a meaningless title, father," she replied. "My worth is not held in a gaudy article of clothing. It never has been."

Luther sighed. "Perhaps not," he said. "Tassel or no, daughter, you have my respect. And my pride."

One by one, Ryan, Wes, Jiane, and Luther worked their way through the pile of debris to join their waiting companions.

Chapter 15

The Crystal Cavern

O N THE OTHER SIDE OF THE ROCKSLIDE, the tunnel widened out into a broad ledge that led off into a narrow tunnel. The collapse of the pass had completely sealed them off from the outside, and the darkness was nearly absolute. Elarie held an improvised torch above her head, but the guttering flame barely cast enough light to illuminate the faces of the companions. The young guardsmen that had accompanied Joachim lay on stretcher cobbled together from a pair of spears from the fallen dragonmen and his own bedroll. His eyes were closed, and he had a bloody gash on his head and another on his leg. Wes made a negligent gesture, and his magelight sped through the opening in the rockslide to take up a position above them, lighting the tunnel brightly.

"You're getting pretty good at that magic stuff," said Ryan appreciatively.

"That's the first spell I learned," Wes said with a shrug. "I don't even have to think about it any more." He looked around curiously. "Where are we, anyway?"

"Hard ta' say," said Anton. "We fell quite a ways, an' the pass fell in behind us. Took us a mite ta' find ye after the drop."

"How do we get out?" asked Ryan. "This might not be the best time to mention this, but I'm not exactly fond of tight spaces."

Gideon cleared his throat for attention. "Wes, are you able to cast that spell you used on the dragonmen? The one that made them disappear?"

Wes shrugged. "Yeah," he said, "but I'm not sure if it'll be any use." He closed his eyes and concentrated, trying to form an image of the pass above in his mind. After a few moments, he shook his head. "I haven't spent enough time anywhere near here," he said. "I could send us back to the jail in Briarton. I could probably send a couple of us all the way back to the Collegium if I really wanted to. But we're so close! I don't want to have to start over."

"You may not have to, boy," said Luther. "These tunnels must lead somewhere. We'll explore 'til we find our way out, and only go back to Briarton if we're left with no choice." He considered for a moment. "But I think you may have just presented us to the solution to another of our problems. Can you truly send one of us all the way back to the Collegium?"

"Sure," said Wes. "One or two of us. It wouldn't be that hard. I spent a long time there before I left, so it's pretty clear in my head. That's a lot more important than the distance. But what good would it do?"

"A great deal, boy. There's an army on the plain above, and the king must be warned. If we can get word to him, he may yet have time to mobilize the people." He knelt next to the fallen guardsman. "Can you hear me, soldier?" The young man's eyes fluttered open.

"Y-yes, milord," was his shaking reply.

"What's your name, lad?"

"Jared, milord. Jared Mulrooney."

"Jared, I need you to listen to me. You know who I am, yes?"

Jared blinked several times. "Yes, milord. You're High Lord Luther."

"And you know what's happened here?"

"I... I'm not sure, milord. Lord Joachim... he's dead, isn't he?" At Luther's nod, the young man sighed. "And he was... he betrayed you."

"More than that, lad," said Luther. "Joachim betrayed the entire kingdom. He was a thrall of the dragon." Jared blinked again, then nodded.

"I had my suspicions of him, milord," he said. "but he was my master. I didn't... I had no choice but to..."

"No, no, Jared, it's not like that," said Luther quickly. "You've done no wrong. But we have need of you. On the plains above the Escarpment, there is an army of dragonmen like we've never seen before. The King must be warned."

Jared's eyes widened. "Yes, sir. I understand. But how?"

"This boy here is a mage," said Luther, indicating Wes. "He can send you to Collegium Keep in an instant. Once there, ask for Diaticus. He'll see you healed. But it's very important that you give him the message. Tell him of the dragonmen. Get word to the King! The armies of Canellin must be mobilized!"

"Yes, milord," said Jared, swallowing hard. "I'll see it done."

"Good," said Luther. "Good lad." He rose and turned to Wes. "Well, boy, can you do it?"

Wes nodded. "I think so. It's dangerous, though. I've never done this with a destination so far away. If I screw up, he could end up almost anywhere."

"'Tis a risk worth takin', laddie," said Anton with a reassuring smile. "The king must be warned."

"Okay," said Wes. "If you're sure. Everybody else, stay back out of the way. I don't want anybody to get caught up in the spell by mistake."

When everyone was well out of Wes' line of sight, Luther knelt next to Jared and laid his hand on the man's shoulder. "Rest easy, lad," the big man said softly. "Diaticus'll have you fixed up in no time." He stood and stepped away from the injured man. "At your leisure, boy," he said to Wes.

Wes concentrated, forming an image of the courtyard at Collegium Keep in his mind. Once he had it firmly centered, he began making the gestures that would activate the spell. "Movare colloqum, vidala luanzir," he chanted. Dancing sparks appeared, swirling around madly to envelop the fallen guardsman. The sparks whirled faster and faster until they totally obscured the man. Then they burst outward soundlessly, and Jared was gone.

"I think it worked," said Wes. "He should be in Diaticus' study right now."

"That's done, then," said Luther. "Now all we have to do is find our way out of these blasted caves."

"Great," muttered Ryan apprehensively. "Just what I wanted to do today, wander around in a tiny tunnel with no idea where I'm going."

"Think of it as an adventure, man," said Luther, clapping Ryan on the back. "Something to tell your grandchildren about!"

"Assuming we live that long," said Ryan cynically.

☙ ❧

Joachim's stallion and Wes' own gelding had made it through the rockslide relatively unscathed, leaving their party short of mounts.

245

The supplies had been gathered from the dead animals, and some time was spent repacking the two surviving mounts as packhorses. Much had to be discarded, and they finally settled on simply packing all of the food they could salvage and then filling out the rest of the packs with odds and ends that might come in handy. Finally, they were ready to proceed, and they left the ledge and started up the narrow tunnel at a walk, Elarie and Jiane in the rear leading their packhorses.

The tunnel they were traveling through seemed to follow the same route as the pass above had. They followed the trail for over three hours before the tunnel began to widen. The passage sloped suddenly downward, widening as it went, and Ryan stopped.

"The passage widens even more up ahead," Jiane said, halting beside Ryan. "Listen. Do you hear that?" The others strained their ears to hear. "It's running water. We could be nearing an exit."

"I don't see how," said Ryan. "We've been moving downward for the past half hour. Who ever heard of a cave with an exit below ground level?"

The sounds of running water grew louder over the next hour, but the tunnel continued to slope steadily downward. It widened even further until suddenly, they found themselves in a vast open space. Wes' magelight wasn't enough to illuminate the entire area. At a nod from Luther, the boy tossed two more lights into the air. They swirled about the first for a few moments and finally spread out to reveal a huge cavern. The walls sparkled with crystalline formations, and the light reflected from a vast pool of water on the far end. The sound of running water was from a waterfall that fell nearly a hundred feet into the pool. The crystals studding the walls refracted the light into a multitude of colors which danced on the floor of the cave in amazing patterns.

"Where are we?" asked Wes.

"Our campsite," replied Luther. "At least, that's the use I intend to make of it." He proceeded down into the cavern, looking around himself in wonder.

"This is amazing," Ryan said, eyeing the huge cavern. The walls curved upward to form the domed roof of the huge cave, and every square inch of them glittered and shone with crystalline formations. The colors of the crystals varied, from blue to red to yellow, green to brown, and even pink, but they cast their dancing lights in every direction.

246

"Better than amazing," breathed Wes in awe. "It's beautiful."

The companions led the packhorses down into the cavern, their eyes dazzled by the shimmering lights. They took the horses to the pool and allowed them to drink their fill before Wes grabbed the waterskins and began refilling them with the clean, clear water. The rest of the party sat on the rocks and rested. Wes returned to the group to find his father admiring the walls of the cavern with a bemused expression.

"You okay, Dad?" he asked.

"Hmm? Yeah, fine," replied Ryan. "The view in here is incredible! We're still underground, but it's nothing like being trapped in those tiny tunnels." He shuddered. "I hate tunnels."

"Don't worry," said Wes. "If it gets too bad, or we can't find a way out, I'll just translocate us back to Briarton and we'll start again from there. We'll lose some time, but we'll be able to find a different route." He gave his father a sheepish grin. "I'm really not in that big a hurry to get there. I'm actually scared to death."

Ryan smiled and put his arm around the boy. "I know you are, kid. And I'm proud of you." He looked down into the boy's eyes. "I've been waiting for you to go to pieces since we got to the cliffs, but I've been impressed. I don't know how you've been able to hold up, or how you made it as far as you did before we found you."

"Rocks," said Wes, blushing.

"Rocks?" repeated Ryan. "What rocks?"

"For my collection," said Wes, grabbing his backpack and unzipping the flap. "I didn't realize I was doing it at first, but even when I did, I couldn't stop. You know how whenever we go someplace new, I always pick up a few rocks for souvenirs? I've been doing that here, too." He reached into the pack and rummaged for a few moments, coming up with an odd shaped, semi-transparent stone. "I picked this up the day Gideon and I were attacked by dragonmen the first time. The day I first cast the translocation spell." He dropped the rock into the bag and pulled out another, much smaller. "This is the rock chip that made Gideon's horse go lame a day or two from Briarton." He fished out yet another small stone. "This one came from the courtyard at Collegium Keep."

"How many of those things do you have in there?" asked Ryan, peeking into the bag.

"A few," replied Wes, his blush deepening. "A lot, really. Whenever I was scared or nervous, or when the boredom got to be too much for me, I'd grab a few cool rocks to toss into my bag. It's kind of what's kept me from going nuts."

"I don't think it was just the rocks, son," said Ryan proudly. "I think you're a lot braver than you give yourself credit for."

By unanimous assent, the group took Luther's suggestion that they use the cavern for a campsite and try to get some sleep. There was no wood to be had for a fire, so they bundled up in their blankets and bedded down to sleep in shifts. Ryan fell into his blankets eagerly, but Wes was far too interested in their surroundings to fall asleep. And so, he found himself standing the first watch with Gideon. Wes made a point of wandering the cave and exploring the multicolored lights being projected by the crystal walls. He even picked up a few small rocks with particularly clear crystals in them to drop into his backpack.

"They're very beautiful," said a soft voice behind him, and he turned and smiled at Elarie.

"Yeah, they are," he replied. "My friends back home would laugh their butts off if they ever heard me say something like that."

"I don't see them about," the girl said wryly, "and your secret's safe with me."

Wes smiled. "You know all that stuff with the Tower of Lore, and the stone?" Elarie nodded, and Wes took the stone from his pouch, holding it up by the thin chain. "Turns out it was a waste of time," he said wryly. "Mages can't use these things by themselves."

"It's very pretty," said Elarie hesitantly. "May I... can I hold it?"

"Sure," said Wes with a shrug. He handed the stone to Elarie.

"It feels strange," the girl said. "The same as it did back in the tower. It almost... tingles."

"Really?" said Wes. "It just feels like a rock to me."

"It's faint. Maybe you just didn't notice. But there's a definite sensation when I touch it." She gazed wistfully at the stone, and then held it out for Wes to take.

"I should probably make sure this gets back to where it's supposed to be," he said, taking the stone. "I mean, Joachim might have been a bad guy, but the stone is still an important part of your history." He sighed. "But either way things happen from here, I won't be going back that way." He handed the stone back to Elarie. "How about this? You make sure the stone gets back where it belongs. I think I can trust you to do that. In fact..." Wes' eyes brightened as he

248

had a sudden idea. He shrugged off his backpack and reached inside, pulling out a sheaf of papers. "Take the stone to Diaticus, and these too. These are spells that I've copied out of the book. With these… well, he'll know what to do with them."

Elarie smiled shyly. "Thank you for your trust," she said quietly. She fastened the chain around her neck, letting he stone hang on her chest. She matched her step to his as he continued his circuit of the vast cave. "I never thanked you for what you did for me back on the plains," she said. "It's very… disconcerting to have something alien inside you, meddling with your thoughts and feelings."

"You got me out of that cell and probably saved my life," said the boy. "It was the least I could do."

"I couldn't have let you and Gideon hang," she said. "Even without whatever that was inside my head, I don't think I'd have let that happen."

"Still, you didn't have to do it." The girl nodded her head, and Wes continued. "To be honest, I figured you'd take off after I got rid of whatever it was you had in you. I thought you'd make a back for Karsenon as quick as you could go."

Elarie shrugged. "The thought crossed my mind," she said. "Once it was gone, there wasn't really anything pushing me to stay with you anymore. I almost turned my horse around right then."

"What stopped you?" asked Wes.

"I'm not sure, really. Something about you, I suppose. What you're doing is important, and I want to be a part of it." She chuckled. "I'd been thinking of getting out of the thieving business anyway. I wasn't lying to you when I told you I was a very good thief. The coins you had Gideon give me were a pittance compared to what I have stashed away back in Karsenon. But I'm not sure what I'd do with myself if I gave up my trade. I don't think I'm cut out for the life of a merchant. Adventuring, now… that might be something interesting to try my hand at for a while!"

Wes grinned at the girl. "Well, you've picked a tough one to start on. I'm not sure anyone expects us to survive this."

"Oh, I don't know," she replied. "From what I understand, you've got quite a bit of magic at your disposal. If I were a gambler, I'd lay my money on you." She winked at Wes, laughing. "Gideon's told me a lot about what you've learned, and what you can do with that spellbook of yours. He's got a fairly high opinion of you. I think perhaps he's right."

"Gideon… he's a good friend," sad Wes. "I couldn't have made it as far as I have without him."

"He seems a solid sort," replied Elarie. "I think you're lucky to have him with you."

"I'm sure of it," said Wes. He and Elarie continued to stroll the periphery of the cave until she finally bid him goodnight and took her leave. Wes watched her go with a strange mix of emotions he couldn't identify. The girl made him nervous whenever she was near.

Wes returned to the main camp area half an hour later to find Gideon on watch. He gave the grizzled soldier a nod, and Gideon smiled back.

"Did you and the girl enjoy your stroll?" he asked with a wink. "Perhaps next time I'll chaperone for you."

"Mind your own business," Wes replied with a grin. "You're the one who said she was pretty!" With a laugh, he settled down into his bedroll to try and get to sleep.

Gideon chuckled. "Funny, that's not how I remember it."

⋙ ⋘

After everyone had had a chance to catch a little sleep, the party packed up and prepared to move on. The cavern had several tunnels leading off in what Anton believed was the right direction, but only one sloped upward, and it was barely wide enough for them to walk single file. Luther and Anton had entered the narrow passage already, leading the packhorses, and Jiane and Elarie were preparing to follow. When it was his turn, Ryan squared his shoulders and marched into the cleft. Finally, Wes entered, and Gideon took up the rear.

Navigating the cramped tunnel proved to be more difficult than they'd anticipated. The roof got lower and lower as they proceeded upward, and the horses began to balk at going further. After a while, Luther halted their march and opened a saddlebag to tear strips of cloth from a tunic. He tied the strips over the eyes of the packhorses to calm them. The blinders seemed to be effective, and they were able to coax the horses forward. The roof of the tunnel finally began to rise, and Wes felt a surge of hope that they were coming to the end of their underground journey. They walked on for hours, plodding through the darkness. Finally, the tunnel began to widen, and Wes gave a sigh of relief.

"Is this it? Are we there?" Ryan's voice was anxious.

"I'm not sure," said Luther from the head of the line. "There's a cave up ahead, and light. It could be an exit."

"Walk faster," Ryan muttered.

Luther dutifully quickened their pace, and they finally came out into a small cave just large enough for them to gather with the packhorses. Ryan's breathing was labored as he glanced around with wild eyes.

"Where is it?" he asked. "Where's the exit?"

"There," said Luther, pointing. A narrow crack in the far wall seemed to glow with unidentified light. Luther moved to the crack and peered through.

"Twenty paces," he said, "but it's narrow. The horses will have a time of it trying to get through here. There's light, though. It may lead outside."

"Twenty paces," Ryan said, eyeing the narrow crack. "No problem."

"We'll have to unpack the horses," said Luther. "And we'll have to make more than one trip to ferry everything out."

The unpacking proceeded quickly, and soon they had their supplies laid out in the small cave. As soon as the horses were unburdened, Ryan grabbed the lead rope of the stallion and began leading him through the tiny crack. Wes came next with the gelding, then Elarie, while the others tried to determine what they could carry and still negotiate the narrow crevice. Wes stayed as close to his father as he could, and was the first to hear Ryan's startled exclamation.

"Son of a…!"

"Dad!" cried Wes. "What's wrong?"

"Nothing!" came Ryan's angry reply. "But we're not outside yet!"

"Then where's the light coming from?" asked Wes in confusion.

"You'll see when you get here. Watch your step, there's a little drop at the end, about a foot down."

Wes led the gelding out of the crack, stumbling over the drop, and stopped in shock. They were in a long rectangular chamber, at least five hundred feet long and half as wide. The walls were carved from the rock itself. There were torches burning every fifteen feet or so in sconces on the wall, and between each was a large wooden door wide enough for several horses to enter side by side. There were fenced in areas running down the center of the room, all of them empty. The chamber resembled nothing so much as a huge underground horse barn. The others filed out into the light, looking around with the same confusion as Ryan and Wes.

"Where are we?" asked Wes, and then laughed. "How many times have I asked that on this trip, anyway?"

"A hundred and forty seven," said Gideon, and Wes laughed harder. He couldn't seem to hold it in. The stress of the past weeks was wearing on him, and the situation was becoming more and more surreal with every moment.

"Quiet!" snapped Luther. "Don't you hear that?"

Wes and Gideon fell silent, as did the rest of the party, and they strained their ears. The sound of clanging metal came to them faintly from behind the doors along the side of the long chamber.

"What is it?" whispered Wes.

"It sounds like forges at work," said Luther. "And it's obvious this chamber is a corral. I think we've stumbled onto a staging area." He walked to one of the wooden doors and pressed his ear against it. After a moment, he moved to the second, then the third, listening intently before returning to where the others waited. "The noise grows fainter as you move down, but it's definitely a forge or ironworks." He smiled. "I think we've reached our destination. I think we're under Dragon Mountain."

Chapter 16

The Prodigal Son

WES' HEART SKIPPED A BEAT with Luther's pronouncement. Dragon Mountain! They'd made it! Weeks of danger, of never knowing if an attack would come around the next bend, and they'd finally arrived! The door was here, somewhere in this mountain. He had only to find it, and he could go home.

Home. Where he was a nobody. Where he'd made too much of a mess of things to ever recover. But home... where his mother lived... his grandparents, aunts, uncles... his friends... everyone he'd ever known or cared about before coming to Canellin.

Canellin was an amazing place. He had friends here, too. And the magic! Could he really give up the magic now and go back to his old life? If his quest was successful, he'd be a hero. He was probably the most powerful wizard on this world already. Back home, he was nothing. Here, he could be special.

Ryan's voice interrupted Wes' thoughts. "So what do we do now?" he asked no one in particular. "How do we find the dragon?"

"I don't know," said Luther. "No one has ever been inside the mountain who didn't come out a dragonman."

"We'll just have to search," said Jiane. "We pick a door and see what we find."

"What about the horses?" asked Wes. "I don't want to risk them in a fight, but I don't want to abandon them, either. I always figured we'd come up from outside the mountain and leave them there when we came inside."

"They'll just get in our way," replied Luther. "Under the mountain or above, it makes little difference. We can leave them here and retrieve them on our way out."

Reluctantly, Wes agreed. They quickly unpacked their belongings and made use of one of the large corrals, doing their best to make the animals comfortable.

"Take only what you need," said Luther. "Don't overburden yourselves. I feel we're close, and taking unnecessary supplies will merely slow us down. One waterskin and one pack per person." The group spent some time rearranging themselves before Luther nodded his approval. "Let's get on with this," he said, leading them to the first great door. "The noise is loudest in this direction. I'll wager it's our best chance of finding the proper path to the beast's lair." He grasped the door handle and slid the door back along its track with a low rumble. Behind the door was a broad hallway that sloped upward gently, torches lining the walls all along its length. Several hundred feet up the corridor it intersected with another running off to the left and right. They shouldered their packs and began walking. The clanging was louder to the right, and so they turned in that direction once they reached the intersection. The corridor curved around gradually, still sloping upward, and they trudged on.

"This is so strange," remarked Ryan. "It doesn't even seem like we're underground anymore. It's almost like we're in a castle or keep somewhere."

"The dragonmen have had centuries to make this place livable," said Luther. "They seem to have been quite industrious."

"How many could there be?" asked Gideon. "In the Great War, the dragon could barely field twenty thousand troops, and we nearly wiped them out. The army we saw has to be more than ten times that number."

"Perhaps they were held back in reserve," said Luther. "Or perhaps they've been breeding. For all we know, the dragonmen who invaded the kingdom this time are only ten years old. Whatever the case may be, we can only hope they've left this place lightly defended if at all."

The corridor continued to curve around, splitting off in several places. The party continued to follow the sounds of the forges in the hope that finding some sign of life would give them a direction to travel. The branching passages showed signs of recent use, tracks apparent in the dust from the passing of a great many horses and booted feet. As the sounds of clanging and hammering grew almost deafening, the passage came to an end, and they found themselves

254

facing a wide wooden door. Luther listened at the door for a few moments before trying the latch. It refused to open, and he motioned Elarie forward.

"Time to earn your keep again, girl," he said over the din. The girl nodded and produced her tools, going to work on the lock, and Luther turned to the others. "We have no idea what we'll find beyond that door. Stay low and be alert. If we can remain undetected, so much the better."

"What do we do if we find a hundred dragonmen on the other side?" asked Ryan.

"I'm not too proud to run away," said the High Lord.

"I've got it," called Elarie softly. As the others joined her, she cracked the door open slightly and peered out. Once she was satisfied, she opened the door fully and crossed the threshold in a crouch, and the rest of the party followed her lead. The door led out onto a wide balcony carved from the stone and overlooking a long chamber. Down one side of the balcony ran a long curving ramp that led into the room below. Lining the sides of the chamber were a dozen forges, six along each wall, their fires burning hotly as dragonmen hammered and pounded. At the far end of the chamber was a single door, the only apparent exit.

"How do we get past them?" whispered Wes.

"I think sneaking is out of the question," said Gideon. "But there are only a dozen of them. Between our blades and Wes' magic, we should be able to take them."

"Count again," said Elarie. "Four more." She pointed across the room to the door as four more figures entered.

"They look different," said Wes. "They're not as big."

"Faster, you filth!" shouted one of the figures, coming into the light. He cracked a long whip over the head of the nearest dragonman. "Yours is the last load, and you're holding up the supply trains!" He pointed back to the door he had just come through. "If this work isn't finished soon, I'll take you to face the master yourselves, and you can try and explain your failure!" He cracked the whip again. "Get to work!"

"They're not dragonmen," said Gideon grimly. "At least, not completely. I've seen their like before."

"As have I," said Luther, and he spat on the stone floor. "They're traitors. These are some of the men who betrayed us during the Great War. They look much the same as they did when they fled the field. Apparently, the dragon decided to leave them as they were. Perhaps they're more useful when they've half a mind to use." He glanced down again into the room. "That one off in the shadows there appears to be in charge. The others continue to go back to him for instructions. Take him out, and we'll have a better chance."

"Their addition to the fray could prove troublesome," said Jiane. "Perhaps we should double back and find another route."

"I think not," replied Luther. "These beasts are the only sign of life we've seen since entering the tunnels. I think our best course is to get through that door. The dragon must lie somewhere beyond."

"Seems like'n it's ta' be a fight after all," said Anton, sounding almost amused. "So be it," he said, drawing a wicked curved dagger.

"We must have a plan of battle," began Luther, but he was interrupted by a shrill battle cry as Anton leaped from the balcony to land among the creatures below.

"What a bloody imbecile!" said Luther angrily. Without hesitation, he also leaped from the balcony, his axe in hand. Ryan and the others ran down the curving ramp into the room below as Luther and Anton engaged the surprised taskmasters, ignoring the dragonmen for the moment.

"Hit them fast!" shouted Jiane. "Surprise is our only advantage!" That was all she had time for before the battle was joined. Jiane and Ryan were each met by one of the hulking blacksmiths, hammers raised as they roared in surprised fury. Gideon engaged another of the workers, and Wes found himself alone with Elarie at the foot of the long ramp. Elarie busied herself throwing daggers with deadly accuracy, taking a charging dragonman in the throat with one and winging Gideon's attacker with the other. Wes chanted spells and threw balls of fire at several others. Ryan's sword took his first opponent through the heart, and Anton's jagged blade sliced through the throat of another. Luther dispatched one of the half-transformed traitors with an overhand strike to the skull. His other attacker, the one he'd identified as the leader, turned and fled toward the door. But when Luther made to follow, he found himself facing a pair of the bestial blacksmiths.

"Ware the door!" he shouted. "Don't let him escape!"

Gideon bounded after the half-man, his sword dripping blood. Ryan and Jiane started to follow, but found themselves set upon by another pair of dragonmen. Gideon was left to face the traitor alone.

He collided with the fleeing creature from behind, and they both rolled to the floor in a tangle. Gideon hurried to try and rise, but the half-man was faster. Gideon rolled to the side to avoid a wicked slash and scrambled to his feet. He drew back his sword for a killing stroke, and then froze.

"Randall!" he cried, his eyes widening. The scales on the man's neck and most of his face distorted the features, but there was no doubt. This was Gideon's eldest son, the son he'd killed on the battlefield so long ago.

"Father!" said the half-man with a hiss. "I should have known you'd come someday."

"Oh, Gods! Randall! I thought you were dead!"

"Of course you did," hissed the scaled man. "It was your blade that slew me! But the power of the dragon knows no bounds, father." Randall flexed his arm, the one that Gideon had hacked off in that fateful battle, as if to demonstrate the Great Dragon's power. The arm was intact and strong, though completely covered in the scales that only mottled the rest of Randall's body. "My master made me whole, and granted me and my fellows more strength than any man has ever known."

"Randall, listen to me," said Gideon, his arms spread wide. "It's not too late, son! It's never too late! You may redeem yourself yet, Randall. Nothing but death is irrevocable!"

"It seems even death can be turned away, Father," said Randall with a sneer. He raised his curved blade and swung a two handed stroke at Gideon's chest, forcing the old soldier to dance back a step. "You'd best finish the job you started all those years ago, Father, because I intend to slay you here, and your friends as well." Randall lunged at Gideon, his sword swinging in a wide arc toward Gideon's neck.

Gideon ducked under the blow and swung up to connect with Randall's arm, and the half-man staggered to the side in pain. "It doesn't have to be this way," said the old soldier. "Randall, you're my son! You're the only family I have left!"

"I have no family," snarled Randall as he dived toward his father with his sword leveled. "The Great Dragon provides!"

"How could you ally yourself with that beast?" asked Gideon, his voice anguished. "Because of the dragon, your mother is dead! Your brother, Conner!"

"Their deaths were necessary," said Randall, darting another furious blow at his father. "All those who refuse to join the Great Dragon must die!"

"Randall!" said Gideon, shocked. "They were your family!"

"Family?" said Randall with a grimace. "Family never gave me anything!" He thrust his sword at Gideon's chest once again, and the old soldier wasn't able to deflect it completely. An inch of steel entered Gideon's shoulder just below the joint. "The Great Dragon told me the attack would come! My task was to make sure the gates were unguarded. Mother's death was foreordained!" He pulled his sword free and slashed again at Gideon's neck. "She had to die! And now, you must die as well!" He lunged again, and Gideon parried his strike. "You must kill me, or you and your friends will die!" He swung a mighty blow at Gideon's neck.

Gideon's parried the blow and spun, his sword slashing down to take off Randall's sword arm at the elbow, the same arm he'd removed before. "So be it," he said grimly as Randall shrieked with rage. Gideon stepped forward, aiming a blow at his son's head. Randall dived to the side, snatching up his sword in his remaining hand. Gideon stepped forward again, swinging his sword at Randall's back. Randall rolled, his blade flashing up to block, and he scrambled to his feet. He returned another cut toward Gideon's chest and the old soldier parried, whipping his blade around to slash at Randall's thigh. Randall surprised him by stepping into the attack and letting it glance off his scaled hide, his own sword thrusting low to slide with awful finality into Gideon's belly and out his back. Gideon slid forward on the blade until they were face to face.

"How does it feel, Father?" said Randall evilly. Blood began to run down Gideon's chin. "How does it feel to know your life's blood is flowing out at the hands of your only living child? You die knowing that it was my blade that returned the killing stroke."

Gideon coughed, the blood bubbling in his throat. "You're wrong," he said. "I die knowing that I've rid the world of a traitorous beast." And he drove the dagger that he'd hidden in his hand through Randall's neck with a twist, opening the half-man's windpipe from ear to ear and tearing his throat out. Randall tried to scream, but it bubbled away impotently, and he collapsed to the floor on top of his father.

Wes turned from the battle, nearly exhausted from his magical attacks on the dragonmen. He glanced up just in time to see Randall's blade slide into Gideon, and the old soldier's final victory. "Gideon!" he shouted from across the long room. The boy ran into the thick of the battle, dodging the blades of friends and enemies alike. He watched as Gideon worked feebly to push Randall's limp form off him, finally succeeding in freeing himself from the dead weight. Gideon struggled to sit up, but it was too much for him. He fell back and was still. Wes reached the old soldier's side and knelt, afraid to touch him. Gideon looked up at the boy, his face tight with pain.

"Wes," he said, coughing blood. "Listen to me. Get home! Forget the dragon! Find your door and go through it, lad! Find it…" Gideon's body shuddered. "Find it, boy, and go home. You have to promise me… you have to…" He reached a hand up to touch Wes' face and then lowered it gently to the floor, laying back with a soft sigh, his breath coming in shallow gasps.

"No," said Wes, despair filling him. "No!" He clutched at Gideon's tunic, burying his face in the man's chest and sobbing uncontrollably. The sounds of battle slowly faded as Gideon's breathing stilled, and Wes felt waves of pain and grief wash over him. He couldn't see, couldn't hear, and his flesh went numb. Gideon was gone, and no magic the boy might try could bring him back. Wes couldn't let go of the man's tunic as he shuddered, unable to even think.

"Wes," said a voice in the boy's ear, and he felt a gentle hand on his shoulder. "Come on, son. There's nothing you can do."

Wes turned and threw his arms around his father's neck.

"I know, Wes," Ryan said softly. "I know. It's horrible, but everything will be all right."

"No it won't," whispered Wes miserably. "He's dead. It won't be all right!"

"It will be, Wes, I promise you. We'll make it."

Wes looked up to see the entire party gathered around him and his father, their faces filled with sorrow and sympathy. Beyond them lay a scene of carnage. A dozen dragonmen and three traitors lay scattered on the floor, their bodies hacked and broken. Wes' companions were relatively unscathed aside from some cuts and bruises, and he felt a momentary surge of relief. Jiane held Gideon's crossbow, a steel-tipped bolt nocked and ready.

"Dad!" he cried suddenly, pulling back from his father. "Oh, my God, are you okay? Are you hurt?"

"No, no, I'm fine, I'm okay," said Ryan quickly. "No one laid a blade on me." He reached up and brushed his hand through Wes' hair gently. "We're going to make it, Wes. We're almost home."

Wes stood and looked down at his friend's body. He took a few deep breaths and wiped the tears from his eyes.

"I know, Dad." He turned to the door with a determined stance, then turned back to look again at the body of the old soldier. "We can't just leave him here."

"What can we do, Wes?" asked Jiane, her voice sympathetic. "We can't take him with us."

"We have to do something. It's not right to just leave him lying here." Wes thought for a moment. "We can't just leave him for the dragonmen to find." He raised his hands quickly and concentrated. The sparks sprang up suddenly, engulfing Gideon's form. The motes of light swirled around him, hiding him from sight, and then burst outward. In moments, it was over, and there was no trace of the man left on the stones.

"Where did you send him?" asked Luther.

"To my room back at the Collegium. It was the best I could think to do." Wes raised a hand and wiped the tears from his eyes. "When you make it back, I think he'd like to go home. To his own village, I mean, where his family lived."

Luther hung his head, and Jiane laid her hand on Wes' shoulder gently. "We'll see to it," she said softly.

Wes nodded absently and turned back to the door. "Thank you," he said. Ryan gripped Wes' shoulders and squeezed. Wes jerked away and walked forward, throwing open the door with a crash. Without a thought for danger, he brazenly walked through into the next room, and his shocked companions had no choice but to rush after him, their weapons held at the ready.

Chapter 17

The Final Battle

THE ROOM BEYOND THE FORGE CHAMBER was a large square with a high roof. There were torches lining the walls, their light showing a broad area with no furnishings. On the center of the left wall as they entered the room was a balcony with a tapestry behind, a dragon woven into the fabric. A broad stairway led up to the balcony from both sides of the room. The other walls each had identical doors to the one they'd just entered. Wes looked around for a moment, but there was nothing else in the room at all. He paused a few feet in and looked around curiously.

"I feel it," he said quietly. "The doorway. I don't know why I couldn't before, but I feel it now."

"Which way?" asked Ryan. "Which door do we take?"

Wes paused, concentrating. After a few moments, he nodded up toward the balcony. "Up there somewhere. I can feel it pulling me."

"Are you certain?" asked Luther. "I see no door."

"Absolutely," said Wes, and without waiting, he started up the nearest stair. The others followed without comment. Wes reached the balcony and began looking around. He gazed out over the room for just a moment, envisioning hordes of dragonmen below awaiting orders from their generals, and then he turned to the wall behind. He examined the wall carefully from a distance before stepping forward confidently and pulling back the tapestry to reveal a small passage. "It's through here," he said, and started down the tunnel.

The passage they followed wasn't long, perhaps fifty feet. It widened out quickly into an enormous cavern. The opposite wall of the cavern was several hundred yards across from them. The cavern itself wasn't like the rest of the rooms and hallways they'd been in. There was no sense that this place had been carved out, but rather that it was a naturally occurring cave. There were several places where large rock formations jutted up from the uneven floor, some as high as a few hundred feet, and the floor was littered with rocks and boulders of smooth black stone. From the center of the room nearly to the opposite wall was a yawning chasm, and on its opposite side was a swirling nothingness in the wall of the cave.

"The doorway," said Wes breathlessly. "We found it." He started across the huge cavern, and the others followed close on his heels. They reached the great chasm and Wes peered down into its depths. A dull red glow could be seen far below.

"I think we're in the cone of the volcano," said Wes wonderingly. "Feel the heat coming up? I'll bet that's lava down there. No, magma. It's underground."

Ryan laid his hand on Wes' shoulder. "But where's the dragon?" he said. "Shouldn't it be here, near the doorway?"

Wes shrugged. "I don't know. I thought it would be." He again peered down into the chasm. "Maybe it's sleeping. But we have to find it. We have to kill it."

"What if it's gone out to join the army?" said Jiane suddenly. "What if this time, the beast means to take an active part in the war?"

"Then we've lost already," said Luther.

The ground suddenly began to rumble, and Wes struggled to retain his balance. There was a sound like tearing metal coming from the chasm, and he looked down into the red glow once again. It seemed brighter somehow. And then, Wes saw a sight that stole his wits from him. He backed away from the chasm, stumbling, and fell backward into a sitting position. He and his companions scrambled back from the pit as the rumbling and shaking grew stronger.

Up the dragon rose from the chasm, flames belching from between its teeth to crash against the roof of the immense cave. Wes stared in awe as more and more of the great beast came into sight. It continued to rise, finally lighting on the lip of the great pit with a huge crash that shook rocks loose from the walls and roof. Wes' jaw dropped open as he surveyed the great beast. It was too big! It was by far the largest thing he'd seen in his life, at least two hundred feet in height, with wings that spanned nearly twice that. Its head almost brushed the roof of the cave, and its wingtips brushed the walls when outstretched.

Without warning, a booming voice began speaking in the minds of the companions.

:*Who dares?:* said the voice. :*Who dares to broach me here, in the seat of my power?:*

Wes staggered back, feeling a strange fluttering in his chest. "It's… it's huge," he stammered. "I didn't… I thought it would be… but…"

:*WHO DARES?:* the voice repeated with more force, accompanying the exclamation with a roar and a blast of flame that passed high over the heads of Wes and his companions. Wes ducked down in terror, but it was quickly replaced by anger.

"What do you mean, who dares?" he cried, standing straight and staring the dragon down. "You know who I am! You've been trying to kill me since I left the Collegium! You sent your dragonmen after me, and your mercenaries and slaves, and I made it here anyway! You killed the best man I ever met, and I made it!" Wes took a step forward, forcing his fear deep down inside him, trying to maintain his anger. "Who dares? I'm Wesley Hal Bellamy, champion of the Gatehouse, and I'm here to kill you!"

The dragon roared again, but it took the voice in Wes' head to make the boy realize it was in amusement, not anger or fear.

:*How wonderful it must be to have such an inflated opinion of oneself,:* the voice sneered. :*My dragonmen were sent out to invade your pathetic lands! My mercenaries, my thralls, my roving brigands, they were all sent out to sow confusion and dissension among mankind! If they caused you strife, little manling, it was no more than happenstance!:* Another roar of draconic laughter exploded upward in a fiery ball. :*You were never more than an afterthought, boy, and even now are barely an annoyance. An annoyance I shall rid myself of forthwith!:* The dragon's head snapped forward, and gouts of flame shot across the several hundred paces toward Wes' party. Wes flung one hand out with barely a thought, and the familiar blue dome sprang into existence, shielding them for more than half the distance to the dragon. The flames washed over the dome for a moment, and then the magical shield shattered like so much glass. Wes fell back a step and dropped to his knees, shielding his face with one arm in fear. He flung his other arm out again in desperation and the dome reappeared, smaller this time, barely large enough to enclose the six of them. Thankfully, the smaller shield seemed stronger, and it held against the dragon's onslaught.

Ryan reached out and grabbed Wes by the shoulders, pulling the boy around to face him. Looking into his son's eyes, he saw nothing but terror.

"Wes!" he shouted over the roar of the flames. "We can't stay here! We need to get to cover!" He looked around desperately, flinching every time a huge rock shattered against the glowing shield. His eyes caught a glimpse of something promising perhaps twenty paces off to their left. "There! That rock formation over there! Will this shield move with us if we get behind that?"

Wes looked at him blankly for a long moment, and then flinched as another large stone shattered against the dome near his head. Finally he nodded, his eyes still wide with panic.

"Y-y-yeah… I can make it go where I want. I think."

"Good," said Ryan. "Luther, Anton, you two lead, Elarie and Jiane take the middle. Wes and I will take up the rear so he can maintain the shield. Move!" No one seemed to object to Ryan's sudden commanding voice, and they followed his instructions. They barely made it five steps before Wes staggered and dropped to his knees, his limbs trembling. Ryan knelt down beside the boy, his arm across his shoulders protectively.

"Wes, what is it? What's wrong?"

"It's… it's too hard!" Wes' eyes were squeezed shut, his face screwed tight with strain. "I can't keep the shield up, make it move, and walk all at once! It's too hard!" The boy shuddered and Ryan held him closer. "It's not just fire and rocks it's throwing. It's using magic too! I can feel it pulling at me, tearing inside me! It hurts!"

"Son… it's okay. It'll be okay! You can do this! I know you can!" He gathered Wes up into his arms, lifting him. "You don't have to walk. I'll carry you. All you have to do is keep up the shield and move it."

"Okay…okay…I'll try…"

Ryan stood, Wes' body limp in his arms. He and the others moved as quickly as the shield would allow. An eternity later, they reached the shelter of the broad rock face, and Ryan gently set Wes' feet on the floor of the cave. With a wave of his hands, the boy shifted the shield. The blue light was now shaped like a half dome that terminated at the rock face, but it was wider, giving them slightly more freedom of motion. When the change was done, the boy collapsed with his back against the rocks, his breathing labored.

264

The dragon had not been complacent during their maneuver. It had levered itself completely out of the chasm and stalked them to the side, its attack never faltering. Its movements were severely limited by its great size. The cave, despite its immensity, simply wasn't big enough to allow the beast to move about freely, and there was no way for it to take to the air. It continued belching sheets of fire in frustration.

Ryan checked on Wes. The boy seemed unharmed, merely exhausted. Reassured, he turned to the other members of their party.

"What do we do now?" he asked. "It's got us trapped. Wes is fighting it with magic, but if it wins that, this shield is gone and we're as good as dead."

"I'm open to suggestions," replied Luther grimly. "We knew when we followed you that our only real hope lay with the boy. Inside this bloody shield, we can't even strike back!"

"Even if we could," said Jiane, "all we have are a crossbow and Anton's longbow. What could we hope to accomplish?"

Ryan thought furiously. "At least we could distract the thing and give Wes a chance!" There had to be a way to strike back at that monster!

"Wes," he said suddenly, "can you make it so we can shoot through the shield, but the dragon can't get at us?"

Wes looked up at his father, his face full of despair. His arms and legs still seemed to tremble slightly, from strain or fear, or perhaps both. "I can't. It's too strong!" The boy shook his head back and forth almost manically. "The spell doesn't work that way anyway." He squeezed his eyes shut and whirled toward the dragon, pushing against an unseen obstacle with both hands. There was nothing there, but it was obvious that he was fending off a powerful force. After a moment, his muscles relaxed. "God, it almost had me…" he said. He turned back to his father. "We're going to die, Dad," he sobbed, burying his face in his hands.

"No we're not!" shouted Ryan, startling his son. "You can do this, Wes, I know you can! You were meant to do this!"

Wes leapt to his feet, his palpable anger overpowering his fear for a moment. "Don't you get it?" he shouted. "I screwed up again! I thought I was so tough, so powerful getting this far, but I'm not! The dragon wasn't even after me! I wasn't even an afterthought! I'm nothing against that thing!"

Ryan looked around incredulously. "Wes… look!"

Wes looked to both sides quickly, suddenly panicked that he might have let the shield slip. To his astonishment, the shield was not only still there, it had almost doubled in size, becoming brighter and more solid than it had been.

"See? You're more powerful than you think, son!"

"It was just because I was mad. That's all it was." The dome began to shrink back to its earlier size.

"Then get mad! Get furious! Don't listen to that thing out there! It lies!" Realization dawned on Ryan. "That's right! It lies, Wes! It was trying to stop you. Remember Joachim? He said his master would reward him for your death. That master! That monster over there! And the storm that almost sank your ship in the channel! The way you described it, it had to be magic, and it had to be after you! You, specifically! It's afraid of you, Wes, so afraid that it threw magic at you hundreds of miles away and sent other monsters out to kill you!"

:I fear nothing!:

Wes stood, looking inside himself. Was it true? Did he have more power than he had imagined? Could he really do this?

The dragon stepped up the ferocity of its rampage suddenly. It began tearing huge slabs of rock from the walls of the cave and lobbing them at the shield in addition to its already formidable flames.

:You cannot hope to prevail. You will all die!:

"I... maybe I can do something." Wes stepped to the center of the dome, holding out one hand and peering at nothing. "If I look just right... if I tune myself... I can see it. The magic." His eyes sparkled, and his face took on a wondering expression. "I can really see it. I've never seen it before, not like this." He took a deep breath. "It's beautiful! It's like threads of crystal flying all over! I think I can..." He paused, looking over his shoulder at his companions. "You better get back behind the rock, just in case." They did as they were told, and Wes continued to reach toward the magic that only he could see. He seemed to strum his fingers along something, and then grasped with his fist and made a jerking twist. Nothing seemed to happen. He tried again, with the same result. His shoulders slumped as he turned toward his companions.

"I'm sorry. I guess it didn't work." He shook his head, unsure what to do next, and a thought struck him. The magic *did* look different, even if the shield didn't. Slowly he knelt, picking up a rock the size of a baseball. He turned, cocking his arm back, and threw the

266

rock sidearm as hard as he could. It sailed toward the dome, and then through it without resistance.

"It worked," he said quietly. "It worked!"

"What did you do?" Ryan asked.

"Something I shouldn't have been able to," replied the boy. He staggered for a moment, still weak. "I changed the spell from what the book said. I took all the... I don't know... hardness of the spell and flipped it to the outside. I made a wall with only one side." He laughed aloud. "But it worked! We can shoot at it now!" He turned to his companions. "So do it! Attack!"

Elarie was the first to move. She rushed to Wes' side, producing a dagger from nowhere. In a movement almost identical to his, she cocked her arm back and let fly. The dagger, too, flew through the shield without resistance, but it fell far short of the raging beast.

"What are you louts waiting for?" she shouted. "An engraved invitation? Shoot it!"

Anton leapt forward as well, his longbow drawn, an arrow flying before he stopped moving. It caromed off the monster's scaled hide harmlessly, but it was followed by another, and another. Jiane joined him, crossbow in hand, and fired a shot as well. She cranked back the string as fast as she could and loosed another bolt. Most of their shafts proved ineffectual against the dragon's tough skin, but perhaps a third of them managed to find weak spots in the dragon's armor or slip between scales. As each one found its mark, the dragon roared in pain and anger, increasing the ferocity of its physical attacks.

"It's working!" said Wes. "You're distracting it from using its magic!" The boy quickly unslung his backpack and pulled out his book. He began thumbing through the pages rapidly, looking for something that would help them.

:*Pinpricks and splinters,*: came the booming voice in their minds. :*You have no hope! You cannot prevail against me with sticks and stones!*: It drew back one of its forelegs and made a throwing motion with its empty paw. Lightning flew from its outstretched claws, cascading over the luminescent dome violently. A bolt penetrated the shield, scorching the rocks at Ryan's feet as he and Wes dived to either side. Elarie and Luther also ducked as another sizzling bolt arced over their heads to blast a chunk out of the rock wall. Anton and Jiane kept up their attack, firing arrow after arrow at the monster.

"This isn't working," said Ryan as he picked himself up off the dusty cave floor. "That thing's right, arrows aren't going to kill it. We have to find something else!"

"No," said Wes with sudden calm. "I have to do it myself." He gave his father a determined look.

"What are you talking about?" said Ryan wildly. "We have to work together, son! You can't go off half cocked. I won't let you get yourself killed!"

"I have an idea, sort of. Something's different about the magic here. It feels... older. I can see it. I can *hear* it. There's nothing in the book about that!" He turned to regard the dome, closing his eyes to concentrate. The lightning stopped penetrating as the dome strengthened even further. "You see? It's the magic. It's like music. It's singing. And I can make it sing!" He turned back to his father, forcing the desperation away so that he could maintain his look of determination in the face of his father's fear. He shoved his book into the backpack and slung it on his back, squaring his shoulders. "I can do this. I have to. It's why I'm here." He looked at his companions one after another. "All of you, just back me up. You'll know what to do when I give the signal. Just..." He faltered, the fear breaking through for a moment. "Just back me up!" he said, whirling, and then ran for the barrier.

Where Wes touched the dome, it seemed to stretch with him, bubbling outward. As he passed the threshold completely, it snapped into place around his body, hugging his form, creating a sort of personal shield around him. He continued to run, stopping when he reached a point halfway between his friends and the great beast. He held his arms out to his sides, palms up, and assumed a cocky pose.

"And I'm supposed to believe you're not afraid of me?" he shouted in a disdainful tone. "When you're here, throwing everything you have at me, and it's not doing you a damned bit of good? You're the one who's nothing!" He whipped his hand forward in his sidearm throw, and an enormous fireball flew from where he stood toward the dragon. The monster bobbed its head, barely avoiding the flames. The ball of fire struck the ceiling, tearing a huge chunk from the stone.

:*Flames, against a dragon??*: The dragon's laughter echoed through his mind. :*Fire cannot harm me!*:

"Mine can," said Wes, flicking another fireball toward the dragon. "You've done your best to kill me! To kill everybody,

268

everywhere!" The ball of flame flew, grazing the monster's wing as it attempted to dodge. The dragon shrieked in agony as the wing joint began to smolder, and then to wither. "You're a plague on the whole world!" Another flaming ball flew wide of its mark, but the dragon danced back away from Wes, shrieking with rage. "You're evil!" The next fireball found its target, striking the great beast on the chest. The scales there sizzled, melting and flowing down its breast in glowing red rivulets. "You killed him! YOU KILLED GIDEON!" Another fireball quickly followed, striking the dragon squarely in the jaw and snapping its head back as its flesh burned. "You don't deserve to live, you son of a…"

:*ENOUGH!*: came the booming voice, accompanied by the loudest roar yet. :*I'll not be bested by a WORM! You will die, now!*: The huge creature slammed down a clawed forefoot with a resounding crash, and arcane energy swept toward Wes with a sound like a whip cracking. Where it struck the boy's shield, dark spots appeared and began to spread. They grew into holes, expanding up from where his feet were planted. Wes cried out in anguish and fell to his knees.

"Now! I've got its power locked on me! Do it now!" Wes shook his head from side to side, trying to shake off the grasping probes that were penetrating his mind. "Hurry! It's trying to steal my magic!"

Without waiting for the others, Ryan charged across the open space, his sword drawn.

"What are we waiting for, gentlemen?" asked Jiane, drawing her slender blade. "They need us."

Anton pulled his dagger, and Luther gripped his axe, and the three of them ran toward the dragon shouting in unison.

Anton and Jiane began hacking and stabbing at one of the dragon's great legs while Luther began chopping at the other like a woodsman. Ryan was darting in and out, slashing at the beast, scoring a hit on its tail, then on its hindquarters, then flashing back to strike at the tail again. The dragon's armor was proof against most blows, but their concerted attacks managed to draw blood.

The dragon hardly reacted to the attacks, its concentration focused on Wes as it desperately tried to wrest the boy's power away and sever his link to the magic.

:*You are nothing, child,*: came the deep voice in Wes' mind. :*You are nothing on your own world, and you are less than nothing on mine. You believe you have destroyed your father's life where you come from? How much more have*

269

you destroyed it here? How he must despise you! He will die, as will you! You will ALL die, because of your arrogance and ineptitude!:

"Get... out... of... my... head," said Wes through gritted teeth. He whimpered as the dragon sent a wave of pain directly into his mind. He felt his magic pulling away from him, and he clutched at it desperately.

"Don't listen, Wes," came a soft voice in the boy's ear. He felt an arm fall gently across his shoulders and realized Elarie had joined him in the midst of the battle. "Your father risked his life for you. He came for you when any sane man would have fled, son or no! Was that the action of a man who despised you? He loves you, Wes, and he's counting on you to save us!"

:Phagh: came the dragon's voice, now silky smooth. *:What use is love? I can give you so much more than that! I can give you power beyond imagining! I can make you like unto a god! Between us, we can rule this land!:*

"You don't have anything I want," said Wes in a hoarse whisper. "Do you hear me? Nothing!"

:Then all I have for you is death, boy!: The beast batted Luther aside with its hind foot, and then stamped on the floor. The concussion threw Anton and Jiane to the ground and staggered Ryan. The beast made a yanking gesture with its forelegs, and the shield around Wes shattered. The boy screamed in agony, rising up on his toes, his arms stretched out to his sides. Elarie lurched forward, reaching for Wes, and stumbled to the still shaking floor. As she fell, the Catalyst Stone on the slender chain around her neck flashed brightly. The sudden surge of magical energy was like a whipcrack, and the girl found her hand grasping the stone.

"Wes!" she cried in panic. "The stone!"

Wes had seen the flash, and his hand seemed to move of its own volition. He reached out, grasping the stone in his fist where it hung from Elarie's neck.

Elarie rose off the floor, being pulled upward as if a string were attached to the top of her head. The tips of her toes lifted from the rocks, and her body tensed as she seemed to stretch out, her arms flung wide. The energy crackled around her, coursing through her, coalescing into a stream that flowed from her to the screaming boy.

"What... what's happening?" Elarie cried.

"I... I don't know!" Wes called back. "It... it hurts!"

270

:It's time for you to die, boy!: The dragon reared its head back and sent a jet of white-hot flame shooting toward Wes.

"No!" cried Ryan, stretching his hand out toward his son, knowing he could never reach him in time. Time seemed to slow, the flames jetting from the dragon's maw moving with the speed of a falling leaf.

I will come to the aid of the warrior in need, said a soft voice in his mind. The scene before him slowed even further.

I will come to the aid...

Luther was frozen in the act of struggling to his feet. Anton was motionless as he knelt over Jiane's prone form.

...of the warrior in need.

Wes floated still as stone, his arms outstretched, his agonized cry silenced, the Catalyst Stone clutched in his fist forming a conduit between him and Elarie. But there was no motion.

Suddenly, the scene shimmered and faded, and Ryan found himself standing in an altogether different cave, the cave below the Wizard's Collegium.

I will come to the aid of the warrior in need, said the voice again as Ryan regarded the great black blade embedded in the stone floor. His thoughts were muddled. He couldn't figure out how he'd gotten here, or what he was supposed to do. The sword began to glow with a blue light. *Your need is great. It is time.*

Ryan felt a sudden compulsion take him. He strode forward and gripped the sword's long hilt with both hands. With a single smooth motion, he pulled the sword from its bed of stone. Blackness seemed to crawl down from the sword as he held it aloft, creeping down his arm, solidifying, becoming rigid. The liquid blackness poured over Ryan's body and engulfed him, and he was suddenly bathed in brilliant light. There was a wrenching sensation, and he was back in the dragon's cave, positioned directly between Wes and the certain death poised to strike the boy. Time lurched back into motion, and he barely managed to raise the sword to block the jet of flame as it descended. The flame struck the sword's edge and split, flowing to both sides, leaving Elarie and Wes unharmed. Wes collapsed to the floor, but Elarie remained in the air, a glowing tendril of energy flowing from her into the boy.

"You two stay behind me," said Ryan as the dragon unleashed another gout of flame at him. He deflected the attack harmlessly.

"Dad? Is that you?" Wes struggled to rise, the energy crackling around him.

Ryan looked at his arms, taking in the ebon armor that covered them. His hands were covered in black gauntlets, the Obsidian Blade held outward in both hands. "It's me. Stay behind me and let me handle this."

It is not your task, said the soft voice in Ryan's head.

"You shut up." Ryan strode forward, sword raised.

You are the Guardian. He is the Champion.

"Dad! Stop!"

Ryan paused, but couldn't look at his son as the dragon sent wave after wave of flame to be batted aside by the black sword. "Don't argue, Wes, just stay back!"

"Just listen to me! I know what to do!" The boy stepped forward next to his father, who was busy deflecting jets of flame. Ryan turned his gaze to Wes and got a good look at his son, his eyes going wide. Wes' body was surrounded by a coruscating nimbus of flame, his body engulfed in energy. "Just keep doing what you're doing. Wherever that sword came from, it's blocking the dragon's magic. I'll handle the rest."

Ryan looked at Wes skeptically, but what he saw in his eyes made him reconsider.

"Fine," he said finally. "Do what you need to do, and I'll keep it busy." He took a step forward, positioning himself between Wes and the dragon.

Wes held his hands out before him once more. He could see the magic in the air, all around them. He could feel it as it thrummed in the air. He could hear it, a symphony of sound meant only for his ears. A symphony he knew he could direct.

Energy continued to pour into him through Elarie, and the aura around Wes continued to grow brighter. He began to draw in the energy, as much as he could hold and more, weaving the webs that only he could see. The dragon continued its flaming attacks, but Ryan blocked each one as if he could read the beast's mind. Wes began to get flashes of the dragon's thoughts... flashes from the first dragonwar... then further back... caves, not like this one, darker and farther away... he could see deep into the dragon's soul... and then he found it.

"It's over," shouted Wes, addressing the dragon. "Give it up and I might let you live!"

:Fool! Let me live? You have no hope of winning!:

"I just did, you idiot" said Wes in triumph, as he made a final twist of his wrist. "I have your name, Dragon. Hralnag! Your name is Hralnag!" Wes laughed, an almost relieved sound, knowing that it was over. "I have your name, and that means I have *you!*" Wes embraced the magical symphony all around him, his hands moving in cadence, directing an unseen choir, an orchestra, chiming bells and flaring trumpets. "I can see your spell, you bastard, and I'm a real quick learner!" He pulled back with all of his might, both physical and mental, and Hralnag's magical power tore away from the beast like so much paper. The power rushed into Wes in a torrent. It was all he could do to keep from being consumed, but he held onto the magic, containing it within him, exulting at the feeling of strength and power.

:NOOOOO!:

"Yes," said Wes, his voice like stone.

:I won't be beaten by a filthy human!:

"You already have been. Now it's you who's nothing." Wes made a negligent gesture, and lights began to dance over the dragon's hide. It began to shake violently, its spread wings colliding with the cave walls and knocking loose showers of gravel. The lights spread upward from its feet, engulfing its legs, spreading onto its torso. They seemed to expand until the dragon's entire form was engulfed in a tornado of swirling light. The light swirled around the great beast maniacally until no part of the dragon could be seen. The raging storm of incandescence seemed to last forever, slowly covering the beast in shining, swirling silver-blue fire. Suddenly, the lights exploded outward in a shower of sparks, and the dragon was gone.

Wes stood, his body still surrounded by that nimbus of energy, the channel between him and Elarie still funneling pure magic into him, Hralnag's magical strength only adding to the torrent. He held onto the power for a moment, reveling in the feeling of omnipotence that consumed him. But it was too much. Even he could tell it was too much for a mortal body to stand. The magic coursed through him, fire running through his veins, and he fell to his knees. With a savage cry, he pointed upward, forcing the pure energy out and into the air. A white-hot bar of light streaked upward, shattering the roof of their cave and escaping out into the skies of Canellin, spreading outward to explode into the ether of the magical world. Wes then forcefully reached inside himself and found the channel between him and Elarie, severing it, and the girl collapsed to the floor in a heap. He knelt on the floor and gasped from the exertion, looking fearfully toward Elarie, but she finally began to stir. She looked up at him with a weak smile.

Luther finally regained his feet and stared at the spot where the dragon had stood. He turned, limping toward Wes, and his face slowly split into a broad grin.

"You did it," he whispered, loud in the sudden silence of the cave. He quickened his pace and raised his voice. "You did it! You killed the beast!" He reached Wes and took the boy in a huge bear hug. Wes grunted at the pressure, and the big man set him down.

"I didn't kill it," said Wes. "I just sent it away."

"Sent it where?" asked Ryan.

"An image I pulled from its mind," replied Wes wearily. "Hopefully back where it came from. At the least, I hope it's somewhere it can never come back from."

Chapter 18

Homecoming

WES STAGGERED TO THE CAVE FLOOR, his breathing labored. The battle with Hralnag had taken its toll on him.

"We did it," the boy said simply. "It's over. We can go home."

"You did it, lad, you and your father. The rest of us were merely bystanders." Luther sat down with a thump next to Wes. "You're heroes."

"We did it. All of us. I'd be dead now, and Dad too, if it weren't for you and Jiane, and Anton." Wes' face fell. "And Gideon. Especially Gideon."

"Gideon will be remembered as a hero. He was a good man." Luther looked Wes in the eye. "He wouldn't change how this worked out, boy. He traded his life for yours, and I know he thought it more than a bargain."

"I know. I just wish I could have told him… I wish I could have thanked him for everything he did for me." Wes bowed his head, tears coming unbidden.

"He wanted no thanks. It was… it was just who he was." Luther struggled to his feet and made his way to Jiane's side, where Anton knelt. "How is she?"

"I'll live, father," Jiane said, sitting up with a wince. "Cracked some ribs, and I think my ankle is broken. But I'll live." She put her arm around Anton, and he helped her stand. The three of them hobbled to the packs and began tending their wounds.

"Dad," said Wes, looking the armored man up and down. "You saved me. That sword, the armor… it was what saved us all. I can feel it from here. It's magic, and it's powerful. What is it? Where did it come from?"

"I don't know," replied Ryan. "That is, I know how I got it. I know where. I just don't know what it is, really." Ryan looked across the chasm toward the swirling gateway. "But it's pulling me somehow. It's talking inside my head. It… it wants us to go home. To the Gatehouse, I mean. It wants us to hurry."

"But…" began Wes, looking at their companions. "Why do we have to hurry? It's over! We won! We have plenty of time now, Dad. We can help Luther and Jiane, Elarie… we can rest… we don't need to leave yet!"

"I don't know why, son. It's… he's saying that it's not over, that we have to get to the Gatehouse." Ryan paused, his eyes glazing for a moment, and he gave the sword in his hand a look. "What are you saying? I don't understand what you mean!" Luther's head snapped up at Ryan's exclamation, and he watched the exchange with interest. Ryan looked up again at Wes, his expression more confused than ever. Turning, he took a few involuntary steps toward the gateway, and then stopped and looked over his shoulder at Wes. "It's time, son. We have to go. We have to go now!"

Wes looked at his father, then back at their companions. All of them were watching now, curious.

"Go, boy," said Luther. "You've done what was required. You're both heroes, and will be remembered in legend for all time. But this may be your last chance. Go."

Jiane struggled to her feet. "He's right. We'll miss you, both of you. But you've earned your reward. Go back to your lives."

Wes finally let himself look at Elarie. There were tears in her eyes. Suddenly, the girl rose, staggering forward to embrace him. She held him tightly for a moment, then pulled back and took his face in her hands.

"I never even got a chance to get to know you," said the young thief. "Even after the spell was gone, I wanted to know you. You're special." She shrugged, looking the boy in the eye. "Go home, Wes. It's where you belong." She leaned forward slowly and gently touched her lips to his. "Go home. I'll miss you."

Wes looked at the girl, unfamiliar emotions raging inside him. He felt a sudden sense of loss as he brushed her hair back from her eyes.

"Why couldn't you have done that sooner?" he asked. "I'll miss you too," he said quietly. "Remember what I asked you to do.

276

Get those papers to Diaticus. He'll know what to do with them." He turned and walked to his father's side. Side by side, they walked toward the gateway. Ryan looked back over his shoulder as they made their way around the chasm.

"Thank you," he said simply, nodding toward their friends.

"No, friend," called Jiane. "Thank you." She raised a hand in farewell. "Thank you," she repeated in a whisper.

"Jiane, are you crying?" asked Luther in a teasing voice.

"Absolutely not, Father," said the young woman gruffly.

"I thought not," he replied, brushing a tear from her cheek.

Ryan and Wes worked their way to the other side of the deep pit, coming at last to the swirling gateway. They both paused at the threshold, and Wes looked at the portal in sudden fear.

"Stop!" Wes said suddenly, and Ryan looked down at him. "Why do we have to go back? Why don't we just stay here?" Wes' voice was almost frantic as he took a step back from the gateway. "We could! Why go back there? Things are bad there, remember? I'm in trouble all the time, you hate your job. Here we're somebodies! With the dragon gone, things here can be great! We're heroes, we're important. Why go back at all?"

Ryan looked at his son silently for a moment. The sword was filling him with a sense of urgency, a painful need to step through the gateway, but he couldn't ignore the desperation in his son's words. He took the boy by the shoulders, looking him in the eye.

"Wes, we have to go back. Our lives are there. Our family. Your aunt Fred, your uncle Jake, your grandma and grandpa. Your mom. All your cousins." Ryan gave Wes a shake. "Everything we know is there. And there's something wrong. Something that could affect our own world. Something that could put everyone we love in danger." He released the boy's shoulders and shook his head. "If things are bad there, we'll fix them, just like we did here. You're not the same kid you were when you came here. I'm not the same man, either. If things are bad, you don't just walk away and forget about them. You work hard to fix them. And we can, son. We can fix things."

Wes considered his fathers words for a moment and knew they were true. Part of him was terrified at the prospect of going home, but he felt a sense of responsibility and renewed determination. He looked past his father and into the swirling portal that awaited them.

"We can strive," he said quietly, stepping around Ryan and through the gateway.

"Exactly," said Ryan, rising. Parental pride filled him. "We can strive." With a smile, he followed his son home.

"This is the dawn of a new age of peace," said Luther pompously after Ryan and Wes were gone. "The dragon is no more, and mankind may finally reign throughout the land."

Anton looked at the man, incredulous. "Peace? Are ye daft, man?" He looked at Jiane, who shared his astonishment at Luther's pronouncement. "Do ye forget the army o' dragonmen, hundreds of thousands of them, ready ta' invade the kingdom? Even without the dragon, we'll have a time riddin' ourselves of them!" He turned away, Jiane's arm around his shoulder, shaking his head in disbelief. They limped slowly toward the exit to begin searching for a way to the surface. "Peace, he says," the man muttered. "Gods above!" Elarie followed, all three wearing identical expressions of amusement at Luther's discomfiture.

"I only meant..." began Luther lamely. "I just thought the moment deserved some words," he said, blustering. The rest of the party ignored him. "Oh, never mind," he said, shouldering his axe and following his companions.

⚬⚬ ⚬⚬

Wes felt the lurching dizziness once again as he stepped through the gateway. He staggered as his feet came down on the polished wooden floor of the endless hallway. He was home! It had worked! He staggered again as his father appeared behind him, bumping him with his own stumble. Far off down the hall, Wes spied Pomander opening and closing doors seemingly at random.

"You're not being very helpful," the little man was saying to no one in particular as he opened another door. "Just let me through, I tell you! I don't know why you're being so difficult!" He slammed the door in obvious frustration.

"Pomander!" called Wes. "We did it!"

Down the hall, the strange little man who had set all this in motion whirled in surprise.

"You!" he exclaimed. "How did you... wait. You did what?"

"I did what you told me to do. I beat the dragon!" Wes looked over his shoulder at his father. "We did it, I mean. Me, Dad, and some friends."

Pomander stared at Wes for a long moment, and then his face split into a grin of pure glee. He rushed toward them down the long hallway, stopping a few paces from Wes and dry washing his hands.

"You did it? The dragon is gone?"

"Yes, it's gone. It won't be any danger in Canellin anymore, at least." Wes frowned, confused by Pomander's behavior. "That's what you wanted, isn't it?"

"Hmm? Oh! Oh, yes, absolutely, you've done well!" The little man leaned sideways to peer around the two returning travelers. "And the portal is still open!" His eyes shone with a sinister light.

Wes followed Pomander's rapt gaze. "Yeah, it's open. Why? What's the matter?"

"Nothing, boy," said Pomander brusquely. "You have done well. You are released from service with my sincerest thanks." He bowed gracefully, then straightened and stepped toward the doorway.

"Released?" said Wes, confused. "Wait, where are you going?" He grabbed Pomander by the arm. "After all of this, everything you put me through, put my Dad through, you're just going to leave?"

Pomander whirled at Wes' touch, jerking his arm free of the boy's grasp. "Young man," he said through clenched teeth, "I have my own business to attend to. You have performed a great service, and I'd like nothing more than to throw you a tickertape parade. But right now, I must be going." He waved his hand dismissively. "I believe you know the way out."

Don't let him get through the door, said a metallic voice in Wes' head.

"What?" he said, looking around.

"You heard it too?" asked Ryan.

"Heard what?" said Pomander in annoyance as he edged toward the swirling portal.

He must not go through the portal or all is lost, said the voice.

Pomander backed away from Wes, who was looking at him with suspicion. "Boy, whatever you're thinking, it must wait. I must go, I have…" His voice trailed off as he backed into something hard and unyielding. He slowly raised his head to see Ryan blocking his path, black armor seeming to soak up the dim light of the hallway.

"Not until we figure out what's going on," said Ryan firmly.

"Well, as to that," said Pomander slowly, looking to Ryan's left and then quickly darting around him to the right.

Stop him! The voice was urgent now. Unable to think of a better plan, Ryan acted on instinct. He whirled his blade around in a lightning arc and stabbed it into the center of the swirling nothingness. The magical energy of the portal flashed brightly and then exploded in a massive concussion, knocking Wes to the ground as Pomander rebounded off a solid wall. The little man battered at the smooth surface where the portal had once been.

"No!" he wailed pitifully. "No, blast your hide! I'll kill you!" Pomander scrambled to his feet and leapt toward Ryan, fingertips outstretched like claws. Still reacting instinctively, Ryan whipped the sword up, catching the little man in his broad belly. The sword completed its upward swing, cleaving through flesh and bone as if it were butter, slicing through the enraged little man's chest and emerging with no resistance.

Ryan stood in shock, sword held frozen at the top of the swing, disgusted at what he'd just done. He had killed before, dragonmen by the dozen, but this was a human being. He watched numbly as the little man fell to the floor at his feet.

But the little man apparently wasn't dead. The body convulsed, and then began to deflate. Ryan's mind had barely registered the lack of blood when he saw a black arm reach up out of the depths of the body through the gaping slash. It was joined by another, and then a head and torso as a small winged creature struggled to extricate itself from the deflating pile of flesh and bone.

"What is it?" cried Wes in horror, backing away.

"I don't know, just stay back," replied Ryan, leveling his blade at the creature. The sword began to glow with a deep blue light as the creature, once freed, looked from one to the other of them wildly.

"No! You've ruined it!" shouted the little creature in a high, hissing voice. "You will pay for this! Mark my words!"

The glow from the black sword seemed to slide down the length of the blade, dripping off the tip like blood until it coalesced into a floating ball of light directly between Ryan and the winged creature. Wes had seen this before, the glowing ball of light... in Canellin, fleeing from Elarie as he forced it out. The beast danced aside with an oath as the shining orb shot past it and slid neatly into the deflated form on the floor. Pomander's body began to re-inflate around the ball, the horrible wound closing itself seamlessly around it as the body began to stir. The creature launched itself into the air away from Pomander's expanding form, taking wing and flying down the long hallway. It was nearly out of sight before Pomander struggled into a sitting position.

"Take that, you little monster!" shouted Pomander, feebly flinging a fireball after the retreating creature's back. It fell far short.

"You will all pay!" came the faint reply, and then the creature vanished into thin air.

"Where did it go?" asked Wes.

"Back to its home, I suppose," said Pomander. "Crowley doesn't need a doorway to travel there, just as I don't need one to travel here." He rose to his feet, patting himself as if to make certain everything was still there. "Well," he said, "that was an adventure, wouldn't you say, gentlemen?" He turned to face Ryan and Wes only to find the tip of the black sword an inch from his nose.

"You," said Ryan menacingly, "have some explaining to do."

Pomander raised a fingertip and gently pushed the blade aside. "Tsk, tsk, my good man. The danger has passed. I believe it's time you put that thing away. It won't allow you to harm me now, anyway." Ryan's armor suddenly faded away, leaving him in his regular tunic and trousers. The sword remained, but try as he might, he couldn't force himself to raise it against the little man. And then the sword seemed to melt, flowing upward toward the hilt to engulf Ryan's hand. It moved upward onto his arm, and then faded from sight. Ryan stared at his arm in shock, but Pomander seemed unimpressed. "Please, if you'll just follow me, all will be explained. We'll be going to my study. Would you care for some refreshments?"

"Are you insane?" Ryan said, thrown by the little man's casual attitude.

"I could us a soda," said Wes, and Ryan shot him a hard look. Pomander smiled up at them knowingly, and then calmly walked past them down the passage.

Wes and Ryan looked at each other, Ryan's expression dark. Turning, they followed Pomander down the endless hallway.

✦✦✦

Wes sat in a comfortable chair in the study, his father seated opposite him on the couch. Ryan held an untouched glass of beer.

Wes, for his part, sipped his root beer again, savoring the taste against his tongue. It was heaven. More than three months without a soda was a fate too horrible to imagine ever going through again!

"So you're telling me," his father was saying, "that it wasn't you who shoved us through the door, it was this creature, this Crowley.

Pomander had spent the last twenty minutes explaining to them what had occurred in the Gatehouse. Wes had only half listened, basking in that sensation of welcome embrace that seemed to exude from the very walls of this place. The feeling had been only a dim memory until the moment the winged black creature had vanished, but then it had returned in full force. His father obviously felt it too, but seemed far too intent on making sense of the little man's words to luxuriate in the comforting embrace.

"Yes and no," said Pomander. "When Wes arrived here, I was myself. But after I was attacked by Crowley, the little beast insinuated a piece of itself into my mind. Yes, it was me who sent Wes to Canellin, but it was Crowley who wanted him there. He was rifling through my memories and influencing everything I said and did. I was unable to stop him, and until I figured out what was happening, I was even a willing participant in his plan. As my best guess, I'd say Crowley primarily wanted to rid himself of Wes' distraction, and if the boy managed to vanquish the dragon, so much the better. Evil or no, the dragon would have been an impossible obstacle to any plans Crowley might have had for Canellin."

"But it wasn't you who sent me through," said Ryan.

"No. By that time, I had deduced what was happening and fled my body. It was entirely in Crowley's control, which is why the House began to actively work against the little beast. When he sent you through the doorway, I followed, and did my best to influence events there. In that state, I was able to act in only very minor ways. A gentle nudge to Diaticus' mind to urge him to trust you, and a push on Luther's sense of honor and friendship to encourage him to befriend you, that sort of thing. It wasn't until you made your rather unsuccessful attempt to draw the Obsidian Blade that I had the idea of using it as a vessel for my consciousness. But before I did that, I decided to try and use a mortal shell instead." He looked almost apologetic. "The girl Elarie was useful to some extent, but I should never have done what I did. It was a horrible misuse of my powers." The little man shuddered. "But taking up residence inside the sword was a course of action I'd not like to repeat, I assure you. The blade has a mind of its own, as I'm sure you're aware by now. Sharing living space with an intelligent sword is a most unpleasant activity."

"So it was you who brought me from the cave to the sword."

"No. The sword chose you for its bearer. I couldn't even make myself heard then. It's very powerful."

Ryan looked thoughtful. "The sword… is it gone?"

"Apparently not," said Pomander. "I'm not certain it's done with you. It seems you're to bear it, at least for now. Be aware, though, this sword has chosen you. Once a bond like that has been made, it's not so easy to ignore."

Ryan shrugged, and then looked down at his lap with heavy eyelids. "I'm still not sure how much of this is real. How do I know you're not just feeding us a line? That it wasn't you who was telling Diaticus to keep me away from Wes?"

"Don't think too harshly of Diaticus, either," replied Pomander. "He's a good man. He longs for magical power, but that's the nature of wizards. And with the papers Wes left for him, and the knowledge you gave him to allow him to decipher them, he will most likely rise in skill. He may even bring about that magical renaissance he so dreams of."

"So what happens now that the doorway has been destroyed?" asked Wes.

"That, I'm afraid, could be a problem." Pomander shook his head sadly. "Necessary as it might have been, the House is now wounded, and I'm unsure if it can recover. But, had Crowley reached Canellin, all would have been lost. If he had managed to alter the portal there, which is very possible, he could have opened a gate to his own realm and cut off our own, allowing other minions of the Unnamed free reign. Canellin would have fallen to the darkness, and there would be no hope of ever defeating the Unnamed."

Ryan sat silently. Wes could see that he was tired, as tired as Wes himself was. They were weary to the bone, and every muscle ached. But they were home, and everything would be all right now. They could go back to their lives, pick up where they had left off, and let this just become a memory of an adventure shared. His father yawned hugely, causing Wes to have the urge as well.

"God, what time is it?" Wes asked.

Pomander glanced at an ornate clock on the mantle. "Four of the morning. We've been at this for some time, it seems."

Wes sat upright as a sudden thought struck him.

"Pomander," he asked quickly, "how long were we gone? What day is it?"

Pomander gave Wes a sly smile. "Ah, lad, there is a very useful aspect of the Gatehouse that comes into play there. It's the wee hours of Thursday morning. You have been gone nearly eight hours, relatively."

"Eight hours!" Ryan was aghast. "And it's the same night! It's been so long, I didn't even think! We've been through all of this, and hardly any time has passed here!" He buried his face in his hands. "Oh, God, I have to work in a few hours! How am I supposed to do that after all this? How are we supposed to just go back to our lives like nothing's happened?"

"I'm sorry," said Pomander in sympathy. "I understand your concern. You were never intended to be a part of this. Your son is the champion, and even he was supposed to be far more prepared before I ever sent him through a doorway."

"God. This is a nightmare. We have to go home! We need sleep, in our own house, in our own beds. And we need time to adjust to being back! We've got to try and salvage our lives!"

Pomander looked at Ryan reassuringly. "It won't be as bad as all that, I promise you. You'll find yourself slipping back into your old life, your old routine, with barely a thought." He turned his gaze on Wes. "And I will be here. We'll be seeing each other again before too long." He rose from his chair and brushed his tunic straight. "But for now, my friends, I believe you have been through enough. You both should go home and rest comfortably. You've earned it."

Ryan looked at Pomander in astonishment. "Seeing each other again? Are you insane?" He stood, towering over Pomander. "We're not coming back here. Ever. We're done."

"I'm afraid not, Ryan," replied Pomander. "Canellin was never Wes' true goal. There is much work to be done, and Wes is the Champion."

"I don't care what he is, he's my son, and we're not doing this again!"

"Wait," said Wes. "I have another question." He looked at the little man curiously. "Why me? Why did you pick me?"

Pomander laid a hand on the boy's shoulder. "My boy, I didn't choose you. The House chose you, the same as it chose me so long ago." He smiled slyly. "And the House is never wrong."

"It's wrong this time," said Ryan.

"Dad," said Wes. "Let it go. You know he's right. Can't you feel it? The House is letting you know."

Ryan paused. "I feel it," he said. "But it's not fair. You're just a kid…" He trailed off, looking Wes in the eye. "I guess you're not, though, are you? Not anymore, at least." He sighed. "Just promise me, Wes. You won't come back here again without me. Ever."

"I promise, Dad," Wes replied. He turned to Pomander, and rose to stand beside his father. "Thank you, Pomander. For everything. In spite of it all, I'm glad we went." Impulsively, he embraced the little wizard. Pomander stiffened in surprise, but then relaxed and hugged Wes back.

"As am I, my boy. As am I." He patted Wes on the back fondly, then released him. He gestured to the door, and the three of them left the study and descended the stairs to the cozy room past the entryway. Wes stopped suddenly as his gaze lit on the empty display table.

"Oh! I almost forgot! I've got some things you should have back, now that this is all over." He pulled off his battered backpack, unzipping the flap.

"No, no, Wes," said Pomander quickly. "Anything you found on your adventure is yours. Keep them for mementos of a job well done."

Wes stopped in the act of pulling the book of magic from his backpack and slid it back inside. It would be nice to keep, even though it was useless to him here. It was going to be hard living without the magic of Canellin. "Thank you," he said sincerely. "There is one thing that I want you to have back, though. I didn't mean to take it, I just wanted to look at it. I forgot it was in my bag until I got to Diaticus' study." He pulled out the ornate sextant.

Pomander reached out his hand and gently traced the pattern etched into the metal. After a moment's consideration, he pulled his hand back and shook his head. "It's yours. It was a gift to me, and now I give it to you."

Wes regarded the ornate device wordlessly. It had meant a lot to him to have this with him, to remind him that the Gatehouse and his old life weren't just a dream. For a moment, he was overcome with emotion. When he could finally speak, all he said was, "Thank you." He carefully placed the sextant back in his bag and turned toward the door with his father, Pomander following just behind. The door opened as they approached. Ryan paused for a moment at the doorway before stepping through. Wes paused as well, reflecting that this would be the step that truly meant he was home. He began to step forward, but Pomander's hand on his elbow stopped him.

"Wes, there's something I have to tell you." The little man was hesitant. "There are rules concerning the Gatehouse and its Champion. They are beyond my control. I just want you to know that what is about to happen is none of my doing."

"What do you mean?" asked Wes, following Pomander's gaze out the door to his father. "Dad?"

Ryan stood on the porch, looking around himself blankly. Wes stepped outside onto the porch and went to his father's side.

"Dad? What's wrong?"

"Wes?" Ryan looked down at his son in confusion. "What... where are we? What's going on? I... did I have a sword?"

"We're at the Gatehouse, Dad, don't you remember? Canellin? The dragon?"

"Dragon... yes, I remember. I..." Ryan fell silent, his face going completely blank for a long moment. Then his expression changed to one of anger. "Wait till I get you home! What got into you? Wandering around in the woods in the middle of the night! What were you thinking?"

"No," breathed Wes softly. "No, no, no! You can't forget!" He turned back to confront Pomander only to find the door firmly shut. He tried to open it, but it wouldn't budge. Pounding on the frame, he shouted for Pomander. "No! Pomander! You can't do this!" He pounded harder, tears streaming down his cheeks. "He has to remember! I don't care about anything else, but he has to remember! Things were good between us finally!" Wes pounded harder, even kicking the door in his frustration. "You can't do this to him! It's not fair! He has to remember!"

"Wes! Stop it!" Ryan grabbed the boy by the arm.

"No, damn it, this can't happen! You have to remember!"

"Wes! I do remember! Stop!"

Wes stopped his furious pounding, but his tears would not subside. "You do? You remember?"

286

"Yes," said Ryan gently, hugging Wes closely to his chest. "I remember. I lost it all for a second, but then it was like somebody turned on a light switch in my head. I remember, son. I remember it all."

Wes squeezed hard, holding onto his father in relief. "You remember," he said softly. "You remember!"

Ryan smiled as he embraced his son. "Yes, I remember." He brought his hand up and smacked Wes on the back of the head with a gentle thump. "That's for swearing."

Wes burst into laughter. "Sorry! It won't happen again!" The two laughed there together for a good long while, and finally descended from the porch. They worked their way toward the woods in silence, simply happy to be home, and together.

As they reached the tree line, Ryan stumbled over an exposed root and almost fell. He chuckled softly. "Better watch that, that's what got me in trouble in the first place. Wish we had a flashlight!"

"No problem," said Wes, making a twisting gesture. A ball of light appeared in the air above his palm.

"Thanks," said Ryan and continued walking. He stopped when the light didn't follow, turning to his son. Wes was frozen in place, staring at the ball of light.

"Wes... what is that?"

"It's a magelight," said Wes in awe.

"That's what I thought it was," said Ryan. As one, he and Wes turned back to the Gatehouse, thoughts of magic and danger storming through their heads. But the Gatehouse was gone. Indeed, the entire hollow where it had lain seemed to have reversed itself, becoming instead a wooded slope, which memory told them was the way it had always been. At least, before they met the enigmatic little wizard.

"Um... I guess we'll tell him later," said Wes.

"Guess so," said Ryan with a shrug. "I know one thing for sure, though."

"What's that?" Wes asked curiously.

"I'm calling in sick in the morning," replied Ryan with a grimace as they turned once more toward home. "I need a vacation."

Epilogue

HRALNAG'S VISION CLEARED SLOWLY. It shook its head, trying to clear it, and saw that it was no longer in its mountain cave. It found itself instead in a smaller, more cramped location. What had the boy done? It lifted its great wings as far as the small space would allow and roared in agony as pain lanced through the injured wing joint. No matter. It would heal itself with its magic and return to wreak its vengeance.

No. The magic was gone. The wing would have to heal on its own, and the dragon would have to find non-magical means to escape this prison. It tried to raise itself up so that it could get a better look at its surroundings, but its hind legs refused to move. It scrabbled at the rocks with its forelegs, but its hindquarters were frozen in place. Craning its long neck to peer beneath its huge form, the dragon realized its predicament. From the middle of its torso to the tips of its toes, it was embedded in the solid rock of the cave floor.

The boy! The boy had transported him somehow! And worse, the untrained, inept child had miscast the spell, leaving this as the result!

Again, no matter. No matter at all. Digging itself out would be difficult, but it could be done even if it took a century. Revenge would be had! It would find a way to regain its magical abilities and renew its strength, and it would return. It would destroy that entire land!

An odd sound, almost like stone cracking, caught the dragon's attention. Its head whipped about instantly, its eyes squinted to peer into the shadows. The cracking sounds continued, increasing in volume and frequency. Ah! There! A narrow passage that looked like it opened into another chamber beyond this one. The great beast snaked its neck around to try and see beyond the passage, but the light was dim. It could make out some kind of debris pile, rocks mounded as high as the roof of the chamber beyond. The sound seemed to be coming from there. As the dragon craned its neck and squinted its eyes, one of the rocks near the top of the pile began to vibrate and then tumbled down, rolling toward the dragon. It came to rest near the great beast's snout, and the dragon finally realized what it was. An egg.

They were all eggs, the entire pile! That meant the dragon was back home, back where its kind had originated! These eggs... they must be a cache left from the great purge, when it had destroyed its brethren. They could have been dormant here for thousands of years. And now, in the presence of one of their own kind, they were hatching!

:hungry: came a shrill voice into the Great Dragon's mind. The egg before him cracked jaggedly down the middle, and out rolled a tiny dragonet no bigger than a common cat. The sound came of more eggs beginning to crack, and more shrill voices speaking silently.

:hungry:

:feed!:

:meat! smell!:

:STAY AWAY, VERMIN! I could crush you with a toe if I chose! You will serve me, or you will be destroyed!:

More and more of the eggs began to vibrate, thousands of them, and more voices penetrated the Great Dragon's thoughts.

:destroy?:

:crush?:

:eat! hungry!:

:what is?:

:is meat! is trapped!:

:Not meat, you simpletons! Master! Follow me, serve me, and we will achieve greatness!: Plans were already forming in the great beast's mind, a way to use this new development to its advantage. The young dragonets would be impressionable, unsure of themselves. They could easily be influenced, brought to heel.

Hundreds, thousands of glowing dragon eyes regarded the great beast from the shadows.

:greatness?:

:be great?:

:be mighty?:

:hsst! is trapped!:

:Will be mighty,: came a surprisingly clear thought from one of the newborns. *:Will be great. Will lead!:* A tiny form slinked forward ahead of the rest. It sat back on its haunches, its half-formed wings

flapping twice as it looked at the great dragon embedded in the cave floor.

:*You... are evil.:* It looked directly in the larger beast's eyes. :*Will not serve you. Will be free!:* The little dragonet turned, seeing the thousands upon thousands of hungry eyes glowing in the chamber beyond. :*But first,:* said the dragonet's voice again, :*will eat!:*

The Great Dragon's eyes widened as every hatchling in the cave rushed forward as one and descended upon the beast, teeth bared, screeching in hunger and excitement.

The Story Continues in:

Gatehouse:
The Door to Justice

Be sure to watch for it in the fall of 2011!

To learn more about E.H. Jones, the
Gatehouse series, and to keep up to date on
upcoming projects, check us out on the web!

http://doortocanellin.blogpsot.com

http://sites.google.com/doortocanellin

www.ingramcontent.com/pod-product-compliance
Lightning Source LLC
Chambersburg PA
CBHW071258170626
46809CB00001B/263

* 9 7 8 0 6 1 5 4 7 8 7 6 0 *